Kristen Arnett is a queer fiction and essay writer. She won the 2017 Coil Book Award for her debut short fiction collection, *Felt in the Jaw*, and was awarded Ninth Letter's 2015 Literary Award in Fiction. She's a columnist for *Literary Hub* and her work has either appeared or is upcoming at *North American Review*, *The Normal School*, *Gulf Coast*, *TriQuarterly*, *Guernica*, *Electric Literature*, *Guardian*, *Salon*, *The Rumpus*, and elsewhere.

MOSTLY DEAD THINGS

A NOVEL

KRISTEN ARNETT

corsair

CORSAIR

First published in the US in 2019 by Tin House Books
This edition first published in 2019 by Corsair

1 3 5 7 9 10 8 6 4 2

A CIP catalogue record for this book is available from the British Library.

ISBN: 978-1-4721-5544-3

Printed and bound in Great Britain by Clays Ltd, Elcograf S.p.A.

Papers used by Corsair are from well-managed forests
and other responsible sources.

Corsair
An imprint of
Little, Brown Book Group
Carmelite House
50 Victoria Embankment
London EC4Y 0DZ

An Hachette UK Company
www.hachette.co.uk

www.littlebrown.co.uk

Problem solving is hunting.
It is savage pleasure and we are born to it.

—Thomas Harris

Happiness is a large gut pile.

—T-shirt proverb

for michael michael motorcycle

SKINNING

SKINNING

ODOCOILEUS VIRGINIANUS— CUTANEOUS DEER FIBROMA

How we slice the skin:

Carefully, that's a given. Cutting with precision sounds like the same thing, but it's not. Consider the following: you've pared the flesh from a mango for a bowl of fruit salad. Have you done it thoughtfully, preserving the sweet yellow flesh, or have you done it with the clinical detachment of a surgeon?

There's gotta be some tenderness. There's gotta be some love.

Our father said this as he slid his knife into the coat of a white-tailed buck. It was unusual. He never let us close to the table while he worked.

You've gotta want it. He pointed to the throat, tapping lightly with a fingertip. *Start below the cape, here. Like you're unzipping a jacket.*

Milo and I crowded at either side of the metal table as our father gently opened the body, his hands blue-gloved and steady, as if delivering a baby. We were nine and ten and treated the shop with its creatures like our personal toy store. Other kids had stuffed animals; we had preserved skinks and mounted bass and antlers coated with Varathane.

Gimme a little elbow room, guys.

We each stepped back half a foot, then moved in close a few seconds later. The buck was large, but I'd seen bigger. The deer had already been drained of its blood and lay limp, limbs sprawled like a dismantled puppet. It was a nine-pointer and the man who'd brought it to the shop was a regular, someone our father had over for beers in our living room.

Why the whole deer? This wasn't just a mount—the entire animal would be processed: chest, rump, legs. I couldn't imagine why someone would keep the whole thing as a trophy; most hunters left the remains to rot out in the woods after their field prep.

Our father's eyes were bright with excitement. It was a new challenge for him, a way to put creativity into his work. He hummed under his breath. It made me want to sing too.

Inside was cool with the constant hum of central air, but still humid enough to draw sweat over my lip. The sign in front of the shop was just as big and yellow as it had been when our grandfather ran the place: MORTON'S TAXIDERMY (& MORE). The marquee promoted sales, whatever was in excess that week: pig ears, deer antlers, rabbit pelts.

Our father didn't look at us while he spoke, just kept his voice at a low buzz that zinged in my brain. *If it's not done with some kind of feeling, the customers can tell. It won't look real.*

Buckets sat at our feet for any leftover innards the customers hadn't disposed of already, white plastic tubs that had at one point housed pickles soaked in yellow brine. Some entrails we saved, some we didn't, but we always made sure the floor stayed clean. The smell of bleach saturated my cloud of dark hair, even when my mother braided it out of the way.

Milo and I both wore old Publix bag-boy aprons, tied around our necks and backs in looping double knots. Though I was older by a year, Milo stood half a head taller than me—taller than anyone in the fourth grade. We leaned close to our father's elbows, trying to catch the knife's movements, until he cleared his throat and we both moved back again. He wore a black rubber apron that he'd rinse off in the back sink, slicking off the intestinal remnants of our daily autopsies with lemon-scented dish detergent. Our mother would wash ours and hang them in the front closet, next to our muddy sneakers and raincoats and the mothballed sweaters that we wore only once a year.

Jessa-Lynn, hold the neck steady. I moved to the front of the table and dug my hands into the fur until the spine and tendons compressed beneath my fingers. I fought the urge to massage deeper, to let my hands crawl spiderlike up the column and embrace the muzzle.

Now come here, son. It's not gonna bite.

From behind the deer's fuzzy cheek I watched my brother take the knife from my father, a double-sided scalpel. On the table beside it sat the half-moon of the fleshing blade he'd use to strip the wet hunks of flesh from the skin. Its curve caught the light, blinking silver under the fluorescent bulbs that lined the paneled ceiling.

Like this? Milo clutched the knife like he would a sharpened stick, something to gouge and mutilate. He fidgeted and nearly dropped his grip as he dug down into the deer hide.

Let me show you. Flex your wrist. Press steady, slow. Not too deep.

5

Prep meant our father would completely skin the buck and assess the skeleton. See where the shot penetrated and reconstruct the animal's body, fortifying it with thick patches of wool and cotton padding and strong wiring to hold the pose. Most shops worked only off prefab mannequins and forms, but my father liked creating his own—even if it meant every piece took two weeks longer than it would at a competitor's shop. Customers looking for specialty work were willing to pay for the extra labor, but most weren't after the art my father wanted to make of their kills. It didn't matter to Dad; he'd put in the time regardless. Even if it meant losing business.

He's got a gristly patch here, push harder.

According to our father, customers wanted something commanding in the animal's pose. Most were hunters, and if they chose to have their kill mounted, they wanted it larger than life, as if the animal might reanimate and attack. They wanted bigger, stronger, more muscled. Our job was to grant that wish, even if the person had shot the animal from behind as it nosed through a garbage can.

Milo sweat through the neck of his shirt. It was cool in the back of our shop, low sixties to keep the inevitable rot at bay, but my brother looked like he'd just run in from the playground. *I'm not sure. Like this?* He pulled up the knife—jagged, moving too quickly. There was a purring tear. *Sorry, sorry!*

Grunting, my father took my brother's hand and guided it back down to the work. *That'll have to be repaired. You'll have to stitch it up after we tan so the lines won't show through crooked.*

Sorries wouldn't fix the coat. There would always be a scar, something out of place to mimic the fat bullet hole behind its

6

tufted ear. Ripped pelts weren't ideal, but there were ways to cover them: mud flecked up on an ankle or the fur combed over in a way that suggested muscle mass beneath the skin. I ran my thumbs down the buck's neck to the softest place at the heart of its throat. Its white hair had grown in a clumped oval, framed by the thicker, slick stuff that coated its back—the dense coat that grew in for winter, even in Florida. Usually my father would brace the deer's antlers in one of the clipped tracks that hung from the ceiling. We'd never been so involved in the process before; certainly never been allowed to use his tools or cut into any of the customers' prized pelts.

There. Push hard, just below the fetlock. You gotta scoop along, like you're pulling open canvas. Let the knife become an extension of your arm.

Our father's cuts were seamless. He'd been doing the work for almost thirty years, alongside his own father, who'd died the year Milo was born. In pictures, our grandfather looked like a harder, grayer version of my father: tattooed and T-shirted and grizzled, the kind of man who smiled only when he needed to stretch his mouth. His picture was still up in the front of the shop, near the register. It sat between the mountain lion he'd shot and stuffed and a BEST OF CENTRAL FLORIDA TAXIDERMY plaque with years pinned underneath it dating back to 1968.

Milo's blade slowed. They'd reached a blockage behind the back right leg. My father took the scalpel from my brother and squatted down to view the situation, lifting the carcass and turning it deftly. One hand pulled the skin taut while the other slid the knife below the lump that protruded from beneath the

7

fur. He quickly sliced the flesh and poked the knife beneath, flicking the tip upward until the mass was exposed.

What is it? Milo's face was ashy gray. His lips, normally petal pink—so pink that boys from school joked that he wore lipstick—had thinned into a pale slit.

Deer tumor. Our father carved out the lump until it began to separate from the fatty flesh and veins that surrounded it. *Pretty good size. Maybe four inches across.* He hefted the mass in his hand, the vibrant blue of his glove clashing with the dark, clotted red of the tumor. He dug into it with the fleshing blade, testing the resistance of the growth. *Hardly ever see any this big. Mostly just warty stuff around the neck. Sometimes the groin.*

Milo covered his mouth with both hands. A deep noise rumbled in his chest, a sound like gears grinding together, and then he turned and puked. We'd had tomato soup and grilled cheese an hour earlier. Most of it went in the big plastic bucket, but some of it splattered onto the concrete floor, with a few bits landing on our father's shoe.

The buck's eyes were open, surfaces glazed and beginning to harden into wrinkles along the corners from where the water had leached. Milo continued to vomit into the bucket as our father stalked from the table. He brought wet rags from the corner sink. He waited until Milo was done, still slumped over on the floor, before thrusting one at him. *Get the mop from your mother out front and clean all this up. Everything.*

The tumor sat on the metal table, my father's knife still stuck in it. He took the blade by the handle and pressed on either side of the mass with his fingers until it pulled free. Wiping it against the other rag, he turned and offered it to me. Overhead, the air-conditioning hummed to life again. The breeze was cool against my neck as I took the knife. It was solid in my palm, the curvature of the handle fitting just inside the crease where my hand closed. He beckoned me around the table and I stood in front of him, contemplating the buck's substantial bulk.

See there? He held my wrist, gently pointing the knife toward the open wound, now taking on oxygen and darkening. *We'll have to work around that. Can you get below the leg and take the seam around the back?*

Being this close, I was enveloped in the odor of his aftershave. It reminded me of Christmas trees: piney and musky, a smell that wouldn't scare off a deer. Behind us, Milo dragged in the yellow mop bucket. Some of the water splashed over the lip and onto the floor as he struggled through the doorway. Our mother called to him from the front of the shop. My father turned away from my brother and leaned down to whisper in my ear.

You're a natural. Just like your dad.

It felt right; it felt like I'd been doing it forever. I could see the exact place I would set the blade and strip the animal, knew how we'd replicate the skeleton with trusses and padding and ruffed forms. I could see where the tanned hide would fit over the preparation: a strong, hardy deer, head uplifted, sniffing the wind. Inserting the tip of the blade into the opening, I pulled forward carefully. I let myself love the buck on the table. I caressed its soft, sweet body.

My father put his hand on my shoulder and squeezed lightly. Leaning forward, I braced my arm against the cool metal of the table and looked into the cavity where the flesh separated from the skin. In the dark heart of its carcass, I saw my future mapped out in gristle.

I was my father's daughter and I loved him fiercely. We had identical hands and neither of us could roll our tongues. Both of us snapped using our ring fingers, which we thought was very funny. There were permanent frown lines etched between our eyes. We liked the crusts off pizza and the tartness of lemons squeezed in water. There was a security in seeing myself mirrored back. Our shared love of the animals; the way we could be in a room and stay silent, comfortable in our skins as long as we were together. No one knew me like him. No one understood him like his daughter.

Not so different from us, Jessa. He tugged my braid. *Just guts and blood.*

We were a family of taxidermists.

We were collectors, dismantlers, and artisans. We pieced together life from the remnants of death. Animals that might have weathered into nothing got to live on indefinitely through our care. Our heart was in the curve of a well-rendered lip smoothed over painted teeth. I saw my father's hand in the ears of the rabbit he created for my brother the one that rode on a small doll's bicycle. It was in the glass eyes of an albino ferret whose lids my father sculpted with the utmost tenderness. We created better than anyone because we loved it more, because we knew those animals better than anyone else ever could. It was ours because we fashioned it to be ours. My father molded me to assist him; to be the one who helped shoulder the load. He was the lynchpin that held our family's world together, but I was the one who supported him. I could always bear the burden because he told me I was strong. Because he told me I was the only one who could.

I tried to tell myself this as I stared down at the blood and matter congealed on the concrete floor of our workshop. As I assessed the droplets that dotted the white cinder-block walls in a Rorschach pattern that my eyes identified as a butterfly, as two men shaking hands, as the entrance to a well that opened into something infinite. Let my eyes follow the sight line of the red mess, which had originated from the soft place in my father's skull. Somewhere near the temple, but I couldn't be sure. It was hard to look at for longer than a few seconds. Hard to believe it was real.

Behind me, softly, the radio played Randy Jackson.

He was in his chair, slumped over the metal counter where he'd spent so much of his life. Face down, head turned to the side so that I could make out the bristle of his mustache. The eye I could see was closed. His wire-framed glasses had slipped halfway down his nose the moment he'd fallen, one side bent crookedly behind his ear so his hair fluffed up to a graying point. He wore his apron over the plaid button-down my mother had gotten him for his birthday so many years earlier; the one I said made him look like the Brawny paper towel man. I could almost make myself believe he'd dropped off to sleep midproject, which he sometimes did. Working into the small hours of the morning, painstakingly stitching hide beneath the

11

light of a gooseneck lamp. If he just woke up and grouched at me for staring at him. If he smiled at me so I could feel okay. If he were breathing. If there weren't so much blood.

It was the whole animal laid out in front of me again; un-natural and unknown. That was the first collaboration with my father. This would be the last.

It hurt to see him that way, wounded and opened up to the elements. I allowed myself a moment to marvel at his face. It sometimes looked much older than its sixty-six years, but death had made him young again: his cheeks soft and loose, lips tender and partially open. His hands, always in motion, finally still.

Though I knew I shouldn't, I took off his glasses and smoothed down the cowlick in his wiry hair. I moved his hands from the table and set them in his lap, one propped on ei-ther thigh, how he always liked to sit at the dinner table while my mother prepped the meal. I unbuckled the watch from his wrist with trembling fingers, the watch that had been my grandfather's before it had belonged to him. The one I'd cov-eted because it was my father's favorite and he cherished it. Things that were his that I wanted to be mine. His watch. All the best knives. The shop. His pride.

I picked up the handgun from where it lay on the floor. I set it on the counter next to the letter he'd left with my name spelled out in all capital letters. He'd taught me how to shoot with that gun. Taken me out to the backyard, just the two of us, and helped me pull the trigger. I was scared, but I wanted to look tough, because my father couldn't stomach crybabies. He smiled and told me how impressed he was with my aim and my confidence. Put his hand on my shoulder and squeezed, how he always did when he was proud of me. He was always proudest when I refused to show weakness.

My little miniature, he said. *Best sharpshooter in Florida.*

Then I went to the back and pulled out the mop bucket and the bleach, staring hard into the water as it churned in the yellow tub. Told myself it was the fumes that teared me up as I dunked the mophead into the liquid, and then began the slow process of cleaning up the mess. I left the letter on the counter until I could get myself under control, wondering if it would say anything to help me understand the animal in front of me.

1

Along with the typical antler sets and knotted pine logs that bracketed our porch, the plate glass window at the front of the shop held a goat, a Florida panther, and a wild boar. The boar and the panther had been around for so long we considered them part of the family. I'd mounted the goat just a few weeks back. It was a black-and-white English Bagot, identified as "vulnerable" on most species survival lists. It had a coat so soft you'd think you were stroking velvet.

But when I came in that morning they weren't in their usual display spots, reenacting a scene from *Wild Kingdom*. Instead, the panther was propped behind the goat, its openmouthed growl suddenly transformed into an expression of uninhibited ecstasy.

"Why?" I turned to my mother, who was wearing her favorite pink floral nightgown with the smocked lace around the throat. She sat sideways on a metal folding chair she'd set in the middle of the sidewalk, holding an empty coffee cup and a cigarette. "Just . . . tell me why."

"It speaks for itself." She took a drag and tapped ash into the mug, which she balanced on her knee.

It was the second time in a month that she'd rendered a sex scene in the front window of our store. While the panther plowed away at the goat, the wild boar leered at the two of them from behind a large plastic ficus I recognized as a decades-long resident of my parents' living room. Even now, in my thirties, I could vividly recall when my parents had brought it home—something green and "living" to chipper up the dull drab of decapitated animal heads that lined the walls behind the couches and my father's recliner.

Binoculars had been propped in the boar's yellowed tusks. There were condoms thrown around, some of which had been opened up, innards dangling from the branches of the potted plants. A second look revealed that the panther's paws were shredded from where the adhesive and pins had originally secured it to an oak branch.

"Take a real good look," I said. "Get it out of your system before I take everything down." My casual morning of stripping skins and sipping black coffee faded into the distance, replaced by the aggravation of refurbishing injured fur and staining new mounts. The panther would likely take days to fix.

The sun was already burning off the morning humidity and warming the pavement. I'd seen Travis Pritchard's pickup pull into the Dollar General parking lot across the street. This part of town was all older family businesses and single-family homes, dirty, flat places with sprawling yards. Pitted streets intersected at odd angles without the benefit of stop signs, stucco ranches in myriad shades of tan squeezed between a coin laundry, a Goodwill, and a shoe repair shop. A used car lot took up most of the real estate two streets over, near a diner where I ate most of my meals, convenience stores dotting the perimeter. It was Wednesday—BOGO value day for the retirement set from the Towers, a gated community comprised of local grandparents and snowbirds. Soon a crowd would gather to view Libby Morton's latest unholy rendering. The thought of fending off scandalized seventysomethings this early in the morning did bad things to my stomach.

I took the cigarette from her hand and got one good drag off it before stubbing it out under my boot. The goat stood placid, assessing me with its slitted yellow eyes. I turned away so I wouldn't have to see it in its indignity. "Can we go back inside now?"

"I'd prefer to sit here."

"I really wish you wouldn't."

My mother shook her head, free of the waist-length hair she'd had since my brother was born. When questioned about the decision to lop it all off, she mentioned a magazine article she'd read when she took my father to one of his doctor's appointments. Something about hair holding grief: how dead cells left on a living body might make pain last longer. Her shorn head took some getting used to. When the light caught her just right, it was like looking at a miniaturized version of my brother. They both had the same strong jaw and sallow skin, a long, narrow nose framed by deep grooves that almost resembled parentheses. Her remaining hair was still mostly dark, but now there were sprigs of white along with bits of bare scalp that poked through in patches where she'd gotten a little overzealous with the razor.

"Please?" I said, looking at the Dollar General. Travis stuck his head through the front door and waved.

She sighed heavily and propped her chin in her hand. "I'm gonna sit here for a minute. You go on ahead."

A morning jogger in bright purple spandex ran past, moving down onto the street to avoid us on the sidewalk, almost stumbling to a collision as she took in the window display.

"What is *that*?" she asked, mouth dropped so far open I could almost count her molars.

My mother placed one hand over her heart. "It's my work."

"I'm gonna go make some coffee." I scrubbed a hand over my face and wished it were late enough in the day to crack open a beer. At least the place next door was vacant. For a while it'd been barely surviving as a subpar kitschy vintage restaurant, but no one had rented it for the last year and a half. My father always said he'd rather eat something *I* cooked than spend money on a place that couldn't even manage to make a grilled cheese.

"Coffee? Mom?" I repeated.

She nodded and waved me off, pointing out various areas of interest in the display. I heard her mention something about the panther's naturally high sex drive as the door snicked closed behind me.

"Good fucking grief."

The mess was even worse up close. Bits of fur and leaves littered the floor, as if the animals had taken chunks from each other's hides. There was a big slash by the boar's tail that nearly brought me to tears. I turned away, disgusted with my mother and with myself for not handling things sooner. Imagining what my father would say if he could see the wreck she'd made of his work, I swallowed hard. He'd be so disappointed.

This kind of shit was getting to be a regular occurrence. The original lewd display had been constructed less than a month after we'd buried my father. That morning the shop was pitch-black and I ran directly into the bear—except I didn't know it was a bear; I thought I'd caught an intruder. When he built it, my father had reinforced its broad torso with two-by-fours. The punch I laid on it almost broke my hand.

I'd tried to wrap my mind around the scene as the overhead fluorescents flickered spastically to life. The futon from the spare bedroom wedged next to the glass, covered in my grandmother's linens. A raccoon I'd mounted the week prior gowned in a satin negligee, bridal veil hanging delicately over its face. Its uplifted hand gestured sweetly at the bear, standing beside the bed in a roomy pair of custom boxer shorts made from two pillowcases. I'd immediately recognized the print; they were from Milo's old Spider-Man bedroom set.

There'd been other incidents too: a parade of animals decked out in lingerie and posed in front of boudoir mirrors, alligator skulls with panties stuffed in their open mouths and dangling from their teeth. I knew my father would mind someone dripping lube on his prized mountain lion. He'd definitely mind the ripped fur. But he wasn't there to say anything about it and my mother was my mother. I had only so much control over what she did. I couldn't help but feel I was letting him down, again. His letter, sitting beside my bed, stayed in my head.

I trust you to handle things. I need you to do this now.

"Do better," I muttered, shaking my head. "You gotta do better than this."

Our tiny kitchenette was at the rear of the store, close to the entrance to the workshop, but still in sight line of the register and the assorted candy bars that kids liked to pocket. I searched through the cupboard for coffee filters and found none, remembering too late that we'd been out for a week. I settled on a wadded paper towel.

My mother used to clean the store, but aside from her new window-dressing duties, she'd stopped coming in completely. Dust coated the sale items, coasting along the backs of baby alligators and the lacquered fish until they looked like they'd grown fur. The neon-hued rabbits' feet were grimy, as if the rabbits had run through mud puddles before losing their paws.

Outside, my mother was still yapping about her pornography. Aside from the runner, she'd managed to snag Travis, who stood looking at the scene like a kid in front of a mall Santa Claus. My mother's pink nightgown turned luminous in the sunlight, silhouetting her legs and torso. I wasn't totally sure she was wearing underwear.

I rinsed out a dirty mug and scrubbed the stains with a rag I found next to the sink. Then I poured coffee and took a scalding sip, settling back behind the register. My mother gestured to Travis and to the runner, who'd pulled out a cell phone and was taking pictures.

The beginning of a tension headache boiled behind my forehead.

Travis was still standing outside when my mother came back into the shop. The bell chimed fretfully as she pushed open the door, the metal folding chair jammed under her armpit. She was in the fuzzy slippers my father got her for Christmas a couple of years earlier. Leaves and mud slopped onto the sides and back of the little bunny faces. It had rained the night before, which meant she'd walked over from the house at God only knew what hour of the night.

"Thanks," she said, taking my coffee and handing me the mug full of cigarette ash. She took a sip and grimaced. "That's awful."

"We're out of coffee filters."

"Somebody should buy some more. Tastes like dirt."

"Sorry about that," I replied, deciding not to bring up the fact that she usually bought the coffee, the filters, and the garbage bags. My father would've taped the grocery list to the steering wheel of her car. He would've said her name in that exasperated way that showed he loved her even though she drove him crazy.

"God, I'm tired."

She leaned back against the counter and her ribs moved visibly beneath the ruffled bodice of her nightgown. She was smoking again, which she hadn't done since we were little. The bags under her eyes were deep-set and very dark, like someone had pressed their thumbs into her flesh. I wanted to shake her and ask why she had to make things harder than they already were, why she couldn't just act normal so we could move forward the way Dad would want us to, but instead I went to the back and called my brother.

He picked up on the fourth ring, voice still thick with sleep. I wondered if there was anyone there with him, but my gut told me he was alone. He hadn't seen anyone seriously since Brynn had left him and the kids. Both of us forever in mourning of her, even though she'd been gone for years. Still, it was late. I'd anticipated he'd be at work or at least on the road. Milo, the guy who could never figure out what he wanted to do with his life. He called in sick every other Monday. His daughter was about to go into high school and she was the one who had to do the grocery shopping because he always forgot things like milk and bread. *You have no work ethic*, our father told him once, and Milo smiled as if it were a compliment.

"Come get your mother, she's done it again," I said, watching her in the pale light that filtered through the window. She'd turned to face the scene at the front of the shop, rubbing a dusty pink rabbit's foot between her fingers.

"Christ. Lemme get some pants on."

"Don't worry about it, she's not wearing any."

"I'll be there in ten minutes. Don't let her leave."

I hung up and wondered how I'd get through the rest of the day, much less the rest of the week. Our father had been dead for a year and I was expected to take over everything; manning the store alone, figuring out what to do with my mother's burgeoning creative talents. It was exhausting.

"One thing at a time," I said, pulling out a pad of old scratch paper. "That's all there is to it."

It was easier to work that way: moving forward piecemeal, performing each small task with the entirety of my focus. One done, then another. Letting them all pile up until there was no room to think about anything else.

Bunch of deer mounts. Bud Killson's bass needed fresh shellac and a couple of new eyes. There was endless fleshing, piles of stuff backed up in the freezer. Pelts to scrape and tan. Flushing out the acid baths and refilling them. Scrubbing down all the countertops in the back, bleaching the floors. There was always something to do.

I'd seen my father work that way all my life. Lists, routines. No time for stress when you've got a schedule to keep.

Remembering that made my limbs loosen and my jaw un-
clench.

I could do it. I just needed to be Dad.

"Your brother's here," my mother called, setting down her
coffee cup. "Maybe he can give me a ride home."

Milo climbed out of the truck and left the motor running.
He looked like he'd slept in his clothes, and he was sporting a
couple of days' worth of patchy beard. Waving off my offer of
coffee from the doorway, he took my mother's arm and put her
into the truck. She didn't argue, just yawned and shuffled her
nightgown so it covered her bare legs. They looked too thin; the
veins ran blue along her ankles.

"Come for dinner tomorrow," she said. "I'll make enough
for everyone."

Dinner at my mother's meant feeling everything. It wasn't
like the shop, with its tools and disinfectants and work. There
was so much of Dad alive in the house: his recliner with the
saggy, loose stuffing in the armrests, paperback crime novels
parked facedown on the floor, his buttonless shirts piled haphazardly beside my mother's sewing machine. The green bottle
of the aftershave he always wore still sat next to the bathroom
sink, its top placed upside down beside the faucet.

"I've gotta get stuff done around here," I said. "Got a customer coming by."

"I'll see you at six."

I didn't argue, just waved as they pulled out of the lot.
When I turned around, Travis Pritchard was standing in front
of the window again. He had his cap in one hand and was rubbing the other very gently along his buzzed salt-and-pepper

scalp. His shirtsleeves were too short, revealing slips of his skin nearly up to the elbow every time he raised his arm.

"Don't you need to get back to work?" I hooked my thumbs through my belt loops and yanked up my sagging jeans. Unlike my mother, I'd gained weight in the past year. I drank in excess, sleeping most nights in the shop. My belly sat over my pants and pushed them down my hips. Nothing fit right. Everything I owned felt uncomfortable.

"Marleen's got the counter."

Our reflections meshed into the scene in the glass: his weathered skin and dark, sunken eyes, my squat frame in the usual gear—old jeans that needed washing, linty flannel, and a round face so full of freckles that I still got carded at bars. We hovered ghostlike over the animals, more voyeur than even the wild boar.

Behind us, a bus pulled into the parking lot, transporting a load of retirees. "Looks like the Towers decided to come in a little early today," I said.

Travis grunted and reluctantly turned to stare across the parking lot, where the bus was letting down the first of the elderly wheelchair occupants. "Your mother's got a real talent, you know that?"

That's not the way I would've described taxidermy propped to resemble fucking, but I let him have his say. My mother had always had a penchant for crafting. Domestic arts, my father called them. She embroidered, made her own clothes, threw pottery, scrapbooked. It was flower-arranging shit, the kind of stuff moms did because they needed activities to pass the time. I knew she liked art because my father mentioned something

about it once while we were stuffing Canada geese. He mentioned how she'd wanted to sculpt, then shook his head and
showed me the best way to place the birds' wings so they didn't
look lopsided. It was just stuff she did. Nothing important.
Nothing to take away from our time together.

Travis walked back over to the Dollar General and I went
inside to assess the damage. The panther was easy to move, but
I knew that I'd have to spend a while on its paws. Aside from
facial reconstruction, feet were always the hardest to render.
It looked as if my mother had actually yanked the cat straight
from the branch. Bits of its fur were still adhered to the wood.

The mount was smoothed with a lathe to make a flat surface. When I turned it over, there they were, carved into the
bottom: *PTM*. My finger followed the groove of my father's
initials, from the delicate swoop of the *P* to the tight peaks of
the *M*. He'd pulled the branch from a larger limb that fell in
our backyard after a thunderstorm. My father had an eye for
scene and setting. He could make props out of anything: discarded pieces of furniture, wooden pallets, old window frames.
He'd looked in that tangle of downed limbs and seen the perfect match, a mount so well suited that it made the cat look
ready to pounce onto unsuspecting prey.

I brought him an abandoned sled the week before he died.
It was ancient, the crackling red paint sloughing off in hunks,
dangling runners spotted with rust. We had ducks in that week.
Pristine white mallards with bright orange beaks and feet. I put
the sled up on the metal countertop beside their bodies and
asked if he thought it was a good match—that out-of-place
pairing.

Perfect, he said. *Exactly what I would've picked out.*

Remembering how he'd left himself laid out on that same counter ruined the memory for me. I threw the branch off into the corner and knocked down a rack of miniature lacquered alligator skulls. They rattled around on the floor, spinning and knocking against each other. A few of them broke, dislodging teeth that scattered across the floor like uncooked rice.

I ignored that mess and focused on carefully removing the condoms from the ficus. My hands were coated in spermicidal lubricant. It took three strong washes to remove the gunk. I was nervous to look at the Bagot's coat, sure my mother hadn't been nearly as cautious. I left it propped in the window. The light threw pastel highlights on the work I'd done to its face and ears, making it look inquisitive and alert. It was the only good feeling I'd had all morning, staring at that goat and knowing that at least I hadn't fucked that up.

In the interest of my back, I left the ficus where it stood. "Come on, buddy." I tugged at the boar's rump until it scraped backward toward me across the linoleum. "Let's take a look at you."

When I removed the binoculars from the boar's tusks, the right end chipped off, sending white dust pillowing onto the floor.

We hadn't had any new business in weeks, aside from assorted small fry and the occasional regular who dropped off a pity kill, but that wouldn't pay the bills. Money problems were another legacy left to me by my father. I'd always thought he was so capable, that he'd handled everything with money to spare for things like groceries and car insurance. What I'd discovered was a black hole of debt. *I'm sorry*, he'd written, his pen digging wounds into the paper. *I'm so sorry*. I looked around at the mess piled up around the shop: the fly-ridden garbage, stacks of bills and trade magazines slipping over the counters and falling to the floor, mingled dust and hair dotting everything.

The bell clanged as the front door opened.

A woman stood in the doorway. Morning sun poured through the gap and shrouded her figure in shadow, but based on the nice clothes and shoes she wore, I didn't think it was anyone I knew.

"What happened to the display?" She pointed at the window. The boar still sat there awkwardly with its broken tusk, like an uncomfortable patient in a dentist's office.

"The what?"

She molded the air with her hands, as if trying to sculpt the image. "You know, the window scene. My friend Denise sent me a picture. She caught it on her jogging route this morning."

"That wasn't supposed to be up."

"Why not?" She stepped precisely around the clutter on the floor. She wore patent leather pumps that made her legs look great and a professional business skirt with a pleat cut in the back. I wiped my hands on my jeans and assessed my work boots, which were stained with an accumulation of varnish and tanning preservatives.

"It was obscene," I said. "My mother's going through a rough time right now."

The woman was a foot taller than me, lean and angular and handsome. She stopped next to the boar and kneeled beside it, assessing its face. One long finger probed the broken tusk. "I'm Lucinda Rex," she said, cupping the animal's face. "I run the gallery over on Morse."

"Jessa Morton." I poured myself a cup of the weak coffee that still sat in the bottom of the pot in order to give myself something to do with my hands, which were suddenly sweating.

"It's fascinating stuff." She looked up from where she crouched beside the boar. Her eyes were dark and thickly lashed. "You did these yourself?"

"Most of them. Some my father did."

"They're very lifelike." She unfolded from the floor and continued standing beside the boar. Its broken tusk pressed into the smooth skin of her leg and left behind a pink scratch.

Lucinda was the kind of lady I liked to look at, but generally avoided because they were way too classy for me. My usual type was a messy woman, the kind of person who'd go out with me on a date and inevitably leave the bar with someone else. "Was there something you needed?"

"Yes. How much for this one?"

"How much?" I repeated, watching her pet the boar's head. Her hands were slender and her fingers were very long. I imagined them touching my face, stroking a line across my collarbone. "How much."

"I'll give you three grand for it."

"What?" The most anybody had ever spent in our shop was just over a thousand, and that was on custom work.

Frowning, she brought her purse over to the sales counter. "Is that not enough?"

I shook my head. "It's not right—the tusk is broken, see? I'll have to fix it."

"I can't even tell." She wasn't looking. "I'd love to see what your mother could do with something like this."

She had to be joking. "Yeah, right."

"I think it looks fine."

It obviously did not. "I'd need to fix it up first."

"Of course. But let me go ahead and buy it from you now. I'll just pick it up later." She looked appraisingly at me, lips set in a thin line. "Or do you deliver?"

"Sure, we can do that." We never did that.

"Wonderful." She unearthed a credit card from a giant pile of them, an assortment stacked up like playing cards. "I'll expect you tomorrow afternoon."

I spent the rest of the day sprucing up the boar. Its tusk was shot to hell and the coat was worn down and scaly from sitting in the dust and sun for so many years. Patching the holes was rough work without suitable scraps. It made fixing fuckups a hell of a lot harder, but I wasn't about to sell Lucinda something wrecked. For a solid three grand, the work would have to be pristine.

My father had patented a few of his own tanning recipes, stuff that he'd perfected over the years, tricks he'd learned from his own father. Left to my own devices, I couldn't do half the work he did. I didn't have the connections or the experience. Most of what I created was based on gut feeling, what he called my natural talent. It had served me well in the past, but that was with my father there to pick up the slack. When I asked him to teach me, he always put it off.

It'll be faster if I just do it, he'd said about his special glazing technique for trout. *Takes longer to teach than for me to just get it done.*

I'd had to turn down three different jobs because I didn't know the glaze and he had never thought it was the right time for me to learn. Since his death, I often wondered if he didn't teach me those tricks because he still wished he had the right son to share them with.

It was a pointless concern. All I could do was what I'd been doing: running relentlessly, every day, until my brain shut down. I worked until my hands slipped and I nicked the pads of my fingers. Gutted fish until my clothes stunk of the lake. Scraped until my muscles screamed. Then I could sleep again and wake the next day, thrust back into my endless cycle of trying, trying, trying. Being what he needed.

Need. It was a word that my father seldom used. I'd heard him say *want,* and *expect.* But there was never anything like *need,* a word that implied helplessness and frailty. A word that made him seem farther from me than ever, drowning, thrashing alone while he waited for someone to save him. For me to save everything. So I worked. It was what my father would have done. *The best way to get through anything at home is just to stay at work,* he'd say, smiling over the top of a mount. We'd laugh about it, him talking about my mother that way. That she would ever be too much for him to go home to. That he would ever need a break from a person who took care of everything for him so he could do the things he loved the most.

"Focus," I said, examining the boar's legs. "Don't fuck this up."

My mother hadn't been too careful posing it, likely because the animal was double her weight. There were long rips along the belly that required re-stitching and one that I needed to resurface completely. I drank unending cans of beer, my mind switching to autopilot, as it always did when I was re-creating. I let my hands do my thinking for me, building something from the tangle of hide and padding and wires. I cleaned the coat. Glossed the hooves. Patched the slippage along the ears. I thought about Lucinda: her long fingers, her long legs. The way her mouth had looked when she half smiled at me in the shop. Wondered if she'd be pleased with the work, then felt aggravated with myself that I wanted to see her again. I generally never wanted to see anyone, and that's how I liked my life: simple, no mess.

Milo stopped by around nine the next morning, carrying a coffee in each hand. I took both from him and sat with my legs splayed out on either side of the table. I smelled sour, my hands stained with dye from where I'd tried to match up scraps on the underside of the animal. It wasn't exact, but I comforted myself with the thought that Lucinda wouldn't know any different.

"Can't believe you're getting rid of him." He petted the boar on its wrinkled snout before inserting two fingers in the nostrils and wriggling them around. "It's like selling a family member."

I slapped his hand away, worried he'd screw up the paint. "The money will help me sleep at night." The first coffee I sipped from was full of cheap, syrupy creamer. I handed it back to Milo, who chugged some before setting it on the metal table next to my tools.

"Don't you feel bad that it was a Prentice Morton original? Not too many of those left."

Sighing, I rolled my shoulders until my spine cracked. "The two of us are the only originals that matter. At least we're getting paid."

He grabbed a chair from the desk and brought it over to the other side of the boar. His face scrunched up as he assessed the side, squinting deep wrinkles beside his eyes. "It looks good, but it'll never be like Dad's. There's something wrong with the coloring, it doesn't match up along the neck."

What the hell did he know about any of it? He'd never had to spend hours in the shop, matching dyes, sweating buckets into the pelt when it didn't want to stretch right. "Fuck you, nothing's like Dad's."

Milo held up his hands. "Just saying you can't do all this yourself."

"Aren't you supposed to be at work?" I asked.

He shrugged and leaned back, drinking more coffee. "Took a sick day."

Since we were kids, my brother was the flexible one, the person who listened and empathized. He'd been home with my mother while my father took me places: out together on early morning fishing and hunting trips, down to the Home Depot to collect gear for a garden-bed project in the backyard. He'd never asked my brother along; he'd considered him whiny and too prone to crying. *Your brother's a little too sensitive about everything*, he told me one day over lunch, digging pickles off his pastrami and passing them to me. *He has too many feelings. I love him. I just don't understand him, that's all.*

"You okay?" Milo asked, leaning closer to me. He'd shaved, finally, and there was dried blood dotting his chin. "You should eat."

"Sorry, I'm just tired." I set down the coffee and stood up. The world blackened to pinpricks for a moment and I waited until the dizziness passed before continuing. "Help me load this fucker in the truck."

We each grabbed an end and maneuvered it through the back of the shop and into the alleyway. Down the street, light gleamed off the lake like a line of silver glitter. It was steamy out and bordering the high eighties. I anticipated that it would soar into the nineties before long, and didn't relish leaving the boar in the back of the bed. The glue and tanners had a tendency to melt in the heat. More than once we'd lost antlers or eyeballs when someone left our work in the car while picking up groceries. Our father always told people to treat taxidermy as they would a live animal: never leave a dog in a locked car; never leave a mounted deer head in the front seat.

I took a blue tarp from the back of the shop and we laid it over the boar, pinning it down with bungees in all four corners. The animal's tusks and back poked up, propping up the middle of the tarp in a bright bulge that made me feel nervous for its safety. We climbed into the truck and Milo pulled down the alley and into the street.

"Let's get something to eat. You can't live off beer."

"I don't think that's a good idea." Our father would never have left a taxidermied animal in the back of a truck, but he also never would have delivered one to anybody. "The boar might get fucked up."

"It's already fucked up, and we need breakfast." Milo rubbed a hand against his concave stomach. He was wearing an old T-shirt from high school, a rose-colored one with a front pocket stretched out from storing chewing tobacco. His coloring was more sallow than usual, a sickly unnatural hue. I hadn't been spending much time with him lately—too busy with work and avoiding the spillover of his feelings—and realized he looked worse than I did. *How is he taking care of his daughter if he looks like this?* I wondered. *How is Brynn's kid getting fed?*

Even thinking Brynn's name made my brain swim with images of her: crooked teeth and wide red mouth, a girl with so much light in her it almost hurt to look at her face. The one who'd taken up my thoughts since childhood. Memories of Brynn put razor blades in my stomach, never butterflies.

But I forced those images down and focused on food. I could do food. I nodded at Milo and he smiled, turning left, down the street to the diner.

"Maybe it's time to talk about selling the business." Milo steered with his left hand, elbow jutting out the window while he punched gears with his right. "The economy's not great, and there's no money from life insurance, since . . . you know."

My brother had never saved a dollar in his life. He looked so smug, talking about something he'd never had to care about. The closest thing he had to a savings account was his daughter's orange-and-blue UF piggy bank. I wanted to smack him. "What do you know about running a business?"

"You'll end up losing everything you've saved. You need to be realistic."

I'd already put most of my savings into financing the shop, but I wasn't about to tell Milo that. Being realistic meant facing our situation head on, and the fact of the matter was that I was the only one taking care of things. There was no one for me to turn to for help. It made me angry, that my brother could drive me to breakfast and tell me what to do when he never had to deal with any of the shit that came with it. He hadn't found our father, head leaking brain matter onto the metal table where we'd cured our first hide.

"Maybe you could chip in a few bucks," I said, peeling at the paneling that was beginning to separate from the dash. "It's your family too."

Milo's grip tightened on the steering wheel, and I stared out the window. I knew it wasn't fair to say something like that. It wasn't his responsibility to help pay for a shop that our father had never wanted him to help with. I might not have under-stood our mother, but at least she always showed she cared. My father treated Milo like an inconvenience, an acquaintance he didn't like all that much, someone taking up space in the house.

"I'm trying to help," Milo said, tentatively putting his hand on my knee. That kind of touching felt forced, not like any-thing we'd ever done with each other. He and I were handshake buddies. We slapped each other on the back when we hugged.

"Let's just drop it," I said. "I'm too fucking tired."

The parking lot of Winnie's was already half-full. I scrubbed at my gluey eyes and blinked to free an eyelash that had lodged itself beneath a lid. The sun beat down on me as I climbed out of the truck, and I spared a glance at the boar, nestled beneath a sea of blue plastic sheeting.

"You good?" Milo scratched at his bedhead and squinted at me.

"He'll be fine. In and out, right?"

The diner smelled like burnt toast and bacon grease. Milo led us to the very back, next to the kitchen. Brynn and I had come to Winnie's for years, just the two of us, and then we'd brought Milo. Then two again: the two of them without me. Waitresses flew through the swinging doors, indistinguishable from each other aside from their brassy hair colors: coppery penny, corn-silk yellow, the magenta of an especially fiery sunset. One bright head stopped at our table with her notepad already jammed down into her apron. Her hands were birds; one fluttered up into her neckline to fiddle with a button, while the other tugged at an earring.

"You guys want the usual?" she asked, mouth slick and red. Her voice was low and scratchy, like she needed to clear her throat. "Regular? Some coffee?"

"Maybe double that, Molly. Jessa had a late night."

Unlike Lucinda with her cool prettiness, these women were aggressively sexual. Milo and I both had a type and Marsha looked a lot like it: predatory, confident, voluptuous. Brynn was long gone, but stuck between us like a divider we couldn't quite pull down. My best friend and Milo's wife, a woman we'd both known our whole lives. She still dictated how we saw each other. How we saw other women.

He worked his wedding ring around his finger in slow, methodical pulls. She'd been gone for years and he still wouldn't take it off. He'd already gotten the best girl; he'd married Brynn, who was curvier and funnier and meaner than anyone. Marsha slid a hand along his neck and Milo laughed that weird, high-pitched giggle he got whenever anyone paid him too much attention.

I stared out the window and kept my eyes on the boar.

SUS SCROFA—FERAL PIG

There wasn't room on the bed for another body, but that didn't stop Brynn Wiley from climbing in behind me. She curled up next to the wall, legs still striped with cocoa butter that hadn't yet sunk into her skin. One socked foot insinuated itself between my calves as I lay perfectly still and tried to pretend my heart wasn't preparing for flight beneath my rib cage.

Two of our friends were propped in front of us on the floor while we watched a movie in my bedroom. It was my sixteenth birthday and I hadn't even asked for a car; I'd wanted fleshing kits and a chance to work a little on the boar we'd gotten into the shop.

Why are you always so warm?

Lips sticky with gloss stuck to my ear. I'd find a red stain there later and wish it were permanent; that it would smear there forever.

You need to shave. Fingertips tapped my knee, dry and scabbed. *You're disgusting, you know that?*

It was hard to know what was happening in the movie when someone touched me in a way that made my skin feel peeled. Every nerve ending was exposed and frayed. Suzanne and Lizbeth laughed, and then one of them passed the popcorn

39

bowl up onto the mattress beside my head. A hand slid beneath my T-shirt. The cold from Brynn's skin radiated all the way to the bottom of my pelvis.

Her hands ghosted, plucking indiscriminately at my flesh. She found the knobs of my vertebrae, pressed her fingers between the slats of my ribs, cupped her palm around the bulge of my hip. The music from the movie wasn't loud enough to cover the sounds my mouth wanted to make: wounded animal noises, whimpers pulled from deep in my chest. I sat up and folded my knees under me, putting the popcorn bowl between us. Brynn smiled, crooked left canine glowing radioactive blue in the light from the television set. She opened her mouth and I practiced tossing popcorn kernels inside, one by one.

When the movie was over, we made a frozen pizza in the microwave because we were too lazy to preheat the oven. Brynn pinched pieces off and threw bits to my mother's Pomeranian, Sir Charles. He gagged the fourth one up on the living room rug next to the quail family of four my dad and I had stuffed two years prior.

We should go out. Brynn was in a Garfield nightgown that she'd had since the fourth grade. It only skimmed the tops of her thighs. Garfield's face was so stretched out over her breasts that he no longer looked like a cat. When she leaned her hip against the kitchen counter, I could see part of her ass hanging out in pink polka-dotted boy shorts.

Milo's bedroom was down the hall from the kitchen. I could just make out his lean shape in the glow of the light from his ceiling fan. He was almost fifteen and already six feet tall, lanky to the point of emaciation. I knew he liked Brynn, knew he liked her because he looked at her the way I did. We talked less as a result, both of us shying away from our unwanted feelings, not willing to disclose the emotions we both wanted to shed like peeling, sunburned skin. Brynn stretched, arms pulled over her head until Garfield's face elongated into a Halloween ghoul, and his door clicked closed again.

Brynn wanted us to take my father's beer and drive to the shop. Brynn wanted us to drink the beer and look at all the taxidermied animals. Brynn wanted us to play hide-and-seek there with all the lights off. It was my birthday and what I wanted was Brynn.

I rode in the front seat of her hatchback while the other girls huddled in the back. We rolled down the windows and let in the humid night air. Bugs approached the car at forty miles per hour, catching the headlights and smashing liquid on the windshield. Brynn smoked and gave me puffs from where her red lips left heart prints. She pulled into the lot and parked up front. We got out and each had a beer, then immediately opened seconds. I let us in the back door, lights off. Feeling along the wall, everyone stumbled behind me, except for Brynn, whose small hand had found the center of my back. Fingers spanned my spine until I swore I could feel all the metacarpals and tendons. When I finally had her, I'd map her skin. Undressing her, I'd know her joints, her frame, intimately understand the mechanics of her body; what it felt like flush with mine.

Lights flickered to life, fluorescents strobing spastically. Suzanne screamed loud enough to maybe wake the boar, half-undressed on the metal table in the center of the room. Its face sagged forward, opened from below, unencumbered of its tusks. Those sat upright, placed side by side like yellow daggers. The boar's naked frame peeked out. Its bones were so human, so like our own. The skeleton was sad and small without the weight of muscles and fat to flesh it out.

I pointed the others to the front of the shop and told them to drink the rest of the beer. Said there were candy bars and bags of teriyaki-flavored beef jerky under the counter, hidden in the cubby next to the cash register.

My father's tools were put away, except for one small knife sitting out on the countertop. I set down my beer and picked up the blade. More than anything, I wanted to show Brynn how capable I was. I knew she'd never see me as someone she wanted, not the way that I wanted her. I was too much girl, too much of the same. But I could show her my worth in different ways.

I'd bring the animal back to life. It would stretch into a run, craning its neck, arched and triumphant. Or I could make it look coy and sweet, a cartoon animal. I'd create anything, everything. My hands commanded the flesh, brought life back from the grip of death. I had that power in me.

This is what you like to do? Skin these things? She ran a hand down the boar's back leg—down its thick femur, scraped and bleached. Then she brought the thumb of that hand to my mouth. She pressed it there for a second, like pushing a pause button, and then leaned into me with an exhale of yeasty breath. When we kissed, smashed up against the metal table, I didn't care that the knife fell, or that her beer tipped over and spilled onto the boar's feet.

Her eyes were slit and sleepy, cheeks dimpled. It was a soft face like a powdered doughnut, all sugary-sweet. Our mouths met again. My heart thumped wildly in my chest, scrambling behind my ribs like a burrowing animal. I wanted to stroke the hair on her arms, mark the wide mole on her neck, skim the bony collarbones visible from the top of her nightgown. She brought my hand below its trailing end, swept it up her legs, sticky, damp with sweat and tacky from the humidity. Pressing my fingers forward into the vee of her crotch, I found the warm, snarling heart of her. I let my fingers jut there, mouths still eating at each other. Rubbing through the cotton, so much like my own.

There was nothing to say, and that seemed right. I tucked into her, through the underwear, both of us breathing hard, listening for the sound of our friends in the other room. When one of them knocked something over, Brynn and I jumped apart. She reached for her beer and nearly tipped it over again before draining the last sip. My own mouth was dry, but I couldn't drink any more. We went into the front of the shop, with our friends. Turned off the lights, played hide-and-seek. Brynn and I hid behind the bear with its shaggy coat. Our bodies like shadows. Hands finding each other in the dark. Lips grazing. Every time we parted I could smell the imprint of her on me: her spit, my spit, hands full of the scent of her.

When we crawled into bed at 3:00 AM, Brynn said good night and then turned to face the wall. I rolled onto my side and watched the clock, but instead of the numbers, I just kept seeing everything I wanted stretched out in front of me. All of it set out neatly, laid cleanly and precisely. Easy to navigate as the skeletal structure waiting for me back at the shop. I just had to set the bones the way I wanted them and it could all be mine.

2

Milo scrounged for quarters in the center console of his truck, unseating crumpled fast-food napkins and dried oak leaves. "I hate all this shitty construction."

The gallery was one of the new places that had recently cropped up. There were vintage furniture stores and craft beer bars in what used to be a strip mall. Newcomers renovated the beat-up sections of the downtown area, painting walls and repaving streets with brick until everyone's tires bounced at speeds of over fifteen miles per hour. It wasn't new to me. It was what Central Floridians did: pave over everything so they could forget what had been there before. Theme parks and chain restaurants were built over homes and libraries. Banks took the place of family-owned businesses. There were highways built over historic areas; places where you wouldn't know something had ever happened unless a person told you or you read about it in a book. The park where the Seminole once lived had been razed to build carnival space, which in turn had been repurposed as a power building that eventually became a Publix. No one ever seemed to remember what came before. A kind of local amnesia, my father called it. That particular portion of Morse held an old appliance store with a run-down

45

ACE sign papering most of the front window, a co-op that sold locally grown food, and the gallery.

Though all of the buildings were brick, Lucinda Rex's place was painted a flat slate gray. Nothing hinted that it was even a business, other than the front door, where REX was etched in glass, as if a dinosaur might be housed on the premises.

"Is it okay that you're missing so much work?" I asked. "Are they going to fire you?"

He shrugged and finally dug free some loose change. "If they were gonna fire me they'd have done it by now." Six quarters nestled in his palm alongside a couple of straw wrappers and an old french fry. "I've worked there so long now I don't think they even remember I get paid."

Milo had parked out in the street in front of one of the meters. It was broken, but he tried putting the quarters in anyway. Instead of taking the change, it kept spitting them back out into his hand.

Another quarter. "Huh," he said. Another quarter.

I loved my brother, but the way he lived made no sense. No rules, no lists. No caring if his bills got sent to collections or if his truck ran out of gas on the highway and he had to walk three miles in the Florida heat to get a refill. He once told me he'd be happy to live in a tent if it meant never keeping a job. Often he slept until noon and stayed up until dawn reading books in bed. As a lifelong control freak, I found it infuriating. I'd never be the kind of person who could stop caring. Brynn had loved his complete lack of anger and outrage. *I get enough of that from you,* she said. *Let him just be Milo. Like a warm glass of milk. Wholesome and happy.*

"I'm gonna go talk to the lady," I said. "Find out where she wants us to deliver the package."

Milo dropped in another quarter and, when it rolled out, put in a fifth. "'Deliver the package'? You make it sound like we're dropping off a kilo of cocaine."

"What do you think's inside the boar?"

"You're so fucking stupid, I can't believe we're related." He stuffed the quarters in his pocket and leaned back against the truck. "I think this thing is busted."

"No shit."

It was weird outside in that part of town. It didn't feel like old Florida. The sidewalk had been power-washed into submission and no plant life remained, aside from a row of very small cacti set in the gravel that trimmed the edge of the building. The door that led into the gallery was darkly tinted with an intercom placed next to the handle. I pushed the red button on the bottom. It buzzed and the latch clicked open.

Milo and I looked at each other and laughed.

"If I'm not back in ten minutes, call the police."

"If you're not back in ten minutes, I'm leaving and you can walk home."

Inside was a solid thirty degrees colder than out on the pavement. It was dimly lit and the floors were painted black. The space was disorienting, and I thought that said a lot about Lucinda Rex—that she was the kind of person who'd want you confused; maybe the type who'd set up a situation so that when you stumbled out the end of the corridor, she'd be there waiting for you, perfectly cool and collected. I was always impressed with people who could think that far ahead. Though I planned out everything, my life was somehow made up of an endless series of unwanted surprises.

The hallway opened into the actual warehouse. Large objects sat draped with tawny canvases. A few nude mannequins leaned against the far wall. Some were missing legs, others arms, and one contorted body in the corner had no head. Light installations dangled from the ceiling, set to strike the walls and the floor and the mannequin bodies.

Lucinda walked out from the back dressed all in black. "Great, you're here. Where is it?"

There was a compelling quality to the way she held herself, so erect a rod might have been jammed into her underwear. I immediately felt myself shifting, trying to stand taller in my dirty clothes.

"It's still outside. I wasn't sure how you wanted to do this."

"Just cart it through the front." She stared at me without blinking and I tried to stare back the same way, then looked at the floor.

I was always drawn to a certain kind of energy. A specific kind of woman, one who was self-assured and knew she could do and have whatever she wanted. Lucinda smiled, all teeth and strong jawbone and beautiful hair. I walked back down the hallway quickly, trying not to smudge up the floors.

Back outside, Milo was checking on the boar. "He looks good. Kinda cross-eyed maybe."

"He always looked cross-eyed."

We unstrapped the tarp and lifted it up and over. Milo climbed into the truck bed and pushed the mount forward until I could pull it off the end. We got it through the door and moved down the long hallway. Boar hair sprinkled everywhere.

"You can put it over here." Lucinda stood in the far left corner of the room, next to one of the canvased objects. Just knowing that she was watching me made my hands tremble. I was forced to clench them hard into the boar's rear.

Once we set it down, I wished we'd never brought it. It looked out of its element and much smaller than it had in the shop, where it had always sat like a king lording over its lesser subjects. I thought of Brynn and how her hand had once touched its leg, fingers sliding up the bone now encased in fur.

Lucinda crouched and assessed the tusk that had broken. Her skirt rode up high, exposing a lot of thigh—she had great legs, sinewy and strong, lines of muscles standing out until I could see where they connected with tendon, slipping over the joint. "This looks much better. Very clean. I can hardly see the break now."

"Good. I mean, thanks."

Milo narrowed his eyes. He knew, I could tell, and it made me feel stressed out. He was watching my hands, which were scrunched around the hem of my shirt so I would stop wiping my palms on my jeans.

"So what are you gonna do with him?" He patted the boar on the rump. Dust flew up and hung suspended in the air.

"He's part of an installation. I was hoping your mother would be interested in collaborating."

"Our mother?" I couldn't imagine what our mother would do in an art gallery. The only public art she'd ever engaged in was face painting at the fall festival. She freehanded everything:

animals, robots, monsters, fairies. The kids lined up around the building for her.

"I'd like to see if she'd participate."

"I don't think—"

"Here. Just give her my card." Lucinda handed me one. It was black and embossed with white writing. When her hand touched mine, I could feel how tough she was; the strength in her fingers, the long, lean line of her forearms. Even seeing those small muscles made me want to slip my hands along her body and feel for the rest of them. Every time I found a woman I was really interested in, I started thinking about her in terms of how I might disassemble her. It was unnerving.

I cleared my throat and stepped back, examining the card. "I'm not sure she'll want to participate."

Milo reached toward the tarp next to the boar and lifted a corner. "So what you got under here? This place is pretty empty."

"Please, don't touch anything." Lucinda took the corner from his hand. "Have your mother call me, I'd love to speak with her."

"Sure thing." Milo nodded and looked at me, motioning toward the doorway.

"Oh, and I'd be very interested in looking at the other animals you've got displayed in your shop. Let me know if you'd be willing to part with them." Lucinda smiled broadly, and I could nearly count all the perfect white teeth in her head. In her black business suit she looked like a beautiful, dangerous predator. I imagined her mounted on a branch, crouched over an unsuspecting herd of deer.

Sometimes I hated the way I was. That I could look at an incredibly lovely woman and picture her mounted like a dead animal made me wonder what was wrong with my brain.

I moved toward the door. "Call if you need anything else, or if you need help with the boar."

Outside, I let the sun warm me until my blood ran hot again. My scalp burned where my hair was parted, the braid hanging halfway down my back. I twisted the hank of hair and yanked, trying to get my thoughts in order.

"What was that about?" Milo unlocked my side of the truck and then walked around the front to climb in his side. "You into her?"

"It was about nothing. We sold the boar. Now we can spend the money on groceries or something."

We drove home down back streets. I rolled down my window and let the air wash over me. It was sunny and warm, but already clouds lined with black were boiling up on the horizon, out over the lake. Lucinda was pretty, but I could learn to forget. I'd done it before.

I scooped a palmful of air, opening my fingers in the wind. We drove past the old convenience store that had once been a Chevron, a Texaco, and most recently a 7-Eleven. "Could you drop me at the shop? Gonna flip a few deer mounts. Need to catch up on work."

"You need to catch up on sleep." He turned down our street, toward the shop. "It's not healthy, how you're acting. Even Dad went home sometimes."

What I could have said, but didn't: Dad had a wife and a family to go home to, not a shitty apartment with no central air and a roach infestation under the scummy kitchen sink. And even then, it wasn't enough to keep him going. He owned a business and his own home, had a wife and kids who loved him. Grandkids, even. With all of that, he left his body behind for someone he loved to find. A mess for his daughter to clean up.

I dug the keys from my pocket. The goat still sat in the window, looking lonesome without its sexual partners. "Maybe we can have Mom set up something more appropriate. Wouldn't hurt to keep her occupied."

"What, you don't want her hanging around that creepy gallery?"

My father would've wanted me to keep our mother home. Would've liked me taking care of her the way he would've: given her a list of tasks, made her feel needed. He wasn't the kind of dad who talked about his feelings, but sometimes he came up with some stunners out of nowhere. Once over beers, he'd smiled and leaned in, like he was gonna offer some sage advice. *Your mother is a little funny*, he said, touching my arm. Laughing. *She does things sometimes that don't make any sense. It's part of her charm, sure, but it means we gotta watch out for her. Don't want her getting into trouble.*

"I think we can find something for her to do a little closer to home," I said. "She doesn't need that kind of excitement."

"Excitement? She's not a toddler, Jessa."

"Well, she's sure acting like one."

He looked unhappy and I couldn't understand why. Did he want our mother given free rein to create whatever animal porn she wanted? Did he like her running around in the middle of the night?

Milo sighed and I got out of the truck before he could say whatever he was about to drop on me. I felt like a nerve rubbed raw, probably from stress and lack of sleep and the fact that I hadn't had sex in months.

"See you at dinner," he finally said, pointing a finger at me through the truck window. I waved him away and went inside, thunder already rumbling in the distance.

All the lights were off and I left them that way. My eyes were gritty and sticky. I was tired of everything. We should've been open for business, but there was no one coming. Most of our work was done piecemeal, calls over the phone from middling hunters looking for price estimates. The drop-ins had dwindled to nothing.

I sat down in a chair next to a rack of outdated hunting magazines and bent down to unlace my boots. The socks I wore had holes in each heel; they didn't match and I hadn't washed them in a while. Every part of me felt achy, as if I were coming down with a mild flu. This happened to me every time I got anxious about the business, and recently everything was about the business. How we had no money, how I didn't know what to do about my mother, how I wasn't the man that my father was or would ever be, but maybe he wasn't the man I'd thought he was. So what did I know about anything?

Leaning back, I propped my head against a rolled-up T-shirt, one with a picture of a deer with red crosshairs super-imposed over its sleek body. I fell asleep there, telling myself it would be just for a minute, and then I'd start working on one of the many pieces stored in the skinning fridge. Everything felt easier on the cusp of sleep.

My parents' house sat lit by buttery circles of dueling streetlamps. There were homes on either side, but no one lived in them. FOR RENT signs perpetually swung in the weedy front lawns. It stayed swampy year-round. Soupy ditchwater bred mosquitoes and their squirming larvae until they clouded the sky. They bled us dry, tiny vampires that hugged our necks and the backs of our calves, leaving behind bright pink welts.

The entrance to the local cemetery was at the far end of the street. Milo and I played hide-and-seek there when we were young. It was where we'd shared our first cigarettes and our beginner sips of whiskey, backs leaned against the lot's sole mausoleum. It belonged to the Laniers, a family that died out before we were born. We traced our fingers in the engravings until we could sign the names in our sleep. They felt like family we'd never met, watching over us as we ran around the weedy tombstones. We forgot about the bodies buried below us in the dirt, so focused on the fun we were having.

It was where we'd buried our father. Our mother's plot was empty beside his, graves they'd purchased in duplicate back when death felt a long way off. Strange to know my father's body was buried less than a block from his own house. Like he could just get up one night and come home, unlock the front door with the spare key, and sit down comfortably, sipping beer in his recliner. Watch *The Late Show*. Fall into bed beside my mother. Sleep like he wasn't gone from us, forever.

I parked behind my brother, pulling over the oil spot where my father's truck used to leak before my mother sold it. That spot would never grow again, and in fact looked smaller to me, the hot beat of the sun and the persistent rain working to erode the memory of it.

Bats clipped through the purple sky, narrowly diving in and out of the branches of the oaks that bookended the house. The light over the door had burned out again and the mail was piled up inside the metal mailbox. I took in the assorted catalogs, bills, a few small packages that felt like they could've been DVDs, and dusted off the dead moths that had made the mail their grave.

I unlocked the door and walked inside, passing framed pictures of our family, studio shots in church clothes. My brother looked tall and gangly and pimpled in his best suit at age fourteen, myself trussed up like a piglet in a frilly pink party dress I wore only if someone threatened death. My teeth were bared in the shot, as if I were restraining myself from biting my brother's hand, which rested awkwardly on my shoulder.

I kicked off my boots right there in the entryway, socked feet sinking into the orange-and-yellow shag. The microwave whirred in the kitchen. My mother was heating a Pyrex bowl full of frozen mixed vegetables, and my niece, Lolee, sat at the counter, cracking open Oreos and peeling out the centers. She stacked them until there were matching piles of cream and cookies.

"Gonna eat those cookies?"

"Nope." The cookie stack was unceremoniously dumped into the same trash can where my mother threw the packaging from a sticky Styrofoam tray of chicken parts. Lolee picked up the wad of icing and rolled it between her palms, forming it into a dense ball. Then she took a big bite. Cream gummed in her braces, she turned to me and grinned.

Grabbing a cookie from the plastic tray, I sat down and peeled free the center, then handed it to her. Before Lolee, Brynn had eaten the filling. We'd sat beside each other in the kitchen, watching my mother make dinner. Nearly every Tuesday she threw together chicken cacciatore made with bottled spaghetti sauce and too many bell peppers, cooked just long enough that it wouldn't give us salmonella.

Lolee had long blonde hair she'd bleached white at the ends. It was crunchy and beginning to turn green from repeated dunkings in the public pool. She was all teenage summer smells: fruity lip balm, body spray, and the strong aroma of chlorine. A miniature Brynn, if Brynn were the kind of girl who'd grown up with adults who cared about her. At Lolee's age, Brynn and I were fucking things up. She was already thinking about leaving by the time she was fourteen, wondering how she could escape, when all the while I was thinking about how to trap her with me forever.

"Ma, you need help?" I asked, not bothering to get up. My mother hated help with anything in the kitchen. She dropped the Pyrex lid on the counter and the clang sounded like a yell.

She brought over a tube of refrigerated crescent rolls and dropped it on the counter. I held one end of the tube while Lolee took the other. She curled back the cardboard while we both pulled. It exploded with a loud pop, and dough oozed from the rift.

"Get the baking sheet," my mother said, pulling something from the toaster oven. "Damn it, this is already burnt."

Kneeling on the floor, I pulled out the best tray, flecked rusty brown from years of cooking spray burned onto its surface. Lolee flung the cookie parts at me. I caught very few of them; most slid beneath the fridge until my mother slapped the back of Lolee's head, then pinched her cheek and rubbed her neck.

Lolee was all odds and ends. Dressed in a T-shirt and cut-off jean shorts, she'd kicked off her flip-flops and kept nudging at them with her toes. She had the brightness of Brynn and my own jaw set—stark, as if the strong line of muscle had come from biting down and holding back. There was a sharpness to her that revealed itself only in slips. I knew that she wasn't mine. These parts were Morton by association, the giving up of genetic material from my brother, but I claimed her in my heart. I'd held her to my breast when she was an infant and nuzzled her fuzzy baby head. The starling bird daughter that would never come from my own egg.

I rolled the dough into small triangles and stuffed the tray into the oven alongside the chicken. Beers were in the old fridge out back, and my tired neck felt one calling my name. I left my mother with her cooking and my niece with her cookies and went out to find Milo.

He was propped in my father's old recliner on the back porch. He'd already cracked open his second beer, the first empty dropped beside his boot on the smooth concrete floor.

"I told her about the lady at the art place. How she gave you a card." He didn't look at me while he said it, just peeled the label off his beer. It was coming off in wet hunks which he then scrubbed down onto his dirty jeans. The bits rolled and pilled like molting flesh. It looked like dying might.

"I wish you hadn't told her that." Milo was usually the one I could count on for stability, but lately he'd been surprising me. Saying things, making decisions. I didn't like it.

There were only three beers left, one in the door and the other two jammed between some racks of venison that had definitely gone south. The last time we'd had any fresh meat was when my father had gone out with Andy Reeling from a few streets over and come back carting two big bucks. He'd mounted both heads and priced them over to Andy for BOGO. Said we didn't need any more heads in our living room, and he was right—already there were multiples mounted on each wall, peering down at guests with their glassy, vacant eyes.

When we were younger, Milo and I had given them the names of the seven dwarfs, plus a few additions we'd come up with: Sleepy was the one with the downcast eyes, Dopey the one with the tongue hanging slightly out and to the left, Happy with the perpetual grin—likely more a grimace of pain—plus Damn and Goddamn for how often our father shouted those words at the television set during Bucs games.

The patio held the relics of furniture past. Our mother's card table with the vinyl top slashed to bits from where she'd used an X-Acto knife while scrapbooking, the wicker-backed rocking chair that had lost nearly all tension in its seat, and a faded floral love seat ripped to shreds from the scratching of the dogs.

I sat on the edge of the rocking chair and opened the beer with my key-chain bottle opener. Dad's old one, the relief at the top the shape of a golden bass, mouth jutting open to bite at the cap. It hadn't been on him when he shot himself, and I was glad for it. Still, as I opened the beer, Milo and I stared at each other and then looked away. I remembered my dad sitting on the back porch with a beer of his own, the bass hanging from his key chain, which always made a lump in his jeans pocket. Remembering soured the beer, made my tongue and teeth hurt. How his hands grasped the fish head, the hissing sound of the air releasing as the cap flung free. Milo and me running around in the yard, watching him drink. I'd wanted to be just like him. Tall, handsome, always unruffled. The kind of person who could take anything you threw at him. The kind of man who could drink a beer in two long pulls and smile afterward, completely satisfied with the life he'd built.

"Remember when Brynn got me that bottle opener to look like Dad's and it broke the first time I used it?"

Of course I did. I was the one who helped her choose it. We were buying Christmas gifts at the mall and she asked me to pick something out for Milo. *You know him better than I do,* she'd said, and they'd already been married a year.

"I remember that you tried to superglue it back together."

"Didn't want her to know I'd already fucked it up."

He'd gotten her a necklace with a heart pendant, one of those things men always buy that women would never buy for themselves. She wore it over to my apartment, and when she took off her clothes, she draped it over a dusty lamp in the bedroom. I saw it dangling there the next morning through the bleary eyes of my hangover. The tiny diamond chips twinkled in the sunlight, laughing at me. She'd never asked for it back, and I'd never offered it.

"Guess I fucked up a lot." Milo's hands fidgeted on his beer bottle, scraping off more waterlogged paper, rolling the tacky stuff into balls between his fingers.

Brynn was a topic we didn't discuss. What was there to say? She was gone. She'd left us. I could barely stomach my own memories; I didn't want to deal with his.

After Brynn, he was less easygoing and more unavailable. Missing even more work, bailing on the kids. A no-show at sports events and dance recitals. Forgetting birthdays. He still smiled all the time, but it wasn't the kind that reached his eyes. Faux happy, the kind of face I'd construct on an animal I was trying to make docile.

I changed the subject before we got too far into maudlin territory. It was too easy to start him crying. "You think Mom should do it. Go work with that lady."

One of his shoulders rolled up into a shrug, a nonverbal *maybe* he'd been perfecting since he was a kid and didn't want to talk. It was my chance to help fix what was wrong, to ask him questions. Get him to open up. But talking about things was never my specialty. I was the one you came to when you wanted something done. Change your oil, build your back deck, grill your fish. I showed my love by changing tires and jumping batteries. Milo was the one who listened. He always made people feel appreciated and cared for. I'd loved Brynn first, but I'd given her up to him, knowing he'd take better care of her. Someone to tell her all the meaningful, romantic things my mouth couldn't seem to spew.

"We just need to find something else for Mom to do," I said. "Keep her busy."

Milo rolled his eyes. "She's already doing that. It's not working out so great."

After Dad killed himself, we'd both talked to her about seeing a therapist. She'd outright refused and hadn't spoken to either of us for a week. She was offended we'd even asked, as if it were perfectly normal to traipse around in the middle of the night, putting together peep shows in our shop's front window. I thought about the boar again, sitting lonesome and small in Lucinda's gallery, and hoped she'd take good care of it. It felt a little like I'd given another woman an ex-girlfriend's belongings.

"You think we should bring up the therapist again?" I asked. "Maybe that would help."

"Don't they have art therapy in counseling centers? Isn't that a thing?"

"Why does she even need to do *art*?"

"She likes it. You know she did it in school before she married Dad. Sculpting and shit." Milo flicked a fat carpenter ant off the arm of the chair. It landed on the floor close to my boot.

"I didn't know she was that into it."

Milo snorted and rocked back in his chair. "You don't know a lot of things about Mom, Jessa."

It hadn't felt necessary to learn more about my mother outside of her existence on the periphery of my life. She cleaned our clothes and bought us groceries. Made our meals, mopped and dusted, trimmed the tree. My father was the one I'd admired. He was the one I'd wanted to be like. But then he'd killed himself and left me the letter, and everything I'd thought I knew turned out to be wrong. I had a lot of working theories as to why my father chose me to find him, but the one that kept me up at night was the idea that he knew I was hard inside. That maybe he thought I'd treat him the way I would a deer carcass.

Would I have done that? I wondered. Was there a part of me that could compartmentalize his death, skin him and treat him like just another piece in the shop?

"Even in art therapy they make you talk," I said. "So she'd have to deal with shit."

"Maybe *you* should go to therapy."

"Fuck you," I replied, but there was no heat behind it.

I was the one who'd called the police. I'd identified our father's body in the morgue. In the span of twenty-four hours, I'd seen the father who'd bought me a Publix sub for lunch that afternoon, the dead one covered in blood that night, and the blue-hued body laid out naked under fluorescent lights in the county hospital at six the next morning. My mother had seen none of that. There were times I worried she didn't really think he was dead, that maybe she just thought he'd left on a fishing trip for a couple of weeks.

"Maybe I can find something for her to do at the shop. Organize shit, or clean up the front."

Humming, he tipped back in the recliner and drained the last of his beer. He set the empty on the cabinet beside him, one of the relics that had cluttered up my bedroom before being relegated to the back porch. Now it housed our empties, some still half-full, holding drowned cigarette butts and the carcasses of insects.

"We'll figure it out." I swapped the bottle from hand to hand, listening to the murmur of voices slipping evenly through the crack in the sliding glass door.

Milo leaned forward again and scrubbed both hands through his hair. The set of his shoulders gave me pause;

hunched forward, he looked so much like our father. "About the business. I was thinking we could hire someone else."

My head ached fiercely, the knots of my braid yanking at my scalp. I wanted to be back in the workshop, focusing all my energy on the hawk I'd been struggling with—looking at the angle of its beak, the movement of the neck, the wings spanned in near flight, almost but not quite catching the breeze. "Milo, come on. You know I can't."

"Just a few days a week, part-time work."

In the backyard, wind scattered yard debris that had accumulated in the months since our father passed. Leaves and grit kicked up against the screen. I stared hard at the old birdbath, cracked and full of brown muck. Sparrows hopped in and out of the detritus, flicking the dirty water delicately off their bodies with brisk shakes.

Milo sat back again, jaw set. "It's part mine, too. I get some say."

"Don't do that."

"I get some say, damn it."

We didn't argue over much, but there was the one thing that continued to hurt my brother, over and over again. The rawboned son with his mother's pale eyes and sloped shoulders, indicators of his uneasy personality. "When did Bastien get home?"

"Last night. He's staying in my old room." Red crept up the bearded shadow of Milo's neck, cloaking everything like a rash. His embarrassment was feral, an ugly, dirty thing I could nearly taste. "Thought he could stay with Mom for a while. That's good, right? Another person to keep an eye on her?"

"I don't know."

"He's been talking about getting one of those tiny homes they keep showing on television. The ones that are like three hundred feet square. Can fit a whole regular-sized house inside?" Milo smiled and shook his head. "Better than an apartment, he says."

I bit into the meat of my cheek, worked the flesh over with my molars. Bastien was Brynn's oldest and had just finished a second stint in rehab. Not related by blood, not to the Mortons, but he looked so much like Brynn that Milo couldn't help but love him. The last time he'd stayed in town, he'd pawned our mother's jewelry and written eight hundred bucks' worth of bad checks.

"He's better. You can see it in his coloring." Milo looked at me and I saw that he believed what he was saying. Saw that he needed to feel like it was true, for a while, to make things seem solid again.

Need, my father had written. To need meant to be vulnerable. It was one of the scariest things I could imagine. Needing anything meant you were open to invasion. It meant you had no control of yourself.

"Only if he's up for grunt work." I couldn't say no to my brother. Not when it was Brynn's kid. "If he fucks up, he's done. I mean it."

"Fine." Milo got up and pulled out another beer for himself. "He's doing good. Just needs something to keep him busy."

Behind my brother, a shadow filled the sliding glass. Bastien stood with his long arm cradled around the door, as if holding himself in place. He looked better than the last time

64

I'd seen him. His skin was clear of the scuzz of acne and he'd lost a lot of the sallowness. He wore a clean white T-shirt and some board shorts printed in varied shades of blue, pale palm trees emblazoned over a navy wash of waves. I recognized them as Milo's clothes.

"Grandma says dinner's ready." When he smiled, his teeth were dark, nearly wooden in his mouth. Already his hairline was receding, crawling toward the rear of his skull, as if escaping from the hard look in his eyes. "Got any more of those?" He pointed to the unopened beer cradled in Milo's palm. "Go good with the chicken."

"Go get the jug of tea from the fridge, tell Grandma we'll be there in just a minute."

I wondered how much he'd heard of our conversation. Bastien was a lot like his mother in that he let you know only what he wanted you to know. Everything else stayed locked up tight.

Milo stashed the last two beers in the mildewed cupboard where our mother liked to stock preserves—they stood upright behind Ball jars of orange marmalade and strawberry jam turned the color of beef gravy. Then we went inside. It still smelled like home, though a faded-out version. There was less of my father's aftershave. Less of the tanners and formaldehyde, a scent he'd always carried on his body.

Smell, I'd learned, was something that would always be able to sucker-punch me.

LEPORIDAE OF THE ORDER LAGOMORPHA—RABBIT KITS

Movement under my hand broke the spell.

Don't stop. Why'd you stop?

Fingers splayed wide on her bare skin, I prayed the fluttering away. Let myself think it was an anomaly. Maybe her stomach was upset, something that could be quickly cured by antacids.

Here, like this. Brynn moved my palm from where I'd cupped her belly button and dragged it down, lower, until it edged the thin lace of her underwear. Shadows licked her skin, dotting her breasts and hips in dripping gray. Rain drummed against the driveway and the wide oaks in a thick, continual beat that slurred into white noise. We were cocooned in a nest of blankets that smelled like my father's aftershave and my mother's lemon talcum powder.

A single tap against my temple. *Where'd you go?* Her nose dug into my neck. She snuffled, rooting around, and I curled my head to the side, trying to trap her there. My arm slid around her stomach and then I felt it again: a kind of squirming, a wriggling set low in her belly. New life burbled and popped. I'd felt it there before. We both knew what it meant. She rolled away and propped her head on her folded arm, staring out the window.

Yeah, she sighed. *I know.*

That morning I'd said *bunny, bunny* to my four-year-old nephew as I walked into my parents' kitchen. He was standing at the counter with my mother as she pressed orange halves on a citrus squeezer. I smiled at him and he smiled back, his mouth a solid block of orange from where he'd bitten down into a stray segment.

Whath nummy nummy, Bastien mumbled, tongue working around the peel. He choked and it was a wet, sticky sound. Poor Florida baby couldn't handle the constant pollen, drifting onto all our cars and staining the roads yellow. It made him hack and wheeze, a forty-year-old smoker's cough, pale eyes forever bottomed out with purple smudges.

Keeps us safe from monsters.

I dug the peel from between his lips, tossing it into the overflowing garbage. Milo never took out the trash, said he was too tired when he got home from work. Brynn said he never had time for her, that they never had sex anymore, and I was fine with that.

It means good luck. If you say it on the first of the month, everything will turn out perfect, just how you want it.

Bastien closed his eyes. *Bunny, bunny.* He held up one finger and blew on it, like you would a birthday candle.

It rained every day that May, sky drowning the world at four o'clock before the sun came out again to boil the leftover water off the pavement. The world cracked open and smelled fresh cut, seeping green over everything. I drove with the windows down and inhaled the world: the dank scent of wet dirt at a construction site, orange clay smoothed into wet puddles at the high school baseball field, the fruity shampoo as my hair whipped around my face. Even the festering Dumpster beside a traffic light held appeal; it all teemed with life. There were birds nesting in the eaves of the taxidermy shop. When one of the babies fell out and cracked its neck, I spent a whole afternoon carefully preserving it for Bastien.

Every day my mother made scrambled eggs with sharp cheddar cheese, Milo's favorite. The three of them had moved back into my parents' house on the premise of saving money to buy one of their own. Milo's old room had been converted to a sewing studio, so the three of them shored up in my childhood bedroom. They slept every night beneath the tattered posters that still clung to the dark wood paneling: bands Brynn and I used to like and movies we'd watched in high school. My brother, whom I loved, curled up with the woman I loved beneath my red-and-white quilt. Milo said he was glad Brynn spent all her time with me since he was always gone. Said he knew I'd take care of her and make sure she was happy. He smiled as he said it, never a moment's pause that I'd be touching his wife as soon as he walked out the door.

How could he not know? I wondered. How could he think anything less was happening, when he knew I'd had her first?

Milo's job at the Lexus dealership was forty-five minutes away. He got up early and came home late, taking overtime and working holidays. It was a low-paying gig that didn't require any previous experience, which was good because his resume took up less than half a sheet of paper. He'd gotten the job through one of his high school buddies. It was the first time he'd ever really tried, and it didn't agree with him.

If I make it through the ninety-day trial period, I'll be set for a promotion, he said. *Just gotta make it through these first ninety and then it won't be like this anymore. Get our own place. Have another kid.*

On his days off, he stayed in bed until midafternoon and then ventured out to the kitchen for a sandwich before passing out on the couch again. He looked tired all the time, skin grayed out and hair lank with grease. His polos were never clean. Brynn sometimes did laundry, but we both acted like kids on summer vacation. She let my mother do the chores as we hung out and watched television. When Milo came home he'd kiss Brynn first thing. She leaned into it so hard I could hear their teeth click together.

You take such good care of us, she'd say, drawing a line down his cheek with a fingernail I'd painted for her. *Who else would love me so much? No one's sweeter than you, baby.*

He'd look better then, and I knew it was all worth it to him—the long hours, the driving, just to come home to her and Bastien. Listening in on these whispered conversations, I tried to imagine myself in my brother's position and couldn't make the image stick. I knew what she wanted from each of us; the things we provided. I watched my brother work himself to death, saw how he was still able to be emotionally there for her, and wished I could be the kind of person who could do both.

I came over every day on my lunch break from the shop, eating leftover crusts from Bastien's peanut butter and honey sandwiches.

I like our little family. Brynn snuck her hand into the crease of my elbow. I'd let it sit there, collecting sweat, mine and hers. Something I could take home and keep at the end of the day when I drank rum and Cokes next to the busted AC unit in my apartment. Drunk, thinking about what kind of person I was: taking from the people I cared about, taking because if I didn't take what I needed, I might die.

We sat at the dining room table and ate ham sandwiches for lunch. Bastien slurped speckled cereal milk from a yellowing Tupperware. Between bites of Cinnamon Toast Crunch, he touched the little bunnies in their basket with a gentle hand— the kits my father and I had lovingly worked on for several weeks, attempting to perfect the downy sweetness found in mammal babies. My father had found them in a cardboard box inside our garage, cuddled in a nest of shredded newspapers and telephone book pages.

Asphyxiated. Carbon monoxide from the car engine. He cupped one in his palm, body the size of a fat dinner roll. When I took it from him, its neck flopped back until the head was lying over my fingers, limp and dangling.

We'll give them to your mother. I stroked its downy back. It was still warm. *Makes a good Easter gift. Peter Rabbit, right?*

We each took two, bisecting the bodies through their tiny white bellies. There was barely anything to remove, they were so young. Their skulls were dainty, the size of an apricot. I scrubbed them carefully with a toothbrush, washing their coats in the workroom sink. I dried them with a blow-dryer on a low setting. Blush from the drugstore stained each round cheek a delicate, precious pink. I darkened the lines of their eyelids with Sharpie. Peter's black eyes were taken from a beaded purse that a well-meaning aunt had once gifted me, a look Brynn described as *fortysomething soccer mom goes on a post-divorce date.*

My mother held the babies and cooed like I'd finally given her grandchildren.

Darlings. She kissed me on the cheek and squeezed my shoulder. *My best-behaved kids.*

Brynn turned to my mother and held up the empty cereal box. *I'll have to leave for the store now if I wanna outrun the storm.* She was still in her sleep shirt and a pair of Milo's boxer shorts. The flap at the crotch was unpinned; pale underwear kept peeking through.

I'll go. My mother already had her purse slung over her shoulder. Her long, dark hair licked the floor as she leaned over to kiss Bastien's head. *I'll be back in an hour.*

Behind us, the fridge clicked on, running hard enough to jostle the boxes of Minute Rice stacked on its flat top. Bastien set down his spoon and milk drooled from its bowl, leaking onto the quilted place mat. His eyes were sleepy; he swayed in his chair. I settled him in front of the television, tucked a throw around him peppered with gray dog hairs and crumbs from the floor. He sucked his thumb and sniffled, allergies flaring up again. One of the dogs came up and curled beside him.

Brynn and I went to my parents' room because I couldn't fuck her in the same place she slept every night with my brother. What had been my bed was now their bed; a bed for two people who'd committed their lives to each other. I could feel him there between the sheets with us, sad and hurt, and it made me want to cry.

We stood in the doorway of my parents' room and didn't look at each other. It wasn't the first time it had happened and it wouldn't be the last. In order to do it, I let Milo drift until he was a far-off spot in my mind, a hazy blot on the horizon that I could pretend was something else entirely. Not my brother. Not any part of me. Brynn leaned into me and let her head fall on my shoulder. Time was always too short. All we had were afternoons, little minutes between work shifts.

Will I ever get tired of this? I asked the question aloud, though I already knew the answer. You couldn't get sick of sustenance when you were starving.

What happens now? She looked out the window, hand pressed against her belly. I curled around her back and put my hand over hers. It wasn't warm enough anymore without the blankets, but I didn't care. We didn't say anything, just listened to the rain lessen until there were only drips pinging off the window's metal awning.

I stroked one finger down her abdomen. *Bunny, bunny*, I wished, mouthing the words into her damp neck.

3

At the back of the shop we kept a storage bin that housed leftover animal parts. It was the stuff my father called *bits and pieces*, things we kept around as supplementary material when there was a rush and we needed extra scraps.

Just in case, he said when I asked why we'd ever need a single duck foot, webbed yellow-orange and black. *I'm not gonna throw out something we could use.*

Thrift was something I'd incorporated into my own work process. *Bills*, a word spelled out in all capital letters blinking neon in my skull, kept me awake at night. If there was an opportunity to cut costs, I was willing to consider it.

Parts disappeared and reappeared whenever an especially large workload presented itself. The cabinet held an odd jumble: severed deer hooves with the ankles still attached, rabbit feet with too many toes, mismatched alligator jaws. We had feathers from cardinals, finches, herons, crows, and jays—ruffled and slick, downy and spiked. There were horns of all colors and shapes, antlers, bone segments, fur swatches, disconnected tails. The bin had clear compartments, every drawer labeled with its contents in blue masking tape. Looking at it from far away, you could almost convince yourself you were looking at a real cabinet of wonders.

It was a good place to go for gag taxidermy parts, and with my father gone, gag taxidermy paid the rent. I pinned antlers to rabbit heads stuffed with foam cuttings, shellacked frogs propped at miniature card tables, boiled a million alligator skulls, mouths stuffed with pointy teeth painted blue and orange for UF football fans. I turned ducklings into mermaids, fish tails shimmering green-gold. The parts bin emptied until I was digging out ratty stuff that had been in the drawers as long as I could remember. A coral snakeskin disintegrated in my hands, looped round a spool that had once held reams of fuchsia lace for one of my mother's sewing projects.

It was always the same old, same old. Even looking at the bin depressed me. I was bored and unhappy and whenever I got that way I started thinking about sex. Lucinda Rex had been on my mind a lot. It was exactly what I shouldn't be doing, fixating on a woman I barely knew, much less a customer. But while I worked, my mind wandered where it liked. It had been a long time since I'd been attracted to anyone in that kind of way. I went out to bars and met women, ones I never saw again after those blurry, drunk nights in hotel rooms or dirty apartments, but they weren't like Lucinda. She was the kind of woman I knew might hurt me if I gave her half a chance.

Often I found myself comparing the limber body of a deer with the long line of her legs or the strong cord of her neck. Disassembling an ancient rack of fuzzy pinned moths, I wondered what noises she might make if I licked the tender spot below her ear. Whenever I thought that way, I ruthlessly shut it down—usually by jamming my thumb against the edge of the flesher. Lucinda wasn't messy like Brynn, but there was a hard quality to her that scared me. They were both women who'd break your heart and smile afterward. It was easier to head to some bar out of town and find someone faceless. After a few beers, I couldn't tell the difference between my hands and theirs.

But lately after I fucked those no-name women, I always thought about Lucinda. Her dark hair, her slender wrists. At night in bed, dreams of Brynn slid into a miasma of Lucinda until it was like I was sandwiched between their bodies. I woke up early, getting to work before the sun came up so I could try to shake free the images sliding through my brain like a looping projector reel.

Want and *need.* Two words from my dad's letter that meant so much and so little. I never knew what I wanted. And I didn't want to need anything. Better to need nothing; nothing never hurt you when it left.

I was alone a lot at the shop most days, but one afternoon Bastien took Milo's truck and stopped by with Lolee on their way down to the lake. The amoeba count had been high that summer. Signs were posted all over Central Florida warning about the danger of dunking your head. The lakes and reservoirs were death traps, bacteria ready to crawl inside ear canals and turn brains to mush. August sun cooked the lakes in town until they felt like warm baths. The smell coming off every body of water was sulfurous.

My niece had a towel looped around her throat like a scarf and wore my mother's wide tortoiseshell sunglasses. She looked like a miniature Brynn, hip cocked and head tilted. The sun leaking through the door made her hair glow white.

"You wanna go?" Bastien sipped orange Gatorade out of a plastic UCF tumbler. He'd attended a single semester, dropping out after racking up hundreds of dollars in credit card debt.

"I'm trying to clean up in here." I hadn't done much, just swept a dust ball the size of my own head into the middle of the linoleum. There'd been one customer in all day and they'd bought only a LOVE MY BEAGLE magnet. It had been a hard sale for a buck fifty.

"I could do it. Stay and watch the shop."

He poked at a stack of trade magazines, half turning to show he wasn't interested either way.

Lolee hung from the door, dragging back and forth so the bell chimed every few seconds. "We can take out the float." The sunglasses fell low on her pug nose and she mashed them back up with her palm. "You can pull me around, like when I was little."

"You're still little." Brynn and I had taken Lolee out a lot on the float the summer Brynn ran off. We'd take turns sluicing it through the reeds, muck and algae coating our legs up to our knees. Brynn bemoaned the heat as she wiped runny mascara from beneath her eyes, told me over and over again that she couldn't wait to live somewhere with weather that occasionally dropped below eighty degrees. Two months later she took off for someplace even hotter than Florida with a stranger she'd met at the dry cleaner. I found his picture once online. A guy who was short, muscular, and balding. He looked nothing like the Morton family. I didn't show that picture to Milo. As bad as it made me feel, I wasn't sure what it would do to my brother. His self-esteem seemed like a fragile thing; a hollowed-out bird egg.

"Where's your father?" I asked. "Isn't he supposed to be raising you?"

Milo was never around. No parent-teacher conferences, no report card signings, no trips to the springs or Disney World. Did he avoid his daughter because she looked too much like Brynn? I saw her mother in the wide set of Lolee's eyes, the dimple in her chin. Looking at my niece sometimes felt like pressing on a bruise. The pain was there but still pleasurable, a reminder Brynn had existed and loved us.

"Please, you never do anything with me." Lolee pouted, long hair nearly scraping the linoleum. The bell over the door jangled and shrieked. "Please, please."

"Fine. Just . . . stop doing that."

I showed Bastien the old yellow key box behind the counter. Told him the phones routed to the back of the shop unless you picked up by the second ring. There was a customer expected at three and they'd paid in advance. The mount was stored in the back beneath a tarp to ward off dust.

Its black eyes gleamed in the fluorescent light as I flipped back the plastic sheeting. Bastien nodded as I pointed out the torque of the buck's neck and the opened mouth—a request from the customer. Its tongue sat behind a row of teeth I'd scrubbed with denture cleanser. The deer had been shot in the jaw and I'd had to partially reconstruct the bone, padding out half of it with wiring and felt. Some of the teeth I'd borrowed from another mount, still stuffed away in freezer storage. I'd nicked myself with the blade digging at the wiring, and some of my blood had wept into the fur. Occasionally when I sent out a piece like that, with little bits of me in it, I felt as if a part of me were leaving for a better life somewhere else.

Lolee and I left Bastien there in the shop and walked down the street to the lakefront a few blocks away. She trotted ahead in her neon-yellow bikini top with the black piping, T-shirt already pulled off and slung over her arm. I held her towel for her, listening to her flip-flops slap obnoxiously against the asphalt. It was blisteringly hot. Sweat itched down my neck before we'd even made it a block.

At the waterfront, speedboats swept across the mirrored surface, tubes bouncing off each other and rocketing into the muggy air. Wake splashed into the reeds and lapped against the shore, leaving behind slimy trails of algae. The air was fragrant with grill smoke.

It was the same when Milo and I were kids, running around by the water with our friends as our mother yelled at us to stay out of the cattails; that there were snakes coiled up down there just waiting for us to rush past so they could bite our ankles.

How were we so old when it felt like only seconds had passed? Milo worn down and always missing, Brynn unreachable. But here was her daughter, her tiny twin. Soon she'd leave too. Everything grew up and flew away.

Lolee walked to a picnic table half submerged in the overgrowth. The sun was less fierce there, and I sat with my back to the trees and rested my feet on a cypress knee. "You can go," I told her. A clump of kids had gathered down next to the dock and they waved to get her attention, arms crossing and uncrossing over their heads. She abandoned her towel and her flip-flops and left me sitting there, sniffing in the warm barbeque air. She climbed onto the back of a Sea-Doo, holding tight to a boy's waist. She yelled as he accelerated, the sound like a blender taking in a root vegetable. When they charged up over the wake, her hair flew out behind her.

Brynn had loved riding on boats and Jet Skis and motor-cycles. She hung on to the sides of Jeeps and stood up in the backs of trucks, shouting at random people in the street. When Milo bought his first truck, Brynn commandeered the back of it. She lounged there on a towel, shorts rucked up into her crotch, unbuttoned and unzipped, working on her tan. He'd take her through the McDonald's drive-thru and let her order dollar sundaes from the bed, handing back money through the open window. He told her he loved her on one of these rides, yelling it up to her as she banged her hands on the roof of the cab. I stared out the passenger-side window and swallowed down my sadness with another gulp of shitty beer.

You don't know what love is, I thought, wanting to smack him. Love was the steady burn of acid indigestion. Love was a punch in the gut that ruptured your spleen. Love was a broken telephone that refused to dial out. Milo told Brynn he loved her and I could see from the look on his face he thought the words were a magical incantation. Say the word *love* and it's there for you; say the word *love* and the other person feels it too.

What I should have told him that day: love makes you an open wound, susceptible to infection. But he was young then and so was I, and I wanted their happiness more than my own. So I swallowed my pain and let myself pretend love could flourish if I didn't stand in its way.

Kids tramped through the underbrush behind me, bodies blundering through the knotted bracken and air potato vines. I turned on the bench, the wood digging into my thigh and threatening splinters. Looked past the hunks of Spanish moss and palm scrub that fanned out like spread fingers.

Two girls with dark hair were crouched in the dirt.

They looked to be about ten years old and were in a small patch of scrub, staring down at the body of an egret. One of its wings pointed skyward, extended as if in flight. Using sticks, they prodded at the bird's underside. The girl with the ponytail pushed hard enough that her stick finally gave way and broke inside the body.

"Look at this nasty gunk."

"Bugs are in the eyes, little black ones. Are we standing in ants?"

"Probably."

The other girl peeked beneath the wing, tangled hair falling over her eyes. "There's a freaking hole inside it."

My boot snapped a fallen branch. They looked up simultaneously, eyes wide. I didn't recognize either of them. The girl with the ponytail dropped the stick she'd been holding. The other girl clutched hers against her chest where it smeared a mess of black against the fabric. She reminded me of Lolee when she was little, kind of bedraggled and dirty, as if she'd just stumbled in from the playground.

"We didn't touch it." She dragged a hand across the stain, trying to brush it off. "Just looking."

"Birds have all kinds of diseases," I said. "You shouldn't mess with them."

"We know that." The girl with the ponytail backed away, and the other followed. They were about the same height. Same coloring, dark eyes set in pinched faces. Sisters, maybe cousins.

"Oh yeah? Then you should know even poking at a dead thing with a stick can let loose bacteria in the air. You're probably breathing it in right now."

Both girls caught their breath at once, as if they might hold it until the danger passed. I stepped back and made room for them to move through the bushes. They did, avoiding my body, rushing forward after they cleared the palm scrub behind me.

I squatted beside the bird. It was a fairly large specimen, but too far into rigor for me to consider mounting. I grabbed one of the discarded sticks and used it to flip the bird over until it was spread out in the dirt, wings opened wide, breast thrust upward, back curved. Judging by the set of its neck, probably two days had passed. The wound in its side was right below the rib cage. It was circular and dark, a small depression likely caused by a pellet gun.

Though the bird was already in decomp, the wings were in good shape. Using my pocketknife, I dislodged them at the juncture nearest the torso. As I worked, a palmetto bug crawled from the opening in its body and scurried out into the brush.

Digging a hole with the heel of my boot, I nudged the remains into the divot and scuffed the leftover pile back over it. I set the wings on the picnic table and waited for Lolee to finish. She was barely visible out on the water, tooling around on the back of the Jet Ski. The driver turned sharply and the force slung her off the back. When she surfaced, she flailed and yowled. He reached down to help her back on and she tugged him down into the water with her, dunking him over and over again.

She looked so much like Brynn it burned a hole in my chest. I stared up hard into the sun until the world turned blue and spotty. When my eyes met the table again, everything moved, as if I'd looked at a Magic Eye painting too long. Everything dots, squiggles, fuzz. Nothing made sense, no matter how hard I tried to decipher it.

"Can I have those?" I'd stuffed the egret wings inside a grocery bag and my mother couldn't stop staring at them.

"Why?"

I was going to put the wings in the leftover bin once I finished cleaning them. I'd already pulled out the dish soap next to the sink at the back of the shop.

"A project."

Who knew what that meant. I'd been contemplating what my brother had told me about my mother's art—how she'd thought it was something she'd do with her life, before she'd married our father and had two kids. I didn't know much about it. Especially not sculpture. I wasn't sure what the body parts of animals would have to do with that. If anything, I assumed she'd go take a pottery class. One of those ones where women drank wine and made a coffee mug to take home at the end of the night, something she could do with some of her friends.

"What kind of project?" I asked.

"An art project."

She didn't elaborate, just held out her hand. I looped the handles around her fingers and she clenched them, bringing the bag in close to her chest. I imagined the bugs climbing up along the plastic, crawling out onto her blouse, and shivered.

"You should let me clean them first."

"Don't you have other stuff to do? Aren't there deer mounts backed up in the freezer?"

She'd already pulled out plenty of things from the bin and scattered them across the table. There was a bat that I'd gathered a couple of years ago, a hole in one of its webby wings like a punctured kite. She'd also snagged a ratty foxtail, petrified frogs, a busted turtle shell, and a pelt from a black-and-white cat run over by one of our neighbors.

"Do we have any more of this kind of stuff?"

"We're running low," I said, poking at a hunk of armadillo armor. It leafed open like mica. "This is about it."

Roadkill was a great way to keep the bins full, but I'd been lax in my early-morning runs since I'd taken over the shop. I couldn't be bothered to troll the sides of the highway, scouting for carrion that hadn't soured in the blistering Florida heat.

I considered handing over road duty to Bastien, who'd vacated the premises after I'd caught him directing my mother toward the bin of parts. The image of him scooping up possum guts in the ninety-degree weather brought me a small measure of comfort.

"I'd just like to know what you're gonna do with this stuff." There was a little hole in the side of the plastic bag. Even thinking about mites made my hair itch.

She rifled through the cabinet next to the sink, scrounging out several jars of glass eyes and pigment paints. There was a nick at the back of her head, which had been shaved again. The cut had dried with a bit of toilet paper stuck to it. It reminded me of the times I'd watched her shave her legs in our bathroom sink when I was little. Shaving cream dripping from an ankle; running endless hot water that steamed up the room and left my skin feeling slick.

"I'm putting together some stuff for Lucinda Rex," she said. "Just a small presentation."

I wished for what felt like the millionth time that my family could stay separate from the women in my life. Already I envisioned my mother inviting Lucinda over for dinner. Maybe she'd sit between Milo and me at the dinner table, running a hand up and down both of our thighs. Perhaps she'd move in there and sleep in my old bedroom. I pinched myself, hard, on the tender skin of my inner arm.

My mother turned back to the cabinet. "Do we have any black dye?"

"Who's 'we'?"

"You know what I mean, smart-ass." She'd already thrown open every drawer in the workshop. Bottles and jars littered the countertops, crammed full of buttons and thick stitching thread and the pristine gleam of cutlery: knives and stout ruffers and scrapers and pliers.

She turned back around and pointed at me with one of the long awls we used to gouge holes in the pelts after tanning. "Well?"

My mother looked healthy. Her cheeks had filled out a little and her skin was a better color: pinker, less sallow. What could it hurt to let her have this one small thing? If it was going to help her deal with Dad's suicide, should I begrudge her access to the shop and the things that were already hers to begin with? I didn't know if that meant letting my mother make her weird sexual art or not. If it were anyone else, I probably would've found it funny: badgers fondling rabbits, a pink flamingo ducking its slender neck to fellate a squirrel. Animals meant to look ferocious suddenly turned vulnerable, predator and prey equalized by the set of a jaw or the placement of paws. The work was good. The fact that it was my mother creating it was what turned me off.

I knelt beside the cupboard below the sink and dug through the boxes of hair dye from the Dollar General. Most of the time we bought whatever was BOGO, so the selection was limited.

"We don't have black."

"How about off-black or soft black?"

"We have nutmeg, deep copper, beige brown, and absolute platinum."

"I don't want any of those." I went to close the cabinet and she put up a hand. "Wait. Let me see nutmeg."

She turned the box over in her hands, squinting at the model on the front. "No, this isn't gonna work. Too brown. I'll have to pick some up."

There was a braided basket on the floor. I'd seen it hundreds of times in my life; it was the one my mother always put her rolls and cornbread muffins in with a folded hand towel. She dumped all the pieces she'd picked up from the bin into the basket. Everything mingled together in the bottom: bits of skin and gristle. I hoped she'd throw the basket out after she was done.

"Gonna work on this from home." She scrubbed a hand along her head, dislodging the bit of toilet paper and unsticking the tender scab that had formed. Blood dripped from the wound, a bright lick that streaked down the back of her neck. "Could you drive Bastien home? Milo's working late again."

It would have been easy to pick up a tissue from the box along the sink, but I didn't. I just let the blood seep down the back of my mother's skull. Let her walk away, the drip migrating in a zigzag pattern that eventually reached the collar of her shirt. I could hear her out front, talking to a customer. The workstations were a mess—bins and cabinets thrown wide, little snips of hair crowding the sink drain. My father would never have stood for it. But again, my father wasn't alive. He no longer had a say.

ARDEA ALBA—GREAT WHITE HERON

In the time it took me to scale the ladder, Milo had climbed onto the roof of the tree house. He was twelve and I was thirteen, but already his body was the length of someone much older, his limbs pulled out thin and awkward, like melting taffy. Milo was tall, but he wasn't big, and he wasn't coordinated. No sports and no friends, other than me. We spent nearly all our time together. The two of us and Brynn, my brother and me trailing after her like a couple of lovesick puppies.

Could you just wait?

I could, he said. *But I won't.*

We'd found the tree house in the backyard of the foreclosed home, three down from ours and directly next to the graveyard. When we looked through the cutouts in the wooden walls, we could see a sliver of water out in the distance. I called it lakefront property, even though the actual view was mostly worn-down headstones that popped up like jagged teeth.

I'm not going up there, I said. *I'll never get back down.*

I don't give a shit what you do. Just gimme my stuff.

Our mother had enrolled us in summer camp, which was actually just afternoons down at the Y making crafts with other kids who definitely didn't want to be there. We were too old for daycare and too young to stay home by ourselves. Kids with money went to sleepaway camps or Bible ministry youth retreats, but not us. Our father had given us time off from working at the shop. He'd said that was vacation enough, or would we rather come by and scoop remnants from the mounts he was fleshing?

I handed Milo his jar, stretching up on tiptoe to reach his dangling hand. At the Y that day, we'd learned how to make butter from a girl only three years older than me. She'd had her long red hair in a side ponytail with one of those looped elastic bands with clear blue bobbles on the ends. Milo said they looked like balls, that she'd had blue balls in her hair, and Brynn couldn't stop laughing. Suddenly she thought Milo was hilarious and wanted him with us all the time. It made me hate my brother, who lapped up the attention and only became more annoying because of it.

I'm not giving you this bread, I told him, shoving the bag down between my feet. *There's not enough.*

I'm not gonna eat butter without bread. That's gross.

We shook our jars. It would take at least thirty minutes to get the lump going in the buttermilk. We'd filled up all our ingredients in the sweltering kitchen and then taken them with us, leaving our mother to hammer out the fleshy pink breasts for the night's chicken Parmesan.

We spent late afternoons at the tree house once the people living in the foreclosed home moved out. They'd been there for under a year. The man was younger than our father, thin in the arms and waist and wide in the hips. He'd built the tree house with a couple of friends in a single day—all of them shirtless and sweaty, drinking beer in the afternoon heat. Milo and I spied on them from the cemetery, crouched behind the plots of Davidsons and Meekins. Our knees bore witness, collecting deep grooves as we crouched for hours in the unforgiving earth. He'd called for *beer* and *more beer* so many times that Milo and I joked it must be his wife's name. We weren't sure why they'd built the tree house. They didn't have any kids.

This is taking too long. Milo's jar was fuzzy with bubbles from all the shaking, but I couldn't see any butter forming yet. Mine didn't look much different.

Don't be a little bitch. Keep going.

Brynn was coming over soon. She had to watch her baby brother for an hour while her mother ran errands. Gideon wasn't what I'd call cute. He was pale with buggy, vacant blue eyes. Brynn always talked about wanting babies, but I didn't think they were anything great. *Don't you ever think about getting married?* she asked me, draping the end of a bedsheet over her head to look like a veil. *Your brother will probably be a good husband. He's kind of getting cuter.* To get her to stop talking about Milo, I gave her the end of my blue raspberry Ring Pop. I never thought about getting married, but I did sometimes wish Brynn and I could just live together when we got older.

Hey lookit. Milo slapped the wall next to my face.

What? I was getting closer to done; I could feel it. Something hard was lumping against the glass with every flick of my wrist, a kind of thump that made me think of the gel-capped vitamin E pills my mother took for her hair and nails.

There's something poking up behind the memorial bench.

Leaning forward over the wooden railing, I felt it give a little under my weight and quickly settled back. There was something waving beneath the bench.

It's a bird.

It's a plane, said Milo, shaking his jar.

Don't be a dumbass. It's an egret. Maybe an anhinga?

Can't be, too far from the water. Looks like a piece of trash.

I'm gonna throw it some bread.

His long arm swung down, snatching at the plastic bag that held the tail end of a loaf. *No, don't! We don't have that much left.*

Calm down. I opened the bag and balled up a white hunk from the heel. *I'll just use a little.*

My aim was pretty good. It curved down in the hot gust of breeze, flipping, and landed five feet from the bench. The bread lay hidden in the straggling weeds, unnoticed by the bird.

Gimme some. I handed up a hunk, larger than mine. His aim wasn't great. The bread ball landed next to some overgrown headstones where we couldn't even read the etchings; something like Adler or Addison. It didn't matter that he'd missed, though. The bird had flopped its body behind the bench until I could see only the tip of its pale wing poking through the slats.

Instead of wasting more bread, I dropped the bag and gave my jar to Milo. *Keep shaking.*

Hopping the fence from the neighbor's yard, I crossed through the clumps of weedy patches, clouds of gnats rising up from the puddles that would never drain during the summer. Mud sucked at my sneakers, which had started as white off-brand Keds but were ending summer the color of dirt, the bumpers black from Brynn writing the names of all the boys she'd loved during the school year. My shoes had said *Brian* and *Rickie* and *David* and then *Brian* again; Brian who sat in front of me in math, Brian with the floppy dark hair that fell over one eye, Brian who always smelled like lunch meat if he'd been playing basketball.

Brynn and I used to sit side by side on the gym floor during PE, trading a single wad of gum between us. I chewed a lined pattern one way and she chewed a lined pattern the other until we made a shape like a Triscuit. She wrote Brian's name and I chewed her gum, concentrating on her fingers, which cupped my ankle while she wrote. The last time she did it, I saw her write an uppercase *M* and felt my heart stutter. I took the marker from her hand. *No more*, I told her. *Draw on your own shoes.*

The closer I got to the bird, the stranger it looked. Its neck was wrenched next to a tree root. One of its wings was bent nearly backward. When it heard me come around the side of the bench, its neck canted even farther until it was staring at me upside down.

Kneeling in the wet soil, I reached a careful hand toward it. Definitely a heron; a big one, pure white with a rowdy orange beak that opened wide on its hinge. It let loose a prolonged hiss. The wing that wasn't bent was braced behind its arrowed body. I noticed one of its yellow feet was turned completely around, likely broken.

Bring me a towel, I yelled. *Hurry.*

When Milo came back, he was carrying one of our good guest towels. They were shell pink with embroidery stitched around the edge; the kind that never dried your hands, just moved the water around.

You idiot. Mom's going to flip out.

He'd brought Brynn with him. She knelt beside me in the dirt, smelling like the raspberry body spray that she'd been dousing herself with all summer; a half-empty bottle she'd found in a drawer at the Y.

Poor baby. What do we do with it?

I'm gonna wrap him up, then we'll take him up to the tree house.

Then what?

Nurse him back to health, I said. *Fix him up.*

Brynn raised an eyebrow. She'd gotten very good at that. She was also good at smirking from only one corner of her mouth, and tipping her head in a direction that made her ponytail whisper down her shoulder. She made me feel that I had no idea what I was doing with my body, that every part of hers was under control. Milo always watched her, too, with a creepy look in his eyes. When he got that way, I'd pinch him until he looked normal again. She was mine to like, mine to look at. But we were his only friends, really, no other girls around for him to ogle. As long as he kept his comments to himself, he could think whatever he liked.

Make a distraction, like flap your arms or something. I flipped the towel out in front of me, like a matador. *Then I'll grab him.*

Milo leaned over from the other side and shook his butter jar in the bird's face. The heron reared back and I brought the towel in, wrapping it around the thin body, picking it up firmly, like I would a wet dog from a bathtub. It struggled a little, but the effort seemed to drain it. The bird went limp almost immediately.

Our processional led down the dirt track that ran through the heart of the cemetery: me carrying the bird, Brynn clomping along in her platform flip-flops, and Milo, who always came last, no matter where we were or what we were doing.

I climbed the ladder one-handed, pressing the bird against my chest, swaddled like an infant. The tree house was mostly made from plywood—all four sides and the roof—with planks haphazardly nailed together for the floor. It sat fifteen feet up in the oak, and its porch was a good space to cop a breeze.

Scoot over, Brynn said, coming up behind me and knocking into the back of my knees. I didn't really want to go inside. Earlier one of the biggest roaches I'd ever seen had been crawling on the ceiling. Those ones sometimes flew. I wedged myself next to the railing while Milo climbed up last. He still had his jar, shaking it around his head.

Can you stop? I asked. *And where's mine?*

He pointed down at the graveyard and laughed.

Let's just go in. Brynn poked a finger under the edge of the towel and flipped it up to reveal the heron's curled neck, ruffled with tiny white feathers. It looked sleepy and sweet, bundled up like it had caught a chill.

Wait a second, I said. *Let me check inside first.*

Jessa's too freaked out about roaches. Milo pushed his foot into the doorway, halfway on the porch and halfway inside. *She's scared of a bug that's like a fraction of her size.*

Come on. Brynn grabbed his elbow. *Just kill it, Milo.*

There was understanding in Brynn's eyes when she looked at me. I really was only a girl to her; one who would be scared of a roach, while my brother, who couldn't even scrape out the insides of a raccoon pelt without turning green, was the one who'd always be turned to for help. Of the two of us, he was the one who was squeamish. I stayed up late with him when he had a nightmare and got scared of imaginary monsters hiding under the clothes hamper. He was the one who cried over sad movies and let our mother comfort him when he hurt himself.

I was the strong one, but because I was a girl, that's all Brynn saw. Milo, scaredy-cat of the highest order, would always be the knight.

I can do it. I pushed forward but Milo pressed a hand against my shoulder, setting me back on my heels.

Let me get it, you hate them.

I'm not scared. I don't care.

We struggled as I tried to shove forward and Milo kept pushing me back. Brynn was wedged between us, her hands coming up to bat at both our faces.

Stop it, she yelled. *You're both stupid.*

There was one last shove from Milo, whose arms were significantly longer than my own. I fell back into the railing and heard it crack, the sound like ice dumped into a glass of warm water. Then the bird and I pitched over the side.

We landed hard in some fallen oak branches. I lay there kicking up leaves, trying to get back the breath I'd knocked out of myself. I turned my cheek into the dirt and listened to the blood rushing hard in my ears, waiting for the world to right itself again.

Someone turned me over. Brynn was crying, and then she screamed. Milo pulled the bird from my arms. The towel was stained with dirt and something darker. I had landed on the heron with my full weight. Its head hung slack from the opening at the top; blood and a thick, viscous fluid dripped from its open beak.

They set my broken arm in a cloth sling. The bone in my shoulder had broken so high they couldn't put a cast on it. The pain medicine made me too sleepy to walk or talk much. I was glad for it; I didn't want to think about the bird anymore, the way that it had looked when Milo held it up above my head, bloody as an aborted baby.

That night in my room I woke from a nightmare, shoulder throbbing, crying for my mother. She held my head in her lap as I sobbed, stroking my sweaty hair away from my face. She cleaned the snot from my nose with the sleeve of her night-gown and covered us both with her long hair, a curtain that smelled of sleep and the yeasty-lemon aroma of her skin.

Her hands stroked cool on my cheeks and under my eyes. *You didn't mean to kill it. It was already hurting. Sometimes we just can't make things better.*

And I knew she was right, but a small, black part of me had seen how beautifully the bird's feathers glistened in the sunshine and wished I could make it stay with me, always. So I cried for that: the fact that I was the kind of person who'd wish death on a creature just so I could make it my own.

4

I trained Bastien up front and got him acquainted with the merchandise. It was strange to instruct an employee on things I'd known since before I had braces. I'd grown up playing with cattle skulls and freeze-dried mice, casually digging my hands into bowls of shark teeth because I liked the sharp feel of them between my fingers.

"How much longer?" Bastien swept the concrete, corralling flecks of foam and antler shards from the deer head I'd been mounting for the past hour.

"I'm not sure."

"Like maybe forty-five minutes? Fifteen?"

"I don't know."

The form I'd chosen was too large. I was having trouble getting the antlers where I wanted them, and instead of pulling off the pelt and starting over, I'd tried to stretch it with my hands. I'd knocked one of the points against the metal prep table and chipped it very badly. It was a rookie mistake, one I hadn't made since I was in high school.

"But do you think soon?"

"Maybe."

It was distracting, having another live body in the room with me. I couldn't concentrate. Bastien liked to talk while he worked. He was twitchy and spastic, moving back and forth across the room to pick up one of the tools I was using, or to fondle a piece of the deer's pelt. He'd pulled out glass eyes of every color and begun sorting them into piles that I'd have to put away before we left. I'd seen him take the tough linen string I used for sewing and wind it around his palm, making what appeared to be a friendship bracelet. Then he'd given up and thrown the knotted mess onto the floor.

"Is there anything left to do up front?" I asked.

"The floor's so fucking clean you could eat off it." The broom stopped for a second. "Sorry."

"What about the mail that got rained on?"

He shuffled over to the corner and used the tip of the broom to grab at the dirt pockets that always collected there. The tops of his ears were red and the back of his neck was a little sunburned. I wondered how he spent his time when he wasn't in the shop working. His friends weren't any good for him to be around.

He gouged at the dust and a couple of bristles broke off. "It's spread out under the front window where the most sun's coming in."

"That's good. Thanks."

"I'd maybe think about moving the goat, Aunt Jessa." He tipped up the broom and riffed his fingers along the frayed edges, breaking off more pieces that sprinkled onto the concrete.

"Why? We've gotten more foot traffic in the past week than we have in the last month."

Dust flicked upward into the air around him, creating a halo. "His fur is fading. It looks powdery or something."

"Shit."

"Yeah."

I set down my stitch remover and flexed my cramped fingers. The deer's opened face looked up at me, half-dazed from the crooked set of its glass eyes. I'd have to redo the whole thing. "Let's move it now. Put something else up, maybe."

Up front looked just as clean as Bastien said it would. The permanent dust that had built up around the shelving had been Pledged to a waxy sheen. Piles of mail next to the register were sorted into a plastic tray system labeled PAST DUE, CURRENTLY DUE, and PAID—the latter a single sheet of wrinkled paper, which I thought might be a mistake.

We each grabbed an end of the Bagot, not wanting to tip it over and spill it; it would likely bust its seams and I'd have to stuff and re-stitch everything.

"Could you pick up Grandma today from the gallery?"

I nearly tripped over an enormous stack of snakeskin he'd moved into the walkway. "You can't get her?"

"I'm not really supposed to be driving."

I hadn't anticipated that I'd need to see my mother's art, at least not right away. I knew she'd been going over to the gallery most afternoons, but I figured it was just a way to keep her contained while she got whatever weird art jones she had out of her system. That plan didn't include looking at whatever she'd created. I was positive it wouldn't be anything I liked.

Bastien staggered back toward the far wall, where the sun from the front window didn't hit. "She wants to show you something."

"Damn it. Fine." I dropped the goat a little less gently than I should have. I examined the muzzle. "You're right, he's looking beat-up." The skin had warped in the direct sunlight. Both ears were crusty and the goat's nostrils had faint crackles running through them. "He'll need to be moisturized."

"I can do that."

"I'll just do it when I get back." Except I had to run to the grocery and pick up Lolee's marching band uniform at the dry-cleaning place and stop over at the post office to ship out some mail orders.

"It just takes some emollients. I'll be careful."

"*Emollients?*"

He squatted down in front of the Bagot and examined its hooves, which were also looking a little flaky. "Yeah, petroleum jelly."

"You've never done this stuff before."

Pulling a pad from his back pocket, he jotted some notes. "I've seen you do some. Grandpa too, when I was little. There's also this thing called the internet. You can look up lots of shit there."

My father would've loved to teach Bastien specialty secrets, if Bastien had ever shown an interest when he was alive: how to perk an ear, the best way to debone small game without ruining the pelts. If he were still alive, it could've been the three of us in the shop, instead of just me trying to half-ass everything by myself. I remembered the first time my father showed me how to clean and reset teeth. It took us all day, but when it was done they looked nearly perfect in the deer's jaw. There was something so satisfying about it: working on a piece until you'd perfected it. I could teach Bastien to create like that, I thought. I could show him some of the things my father had shown me.

"Okay. We'll see how it goes." I grabbed the keys to my truck from behind the counter.

"Right." He rubbed at the back of his neck and stared down at his notes. "I'll just start with some of the small stuff and you can check my work after."

When I left, he was sitting on the floor in front of the goat, measuring the neck and face with his hands. He looked ready to speak and so did the animal, as if they were already communicating.

There were groceries to pick up and Lolee's uniform, but what I wanted more than anything was a beer. I drove past the tiny air-conditioning repair shop with the words HEATING & COOL-ING stenciled in black script across the windows, the barbershop where Milo and I had gotten our first haircuts, and pulled into the parking lot of the only bar my father and I ever drank at. There were no cars out front and I took that as a good sign.

A couple was wedged into the same side of a corner booth, but aside from them and the bartender I was alone. I sat on one of the red vinyl barstools and the bartender dropped a beer in front of me. Jimmy was around my father's age. They'd gone to high school together, the same one Milo and I'd attended. He wore the kind of shirt my dad always hated to see on Florida guys: a pink floral thing with palm trees in a Hawaiian style, unbuttoned enough to show a grizzled patch of chest hair. A gold chain necklace lay tangled in the nest of it.

I liked being there. It felt cool without the dampness, lacked light in a way that made my eyes comfortable. Outside, juicy green pressed in on you from all sides and sunshine bled so aggressively that you were guaranteed cataracts by age sixty-five, but in the bar you could pretend the world outside didn't exist anymore.

Classic rock played and the bartender hummed along. I drank my beer in long, slow pulls and asked for another. My father and I had come to this place for years, usually on Thursday or Friday nights after we'd closed the shop. We'd each have a couple and sit quietly, no need to talk about anything specific. My mother waiting at home for my father, nobody waiting for me. He never asked about my dating life. Never once questioned why I was always alone; why I'd never brought anyone to dinner or to meet the family.

Anything having to do with sex made him extremely uncomfortable. He didn't like off-color jokes; he threw out my mother's Victoria's Secret catalogs because he found the pictures offensive. *This is trash*, he said when he walked into the living room and found Milo and me watching a comedy in which two people were awkwardly having sex. Milo had protested that it was supposed to be funny, but our father had simply turned off the television and told us sex wasn't anything to laugh about.

Our family wasn't religious. Neither of my parents ever talked about the moral rightness of anything. We just didn't discuss each other's business. Mostly we retold the same old stories, nostalgia over things we'd rehashed a thousand times before, varnishing the memories so they shone and hiding all the bad parts. I often wondered why we couldn't talk about the present, why the past held all the promise while the future sat before us like stagnant water.

My father and I had come in for beers the week before he killed himself. He sat beside me on his barstool and made a dumb dad joke about polar bears. I laughed, not knowing I'd find him in a puddle of his own brain matter less than three days later. I drained my second beer quickly and didn't enjoy it as much as the first.

In her work apron, my mother resembled an elementary-school art teacher. It was a small black thing with overlarge pockets, and she'd pulled it over a T-shirt from when she'd repainted the house. I didn't recognize the jeans she had on, but that might have been because she never wore them. My whole life she'd said they made her ass feel constricted.

"Mmph." She squatted and the jeans pulled tight enough across her butt to turn three shades lighter. "Mmmph."

A pencil jutted from her clenched teeth. It seesawed up and down while she considered the pile of parts in front of her. She squatted lower, leaning over so far I was certain her pants would rip in half. I tugged at my own jeans, which were creeping steadily up my crotch, and tried not to say anything mean about the monstrosity my mother was compiling.

There were myriad cans of liquid latex, hair dye, and glittery puffy paints that we'd used on T-shirts back in middle school. She'd dissected most of the animals taken from the parts bin, freeing the wings from the bat, carving off the face of a small squirrel. It lay awkwardly apart from the rest, staring raptly at the work she was piecing together with an industrial hot glue gun.

She dropped her pencil. It rolled across the floor, landing near a couple of cans of spray paint. "Shoot," she said, crawling after it.

"Isn't it something?" Lucinda Rex looked as casual as I'd ever seen her, jeaned and smocked and T-shirted as my mother. Her dark hair was bound back with a pink elastic band. She wore glasses, large frames that took up a lot of her face. It was overall a very cute look and I felt my hands start to sweat again.

"What exactly are you all doing?" I asked, wondering if my own hair was doing that weird thing where it frizzed out of my braid.

"Your mother's trying out some new techniques. I think the work's coming along nicely."

"Sure." It looked to me like a truck had backed over a garbage can full of roadkill, but I wasn't about to say that to Lucinda.

"Do we have any Spackle?" My mother had picked up the squirrel's head and was attaching it to a loose armadillo plate using the hot glue. When she pulled back the gun, the string broke midair, giving the squirrel a plastic toupee.

"Of course, Libby. Let me go see what I can find."

On the floor beside my mother was a wheeled tray. It was covered at the top, as if she were about to enjoy some room service. The cloth was white and crisp.

"You gonna have a sandwich?"

"What?" She gouged at the armadillo plate with an X-Acto, digging free random chunks. "Oh, lunch. I forgot again."

"What's this then?" I flipped back the napkin and looked down at a wide array of anatomy. "Are these . . . ?"

"Couple of vulvas. There's a scrotal sack somewhere . . ." She yanked the cloth from my hand and revealed the rest, a large metal tray covered with sexual organs. "Ah, here it is." She jabbed her knife at a wrinkled wad rolling in the corner.

"What are you gonna do with those?"

"You'll see."

Her attention went back to the X-Acto; she continued ramming her knife into the side of the armadillo plates, whittling holes roughly the size of quarters.

Lucinda brought back several tubes of adhesive. "Here you are. Wasn't sure what would work best, so I just brought everything we had."

The work perverted all the things I loved about taxidermy. Our pieces, done right, left the animals whole and lifelike—as if they could step off the mount and wander right back out to the woods. My mother's animals were mangled and misshapen, slopped together like trash. It took away their dignity.

"Could we go now?" I asked, pinching the bridge of my nose. I wished I'd stayed for another beer at the bar, or that I'd called Milo to pick her up.

"Go sit out front if it bothers you that much."

"It doesn't bother me." I stared at the squirrel, its face stretched into a grimace of pain, though I knew it could no longer feel anything.

"Of course it does. But you know what? I don't care."

My mother slashed open the armadillo shell, spreading it like sandwich bread. From there, she began adhering the whole of it to a wide white canvas, set up on an easel beside her. It looked like somebody had tried and failed to put up drywall.

The tiny dark nose emerged from the Spackle, snorkeling for air.

"It's awful," I said, unable to take any more. "I can barely look at it."

"Oh, really? It's awful?" She opened the largest tub of glue and smeared it onto the canvas and over the armadillo plates, slathering it until the squirrel was completely submerged. "So it's more awful than gutting animals and scraping out their insides? More awful than stuffing heads and mounting them on people's living room walls?"

"Dad would hate this." That much I knew; my father would've taken one look at that pile of sex organs and taxidermied parts and wanted to burn it all.

"I'm glad." An especially rough jab left a hole in the canvas. "Oh, damn it." She wheeled around, chin set angrily. "My entire adult life that man told me what to do. What I could like, what was acceptable to talk about. It was like living inside a clenched fist."

"That's not true," I said, though I knew it was. "He just cared about you. He wanted what was best."

"I don't have to care what he'd like, do I? He's gone. It doesn't matter."

Her pupils enlarged and swallowed up the rest of the irises. It felt as if I were yelling at a little kid and I didn't have the patience, not with the two beers rolling around in my stomach. I wanted to go home and take a nap. "I'm heading up front. Find me when you're ready."

I passed Lucinda on my way out. She was leaning against the counter, talking on her phone. I knew she must have heard us arguing, and I felt embarrassed that she'd know the intimate details of our personal business. Then I got angry, wondering why she'd let a woman who was obviously in need of a grief counselor mess around with a bunch of genitalia and dead animals.

She waved her hand excitedly toward the middle of the room, across the black lacquered floor. She mouthed the word *amazing*. Gave me a thumbs-up, then gestured again.

The boar I'd brought the week before stood upright on a platform, sliced down the middle. Intestines spilled from either side, liquid red that actually puddled onto the floor with a splattering sound that came from a speaker lodged in the ceiling. It wore a stethoscope, which dangled down and ended in a spangled resonator bedazzled with a ton of clear crystals. Grossly enlarged phalluses sculpted from what looked like Play-Doh were rammed into the intestinal bits. The boar's tongue had been yanked from its jaws, pulled out and draped to the side, painted the same viscous red, cartoonish in its slavering. One of its own intestines had been pulled to the front and hung from the other side of its mouth alongside a horrifically large flesh-toned dildo. Its eyes had been replaced with two green objects. I wasn't quite able to make out what they were.

I turned back to Lucinda. "What's this?" I held up two fingers to my own eyes, and then pointed them over at the dismembered boar.

She leaned over the desk to hit a switch. Bulbs flickered and lit the animal from the inside, blinking spastically—red and green, snaking around the intestines and puddling down on the floor. The eyes glowed witchy, stared down hard at me over the two yellow tusks that remained untouched.

"She found them in her attic." Her eyes widened and she nodded emphatically, glasses sliding down her nose. "Christmas lights. Your mother is a genius."

MACACA RADIATA—
BONNET MACAQUE

At eleven years old, I'd never had a pet of my own. Countless dogs littered our home, running wild when they weren't out hunting with my father, skulking the property around our dead-end street like a pack of sugared-up children. There was the Pomeranian, Sir Charles, but that dog would bite anybody that wasn't our mother. If we were lucky, sometimes Milo and I might find a clutch of feral kittens hidden beneath the shed out back. They were black and calico-speckled, eyes milky with pus. We tried to name them, but by night they went back to being homeless. Our father wouldn't let us keep them.

Too many fleas, he said.

For Christmas, I asked for something wriggling. I didn't care what. It could have been one of the tarantulas I'd fondled down at the pet store or the lizards basking on their fake rocks. I liked the tiny frogs with their neon skins, smaller than my thumbnail. Gerbils. A turtle. I just wanted something I could hold; something that would move and breathe and reciprocate my affection.

What the hell do we need another animal for? my father asked, half asleep in his recliner. He looked groggy, in and out of naps all afternoon, buried beneath a mound of blankets. *There's too many bodies in this house as it is.*

The months leading up to the holiday had been tense. Our father was home most afternoons, grumpy and sick. His skin, always too oily, had turned dry and papery, and his normally wild head of hair had diminished along his skull until he'd shaved off the whole mess. He'd even gotten rid of his mustache. It scared me, seeing that stranger's face in my living room. Milo and I stayed away from the house when he was there, unsure what might set him off. He yelled when we talked too loud, told us things smelled funny. I overheard him throwing up in my parents' bathroom and groaning like he was about to die. When I asked my mother what was happening, she told me he'd caught a bug.

We're going bankrupt, Milo whispered one night as we hid out on the back porch. Our father was yelling about something for the third time that night and our mother was trying to calm him down. *That happened to a kid's family from school and then the parents got divorced.*

I don't think we're broke. Dad hadn't been at work, but there were still a lot of regulars. He'd gone in only two days that week before spending the rest of his time holed up in the bedroom. I walked down the hallway quiet as a ghost, sure my footsteps might wake him. He'd piled on several different quilts even though the house was humid and stifling that winter.

My mother looked almost as worn out as he did. She called our aunt more than ever, and she did that only when she was really stressed. *It's not going well*, I heard her say into the phone as she snuck a cigarette. She blew quick puffs of it out the open kitchen window. *He can't stand being helpless.*

Strength was important to our father, in all areas of his life. He kept himself fit using a weight-lifting set in our carport. He used hand strengtheners regularly, working the muscles in his palms and fingers. His body was his temple, the thing that enabled him to do the work he loved most. *You can't be a taxidermist if you don't have the right body for it,* he told me, pointing out the strong line of his biceps. *Gotta cut through meat. Gotta saw through bone.*

My father was tall, but we both had the same type of body: naturally muscular and built like bulldogs. My brother, willowy and slight, could barely lift the smallest barbell over his head. Our father tried to get him to work out, but Milo wasn't interested. He liked reading. He wanted to spend his time playing video games. He talked about his feelings in a way that made my father cringe. *Strength is here, too,* my father told me, tapping his temple. *Can't be strong in your body if you're not strong in your mind.*

On Christmas morning our parents sat with mugs of coffee, sweat beading their temples as we opened gifts out on the back patio, the only place in our house where we could actually fit a Christmas tree. Our mother liked to decorate all the taxidermied pieces inside. She put Santa hats on the deer mounts and hung tinsel from the squirrels. Shiny red bulbs dangled off the ears of the arctic fox that my father kept in the den.

Milo and I sat cross-legged on the floor. The wrapping paper adhered to our sticky fingers, the cheap dollar-store kind with colors that melted onto our hands, giving us radioactive fingerprints that smeared onto everything we touched.

Oh my God, my mother crowed, as I pried open a thrice-recycled J. C. Penney box. Amid the tornado of white tissue paper was a crimson sweater set. *You're gonna get a lot of use from that. So pretty.* She grabbed it and held it up to my chest. *Wow, beautiful.*

My mother bought me stuff that would never leave the house, much less have the tags removed. Sometimes Brynn would take things I didn't want, like the makeup or the gummy lip gloss that always smeared my chin, but most of the clothes were too big for her skinny frame.

Milo opened packages of socks and underwear, several knives, and a killer sharpener that would make its way into my bedroom. The last gift my father set in front of me, wrapped in butcher paper. He was sitting pale in the sunlight, barely able to sip his coffee. It scared me to see him looking so sick—my mother kept reaching over and rubbing at his thigh with her hand, as if she were trying to warm him up.

C'mon. Let's see it. He used the tip of his finger to pry open an end, Scotch tape already pulling free in the humidity. My heart beat hard inside my chest as I envisioned a little buddy that would live in my bedroom. The box was too small to hold a puppy, but I thought they might have gotten me an iguana, or even one of those desert tortoises that could eat lettuce from the palm of your hand. Milo looked over, eyes darting between the box in my lap and our father, who'd handed him nothing.

Fur poked from the flap at the top. I pulled out a monkey dressed in a top hat and tails. It had a monocle over one brown, beady eye. It looked a lot like Mr. Peanut.

You like it? My father tickled the fuzz that tufted the top of its minuscule cravat. *My dad made it for me when I was your age. Now it's yours.*

114

A silk rose was pinned to its tuxedo jacket. It was very well rendered: the mouth proportioned perfectly, teeth set in even white lines. Its tail curved around its body, swirling into a gentle swoop that wrapped around the top of a tiny lacquered cane. I stared at its small, snickering face and wanted to throw it off the porch. It looked just like the monkey from that movie that gave everyone the plague.

Thanks, I love it, I said, trying to hide my disgust. Its fur felt too slick, like it was wet.

I held it gingerly as my brother ate pink and yellow Pez straight from a Batman-shaped dispenser. My mother gathered up the breakfast plates, gluey with cinnamon roll remnants, juice glasses peppered with pulp dried along their sides. Staring down at me, my father took a sip of his coffee and grimaced. His lips were pale and there was a bright red sore in the crease.

Where's mine? Milo asked, shuffling on his knees in the wreck of wrapping paper. *Do I get something special from Grandpa too?*

Our father got up without responding and left us out on the porch.

You wanna hold it? I held out the monkey and wiggled it, the hat flapping back and forth on its head.

Milo sucked his lip between his teeth and blinked rapidly. *Keep it,* he said. *It's ugly.*

That night my father cleared a space on the shelves opposite my bed, shoving down the music box with the ballerina that twisted awkwardly to the tune of Beethoven's Fifth and the Russian nesting dolls that told the story of the three bears. He set the monkey, named Captain Peterbrook, smack in the center. The monkey leaned on its cane, one spindly arm permanently raised to its monocle.

Now that looks pretty good. My father adjusted it a few more times, carefully twisting the body so it'd get the best light. He coughed and leaned against the wall for a second before adjusting the monkey again. *There. Perfect.*

My parents left the door open as they always did, light from the hall coming in to cast a glow across the popcorn ceiling. A stripe lit Captain Peterbrook, who looked like an escapee from a mental asylum. I turned and focused on the opposite wall, trying not to think about the monkey climbing down in the middle of the night, its cane tapping lightly against the floor. I was still awake an hour later, listening to the murmur of my parents' voices from the living room.

If I get through this, it'll be a miracle.

Could you please stop. My mother's voice sounded thick, as if she'd been crying. *Just for one day. It's Christmas.*

I am telling you, I will never do this again. There's no goddamn way.

Captain Peterbrook leered down at me from its perch, teeth bright and sharp.

Brynn loved it. She rocked it like a baby and cooed nonsense at its ugly face, wanting to undress it like a Barbie doll. *His little outfit! It's so sweet!* She clutched it too tightly to her chest and its hat dislodged. *If you don't want him, can I have him?*

I didn't want the monkey, but I worried what my father would say if he saw it missing. He hadn't gone into work the entire week after Christmas. His face was gaunt as a skeleton.

The red chafing at his lips had gotten so bad he'd started rubbing Vaseline on the corners. *Just play with him when you come over.*

She pulled a plastic comb from her purse and brushed the fine, soft fur of its belly under its tuxedo jacket. The monkey lay facedown on her lap, one of its sly hands partly up her skirt. *I'll take such good care of him, I promise.*

A frog tank would have fit perfectly on the shelf, or even a cage for a hamster. Instead there was only the monkey, a pinched, ugly thing with its dusty coat of fur and its creepy undertaker's suit. It was the exact opposite of what I'd wanted—something warm and loving, something brand new that could've been only mine.

Brynn took the monkey to school and let everyone have a turn playing with it. By the end of the day, it was completely undressed. There were bits of it on the school bus, fur lining the floor, sticking to people's shoes. Without its clothes, it looked more human and ashamed. There were holes in its neck from where the tuxedo shirt had detached. I felt like crying to see it like that, all bare and helpless.

Alone in my room, I stared at the empty space on the shelf where the monkey used to live. Something living—a lovebird, even a goldfish—would have made any of this seem more bearable. I took the other taxidermied pieces from my room and tossed them under the bed: the hummingbird sipping at a delicate pink hibiscus, my orange kitten with its eyes sealed shut, the deer skin I kept at the foot of my bed the way someone might throw a blanket.

I wrote Brynn's name in Sharpie on the bumper of my sneaker, next to my own. I connected our names with fat, lopsided hearts, pressing my fingers to my lips and then to the rubber. Then I scrubbed everything out until there was just a big black mess.

5

Lolee and I sat at the kitchen counter at my parents' house playing Jenga and swapping period stories. They got progressively more graphic as we pulled the blocks free of the wobbling stack, placing them gently on top.

"This one time I passed a clot the size of a garden slug. It got stuck to the side of the toilet. When I crushed it in my fingers, it felt like one too." Lolee dropped her tile lightly, barely wiggling the tower.

I poked at several likely prospects. "Once I pulled out a tampon in a public bathroom. When I threw it at the little metal garbage can, it fell on the floor and rolled under the stall. Landed next to a woman's shoe."

"Never happened."

"Swear to God."

"Did she step on it?"

A block slipped free and everything swayed, but didn't tip. "She kind of kicked it a little."

"Nasty." The electronic timer went off for the slice-and-bake cookies. She grabbed the oven mitts, two cartoon dinosaurs that bit either end of the baking sheet. We were playing at a slumber party, but really I was babysitting because everyone else was busy and Lolee was at an age deemed *too young* to stay by herself, which roughly translated to *might invite a boy over to the house and get promiscuous.*

It was something my mother had asked of me, not Milo. My brother never knew what his daughter was doing. When Lolee needed someone, she called me or her grandmother. Milo was like a fun uncle who remembered to bring home ice cream, the kind of dad who took you to the amusement park instead of making you do your homework. Lolee loved him, but I could tell she didn't trust him to be there for her. Milo would tell you he'd show up for breakfast, and you'd see him two weeks later when he stopped by with beer. No clue what he'd done. Smiling, happy. Nonchalant.

I was the one who'd talked to Lolee about her body and what she could expect from it. I'd stumbled over my words, showing her the instructions from the box of tampons as a kind of how-to guide. Pointing out the uterus, the cervix, the little line drawings in baby pink and white, cartoon fingers and cartoon vaginas. She'd laughed and then I'd laughed, and it was awkward, but at least it was done.

Lolee sat back down across from me, hooking her bare feet onto the rungs of my stool. "I stained the mattress pretty bad one time," she said. "Bled through my underwear, my nightgown, both sets of sheets, and the comforter. I was having a dream that I was swimming in the lake."

"I've had that one before."

We picked cookies off the metal sheet, burning our fingers, licking melted chocolate chips from our palms. Every time we touched a tile, we left behind grease stains.

"Here's a good one," I said. "One time I was messing around with a girl in the back seat of her car. It was really dark and we didn't realize that she'd started her period until she drove me home."

Lolee paused mid-poke. "You're lying."

"I opened the car door and the overhead light came on. That's when we saw the blood. We had to go to a gas station and wash ourselves in the bathroom sink."

"Oh my God. That's disgusting."

The tower fell and rained Jenga tiles all over the kitchen floor. One of them slid beneath the stove. I got down on my hands and knees to retrieve it. When I couldn't reach, I grabbed the spatula we'd used for the cookies and swept broadly beneath the appliance, jettisoning the tile along with a variety of crumbs, a few old tater tots, and something that might have once been a chicken nugget.

"Who was the girl?" Lolee dug at stray cookie guts with her fingers.

"Nobody you know." How could I tell her that the girl had been her mother? That when Brynn saw the blood all over my hands, she'd laughed until she'd cried? That there'd been a corona of brownish red surrounding my mouth from where I'd sucked the life straight out of her? It was a bittersweet memory. The next night she'd gone out with Milo, and when he'd come home after the movie, there were lipstick stains on his neck. We hadn't talked about that; we never talked about that.

My mother normally watched Lolee, but she was out at the gallery again. She'd been there every night for the past few weeks, setting up for some kind of arts showcase, or at least that was what Lucinda had said every time I'd gone to pick up my mother. She described it as *incredible, innovative, one of a kind*. All those expressions led me to believe I'd hate every part of it, but Lucinda was pretty and I wasn't going to tell her something mean.

Lucinda had a raspy voice that made her sound like she'd caught a perpetual cold. She kept her hair knotted on the top of her head and one loose strand curled cutely by her ear. Beautiful in a way that felt effortless, the kind of woman whose entire life is mapped and planned and perfectly maintained without needing to do any work at all. Someone like that would absolutely bail at the first sign of disorder. If I told her our family history, all the death and abandonment and freakish behavior, would she cut my mother off? The embarrassment might be worth it, if it meant my mother would stop shoving her taxidermied porn in people's faces. But the question was moot, because I could barely string three words together in front of her.

Lolee put on a movie and we sat cross-legged on the floor. She painted my toenails with gummy green polish and I tried to sit still. She drew a stripe down my big toenail and then texted something on her phone; did another stripe, sent another text. She took a picture of my foot and then sent it to me.

"I'm right here. We don't have to text each other."

"Shut up and hold still, you're gonna smear it on the rug."

Afterward she painted the nails of all the mounted animals in the living room. The jackrabbit on the mantel got baby pink; the snowy ferrets beside the TV got navy blue. I picked red for the clawed talons of the marsh hawk. It made it look like it had just swooped down and killed something.

"Get me some fries." Lolee pulled on her gray hoodie. It had bunny ears attached to the top that flopped around whenever she shook her head.

We piled into the front seat of my truck. I had on her flip-flops because she said my boots would wreck the polish. They were a size too small, and my bare heel scraped against the sandy floorboard whenever I hit the clutch. She played with the radio and I drove around aimlessly, grabbing fries at the Mc-Donald's drive-thru and then getting ice cream from the gas station. It was freezer-burned, and we had to eat around the bad parts with little wooden spoons they kept by the register.

If I looked at her from the corner of my eye, it felt like driving around with Brynn. She put her feet up on the dash and yanked my hair when I made fun of her baby lisp. Her voice sounded the same as her mother's, kind of throaty with a propensity to trail up in pitch at the ends of her sentences, especially if she was whining about something. I wasn't the kind of person who made friends easily. I'd been closest to Brynn, and there was Milo, and then my father. Brynn had left, my father was dead, and Milo was so stuck in his own head there was no talking to him about anything. I spent lots of late nights parked in front of my television or in the shop, drinking beer until I couldn't see straight and didn't care if the pelts refused to talk back to me.

Need, I thought, was a stealthy invader.

We took our food down to the lake. There were a few lights still on in the parking lot, but it was mostly dark. Our steps down to the dock were guided by dumb luck and milky moonlight glowing through cloud cover. Lolee clung to my arm and

I held the sack of leftover fries, grease soaking the paper bag and dirtying my shirt.

A dank mineral scent was coming off the water. It lapped the dock in smooth bursts, wake smacking the shore and leaving behind slick trails of muck from the reeds.

"I wanna swim," Lolee said, kicking off her shoes.

"It's too dark."

She pulled off her T-shirt and shorts, jumping into the water wearing just her underwear. The water rippled. When she emerged again, her head was sleek as a seal.

I fed her fries when she paddled up to the dock, clinging to the wood with her pruned fingers, complaining about splinters. Her lips were spitty and shone in the moonlight. It reminded me of when she was little, how she only ever wanted to eat if someone else was feeding her. Brynn called her "baby bird," and she'd looked like one with her little peaked face and beaky nose. She had colic so bad it kept the whole house up every night. *I'm never doing this again, never having another baby*, Brynn said. She handed off Lolee any chance she got—to my mother, to me, to strangers in the grocery store. *I just want a break*, she told me. There were purple circles under her eyes like they'd been drawn there with marker. *If I could do it all over again, maybe I'd take a harder look at college. Maybe I should have left right after Bastien.*

"There's too much algae down here." Lolee kicked hard and the wake spilled up onto the shore from the force.

"It's probably a snake."

"Yeah, right." She splashed me with a cupped palm and I moved the bag out of the way so it wouldn't soak up the lake water.

"I'm standing on so many cypress knees. I'm gonna fall and bust my ass when I get out."

"I'll pull you up this way."

She swam out farther, legs churning white. "Nope. I'll get splinters."

Our fries were cold, but I wasn't really hungry anymore. Just playing with my food. I doused the whole sack in ketchup and watched her swim out farther, far enough that her head was only a dark speck bobbing on the surface.

"Come back now," I called, barely able to see her. She splashed more, naming every stroke she'd learned in swimming lessons.

"Breaststroke, doggy paddle." She moved in jagged spurts, the water parting around her. "Butterfly, doggy paddle. Free-style, doggy paddle."

Panting, she reached the dock and held up a hand. I pulled her up quick, but she still scraped the top of her thigh.

"Jesus! Told you I'd get splinters."

Lights illuminated the water red and blue, smearing together and staining everything purple. A car door slammed, the sound echoing off the lake.

"Hurry up and get your clothes on." I thrust her yellow T-shirt at her when she was too slow to grab it herself. Her tiny shorts got stuck halfway up her legs as she yanked them over her wet skin.

The police officer walked down the dock and shined a flashlight in our faces. I moved in front of Lolee, who finally managed to pull her shorts over her underwear.

"Park closes at sundown."

"Just having dinner." I held up the crumpled paper bag, but the light never left my face.

"You eating in the water?" The flashlight's beam shifted to Lolee and swam around her wet head, two damp circles delineating where her bra had sopped up the lake.

"We were about to leave."

"Let's see some identification."

The officer was young and I didn't recognize him. Very blond with a sharp jaw. He smelled musky, like cologne that had been sitting on someone's shelf for too long. I dug into the back pocket of my jeans and pulled out my wallet. It was Velcro and made an embarrassing noise when it opened.

He took my license and gestured at Lolee. "I'll need yours."

"She's fourteen." He flashed the light back in my eyes. It burned there, a lit cigarette butt pressed to my brain. I tried to smile. "She's my niece."

He still had my license, looking at it hard like it might change if he shook it. "This your idea of babysitting?"

"We're just having some fun. It's Friday night."

The beam flicked off our faces and danced along the waterfront, through the swaths of cattails and reeds. Glowing green-blue pinpricks lit in pairs of two. "It's gonna be real fun when we have to come down here tomorrow and drag the lake because a gator bit off your arm."

It had happened before, a couple of summers after high school. We watched it on the news in my parents' living room, Brynn parked in Milo's lap and me holding Bastien. *I hope you kids would never be so stupid*, my father said, shaking his head. Brynn and I looked at each other and tried not to laugh. The three of us swam in the lake most nights in the summer, not usually wearing clothes. *Gators are disgusting*, Brynn replied, shuddering, and then Milo dug his hands into either side of her waist and yelled *gator bait* until she screamed and I walked Bastien in the other room so I wouldn't have to watch.

The officer handed me back my license and escorted us to the parking lot. He continued to lecture me on the dangers of night swimming in Florida lakes while staring at the wet circles over my niece's breasts. I handed her the hoodie she'd brought and helped her put it on, zipping it up beneath her throat.

"If you do this kind of thing again, I'll have to take you in."

I couldn't think of a bigger waste of tax dollars. "Absolutely."

The officer got back in his car and drove away. I stood there feeling stupid and aggravated with myself, wondering what Brynn would think of me doing something so pointless and dangerous with her kid. Probably laugh. Probably do the exact same thing herself. I threw our trash in the Dumpster next to the lot, and a horde of black flies flew up and settled back down. Fragments of pinecone bit into the sole of my one bare foot.

Lolee put her hand on my arm. "Where's the other flip-flop?"

"Floating around with the alligators. I'll buy you new ones."

We drove home on the back roads that bordered the lake. I watched for flashing lights in my rearview, but the streets stayed dark.

An espresso maker sat in the back office of the gallery. As soon as I came in, Lucinda would duck behind the slick black-and-white counter and I'd hear the coughing sputter of the machine. The burnt smell covered the awful odor of wet paint that haunted the place. She'd hand me a cup then and stand quietly while I drank it. The ritual of it helped. Most times I walked in a zipping snarl of nerves, too keyed up to think straight. I didn't like being places where I felt out of my element. I liked stability, the comfort of knowing my surroundings and what to expect.

Lucinda stood there in her beautiful clothes and looked like she already knew I wasn't worth the time. With Brynn, I'd held a constant pit in my gut. The burning knowledge that I'd never get to keep her. Never really have her the way I wanted. This was a different experience. It felt like Lucinda was waiting for me to make a wrong move.

"Another?" Lucinda asked, pointing toward the back.

I shook my head and barely sipped the one I held.

Up front was better. It was too hard to watch my mother dissect animals that my father and I had spent so long constructing. She unraveled stitches and shredded hide, yanking the seam ripper through fabric and wire. Glued green sequins onto nostrils, dripping strands of spangled snot. Built fluids from latex. Made puddles of gore. Then there was the bondage gear acquired from online stores. They shipped unlabeled boxes to my mother's house that piled in listing towers outside the front door.

I couldn't process the way my mother used sex in her art. It was as if my father's death had set something loose in her,

bottled up for the entirety of their marriage. When my brother
and I were growing up, my mother had never talked to us about
sex. Never mentioned a single thing that would lead me to believe she'd be capable of creating sex-toy art. She'd sometimes
joked around with Milo, teasing him about girls, but it was
always lighthearted. Never anything graphic or profane. She
hadn't even liked touching most of the taxidermied stuff. Had
never once asked my father if she could help out in the store,
as far as I knew.

Let me talk to you about it, she had said as she pulled S&M
gear from boxes. *There's a lot you should know.*

I didn't want to know any of it. I wished I knew less.

My mother plugged ball gags into mouths broken open
with pliers, wrenched out teeth and sliced off papery tongues.
She stuck these inside a clear plastic pouch that hung from the
back end of a beaver, the anus an open wound surrounded with
more sequins, these ones red. There were handcuffs lined with
orange-red fox fur. She used a nail gun to adhere nipple clamps
to a female elk whose legs she'd sawn off at the knees.

It felt like watching a low-budget slasher film. I wanted
to fast-forward to the end, to get to the part where we could
pretend none of it had happened. This wouldn't be one of
those things we'd be able to talk about fondly, a funny memory
we discussed over coffee. It was going to be something that
wrecked us all and made it so we couldn't ever look at each other again. The previous week, when I refused to go into the back
to look at the pieces, my mother brought up my father again.

*If you knew how often he had his way, how many times he took
from me, you wouldn't begrudge me this one stupid thing.*

Tired of thinking about it, I put my cup on the counter and rubbed my eyes.

"Would you like to sit down?" Lucinda asked. "Come on."

I hadn't seen anyone but Lucinda go into the back rooms aside from one other person—a short woman, decidedly more butch, who usually wore work boots and a beat-up denim jacket with a ripped collar and pins for bands I absolutely did not know. We'd nodded at each other on occasion, but she never spoke to anyone, aside from Lucinda. They seemed . . . close.

Maybe she was another gallery artist. Maybe she was creating a bunch of horrific exhibits that *her* family could feel embarrassed over. Although she didn't seem to be there for the art. She seemed to be there for Lucinda.

It was cooler in the back. AC flooded the vents and ruffled the wisps of hair at my temples. A desk that was much too large for the room took up a whole corner of the office. It was stacked full of messy paperwork and empty mugs. The espresso maker was on the small cabinet opposite, and the papers around it were covered in dark spatter. Crumpled napkins and plastic sandwich containers lay scattered around an overflowing garbage can. I put my own cup down on a stack of envelopes and had to catch it when an avalanche of them spilled onto the floor.

"This is your office?" I asked. It was the antithesis of her public persona. Everything was dirty and unorganized. Open boxes and tissue paper littered the floor. It was hard to maneuver without tripping over something.

"It's where I keep all the office stuff. Invoices, whatever." She was more relaxed here than out front. Her shoulders sloped downward and her mouth looked less severe, more tender. She stroked a hand through her hair and stared at me. I looked away.

Framed posters covered the walls. Two were black-and-white comic strip art, vintage ones featuring women dressed in 1940s garb: hats and boxy jackets. The others were color prints that looked like they could have come from the front of old novels. There were titles like *Women in Shadows* and *Queer Pulp.* I turned toward the doorway. It felt safest to look there.

"I like your art," I said, then cleared my throat. "It's nice."

She laughed. "This art you like." All her hard angles softened when she smiled. It made her look younger and a lot more approachable. Her chin rounded and her eyebrows lifted. "What do you think of your mother's work?" One cheek dimpled. The left cheek. It held its sharp indent, as if someone were digging into her with a fingernail.

"I hate it," I said, surprised she even needed to ask. "It's god-awful."

"Why do you think that?"

"Are you kidding?" I wondered if she was fucking with me. All her softening and disorganization possibly just a ploy to loosen me up. I picked up a paperweight from a shelf crammed with books, tossing it back and forth between my hands. It was marble and shaped like an egg. "All the sexual stuff. You've seen the props she's brought in. Toys and whatever."

"That bothers you?"

"Of course it does. She's my mother."

Lucinda unbuttoned her jacket and laid it over the back of the desk chair. She had on a thin white shirt that was nearly transparent. "And it's not because she's deconstructing your work?"

She was still smiling, bigger than before, and I decided she was fucking with me a little. "I don't like that," I admitted. "But the sex stuff freaks me out. It doesn't make sense."

"I'm sure she'd explain it to you, if you asked. She told me all about your father's repressive influence. She's just disgorging all at once."

"She talked to you about my dad?" I held up a hand. "Never mind. I don't want to know."

I poked around the office some more. An open cardboard box sat nearest the door. A wad of wrinkled gray flesh poked out. "Is that what I think it is?" I asked, hoping it wasn't.

"Just delivered today."

The closer I moved, the more jealous I got. "Please tell me you're not gonna let my mother anywhere near this."

"It's going in the showcase, yes."

Long ivory tusks curved from the base of the skull. The trunk was coiled around the head, its ears pulled back and cupped around its docile face. Its eyes were thickly lashed; it looked ready to blink at me. "Where the hell did you get an elephant mount?"

"Favor from a friend."

What my mother would do to the beauty of this thing I shuddered to imagine; probably cut out its tongue and replace it with a giant rubber dick. "Lemme buy it from you."

"You couldn't afford it." She sat down in the leather desk chair, rocking backward and crossing her legs.

"I'll give you back the money you paid for the boar."

"This cost way more than that."

I didn't doubt it was true. And it didn't matter—I'd already spent the money she'd given me, plus all the funds from my savings account.

"What will she do with it?" I asked. Images of the elephant covered in bondage gear stampeded through my brain. "God. It's going to be terrible."

"It really bothers you that much?"

"What would you think if your mother shoved a butt plug into a taxidermied coyote and then put it on display for everyone to see?"

"I'd ask her why she did it. What it meant to her."

The air in the room felt too close. I could taste the scent Lucinda was wearing. It had some kind of dessert smell to it, coconut, or maybe almond. "You're not supposed to have to ask your mom why she's playing around with sex toys, or why she's butchering all the stuff you worked so hard to create in the first place. If she's grieving, why wouldn't she go talk to somebody like a normal person?" The elephant's eyes were deep and brown. There were soft pouches of wrinkles beneath them, little divots where the flesh had puckered. "I just wish everything would stop being so fucking weird all the time."

There was something yielding about Lucinda in that moment, in her silence. Maybe it was the disorganization of her office. I would never have done that with Brynn, who'd unloaded on me constantly, but God forbid I ever needed to talk about anything. She'd run straight for the door.

"Let me take you to dinner." Lucinda smoothed her long fingers along the leather stitching in the chair. Her nails were painted a very shiny clear coat, the tips like white half-moons. They were pretty nails. Lady nails.

"You don't have to do that." I felt embarrassed, like I'd thrown up in front of her. My stomach hurt.

"I want to." She gestured to the box. "You can touch it if you want, you know."

I'd never worked on an elephant. In fact, I'd never even seen one in person. It had a beautiful weathered texture that felt surprisingly soft. I wondered what it would be like to work with skin so wrinkled and thick. How had they curled and set the trunk, manipulating the ligaments? Had they used wire or wood bracing for internal support? Padding?

"Drive your mother home and then we'll get some food."

It seemed likely the woman who kept visiting the gallery was going to be a problem, but for once I just didn't care. It felt good to have someone else make a decision. When she got up from the chair, I got whiffs of the bakery smell again: sweet, like a sugary cake. She stood a foot taller than me in heels, but I'd never felt so slight, even though I must have outweighed her by at least thirty pounds. Her arm snuck around my waist and my muscles relaxed, the flesh loosening incrementally, as if I were falling asleep. It didn't feel sudden. It felt inevitable, as if she'd been tugging at me for a long time.

"You haven't dated a lot of women, have you?" Her mouth was close to my forehead, lips smooth and clean and just a little pink. Her breath was damp against my skin.

"I wouldn't call this dating," I said. When I reached up to kiss her, she smiled and leaned down to embrace me. She tasted like her last sip of coffee. I closed my eyes and slid into it.

ALLIGATOR MISSISSIPPIENSIS— AMERICAN ALLIGATOR

Guys at our high school baited gator. Brynn didn't like it, but she usually tagged along, which meant that I'd go too. They brought cases of cheap beer and built bonfires out of old Christmas trees down at the river, which ran about forty minutes away from our neighborhood. We'd carpool out in all the boys' shitty cars with no air-conditioning, struggling souped-up engines, windows rolled down until we were nearly coated in condensation.

Could you sleep in the car? Brynn asked, cuddled up with someone in front of the fire, or drinking beer with another boy out near the water. *Please? We need the tent.*

Drunk dudes crowing, whooping, yelping, the high beams from their trucks boring holes into the reedy waterfront. Gator eyes, bright as stars, blinked at us and moved to deeper water.

I sat close to Brynn while she let me. Loud, aggressive rock pumped endlessly from truck stereos. Lights bounced off the water, and after a few beers your body drifted loose and floated out there with the wildlife. You'd feel as if you could disappear into the woods and it wouldn't matter; feel like you could never be heard from again and that would be just fine.

Once the bonfire lit, I lost her. The trees were yanked from yards or begged off households long after the holidays were over. Some of them were already dark brown and flicking off needles, coats shedding in the back seats of cars, making our clothes reek of pine sap. The fires started small, but at some point they got serious, near arson levels, boys ready to light everything they could strike a match against. We crouched next to the tents as the trees went up like thousand-watt bulbs, shooting shards of tinsel into the river.

Brynn's face lit peachy pink, wondering at the magic. She watched the fire, the boys; I watched her.

Milo wasn't friends with those guys. Sometimes he drove out and sat with me, both of us watching Brynn, neither of us talking about what that meant. When we spent time together, we only talked about family stuff or stupid shit, watched TV together, drank beer out in the cemetery.

Milo was his tallest by then, taller than our father, but not filled out. Lean, our mother said. By contrast I was an oak, a sturdy base with wide hips and thick thighs, my ass not large enough to compensate for the round, doughy bowl of my stomach. Brynn was my opposite in every way: blonde where I was dark, thin where I was plump, breasts high and full where mine were small and sagged.

You're like a mole. A little mole person, Brynn said, poking at my stomach, at the back fat rolling out from my bra strap, grabbing for the soft, fleshy places on my thighs. *Sweet little moley Jessa.*

Taxidermy needed muscle. The universe had organized my shape into what it would be most useful for: standing upright for hours, bending over carcasses. My tough hands were capable of pulling together threads and hacking at gristle, eyes squinty and narrowly placed, ready to analyze the tiniest defect in a pelt.

Older men prowled the perimeter of these campouts, grizzly, bearded guys with teeth discolored by chewing tobacco. They liked to circle the riverfront, calling out slurs that were meant to sound like compliments. One had a van straight out of an after-school special: white and rusted, the words GOOD TIMES spray-painted on the side. He called to us from a rolled-down window, asking to play us some music.

Brynn and I leaned against each other on a stumpy log while most of the boys were out in their boats riling up each other and the wildlife. Milo sat in the dirt at our feet, picking apart a palm frond and braiding the strips around a can of beer. Lindy was with us, one of the girlfriends that we didn't know. She wore a pale blue cami and some cutoffs, what most girls wore at our school. Her hair was so bleached that she'd had to cut off most of it below her ears; bright white, kind of glowing under the lights from the van as the guy inside leaned through the open window and called to us again.

Brynn nudged me until I almost fell into Milo. *He's talking to you.*

I don't want to talk to him.

He was older than my father, face leathery and sun-beaten. His gray hair stuck up in greasy spikes, as if he spent most nights sleeping in his van. His shirt was stretched out around the neck.

Just go. You never talk to anybody.

137

By *anybody* she meant boys. None of the guys ever wanted anything to do with me, and that was fine. I didn't want to curl up with them in their trucks or listen to them swear at each other, swaying on their feet, sweating out the cheap liquor they never managed to hold down. I hated the way they all smelled like wet dogs, crotches outthrust like they thought someone might want to look. They weren't like my brother. You couldn't talk to them.

Milo knew when to talk and when to shut up. He didn't get grossed out by periods or make stupid comments about how women were weaker than men. He liked sappy, emotional movies and was tender to animals. The compassion he showed to other people made me wish I could be more like that. It was scary, to watch him be that open. It meant your heart could get yanked out and dissected.

Brynn pushed me the rest of the way off the log and my ass landed in the wet dirt. Lindy laughed and took my seat, the two of them snuggled together with a bottle of Fireball that Lindy's boyfriend had gifted her before he rode off in the skiff. Brynn laid her hands on Milo's shoulders and he leaned back into her, resting his head against her knees.

He didn't look at me. Just turned and stared out at the water as Brynn drew little circles around his neck with her fingertips. *I'm going to do that goose-bump game on you*, she said, and I stopped watching.

I loped awkwardly toward the van, unfolding the cuffs of my flannel shirt until they hung past my hands. It was brown, like everything I owned, and worn in. It'd been Milo's before he'd outgrown it. It swam on me six months earlier, but the middle had begun pulling forward, buttons over my stomach threatening to pop. When I reached the van, I looked back again. Brynn motioned me ahead and then turned away, leaning down to whisper something in Milo's ear. He ducked a little and smiled, reaching a hand behind him to cup at her neck. My throat hurt to see them touch so intimately. I turned back around and opened the passenger door.

The inside of the van smelled like spilled beer. The man leaned back casually on the seat, legs spread around the circumference of his steering wheel. He had a wide red face with an incoming scruff of patchy dark beard. His clothes were damp and clung to his body, as if he were sweating, though the van was air-conditioned to the point that my hair stood up on my arms and legs. I climbed in beside him, but stayed close to the door.

You're a little munchkin. You want something to drink? He pointed to a case of good beer lodged on the floorboard, not the shitty kind we always stole but the kind that cost money, with names that made you think of Northern states. Brick buildings. He kept smiling, lips wet with spit. Teeth gapped and dark at the root. He looked like every single friend of my dad's. It felt safe enough, so I took one of the beers. *Thanks.*

He shrugged and took a pull from his own bottle. *I'm Thomas. Tommy. Here, lemme show you something. It's not far.*

We drove past Brynn and Milo, skimming piled logs and debris along the beachfront. I could still see the boats out on the lake, the boys shining flashlights down into the water, stirring up gator while they tried not to drunkenly overturn themselves. The man parked his van between two trees, facing away from the road. The moon was out, high and white, shining on the wake rushing the cattails.

C'mon. He didn't touch me, just pointed through my open window. *Down there.*

We took our beers and walked down to the shore. My boots soaked up muck from where the water lapped the weeds. He was tipsy, lurching as he pressed forward.

Now you see that, there? Down by the edge. He picked up my hand then, pointing it toward where he meant. *See that black lump?*

I did see it. It was long and fat, and it smelled like raw chicken left out in a garbage can. I walked closer, him clutching my arm like an invalid, stumbling as I steadied him, stopping less than a foot from the decomposing alligator.

A cloud of bottle flies lifted and resettled on the flesh. *It's not safe,* I said, pulling him back. *Anything dead at night next to the water will attract live gators.*

My father and I stuffed gator heads. Most of the time we just lacquered the skulls, dipping the open jaws into the clear coat, replacing the eyeballs with plastic replicas, though they looked real enough once we pressed them into the sockets.

I never seen a dead thing like that before. He let go of my arm and crouched down by the gator, jabbing it with a piece of fallen palm scrub. He fell forward, steadying his hand against the side. *Oh shit. Didn't mean to touch it.*

I could hear the boys out in their boats and wished I were back by the fire, with Brynn, sipping Fireball. Wished that Milo had just stayed home; that she were running her fingers along the back of my neck instead of my brother's. When Milo asked what I was doing that night, he had a look on his face like he expected me to tell him to get lost. Like he knew I didn't want him there. I couldn't tell him no. Beer combined with the rum I'd had earlier made me feel depressed and hopeless, so I decided I should get much drunker. I took another pull from my bottle and helped Thomas to his feet.

You're really pretty, you know that? The hand he'd pressed to the gator slipped into the fuzz of my hair, petting the frizzing strands at my temple. I let him do that for a while as I watched the lights flicker out on the water, past the shore, the boys still yelling.

We went back into his van and I let him touch me, briefly, under my shirt. He grabbed my breasts through my bra, twisting at my nipples. I closed my eyes and thought of Brynn, but I stopped him when he tried to undo my pants. Instead I undid his, examining the fleshy contents of his sour boxer shorts. Everything smelled musky and unclean. He didn't seem that excited, either; mostly soft and shriveled. He made some crying noises, eyes squinted like a baby. Midway through, he leaned out his open window and threw up whatever he'd been drinking. I wiped my hands on my jeans and left him there to sleep it off, walking the long, twisty road back to the campsite.

Brynn was still perched on the log, taking swigs from the bottle. Milo sat beside her with his arm draped across her shoulder. He nuzzled his face into her neck and his free hand was wedged between her thighs, thumb rubbing circles on the bare skin. It kept happening, the two of them pawing at each other. I wondered if it was her way of being with an acceptable version of me, a masculine one she could take out in public. I wondered if she liked how his hands felt better than mine. If he kissed better. Milo turned to me and smiled. Lipstick stained his teeth.

Well, she asked, looking up at me. *How was it?*

6

Lucinda wanted to spend the night, every night. She wouldn't ask, just curled up next to me after we fucked, both of us sweaty and broiler-hot. It was strange to wake up in the morning and see another body sprawled beside my own. I was so used to sleeping alone. Now there were legs twisted in my sheets, stray hairs in my brush a different color from mine. Damp toothbrush from someone else's mouth and the cap left off the paste. She peed with the door open. Cleaned her ears with my cotton swabs and left them sitting out on the countertop, stained waxy yellow.

"Tell me your best childhood memory," she asked, licking a stripe up the underside of my breast. "What was your favorite food growing up? How big was your house?"

I couldn't answer these questions without talking about Brynn; without making Lucinda feel like she was a bigger part of my life. It was easier to find better uses for our mouths and let the blunt edge of sex shut us up.

No matter what time of the night we stumbled back to my awful apartment, she was there the next day, making breakfast from whatever I had in my fridge. Stuff I'd thought was expired became gourmet; delicious meals scrounged from scraps.

I never said thank you, never told her I was happy to see her in the morning when the sun lit her dark, curly hair. It added too much to the feeling of intimacy, to acknowledge her doing that loving, domestic stuff. If I thanked her, it made what she was doing into something expected. Better to pretend it wasn't happening. Then it wouldn't matter when it inevitably stopped.

"You want eggs?" She leaned over me in the morning, her mouth already half-open, ready for a kiss.

"I don't have eggs."

"Sure you do. I know I saw some."

"I know what I've got in my own fridge. There aren't any."

"I'm gonna look."

I snuggled into the dirty comforter and waited for her to leave the room. Tried to wrangle my messy thoughts into something that would provide distance, the space I would need to reacclimate to how I was before she came over.

Once morning lit my apartment, I knew I shouldn't have her there. It was filthy, not a place for someone as promising as Lucinda, a woman whose underwear always matched, whose clothes were so clean I hated to let them fall on a carpet I hadn't vacuumed in months.

When I finally stumbled out wearing a T-shirt and some saggy shorts, I found her in the kitchen, scrambling eggs on the only skillet I owned, making toast on the stovetop using the coils from the sad, terrible burner that worked only half the time. She poured coffee for me, black, just how I liked it. Setting the cup so softly on the counter that it barely made a sound, she ran her fingers through the long length of my hair. I closed my eyes and let myself be pet, a kind of feeling I could sustain for only a minute before I'd tense up again. Remember-ing other hands.

We could play house all we wanted, pretend like we were something larger than the six hundred square feet of my ratty apartment. But when it came down to it, I had nothing good to give and she was already giving it up for someone else. I knew there had to be somebody. It was how she stood with that wom-an from the gallery. The one who looked a lot like me. Their body language—how women who are fucking lean into each other like magnets. Bodies ready to connect again. The woman had nodded at me more than once. Short hair. Dimpled cheeks that made her look younger than I thought she might be. Forties, probably. Eyes that scanned over me and landed on something prettier, usually Lucinda. This woman had a type and it wasn't me. But I never really liked myself either. Always out looking for someone who'd remind me of somebody else, somebody differ-ent enough to make me forget I had a body of my own.

Lucinda liked to wear my cast-off shirts around the apart-ment. They swam on her in a pretty way, her legs long and dark beneath the hem. Looking at her in my clothes gave me a feeling so sharply pleasurable that I worried it would show on my face. I squashed it as a radical invader, a thing I wouldn't let live inside of me. After she left I'd sniff the shirts, her clean, sunshine smell embedded in my clothes. A reminder that this good thing existed in my life.

She squeezed fresh orange juice, a thing I'd seen done only on TV or in movies. I knew that I didn't buy oranges, that I had maybe never bought them in my entire adult life. Why buy oranges, ever, when they grew everywhere for free?

"Where did these come from?" I asked, sipping it slow, letting the juice cool my throat. I was hopeful for some vodka to mix up a screwdriver, but I knew there wasn't any more of that in the cupboard. We'd finished the bottle together.

"Picked them from your yard."

"I don't have a yard."

"You know what I mean. Outside."

The apartment complex had a dingy central courtyard that boasted a shriveled acacia and what I'd thought was a stunted lemon tree. The peels in the garbage can were greeny yellow and small. I wondered how she'd even known they were good.

"Why don't we have this on the balcony?"

I thought about what it would take to get the plates and cups outside; the glass top was filthy and so were all the seats. It had rained on and off through the night, and frogs liked to hide underneath the chairs, sometimes reaching out a small hand to tap stickily at your legs. It made me scream, no matter how many times it happened. I didn't want Lucinda seeing me like that, ever. Goofy and afraid of a tiny amphibian, like I didn't slice open animals for a living.

"It won't kill you," she said, and I nodded, already feeling squirmy. I followed her through the sliding glass door and breathed in the humidity. She held both our plates, leaving me just my coffee to hold while I looked around sheepishly, scared a frog might pop out.

My balcony overlooked the parking lot and some scraggly palm trees that waved over the adjacent rooftops. Outside normally smelled like other people's food, pungent aromas of meats and spices steaming all day in Crock-Pots. I kept all my windows firmly shut in an attempt to keep out everyone else's business. But that early, with the wind blowing heavy with unshed rain, it smelled more like the earth turned up next to the water: the heavy odor of crushed plants, mud teeming with life.

Lucinda's hair caught the sun and glinted shades of red. Brynn's hair always caught blonde, sometimes amber. She'd loved the sun, but hated getting up early. Brynn always ate breakfast after 2:00 PM. The week before she left, I made her Belgian waffles on an iron I'd bought at a garage sale. She seemed so happy, ripping the waffles apart with her fingers and dipping the mess into whipped cream. We fed each other pieces and took a nap together, drifting off in the afternoon sun. She leaned into my ear and told me she loved me more than anything. How can a person seem that happy and leave you a week later?

"This is nice, right?"

"Yeah," I replied, sipping my coffee. No frogs in sight. "It's nice."

We ate our eggs in silence, dipping crusts into the drippy yellow yolk, watching cars slide past on the street. It was relaxing, the kind of lazy morning I'd watched my parents share growing up. Lucinda handed me the paper and I opened it while she sipped her juice, wondering if we were gonna do the crossword or some other weird, coupley thing. It felt strangely normal, a domestic scene I'd only ever thought about when it came to other people. I took the rest of the eggs off her plate, she snaked my last bite of toast. I knew I could ask Lucinda for a crumb of affection, the barest bit, and she'd stay over the rest of the day. Did she have someone else she went home to when she left me? I didn't know, but it seemed likely. The stocky woman I'd seen coming and going from the art gallery talked with Lucinda the way I wanted to; with a hand on her arm, thumb stroking the crease of an elbow. Lucinda was the kind of woman who would make someone's life easier. If I wanted, I could ask her to stay and maybe she'd do it for a while. Instead, I sat silently while she waited for me to ask. When we were done, she gathered up the breakfast dishes and carried them inside. The shower turned on and I went to get dressed, pulling on a pair of holey old jeans that were coming apart at the seat.

Once Lucinda came out from the shower, she was inaccessible again. She allowed me to kiss her cheek goodbye, but wouldn't give me her mouth. I watched her walk out, taking all the good of the morning with her, and wished the room would swallow me.

Because he'd lost his license and didn't have ready access to a car, Bastien needed rides to work. I picked him up from my mother's house as soon as Lucinda left, and the two of us got coffee at the gas station down the street from the shop. It tasted burnt and was always full of grounds, but we could refill our giant foam cups all day long. Chugging from our bottomless supply of tarry black acid, we stood side by side in the back, working over the pelts and mounts. Sometimes he'd do the scraping, sometimes I would, but we took turns with the most monotonous tasks: stitching work through the legs, boiling flesh from skeletons until our hands sang with blisters.

I preferred the tedious work. It got me out of my head. Bastien didn't seem to mind it either. He took every task I gave him in stride, even petrifying hamsters. Once I let him work on the pieces with me, we got into a good groove. It was comfortable now, most of the time. He'd learned my routines. How to be quiet. Minimal talk, just another warm body. He studied reference material for the various animals and how to utilize the death masks to find the best angle for the neck and ears. He kept his own scrapbook with tabbed indicators for different species he'd worked on: rabbits, squirrels, foxes, deer.

Being alone too long, staring into the dead eyes of an animal, had a way of making you feel you were nothing but a sack of meat. Working with Bastien reminded me a little of being with my dad, who'd known exactly when I needed a specific tool or a cut of thread. Like my father, Bastien had a natural way with bodies; knew what to do with their legs and how to pose their necks so they didn't look stiff. He turned out deer capes faster than Milo ever had, and sometimes gave me a run for my money. These parallels to the past gave me vertigo: I was my father, Bastien was me, and those dead animals—always the same empty faces—forever perched on the table between us.

"Are you going out early?" he asked, finishing up the last pelt of the day. We'd been working for hours, hunched over a stack of deer mounts. Sweat plastered his hair to his neck, dripping a damp line into his shirt collar.

I took a sniff of my armpit and winced. Sour. "I'm meeting a friend for drinks."

He scrubbed his face with a clean rag and tossed it in the direction of the sink. "Okay. Guess I can close up." Bastien

didn't ask me about my personal life and I didn't ask him anything either. The feeling—that neither of us needed any addi-
tional baggage in our lives—was completely mutual.

"Call your dad."

"Right. Guess I'll be here for a while." Milo wouldn't be off
work himself for another few hours. If he'd even gone in; it was
hard to know where he was or what he was doing. It was just as
likely that he was home sleeping. He hardly ever answered his
phone. Most of the time he didn't even have the thing turned
on, just kept it tossed in the back of his truck, a lifeless brick.

"I'll see you in the morning," I said, grabbing a spare shirt
from the cabinet near the door. I pulled the dirty one over my
head and Bastien turned around to give me privacy, fiddling
with some of the tools he'd already cleaned. "Good work today."

"Right."

I knew he was disappointed, but I didn't care. Only drinks
and the dark, close hours I spent with Lucinda in the wreck of
my dank apartment made me feel okay anymore.

We met at the bar and holed up in the back, drinking
pitchers of shitty domestic beer and making heavy eye contact.
As I took that first sip and stared across the table at Lucinda, I
couldn't seem to care about how sorry my guts would feel come
morning. I didn't dwell on Brynn or my mother and father, or
any of the worries that burdened me all day at work. There was
nothing but the drinks and the smooth coolness of Lucinda's
fingers dragging across my forearm.

"Why don't you keep taxidermy in your apartment?" Lucinda poured us each a taster's sip. That's what she called our
first glasses, doling out an inch. We'd see how long we could

last until one of us broke down and drank it. Then we poured full glasses and really went to work. The pitcher sat between us, a safe space to rest my eyes when I looked too long at Lucinda's cleavage.

"Why haven't I been to your apartment?" I let the smallest edge of the beer touch my tongue. It fizzed there and lingered, yeasty as bread.

"I don't have an apartment. You don't like taking your work home?"

She wore three gold bangles on her wrist. The wires were thin and chimed when they clicked together. Light bounced off them with every delicate turn of her hand.

"No, it's not that." I took my first full sip and let my taste buds weep. "You got a house?"

"I live in a condo. I have a roommate." She smiled as I took another mouthful, and then took one of her own. "You're losing fast today. So, if you taxidermy animals for a living and you don't keep any in your own home, what does that actually say about you?"

I drained the last of it and let Lucinda pour me some more, still stuck on the word *roommate* and trying to wash it out of my head. "It says I don't keep them in my apartment. Who do you live with?"

The last of her own slipped past her red mouth, lip prints gumming up the rim. *Roommate* could mean anything, but the way she said it, it sounded like *wife*. The woman from the gallery. I mean, I'd already known. Could tell from the body language. A hand. An elbow. That single stroke of flesh against flesh; I knew what that meant. I'd spent too much time watching their faces when I should've been watching their hands. I poured her more, but she stopped me when the beer reached the middle of the glass. "Why don't you keep taxidermy in your house?"

One long sip for me. "I don't want it to feel like home."

Two more for Lucinda, who wore a black velvet top that clung to her body like a second skin. "That's sad, Jessa. Everybody needs a place they feel safe."

Home and safety weren't synonymous. The times I'd felt most vulnerable had always been with my family. There was my mother, with her sudden deviation from anything I'd ever known or expected from her. My father had killed himself in a place where he knew I'd find him, leaving me a note that said it was my responsibility to take care of the things he wasn't strong enough to handle. The only woman I'd ever cared for I'd shared with my brother, a person I simultaneously loved and hated for it.

Lucinda rubbed her finger along the indentation of her lip and I wanted to smack her hand away, ask why she was turning something that was supposed to make me forget into another agony of remembering. I wanted to kiss her, badly. I wanted to feel something else.

"Jesus Christ, could you just answer the question," I asked, pouring the rest in my glass. *Roommate*, a word that you could use for a friend or a fuck buddy. Even though I'd fought to keep things casual between us, I wasn't sure if I was up for another person I had to share. Based on the way I'd seen them together in the gallery, it didn't feel like it was over. At least, it didn't look like it was over based on the other woman's body language. I knew what it looked like when you still loved someone after the person had long given up the ghost of romance. And that woman had longing written all over her butch baby face.

"I have a roommate because I bought the condo with that person and now I can't ask them to leave without dividing up the property." Leaning forward, she slipped an arm across the table and dug one of her fingers under the band of my watch. She left it there, wriggling below the face.

"I don't keep photos in my apartment either," I added. There was no art, nothing but the cheap eggshell paint that they'd slopped on the walls long before I'd arrived. "It's just a place to sleep."

The finger, still wriggling, slowly worked to undo the band. "You know I'm here for you," Lucinda said, thumb smoothing into the crease of my palm. Her voice took on an edge. "All you have to do is ask. Give me a little, Jessa. Trust me not to hurt you."

Trust was a word that carried too much with it. Things were already moving too quickly; unsurprising given the fact that so many queer women U-Hauled after the first date. It wasn't how I operated, that level of emotional openness, but even the ladies I casually slept with occasionally tried to make things more than they were. I could feel it happening with Lucinda: I thought about her constantly, ignored her when she wanted attention, then got upset that she might be seeing someone else. *Knew* that she was seeing someone else. I didn't know what I wanted. I exhausted myself.

Lucinda took the watch from my wrist and turned it over. My father's, the one he'd died in. I wore it every day, the band slid smooth from his skin and my skin and my grandfather's too. I could tell her all about me, maybe feed her bits of myself.

But what happened when you chummed the water was that the biggest predators showed up and ate everything. There was no giving a little. It was all or nothing.

Large patches of sweat lined the back of my shirt and ran below my arms. I drank the rest of my beer and then I drank hers. "I'll go pay the check," she said once I'd drained everything and was looking around for more to dump into myself.

Outside was dark and unusually still, no noise, not even a rumble from the cicadas. Lucinda placed her hand at the meaty joint of my hip and squeezed, twice. I clenched up both times. "It's quiet," I noted stupidly. Lucinda nodded.

"How come nobody ever sees cicadas?" She leaned into me, smelling like the cinnamon mints she always chewed after drinking.

"What?"

"You hear them all night here, especially in the summer. So how come we don't ever see them?"

It was a good question. Cicadas always hung out in the tops of the oaks, secreted away in the bark, or tucked below thick clumps of Spanish moss. There was a lot of shrieking, but I'd never seen them crawling anywhere. "I have part of one," I confessed, breathing in her sweet smell and licking my lips. "The shell. It's called a carapace."

Lucinda's hand crept down to the vee of my jeans. She pressed there lightly, waiting. There was no one else outside. The sole streetlight flickered overhead, one spasm, two, and then went out. Darkness overtook us. I leaned back into the side of my truck and let her navigate. She rubbed me gently, then stopped with her other hand wedged beneath a breast.

"Tell me more about the cicada." She licked the lobe of my ear, sucked at it. "Everything you know about them."

"Not a lot." I breathed out slowly, considering my words. "I just have the shell. Found it in my backyard." Every sentence prompted the movement of her hand to a different place on my body. First, she rubbed the tender inside of my forearm, then slipped below the hem of my shirt to stroke the skin above my navel.

"What else?" Her breath was a heavy, live thing in my ear.

It was hard to collect the memory. Her fingers crawled over my ribs, slipping delicately beneath the wire of my bra cup. "It was under the basketball hoop, by the shed. My brother tried to crush it with a basketball, but he kept missing."

One finger lazily swept along the bottom of my breast, just barely grazing my nipple. "What did it look like?"

"Waxy yellow. Like cellophane tape."

"What did it smell like?" With the other hand she scraped along the seam of my jeans, back and forth. Lightly at first, and then hard enough I could hear the scratch of her nails against the fabric.

I took in more air and paused, the memory bursting from static fuzz at the back of my brain. "Nothing. There was nothing to smell."

What I'd done was taste it, licking a hole right through the middle of the thorax. Brynn dared me to do it. Dared me to touch my mouth to the hollow shell, holding it up like she wanted me to give it a kiss. A bit of shell had come away from the body, stuck to the tip of my tongue. It melted there, gluey, the way that tapioca pearls tasted when stripped of the pudding.

Brynn screamed and ran back into the house, leaving me there. I'd cupped the body in my hands like it might try to escape too.

Lucinda rubbed hard and fast and I came, teeth digging into my lip until I could taste the copper of blood almost bursting through the skin. I grabbed her wrist when she kept going and the spasms were undercut with the roughness of my jeans grinding into my crotch.

A man opened the door to the bar and light from inside expanded outward in a bright circle. We climbed into the truck and I let her take us to my apartment. She drove five miles under the speed limit, struggling over the clutch whenever she tried shifting higher than second gear. Hunched over the wheel, white-knuckling on the stick shift, she looked frail and small. Not the kind of person who could bring someone to orgasm in a public parking lot. There was danger in being around a person so malleable. She could be anything I wanted: sweet, shy, hard, careful. Loveable. Her layers were cracking open. I worried what I'd discover about myself if I dug into her too deeply.

"You're stripping the gears," I said, laughing at her pinched expression. She drove like an old lady. She drove, I thought, like my mother. "Get a rhythm going. Sex rhythm. You know that, right?"

Lucinda slapped my hand when I tried to shift for her. "Next time don't drink so much, you can drive."

"Fine." She was cute, weaving all over the road. Cute, but scary. "Speed up, we're gonna get pulled over."

The truck lurched into third and I clutched the seat, hoping we wouldn't stall out.

Back at my apartment, Lucinda asked to see the cicada. I pulled a Tupperware from the back of my bedroom closet and found it shrouded in newspaper at the very bottom of the bin, buried beneath a couple of Brynn's old T-shirts and stacks of Polaroids I couldn't bear to look at. Us at birthday parties, sleepovers. Opening gifts at Christmas. Pictures of Brynn holding the kids, wearing only a nightgown. The two of us crunched together on a dirty, strange couch in purple and pink Halloween cat ears.

The shell had disintegrated a little where my tongue had poked through, but the head was still completely intact. It sat cupped in my hand as Lucinda hovered over it, drinking the last cold beer from my fridge. Why was another woman always finishing my beers?

"I should get you some art. For the apartment. It's sparse in here."

"I've seen the kind of art you're into. Pass."

She didn't respond to my jab, just leaned over to examine the insect shell. Condensation dripped off the bottle and landed on my palm, squirreling down toward the carapace. I tilted my wrist so it dripped down my arm instead.

"Fine, no art. Put up some photos, Jessa. Mementos." Lucinda set the empty on the coffee table next to the others we'd killed. Her fingernail gently traced the translucent wings, tapped at its empty, bristled legs. "It's incredible. Perfectly formed, but completely hollow."

Its eyes were milky spots that stood out like bits of bubble wrap. "I like how cicadas sound," I admitted, rolling the shell back and forth in my hand. "They make me feel like the whole world's about to go to sleep. Reminds me of being up late with my dad."

Lucinda took off her pants and shirt, opening the bedroom window in just her black underwear. Her breasts were high and small, so different from my own, which sagged like spent party balloons. My skin wrinkled up whenever she lifted a nipple to suck. It hurt a little, but it was a good kind of ache. When she came back to the bed and tried to kiss me, I pushed her away and kicked off my boots, my jeans. I thought about her *room-mate*, a woman just like me, waiting at home for her, and then I kissed her to make myself forget. Forget all about it. Think only about the body—how it would open for me, be the thing that I needed.

She lay back on my unmade covers, still rumpled from the night before. Had me set the carapace of the cicada on the plane of her stomach, in the fallen divot between her ribs. We watched each other through the open hole of its body. I could hear the live ones screaming again outside in the trees, high and shrill. When my mouth touched the opening to her body, her chest rose abruptly. The cicada rolled forward, ready for flight.

Lucinda got up early the next morning. She pulled on one of my shirts and put her hair back into a ponytail that sat twisted to one side of her head. As she leaned over me in the bed, I could smell my own toothpaste on her breath.

"I'm gonna go down the street and pick us up doughnuts," she whispered, smoothing a hand along my cheek. "Then let's talk about tonight. We should have a game plan for your mom's house." I grunted and rolled over, pretending to fall back asleep.

When the door closed behind her, I sat up and let my hangover sit heavy in my head, dreading the fear and exhaustion that always came with morning sobriety. The cicada was on the nightstand. I held it up to the light, streaming bright through the broken vertical blinds. Its wings were translucent, body yellow stained glass.

Brynn once asked me to make her a dragonfly costume for Halloween. It took me weeks, selecting shiny fabric scraps and molding shimmering wings, holding them up to her back, measuring her for something fluttery and fragile. It fit her perfectly.

Jessa made this for me, isn't it great?

She told this to anyone who'd listen, spinning in circles in the middle of a party, flapping the sparkling wings. I'd dotted them with painstaking rows of tiny rhinestones. She liked the costume so much she'd worn it three years in a row. A beautiful, shining creature.

I left before Lucinda got back and drove to the shop. I drank dank leftover coffee in the dark, broodily, until my stomach pitched and I switched to water.

Everyone was meeting at my mother's that evening for a preview of her showcase. She'd invited over some of our family friends: Vera and her husband, Travis and his wife. I wasn't looking forward to it. I didn't like the unknown aspect of what might be shoved in my face. I worked on some mounts, half-heartedly, then scrubbed down the already pristine counters with bleach. Milo called a couple of times and so did Lucinda. I set my phone to silent and tried to take a nap on the cot in the back, but my brain wouldn't let me rest.

The cot, wedged at the back of the shop, directly faced the gleaming metal station my father favored working at. Slitting my eyes, I could easily imagine him there. Images from the past layered over each other, two films running at the same time: him young and bearded, smiling, hacking into deer meat, and then the way I'd last seen him, splayed out and graying. Lifeless. What had he thought in those final moments? That the letter was explanation enough? Did he think I'd consider him another piece to stuff, something I could mount and set around the house? I fell into a fitful doze, dreaming of my father's face stretched out eerily, as if the skin were ready to be tanned.

I woke groggy and aggravated at twilight, neck cricked into a thousand tiny knots that would only get worse as the night progressed. I pulled on my boots and then drove the short distance to my mother's house, singing along to the radio in an attempt to wake myself up. The lawn was high with Bahia grass and daisy weeds. It had rained for two weeks straight and no one had mowed. The sod, neon green with new life, towered damply over the yards at either side. Lucinda's car wasn't out front and I felt relief that quickly morphed into dread. Rather than talk about things, I'd manufactured a situation where Lucinda would be upset I'd bailed on our plans, plus I'd have to deal with my mother's art at the same time. I hoped Milo had bought beer.

Inside the house, Lolee sat on the floor in front of the television, scraping chipped polish off her nails and letting the flakes fall into the carpet. Milo and Bastien were on the couch, each holding plates full of roast and a cauliflower salad so saturated with mayonnaise it resembled pudding. By the sliding door, Travis Pritchard talked with Vera Leasey's husband, Jay, who'd propped a boot up on an end table to show off a tiny hole near the heel.

"Snake bit." He tapped at it with one thick finger. "Nearly pierced the skin."

"What kinda snake?" Travis asked, leaning in close enough that his nose nearly bounced off the leather. "Rattler?"

"Naw. Moccasin. Out near the south end of the lake."

Vera was in the kitchen with my mother and Travis's wife, Bizzie Lee, whose hair was pulled back with a large purple butterfly clip. Bizzie was a very thin woman with a long nose that kind of curled under at the end, witchlike, but her eyes were sweet. Milo used to say that if she covered the bottom half of her face with a scarf, she probably could have gotten somebody a lot better-looking than Travis, because Bizzie was pretty nice and always gave out double candy at Halloween.

"What do you want in your coffee?" Vera held up the pot. She was wearing a bright blue dress that used to be my mother's. They were friends that way, "girlfriends," sharing clothes and trading recipes. Vera had been a fixture in our home since I was born.

"Black," I said, already anticipating her response.

"Have a little of this cream, I got it out at the dairy today."

It was no use telling Vera I didn't want anything in my coffee. She heard only what she wanted, which was why she and my mother had been friends for so long. I wondered if Vera knew anything about the work my mother was doing. It seemed unlikely. She was conservative and drove around with one of those yellow CHOOSE LIFE license plates on the back of her car. I couldn't see her getting into my mother's gruesome animal porn.

"Grab a plate, everybody's already eaten." My mother pulled a couple of pies from the fridge. A big, gelatinous strawberry one sat on top of the stack, covered with a layer of blue cling wrap.

"Your mom seems like she's doing so much better," Vera whispered in my ear. "This art stuff has been good for her, huh? I know she's always had such a creative way about her. So talented. What's she doing, watercolors? They have that now over at the senior center. Got a class taught by this young guy with a ponytail. Wears jeans so tight you can see *everything*."

I couldn't think of something I'd like to hear less than what was in the male art instructor's pants. I picked up a plate just to give myself something to do with my hands. "Her art's a little more . . . sculptural," I said, digging into a pot of mashed potatoes. *Sculptural* was one word for it. "Contemporary stuff."

Vera groaned and leaned against the counter. "God help us, I hope it's not some of those flowers that look like vaginas. Women get a certain age and they just fixate on that crap."

It was going to be a lot more than that, but I wasn't going to be the one to tell Vera. "Do we have any more gravy?"

"Lemme get it for you." Vera dug the boat out from behind an open loaf of white bread. "She seems less sad. About your dad, I mean. She would just cry and cry all the time before. Now she looks better. Happier."

I'd seen my mother cry only at the funeral. I remembered her leaking a little, like me. Milo had sobbed through the whole thing, burying his face in her neck like a little kid. She'd sat upright and I'd done the same. Both of us stoic. Disbelieving.

"Let me do that, honey." Bizzie Lee took the scrubber from my mother's hands when she went to tackle the roasting pan. "You're gonna get your dress all filthy."

My mother was wearing a strapless red dress that looked as if it had been made for someone Lolee's age. Tight around the hips and chest. She'd slipped a silky scarf over her bare head. It had some kind of a paisley pattern, knotted at the base of her neck. If I'd seen her from behind, I wouldn't have recognized her.

Someone knocked at the front door. It had to be Lucinda; anyone else who knew our family would've barged right in. I wasn't sure how she'd gotten my mother's art over to the house. I doubted the large-scale pieces would fit inside her tiny sedan, but then I remembered she'd asked me if she could borrow the truck the night before, right when I was drunk enough to say yes. Now I could count on her being upset with me for abandoning her and also her outrage over the fact that I'd left her no way to transport the art.

Thank you so much, this means a lot to me, she'd said, snuggling naked into my side. I'd run a hand across her stomach, flatter than Brynn's, without the bumps and divots of childbirth to mar the flesh. Did she want kids? Was it something she'd talked about with her roommate, the woman she lived with in her condo? Her *wife*? There would never be kids for me. Never love. I'd rolled over to face the wall, trying to physically squash the ache in my chest. What a way to think of another human being. That they would love another person so much that there would only ever be scraps left for me.

More knocking. Louder, pointed. It was Lucinda, all right. "I'll get it," I said, dumping my plate on the counter. I'd eaten only two bites, but I was done with food for the night.

When I got down the hall, she was already inside, dragging a big cardboard box behind her. She stood up and huffed a swath of curly hair out of her face, reaching up under her armpits to yank at her bra beneath her suit coat. Turning, she saw me and made a sour face.

"Don't," she said. "I don't want to hear it."

"I didn't say anything."

Kicking it the rest of the way down the hall, she stopped and fixed her hair again. "Just remember, I could have made this better. Whatever happens now, it's on you."

"What the hell is that supposed to mean?" I asked, not sure I wanted to know. Unsettled by the rage in her voice, I followed her into the living room, where everyone else had already gathered.

"Find a seat." My mother cradled two pies in one arm, her coffee mug and a fistful of forks in the other. She looked like a domestic cocktail waitress. "Vera, can you get the plates?"

More chairs had been brought in, including the mildewed ones we kept on the back patio. I sat on a metal folding chair nearest the end of the couch, by Milo, who took one of the pies from my mother and put it on the coffee table. There was strawberry and an egg custard, my father's favorite. Milo cut me a big hunk of the custard, also my favorite, and handed it to me on a plate. I knew whatever was coming would be very bad.

"Welcome, everybody. Make sure you get some pie; the strawberry is Bizzie's and you know how good those are." My mother gestured strangely around the room with a sweep of her arm, as if the strapless dress made her feel compelled to act like Vanna White unveiling the letters to the final puzzle.

Lolee scooted back by my feet, messing with the laces on my boots until I kicked at her to stop. She turned around, smiled, and bit my knee through my jeans. Lucinda stood against the wall beside my father's cape-eared owl, one of his earliest pieces, a real showstopper. He'd rendered it mid-flight, clutching a taxidermied mouse in its talons. He'd won a prize for it, some contest. Lucinda's eyes darted between me and Lolee. I put a hand on my niece's neck and spun her back around.

"If we're all settled?"

"Oh, go on and show us, Libby. Stop screwing around." Vera sat in one of the dining room chairs, pie plate tipping sideways on her lap until strawberry juice threatened to spill on her dress. I prayed it would spill and we'd have to take thirty minutes to find a stain remover stick. Then we could forget this whole train wreck of a night and get on with our lives.

"Lucinda, could you assist me?"

Scooting around the owl's outstretched wing, Lucinda looked at me one last time before she disappeared down the hall. She mouthed something that looked like the word *sorry*. My fingers tightened on Lolee's neck until she let out a squawk and swatted at me.

My mother stepped to the side and flicked on the light switch next to the standing lamp. The hall lit up, profiling a large animal, moving forward jaggedly. Bizzie Lee screamed and pressed a hand to her throat, snagging her husband's arm. Vera's plate finally tipped all the way over. A puddle of strawberry juice pooled in the middle of her skirt.

It was a water buffalo, or it had been at one point in its miserable life. The beast sat on a wheeled platform pushed by Lucinda, who stared resolutely down at the floor and refused to make eye contact with me. My mother cleared her throat and unearthed a stack of index cards from the top of her dress. She read from them and gestured, pointing at various parts of the animal.

"Now, this is just a teaser. The show opens in two weeks. It highlights similarities between sex acts in the animal kingdom and those in modern suburbia. Grief and anger. Specifically correlations to myself and my late husband, Prentice."

Milo was stabbing at his pie like he wanted to murder it. I set my plate down on the floor and then picked it up again, not sure what to do with my hands. No one else was eating.

My mother continued, smiling. Shuffling through her index cards. "I want to use his taxidermy to illustrate the repressive nature of relationships and sexuality. There's a strong connection between sadomasochism and how modern domestic marriages set us up for cyclical punishment. These works explore that."

She stuffed the cards back into her top and grabbed a rope attached to a ring in the water buffalo's snout. She yanked hard. It stuck for a moment, dragging through the shag carpet we'd had since before I was born, then trundled the rest of the way into the room. There it sat, dumb and mutilated, between Jay and the coffee table full of pies.

"What have you done, Libby?" Vera pointed and then quickly retracted her finger, as if the thing in front of her might contaminate it. "What *is* this?"

The buffalo's body was festooned with whips and paddles of various sizes. Chain mail and leather gear were sewn over its torso. Between its horns sat a ludicrously tiny studded leather cap. The buffalo's mouth hung open in a snarl, tongue dangling lasciviously.

Lolee leaned forward to get a better look and I pulled her back against me, trapping her in place with my knees.

"Mom." Milo rubbed his face until I could hear the scratching of his beard under his palms. "Please tell me that's not who I think it is."

"Dear Jesus." Travis breathed out reverently, his eyes huge. "He's right there on top."

Mounted atop the buffalo's back was a mannequin. It wore a tight suit made out of patent leather, showing off lean muscle in the thighs and chest. Almost the entire body was covered, aside from the face, which peeked ghostlike from the opening in the leather.

It was my father. Wasn't it always him? Sprigs of dusky gray hair showed just below the press of the black patent leather coating his skull. His mustache was full and bristling above a gentle smile. The glasses were missing, but it was unmistakably his face—the one that hung over me when he tucked me into bed at night. The eyes that squinted into narrow slits when he laughed. His full cheeks. Crooked nose. Unlike the buffalo, with its snide look of dripping lust, my father seemed nearly beatific. Peaceful, for once in his life.

"He doesn't have anything covering his ass," Bastien said, laughing. "It's just hanging out there for God and the world to see. Holy shit."

My mother stood there, admiring her work. She kneaded the buffalo's coat, combing through it like dolls' hair. My faux father's knee glanced against her shoulder. She patted it absentmindedly. Even though I'd known what to expect—more so than anyone else in the house—it was still unnerving to view the piece in my childhood home. How many times growing up had we spent Thanksgiving dinners just this way: friends and relatives sitting on folding chairs, eating food everyone had prepared in our family's kitchen, sharing stories we'd all heard a thousand times. Eating pie. Drinking too-sweet coffee. Here we were, back again, except my father, instead of lounging in his recliner, sat astride a buffalo in S&M gear. It was surreal to see him on display, to watch people we knew look at our family; watch them reassess everything they thought they knew about us.

"That's really something." Vera set the plate down on the floor beside her chair and scrubbed at the strawberry juice with a napkin. "That's just ... really something."

My mother took a deep breath and smiled, hand still cupped around the figure's knee. "I have a couple more things I'd like to show you all. But first, who'd like some more pie?"

PROCYON LOTOR— COMMON RACCOON

Gripping the pelt made me feel less like ripping out my own hair. I wanted to pull handfuls of it straight from the root, until the pain in my scalp forced me to stop thinking. Instead I dug mercilessly into the still-wet raccoon, gouging holes in the soft spots closest to the tail. Its skin hung limp, too big for its baby body.

The skeletons sat beside me at the table next to a collection of felt and wire. Thread unspooled and dripped onto the floor. The bones were nearly ready for an acid bath, but I couldn't stop shaking long enough to scrape free the last of the gristle. Flipping the pelt again, I looked at the places where my thumbs had torn angry divots into the snout. The baby was tiny. Its jaw still held milk teeth.

Setting the raccoon down on the table next to its twin, I wiped a mixture of blood and sweat on my jeans. Then I pulled my braids from their elastics and took down my hair. Digging my fingers into it, I yanked and yanked, but it didn't help. As usual, I felt nothing.

Earlier:

Milo said that when he hit the babies with his car, they'd just been sitting together in the middle of the road. Instead of leaving them there, he felt the old taxidermy impulse kick in. We couldn't ever leave roadkill behind. Something inside us always made us stop to pick up dead things.

Funny, right? Hit a dead animal and I immediately think of Dad. Don't be wasteful, Son. *Couldn't help but bring them home.* He'd carried them beneath his arm like a couple of stuffed toys.

He laughed, but it was the flighty kind that verged on tears. Wiping his nose on his bare arm, he left behind a shiny trail of snot. I glanced inside the plastic bag and saw them curled up against each other. They were fully intact. They could have been sleeping.

It was late and I was tired. *You didn't mean to. Don't get upset.*

I know that! Milo's eyes leaked steadily. They'd been blood-shot for weeks and he just let them drip, like he couldn't even feel tears anymore. My own eyes were so dry they felt tacky with grit. He stood there looking shamefaced and I couldn't even empathize. I just wanted to smack him.

Brynn would've told him to suck it up. She'd have dug a finger in his side to try to make him laugh, even though he hated to be tickled. He sniffled again, and my fingers clenched on the bag's handle, dead bodies rustling against the plastic. Most taxidermists didn't even take on raccoons, and he should have known that. The threat of rabies was too great.

There wasn't time to clip the wheel, he said. *They just looked so surprised.*

Don't worry about it.

It was hard to talk to my brother without yelling about everything he'd done wrong. Wasted tears over dead raccoons when he should've been doing anything to fix what was actually broken. All those years fighting to keep Brynn with me, bottling my feelings because I knew they made her flighty, and he'd dumped his emotions over her like a leaky roof. Yet there he sat, crying, knowing Brynn would never stick around for it.

You did this to us, I thought, hating the stupid, woebegone look on his face. *You did this, and you knew better.*

It was two o'clock in the morning and pitch-dark, no stars out to pinprick the sky. Lolee was curled on one end of my parents' couch. She'd tried waiting up for Milo, her back rigid, like maybe if she sat up tall enough, she'd keep her eyes open. The news came on, then a movie I didn't watch. There were car chases, gunshots, wrecks, and siren shrieks until my father came out and dialed the volume down to a low whimper. Lolee fell asleep with her head buried between the cushions. As the blue lights bounced off her pale, wheaty hair, I thought how strange it was to see her sleep the exact same way as Brynn, knowing that it might be the only way I'd ever see Brynn sleep again. Through her children.

But back to the work.

I finished my last beer and carted the raccoons out to the truck. Milo had fallen asleep in my father's recliner, so I'd put Lolee to bed myself, knowing he'd never do it.

The raccoon bodies were still warm, as if they might wake up and crawl out of the bag and onto my lap. There were no open wounds. Nothing stained the bag, no blood or fecal matter.

They could've been mistaken for sleeping if it weren't for their necks. Their skulls lolled, flopping back limply against their tiny backs. Nothing made an animal look less alive than tension leaked from the spine. It was why we worked so hard to pose our taxidermy just right. Too loose or cricked and you couldn't help but imagine their death.

I'd only ever seen it once on a human body.

Before Lolee was born, we'd gone out to the lake as a family. It was just the four of us down at the water: Milo, four-year-old Bastien asleep on a towel, and me and Brynn splashing each other in the wake from the boats. When my brother picked Bastien up to take him to the shade, his head rolled all the way back, hanging limp over Milo's arm. Brynn screamed and crossed the lakefront in wild strides, the towel around her waist flopping off into the water. When she grabbed him from Milo, I worried she might accidentally hurt the kid.

Don't you do that, she muttered into his neck. *Don't you ever, ever do that!*

Bewildered, Bastien clung to her and cried. They stayed like that for a long time. Her clutching him, his chubby kid legs dragging down her body. Her top had twisted to the side, nearly exposing her breasts. Milo tried to drape a towel around her shoulders and she turned away jerkily, baring her teeth.

When she got like that, I knew from her body language to leave her alone, but Milo never knew when to quit. He was good at listening and empathizing, but he was always too close, too present. Sometimes Brynn needed space; she needed to feel bad and be by herself. In that moment with Bastien, he wanted to touch her even though she looked feral. When he dropped a hand onto her shoulder, she tensed, but let it rest. I gathered up our things while the three of them huddled together. She'd needed that and I hadn't known.

Brynn liked the solidness of married life. She told me this constantly, pointing to her mother as an example of what she never wanted to be: thrice married, living in a trailer, working at the same shitty job for fourteen years to support kids she never spent time with. *If my marriage doesn't work out, I'm not sticking around. I'm not gonna be one of those women who stay in the same place all their life. It's too fucking depressing.*

I knew her marriage would work out because I'd given her exactly what she wanted: a stable household, kids she hardly had to raise, and a normal husband who'd love her despite her flaws. Someone who was thoughtful, did romantic things like buy flowers for three-month anniversaries. A guy who'd listen and care about her hurts and share his own feelings. I'd given her someone I could trust. I knew he'd love her almost as much as I did. Almost.

Where was I?

I made my way through the dark store with practiced ease. I knew how many feet from the register to the shelving units on the opposite wall, knew the breadth between the boar's tusks and the magazine rack. I knew where the bin of gator heads sat and where to walk to avoid knocking them over. When I flipped on the lights in the back, they produced the familiar buzzing that signaled peace to my brain.

I set the grocery bag on the metal table and removed the raccoons. They lay pliant. Eyes liquid, hands still reaching for each other.

Where's your mother? I asked, picking up the one on the left. Stroking a finger down the length of its soft back. *Where's your kin?*

I busied myself with the prep work that usually calmed me: laying out the tools in neat, orderly rows. The coupled fleshers, the scraper. Small scalpels and sharp kitchen scissors I used to clip the tough bits of ligament. I washed my hands, waited for the water to warm up, and then washed them again. Pulled out my apron from the closet and settled it over my body like an afghan. Standing in front of the table again, I looked down at the raccoons and to my amazement found I couldn't concentrate.

I grabbed a six-pack from the fridge and set it on the metal prep tray before cracking one open. Then I picked up one of the scalpels, testing the blade against the ball of my thumb. Maybe they weren't sharp enough. Pulling out the whetstone from the drawer below the sink, I sat down and methodically sharpened every blade. The steady scritch-scratching added to the cloudy fog the beer had already stewed in my brain. Once everything was sharpened and I'd finished my drink, there was nothing left to do but look at those two dead babies.

Hands smaller than half-dollars. Soft, tufted ears. Their faces looked nearly human. I picked up the one on the left and turned it over to make the first long incision across its belly.

Back, back.

Whenever Brynn talked about leaving, she made it seem like a big production, like the plot to one of those stupid movies she liked on the Hallmark Channel. Never anything remotely believable. *I'll go to California and live next to the desert*, she said, cutting crusts off the kids' PB&Js. *There's still time for me to get into acting. Like, I could do character work or something. Only wear linen dresses.*

What about Milo? I asked, pushing a hunk of dirty hair behind her ear. *You're gonna abandon him and take the kids? Heartless. Beautiful and heartless.*

She laughed and kissed me. *You know I'd never leave you guys. Who'd take care of me?*

It was true that we both knew what she wanted. What she liked. We were willing to give those things to her, no questions asked. Milo worked, brought home money, and listened to her when she was upset or hurting. We both took care of the kids without complaint, soothed her fears when she worried and fretted and hated herself. I gave her friendship and passion and provided an outlet for her anger. Milo was the one who could calm her, make her feel sane again. When I wanted to strangle her, he was there with a hug and a sweet, romantic gesture like a stuffed toy or some stupid candy she liked. When he was too sentimental, I let her be selfish. She could be kind and sweet around Milo and not feel vulnerable. She knew she could be mean and awful around me and I'd love her anyway.

I'm too much for one person, she whispered to me once, biting the shell of my ear.

But she didn't go to California, and she didn't take the kids. She left us all a little after lunch on a Tuesday. There was nothing special about it. No precursor to the event, no giant fight or ultimatum. It was like any other day.

I thought about that a lot, after. How mundane it was. It was so unlike her to make it into nothing. Just a regular, average afternoon with lunch and work and home. I felt cheated.

We all ate together. My father and I home from the shop, my mother heating bowls of chicken noodle soup in the microwave. Milo was working a late shift, and when he left, Brynn kissed him hard on the mouth and smacked him on the ass. She brought out a roll of paper towels and gave Lolee and Bastien their soup. When one of the kids spilled a Coke on the table, she didn't even get upset. We cleaned the dishes together, and I stood outside with her on the porch while she smoked a cigarette. She wore an old dress, faded blue and sleeveless, and scuffed around in my brother's oversized flip-flops. Then my father and I left to go back to the shop, and my mother ran to the store.

I was only gone for twenty minutes. My mother shook her head, as if trying to calculate how Brynn could've gotten all her things together and left in such a goddamn hurry. *I never thought she'd leave the kids there, not alone.*

But she did. She put Lolee down for a nap and turned on a movie for Bastien, one of the Disney ones they'd already watched a million times. Then she gathered most of her clothes, got in her car, and drove away. When my mother got back, Lolee was asleep and Bastien was still sitting on the couch. Neither knew where their mother had gone.

Brynn didn't come home that night, and she didn't answer her phone. I called over and over again, sure that if I could talk to her for just a few seconds, she'd come back. The phone stopped ringing through after a couple of days. It just went straight to voicemail.

Work. Always, there was work. If I could focus on that, I'd know where I was. I'd be safe.

I scraped methodically at the raccoon skin but couldn't disengage. I was so out of it I hadn't stopped to put on gloves. Raw meat slid under my fingernails, lodged in the cuticles. The bones were slick with blood and hard to separate. Intestines had burst inside the first raccoon, smearing everything in shit and bits of digested food. Halfway through the first animal, my stomach roiled.

The raccoon's eyes were glossy. Its lashes folded over the lid in a charcoal fringe that made it look sweet and bashful. When I pressed down on the back to get better leverage through the rear legs, the lids slid down in a slow blink and opened up again. Brynn had always wanted a raccoon for a pet. She liked how wild they were—one second sweetly playing, the next hissing rabidly at you from a garbage can. *Never tell if they're gonna bite you or hold your hand,* she said, showing me a video on her phone. *We should get one, Jessa. Little tame raccoon we could take on walks around the neighborhood. Wouldn't that be cute?*

I set the bones into a dissolving bath and walked straight into the bathroom. I stared at my reflection in the mirror over

177

the sink, breathing in through my nose and hissing air out through my teeth. A bit of raccoon flesh dotted the toe of my boot. I leaned over the toilet and retched up all the things I'd eaten that night: chips and salsa, the beers.

When I was done, I wiped the flesh off my shoe with a square of toilet paper and flushed it down with the rest. I slapped at my face until color came back into my cheeks. Then I cracked open another beer from the fridge and drank it, ignoring the rawness of my throat.

I flipped the second body, setting it beside the newly stripped pelt of its brother. Taking the scalpel, I dug a track through the middle of its belly that opened into a deep well of gore. It was the worst trauma I'd ever seen. The raccoon's entire system had been obliterated; but from the outside, it looked totally normal. Emptying the mess of it into the gut bucket, I started the whole process over again.

How to leave the past when it's staring you in the face all the time? When it's got its teeth dug into you like a rabid animal?

After Brynn left, I thought about transitions a lot. The sameness, the dullness of everything. How nothing in my life ever felt like it was moving fast enough, but at the same time I couldn't stand to leave the one place where Brynn had left me. The last place we'd loved each other.

Limbo to me felt like remembering pain. The memory of slamming your fingers in a car door or smashing your littlest toe into a wall. It was the shivery feeling you got if you remembered ramming your shin into a desk. You could re-member feelings over and over again and they never changed or got any better. They always hurt the same, and it seemed they always would.

Where did Brynn go? Nobody knew, especially not Milo, who was never home the month before she disappeared. Work-ing overtime at the dealership so they could afford to buy a house instead of throwing money away on rent. It should've been funny, Milo working so much though his whole life he'd done anything to avoid it, when in reality it was the work that allowed Brynn to slip away, unnoticed. If he'd stayed home with her, lost that job or just worked at the gas station, would she have ever left?

I could barely stand to look at him. My whole life I'd loved my brother without fail, without question, but Brynn's depar-ture had severed our closeness. I'd go to my parents' house to see the kids and he'd sit beside me on the couch, asking unan-swerable questions:

Have you heard anything?

Do you think she'll contact the kids?

Doesn't she love me?

He cried, often. Talked about how happy they'd been, describing their relationship in minute detail, searching for the trigger that had blown up our lives. Their marriage. Their kids. The house they'd wanted to buy—furniture she'd already picked out from the rent-to-own place downtown. I couldn't tell if I was angry at him for not anticipating her leaving or just mad at myself.

One month, two months. After the third month with no word, Bastien stopped asking about her. She'd missed his tenth birthday. There was a party at the bowling alley down the street. A lot of people showed up. Lots of balloons and pizza and streamers. It was one of the worst days of my life.

Milo bought gifts haphazardly and with very little thought: sports equipment Bastien didn't want and video games he already owned. They were the kind of gifts my own father would have bought for Milo. The kind of gifts that said *I know nothing about you; you're a part of my life I ignore and your birthday means that little to me*. I took everything back and exchanged it for the stuff Bastien actually asked for. I put Milo's name on the front, barely restraining myself from writing Brynn's alongside it. Hopeful she'd remember her son's birthday and show up.

We served cake and half-melted ice cream. Nine kids came and bowled three rounds. I handed out tokens in little Dixie cups to play the outdated arcade games: *Ms. Pac-Man, Donkey Kong, Galaga*. When we were growing up, Milo'd had two birthday parties there and I'd had one. Brynn and I'd taken so many pictures in the photo booth we could've papered a wall with all the photo strips.

I hated being around Milo's wallowing, but I couldn't stand to be alone. In my apartment I sat up all night drinking and watching TV, praying I'd hollow out and stop caring. Every place that used to feel comfortable to me just felt filled with Brynn. Every place in town held a memory. The movie theater where she'd barfed Sno-Caps. A gas station parking lot where we'd gotten strangers to buy us lime-flavored wine cooler. There was no escape.

I spent all my free time at my parents' house with the kids and used them as a distraction. We built forts, played in the sprinklers, wandered the graveyard. My mother said nothing, just stared at us with sad eyes and made too much food.

When I was over there, I found myself looking for traces. Clues. Brynn wasn't the kind of person who'd kept a diary. She liked shouting her feelings at the top of her lungs so everyone could experience them with her. I knew every bad thing she thought about anyone, including myself. No one knew her better than I did, but I couldn't think of a single way to reach her.

Her mother had moved down to Boca a year after Brynn and Milo got married. They weren't on speaking terms. When I couldn't stand it any longer, I snuck her number from my mother's address book and called. As the phone rang I prayed Brynn would be the one to pick up. Knew I'd be able to tell it was her even by the way her breath touched the receiver.

A man answered. He sounded boyish, even for Brynn's mother, whose taste in husbands ran toward half her age.

Can I speak with Marsha?

Who's calling? The voice was sullen, kind of defensive.

Tell her it's Jessa-Lynn.

There was a pause and the tone brightened. *Hey. Jessa. It's Gideon.*

The last time I'd seen him was before he'd hit puberty and still sounded like a chew toy someone had stepped on. Brynn's little brother—half brother, I amended, just like Brynn would have done.

Is your mom there?

Nah, she's at work. Probably won't be back till pretty late tonight. You know Mom.

The day stretched out in front of me like an endless nightmare. Even if he gave her the message, there was no guarantee she'd call back. Marsha Wiley was even flakier than her daughter. *Could you give her my number? I need to talk with her.*

There was laughter in the background; maybe a television set. Maybe the radio. He sighed. *You can ask, you know.*

I was too needy to pretend I didn't understand what he meant. I went ahead and asked if they'd heard from her. I promised not to tell Milo. I'd have promised anything for an answer. Anything to explain why this had happened.

Not recently, he said. *But yeah. She's been by.*

It was a careful response; one I'd anticipated. *Is she okay?*

She's fine. The same Brynn.

More muted laughter, a door slamming. Was it her? There was no way to know. I dug my fingernails into my palm and focused on the burn.

I'll tell her you called, he said, and then he hung up.

Wait. There was still work to finish. Wasn't there always something?

Handfuls of hair littered the counter. My father had always called it "a woman's crowning glory." He'd told me never to cut mine, that it was as beautiful as my mother's.

Gingerly I touched the places I'd torn fistfuls straight from the root, rough patches where tingling radiated from the skin. I'd torn two nails down to the quick and blood welled beneath the pinky on my right hand. My whole body jittered and shook.

I pressed my face to the cool metal of the table and wept until I couldn't breathe. Cried until my chest wanted to collapse.

When I was done, I wiped my face with the hem of my shirt. Gathering up the handfuls of hair, I separated the collected bundle into two sections and rolled them. Then I opened up the raccoon bodies and slipped a knot of my hair into each tiny stomach.

I drank one more beer and cried again. My eyes burned as if I'd rubbed sand in them. Wiped my face again, finished the beer. Threw out the empty.

Turning off the lights, I left the work half assembled on the countertop and fell asleep on the cot. When I woke the next morning, the raccoons were gone. My father had covered me with his Florida State sweatshirt, a huge thing that he always wore in lieu of a coat on the five occasions a year it actually dropped below sixty degrees in Central Florida.

He squeezed my shoulder, then cupped the side of my head with his warm hand. *Pull up the hood, sweetheart. Your hair's a wreck.*

7

After the unveiling of the buffalo, Milo's eyes looked glazed, as if he were trapped underwater. We both turned our attention to the TV set, which was playing a rerun of some crime show. On-screen, a woman sprayed luminol onto a linoleum kitchen floor. When an investigator turned out the lights, the room glowed like a radioactive chamber.

"It never looks like that," Bastien said, cutting himself another slice of pie. "Way too bright."

"What are we going to do?" I asked my brother. People milled around, acting as if there weren't a gigantic buffalo covered in S&M props taking up half the living room.

"About what?" He picked at the crust of his egg custard until Lolee took his plate to scavenge the remains. I put my hands over her ears.

"About what just happened, you fucking dummy. Mom obviously had a breakdown." I nodded vaguely toward the monstrosity, unwilling to raise my eyes above its broad sides, where the patent leather leg still dangled.

"It's gonna be fine. Probably good for her, right? Get it all out of her system."

It was the complete opposite of fine. My brother, the one with the insight and empathy to understand what people needed, couldn't even be trusted to look at our poor mother and know that something had gone horribly wrong.

He stared at the TV, wiping his clean lips repeatedly with a folded napkin.

"You're delusional," I said. Lolee got up and moved toward the water buffalo and I snagged her back by a belt loop. "Go play outside," I told her, pushing her toward the back patio.

"I'm with Aunt Jessa, Grandma has fucking lost it." Bastien dug into his pie, crumbs clumped in the corner of his mouth. "Weirdest shit I've ever seen."

"Shut up. Go help." Milo pointed at the empty plates. "And take those in with you."

Bastien made a face but did as he was told. I turned to Milo and tried again. "I'm honestly worried about her mental state. She thinks this is a healthy way to grieve Dad. What does that tell you?"

He shrugged and leaned back against the sofa cushions. "I dunno. People all handle shit different, I guess."

I couldn't understand why he was acting this way. I took a breath, trying to think up something reasonable to counter his argument. "That is the stupidest thing you've ever said."

Jay and Travis stood talking beside the buffalo while they finished their coffee. Travis smoothed a hand up and down its neck, perilously close to the leather figure's thigh. "This is real well done," Travis said, picking up a wooden paddle studded with blunt spikes. "You ever seen one of these before?"

Jay looked like he was going to respond, but Vera shot him a look that promised death. "Nope, don't think I have."

I tried again. "It's not right. She needs to see a therapist, something."

"What do you expect us to do about it, Jessa?" Milo rubbed a hand across his forehead. "She's a grown woman. She can do whatever she wants."

"Well, I'm putting a stop to it," I said, trying to convince the both of us.

I found Lucinda in the hallway, examining some of our family photos. She touched the edge of a frame, one where the four of us posed in front of a craggy waterfall. Milo and I were both wearing overalls. My mother had on a denim dress with a red bandana tied around her ponytail, my father with a matching one around his neck, his arm looped around her shoulder. It was the most ridiculous picture of our family, and I'd always loved it.

"This is adorable," Lucinda said. "Look at that bowl haircut. You still have those overalls?"

"Can we talk?" Instead of waiting for an answer, I walked down the hall and out the front door. Bugs zapped in the piss-yellow light from the front porch fixture. A large, fuzzy moth repeatedly battered itself against the dirty glass.

The air was fully saturated, cars already covered in condensation. We stood close to my truck and I remembered the way she'd pushed me against it, how her hands felt on my skin.

"This show cannot happen," I said, crossing my arms so I wouldn't try to touch her. "I mean it."

"That's not very reasonable." She leaned into me and rubbed her hands briskly up and down my arms, chafing the skin. "Also it's pretty ballsy of you to ask for anything after bailing on me this morning."

"Stop it." I put another foot of space between us. "That is my mother and there's something wrong with her. It's not okay."

"What do you want me to do? I can't just tell her no. I've invested a lot of time and money."

I was sure she had, and probably a ton of it. Lucinda didn't talk about it much, but I knew everything she owned was tied up in her condo and the gallery—a pretty significant chunk of change. What little I'd managed to uncover about her finances had come from rooting around her office while she was preoccupied with my mother's work. There were always massive piles of mail stacked on the desk, mostly addressed to Lucinda Rex, but also some made out to a Donna Franklin. Her *roommate*, that word again that could've meant anything but likely meant partner. Maybe wife. A person Lucinda was probably sleeping with, sure, but it was also someone else investing in my mother's work, who'd put money into it. Someone who might be able to see reason when it came to stopping this atrocity, if she had a little distance from it.

And if I got a little more info on their relationship at the same time, even better.

"What can I do?" she repeated. "What do you want from me?"

"Figure something out." I climbed inside the truck and started the engine. It took three tries to turn over, I was so stressed. When I backed out of the driveway, she was still standing there looking at me, her face glowing unrecognizable in the beams of the headlights.

Driving straight to the bar, I drank until I was so drunk I couldn't unbutton my pants in the bathroom. There were other women in there with me: a brassy blonde with a tattoo of a dolphin on her shoulder, an older woman who wore a sweatshirt with a Christmas wreath puffy-painted on the front. I wished I could be either of them, that I could trade bodies and go back to whatever their lives were so I could stop staying in mine. Husbands, children. Families that didn't need so much care. I took a cab home and puked up everything I'd had to drink in my kitchen sink. When I woke the next morning, bleary and sick, I called Bastien and told him I was taking the day off.

I spent my time at home sleeping, dreaming about my mother and Lucinda and Brynn, all mixed up in a strange sexual miasma. Vague, sticky figures cavorting with the animals my father and I had taxidermied: the bear, raccoons with small black paws that grabbed with scratchy fingers. I woke at dusk and stumbled into my living room. A steady stream of ants marched their way down the wall next to my head, following a crooked path into the kitchen. There were dishes piled up in the sink, crusted with food that had long ago fouled. The air was sour and thick with garbage.

It had been only a day since we'd fought, but I couldn't be alone in that apartment anymore without going crazy. I called Lucinda and asked her to meet me for drinks.

We met up that night. Then we met up the next. I didn't bring up what had happened at my mother's house and neither did she, but it sat there between us, another of the unspoken hurts in my life that worked to rot something good from the inside out. It was all cadaver flesh. I refused to step foot in the gallery, unwilling to support it even by acknowledging it. Alone at home, I went online and looked up stuff about Lucinda. About her life before me, outside of what we had. I wasn't very good at it—my brain didn't like processing things on a screen; I was used to tactile work—but I knew enough to figure out she was married. Donna Franklin, I learned, was eight years older than Lucinda. Before they'd bought the gallery together, she'd lived in South Carolina and owned a woodworking business, one of the gayest professions I could imagine. There were some pictures of her when I googled further. I stared, wondering if we were a similar gay type. We shared a body shape, for sure, both of us stout with faces more likely to frown than grin. At the bottom of one of the outdated websites, I found contact information. A phone number. I wrote it down on a Post-it and kept it hidden inside an old magazine in my bedroom. There it sat, stuffed between the pages of a 1994 *Better Homes and Gardens* showcasing water features. Just in case.

My relationship with Lucinda continued, but it wasn't like before. We didn't talk. There weren't moments where sex verged on tenderness. We fucked against walls or on my ratty sofa; sometimes leaned over the coffee table or slammed against the sticky kitchen countertop. I knelt on the rug, pressing my face against her crotch until I thought she'd absorb me into her body.

We never fucked in bed. I kept the door to my room closed and directed us anywhere else. The harder I pushed her away, the more often she called. I touched her like I wanted her to combust, exploding into pieces sharp enough to draw blood. Donna could take care of the intimacy I lacked, I thought.

Donna with her short hair, Donna with those wide, strong hands, just like mine, Donna with her soft, dimpled baby face. What did it matter if Lucinda said she needed me? Someone who says she needs love when she's really just looking for some on the side isn't talking about romance; she's talking about the demands of the body. The grunting sexuality of the physical. Well, let Donna keep her sweetness, I thought. Let Donna have her love, whatever the hell that meant. I could focus on the happy little deaths we inflicted on each other. I could have that, if nothing else.

I took on more work at the shop, happy to let Bastien man the front. I slipped skins with relish, slicing and curing, my fingers clenched into the shape of the tools long after my shifts were done. When I got home, arms aching from the strain, there'd be globules of gristly muscle stuck to my clothes. I drank and slept hard; I didn't want any more dreams.

The shop was doing well. Bastien fielded marketing and added social media, something my father would never have done and which I barely understood. Our client base grew until we were pulling in a fair amount of work again. The old business was dying off, but we found new footing with a younger crowd that I'd never imagined would be interested in taxidermy. It was good money, though, and I didn't care what they wanted. I never questioned any of it until a woman approached me one afternoon with a coupon.

"Excuse me. I have one of these?" She waved a wrinkled paper in my face. "This is Morton's, right?"

She couldn't have been more than twenty-two. She wore red corduroy shorts and a white middy blouse cropped above her navel. Not our usual kind of customer; those were always cranky men in their late fifties who talked *at* me, like they thought they could teach me something.

"Yeah, that's us, but we don't have coupons."

The woman thrust the paper under my nose until I was forced to take it from her or inhale it. It was printed and the ink had smeared along the top edge, but there was our logo, smack on top: MORTON'S in all caps with the weird apostrophe that almost looked like a demonic tadpole.

"I heard you might be getting in some peacocks?" she asked, as I shrugged and contemplated our ad, in print. New things happening in the store now, all the time.

Bastien laughed and I turned to look at him, curious what was so funny. He never laughed unless someone fell down or made a joke about using the bathroom.

"Later this week," he told her, snagging the paper from my hands. "Gotta pick 'em up first."

Bastien and I grabbed Lolee on the way to get the birds. She spent most nights at her friend Kaitlyn's house since my mother was always holed up at the gallery. Kaitlyn was a short girl with a bulldog face and a sweet smile. They played in the marching band together, both of them flutes. Lolee liked being over there, and I didn't blame her. My mother was so busy that she'd stopped making regular meals. Last time I'd been in the house, every leftover was gone and there was nothing to eat but some questionable milk and half a box of stale cinnamon Life cereal.

Bastien drove my truck down purpling streets while I drained my first beer of the night. It sat wedged between my knees. He flew into Kaitlyn's driveway and my sip dribbled down my chin and soaked the collar of my shirt.

"Where we headed?" I asked, cracking open another and wiping the condensation off on my jeans. "Is there a wholesale outlet? Never did one of those."

"Nah, not that. Something else. Fresher."

Lolee wandered out in ancient pajama shorts and my old high school sweatshirt. "Climb in the back," Bastien yelled through the window. She boosted herself along the bumper, flip-flops slapping at the corrugated bottom of the bed.

Pressing her mouth to the back window, she made a monkey face, tongue streaking the glass with her spit.

"Keep your shoes on," I said. "There might be broken bottles back there."

Bastien drove haphazardly, zigzagging across a few of the wider residential streets, making Lolee screech as she tumbled around in the back. Instead of taking us out one of the exits, he circled closer to the heart of the neighborhood, nearing the golf course that ran through the middle. Despite its name, Fawn Creek didn't have any kind of running water, just retention ponds. A fountain spewed water from its center, turning colors on holidays: red and green for Christmas, patriotic hues on the Fourth of July.

Dusk came quickly, shepherding in a horde of bats. They fluttered spastically in the orange-washed sky, tripping over each other mid-flight. Bastien turned down a side street. It was poorly paved; the truck bumped along the divots in the asphalt, bouncing my beer until some spilled on my pants.

"Slow down, dick," Lolee yelled, slapping her palm against the glass. "I'm gonna crack my head back here."

Bastien laughed and revved the engine, then cut a tight corner at the back of the golf course. I'd never been to this area before. It was where the workers came to unload stuff. I had a sudden memory as he parked his truck near the cages of balls and unearthed a key chain from his pocket.

"Didn't you used to work here when you were in high school? Like a caddy?"

"Nothing that glamorous." Bastien hopped down from the driver's seat and cracked his back, stretching his arms high overhead. "I mowed the grass. Sometimes I drove the truck that picked up the balls people shot out on the driving range? It sucked."

Lolee stood up along the side and the whole truck dipped under her weight. Bastien helped her down, dropping her in the grass with a grunt.

"You're not as strong as Daddy," she complained, then leaned over to massage her calves.

"I'm not as nice, either." He pressed down on her head until it went almost between her knees. Lolee screamed and swatted at him.

"Okay, seriously." I drank the rest of my second beer. There were three still in the truck and I thought I might need them soon. "What the hell are we doing here? I'd like to get dinner."

Bastien's chin had a scraggly growth of beard coming in. His eyes were colorless in the foggy evening. "Shouldn't take long."

I ghosted along behind the two of them as we moved farther away from the lampposts that dotted the periphery of the smoothly mown green. It was quiet except for the occasional switch of our legs sliding through the grass. There was a dank, creepy little shed near the back of the lot. I stopped to look while Bastien and Lolee trudged toward it.

"Hey," I called. Lolee turned around and trotted back. "What is this, what are we doing?"

"Getting the peacocks." Lolee pulled her hair up on top of her head and knotted it with one of the elastic bands she kept looped around her wrist. She danced around me, spinning, twirling like a little kid.

I could barely make out Bastien in the murky light. Our shadows were long and fragmented over the shitty grass that made up the far corner of the course. Lolee and I walked together, swinging our arms in tandem. I wondered when I'd get home so I could drink in peace and forget about the day.

Closer up, the shed looked less like something out of a horror movie and more like something from *Little House on the Prairie*. The roof was slanted and angled with wooden planks, and a long gravel drive sat behind it. Someone had painted the slats slate gray at some point, though they had started to peel in the humidity. A sign posted on a two-by-four out front said NO TRESPASSING in very collegiate font.

Close to the shed, the air turned thick and gamey. A peacock stuck its pinhead out the door. Another appeared above it, creating the comical impression of two kids peeking around a corner during a game of tag.

"Are those alive?" I asked. "They're fucking *alive?*"

Three peacocks strutted through the open doorway. Bastien followed along behind them, golf club tossed over his shoulder as if he were about to tee off. The birds walked ahead of him, feathers glossy gold-green in the moonlight, unafraid.

Lolee continued playing with her hair, braiding the small pieces that drifted down from the sides into little spikes that stuck out from her temples. Completely confused, I followed alongside Bastien, who shepherded them back toward the truck.

"The fuck are we going to do with live birds?" I asked. "The fuck, Bastien?"

"Do you know if that new Chinese place opened yet?" He swung the club gently to the right when one of the birds fell out of line to examine something crawling in the dirt.

"What Chinese place?" The birds looked stately and regal, like emissaries headed to an important event.

"That one by the bus station. Near Bennett."

"Oh. I didn't even know there was a new place opening. I always go to the one by Grandma's house."

Bastien laughed. "That place closed like three years ago." The golf club swung again, tenderly guiding the last bird back in line.

Back at the truck, he handed off the club to his sister and climbed into the cab. The birds milled around in the high weeds in front of the tires, pecking at dust and gravel. They fluttered a bit when the engine turned over, but then went back to digging, feathers glistening and iridescent in the glow of the headlights.

He revved it hard and they startled, landing awkwardly on top of each other before running back in the direction of the shed. Bastien drove after them, taking the small hill up into the course. The birds shrieked and so did Lolee, who ran behind the truck. Bastien swung wide doughnuts in the middle of the grassy lawn while the peacocks screamed, sounding nearly human in their terror.

One keeled over immediately. It flopped belly-first over its legs, skidding into the grass. The second fell right alongside it, feathers fanning over both their bodies. Lolee ran after the third, which was half flying in any direction that might take it away from the truck. It had almost made the tree line when Bastien swung back around and nearly drove over it. The bird rushed toward me, screaming, and then fell over mid-stride.

Bastien drove to where the first two lay. He left the truck running and climbed out, picking up both birds and dumping them into the bed.

Lolee skipped to the third and poked at it with the golf club. Its neck flopped, but it didn't stir. "Got 'em all this time!" she called to her brother, before heaving the dead peacock over her shoulder.

PAVO CRISTATUS—INDIAN PEAFOWL

Brynn's mother was *between husbands.* That's what she called it, as if it were only a matter of time before the next one wandered into the justice of the peace and put a ring on her finger. Marsha Wiley spent most nights out at the bar looking for marriage material, even though she'd warned fifteen-year-old Brynn that bars were the absolute worst place to find a man.

Too many losers. She leaned back in the beach chair, mirrored sunglasses perched at the end of her tiny nose. *Everybody's already been married before and fucked it up. If they're not married, they're too fucking old.*

She pitched her half-finished cigarette into the planter. Brynn's eyes followed the butt, and I knew she'd fish it out after her mother left.

All your husbands are old. Brynn was still in her nightgown. We'd spent the night at the trailer. Her mother had stayed out till three in the morning on a date, and we'd kept an eye on Gideon.

That's not what I mean. These guys are, like, old horses. Like they've been trained to work a certain way and once they pass fifty, it's no can do. No changing. They're just gonna keep living the same bachelor lifestyle they always did.

Couldn't you find one who's not gonna change but you don't mind it? I asked, eyeballing her long legs. They still looked really good, very tan and smooth. Not as thin as Brynn's but muscular, like a runner's.

Marsha smiled and slid a hand down my arm. *Oh sweetheart, these guys are like little kids. They have awful hygiene, they can't hold down a job. Letting one in your house is like taking in a pig.*

You make men sound fucking disgusting. Brynn pulled her hair back into a ponytail that sat high on the crown of her head. Bald patches of scalp showed through the grease. Neither of us was clean. I could smell the dank odor of my armpits through my T-shirt.

Watch your mouth. Marsha picked up one of our plates from the night before and scavenged a leftover pepperoni. *Did you eat all the pizza? Now what'll Gideon have for lunch?*

Let's dig out the kiddie pool. Brynn dragged me back inside the trailer. I looked for it while she put on her bikini. Digging around in the front closet, I pushed past plastic Publix bags full of discarded clothes and car parts that the last boyfriend left behind. The pool was buried under a stack of old school stuff and expired coupon mailers. It looked like there'd been a leak. The papers were all damp and warped, curled up on the corners. I saw Brynn's name in shaky, childish scrawl on a painting of an orange cat. It had leached a bright wash onto the sleeve of an abandoned sweatshirt.

We dragged the pool outside and down the splintery wooden steps of the porch. Brynn crouched in her bathing suit, flattening the plastic over the crunchy dead grass and sand-spurs. A guy working on his truck a couple of trailers down yelled something in a grunting voice that made me uncomfortable, but Brynn just ignored it.

It was exhausting work blowing up the pool. We took turns, huffing our bubblegum breath into the small rubber nipple. Once it got halfway inflated, Brynn sealed it up and tossed it down in the weeds.

Good enough, she said, yanking out the hose from where it rested under a corner of the trailer, looking like a snake someone had run over with a car. She turned on the spigot, and the water came out boiling hot. Everything smelled like chemicals and damp dirt.

Marsha came back out wearing a neon green sarong and a sparkly pink bikini. On her hip she carried Gideon, who was still dead asleep. She dropped down in her beach chair and it creaked ominously, sagging nearly to the ground from their combined weight.

Brynn and I sat in the water and let the hose flush up on us like a fountain, the sun beating around our heads, flies buzzing in the neighbor's garbage. The guy working on his truck was listening to loud country music and singing along. He didn't seem to know too many of the words.

Marsha kicked off her flip-flops and scooted forward until her feet reached the water. She stuck them in beside my legs. Her toes wiggled around in the bottom of the pool, nails coated with bright teal polish. The same color flashed on her fingers. She was the only mother I knew who wore her teenage daughter's clothes and makeup.

You sure you don't wanna borrow a suit? Marsha tangled her fingers in my hair, combing it out until I wanted to fall asleep. *You gotta be hot in that getup, baby.*

I wore some of Milo's old cargo shorts and a bass-fishing T-shirt with the neck stretched so wide you could see both my dirty white bra straps. *I'm okay*, I said, leaning back into her fingers. They scratched and rooted, searching out knots.

Oh please, Jessa'd never show that much skin. Brynn flopped over onto her stomach, bikini bottom riding up the crack of her ass. I tried not to stare, pulling my knees up to my chest. Just concentrated on the fingers rubbing circles along my scalp.

Leave her alone. Jessa doesn't need to show a bunch of skin.

Why not? Brynn wriggled around until her legs hung off the back of the pool. Water spilled over the crushed lip, streaming miniature rivers. Muck floated down the dirt driveway out into the street.

Because she's got a great body. You can see it without having to show it off. She's got a really classy way about her.

Brynn snorted. *Right. That bass-fishing shirt is classy as hell.*

My muscles loosened until my shoulders drooped and my head dropped down onto my knees. *I'm so classy that I'm going to pretend I didn't hear that.*

You're such a little bitch. Brynn cupped her hand and sent a tidal wave of water down my front. The next scoop went over me and landed on her mother and Gideon. He woke abruptly and started wailing.

For God's sake, Brynn. Marsha stood up, half her sarong dangling off her arm, while Gideon struggled and rubbed his eyes. The back of his head was sweaty and wet. *Take him inside and give him a Coke.*

Brynn groaned and stood up, shaking water onto me like a wet dog. She took Gideon from her mother, staggering under his weight. His legs hung down around either side of her body, nearly dragging to her knees. *This kid's about to pull my top off, Christ Jesus almighty.*

Brynn kicked the trailer door open with her foot when it jammed in the frame. It slammed closed behind her.

Marsha went back to playing with my hair. I could feel her separating the strands, braiding them loosely, letting them fall down again before she picked them back up to start over.

You're getting a little pink. Marsha ticked a fingertip against the shell of my ear. *You need some sunscreen.*

The chair creaked as she got up again and went into the house. She came back with a brown plastic bottle that smelled like coconuts and pineapple. She dabbed a little where she'd touched before, smoothing it down and around until my whole ear was covered.

Working at the store this summer?

Yeah. Gonna skin some deer mounts tonight. My dad's gonna show me how to set the eyes. Last one I did ended up cross-eyed.

I relaxed again into her strokes, and the scent of the lotion filled my nose. She pinned my hair at the top of my head and began working on my neck, which was so tense it felt gristly and only half-human.

When she bent low to talk, the smell of her cigarette still clung to her breath. I breathed in and out, coconut and cigarette, cigarette and pineapple.

You're so knotted up. Her hands worked lower, dipping down into the neck of my shirt, fingers feathering across either side of my spine, sliding under my bra straps until they hung limply from either shoulder.

It's from sewing. I have to use the tiniest stitches. Dad makes me redo them most of the time.

Hands smoothed over my shoulders, fingers dipping into the valleys of my clavicle. My nipples hardened as her hands lowered incrementally. Breath shored in my lungs.

Your skin's like a baby. Smoothing, down, farther down, until the tip of one finger rubbed against the edge of my areola. *How are you so soft?*

There was a loud, drawn-out honk. Marsha's hands left and I stayed in the same position, simultaneously hopeful and scared that she'd put them back. Wondering what would slow the steady, awful pounding in my chest. Even my eyeballs felt like they had a heartbeat.

The man who'd been working on his truck waved over at Brynn's mother. He had a bandana shoved into his back pocket. When he turned around, it looked like a wagging of tail feathers, a bird showing off plumage.

Come take a look at this. His shirt rode up, revealing a lot of his tanned back. Marsha got up right away, leaning on my shoulder to balance as she slipped on her wedges. I stared at her toes, covered in dirt and stray bits of weedy dead grass.

She padded down the dirt driveway, sarong flaring out wide and bright behind her, ass swaying side to side as she made her way across the street. The rhinestones sewn into the fabric spit with light. I was thirsty all of a sudden. I picked up the hose and drank the rubbery, cold water until my stomach felt full enough to burst.

Fucking finally. Brynn stomped back down from the trailer and sat with a splash in the water next to me. She flopped her legs over mine, sticky with coconut lotion. Some of it slicked off into the water, leaving iridescent rings like an oil spill. *Can we eat dinner at your house tonight? I know my mom's gonna try and talk me into watching this kid, and we ate all the good stuff. She won't get anything else until her next paycheck.*

Marsha laughed at something the man said, her voice trilling up high and sharp, almost screeching when he reached out and dug a finger into her side.

I'm working the mounts tonight.

Please. I'll just stay at your house and we can hang out when you're done. I'll play cards with your mom and Milo or something. Anything's better than this.

We both stared at her mother, who was leaning hard over the open guts of the truck. One sandal dangled from a lifted foot.

I guess. Lemme call my mom first.

Brynn shot up out of the water and shook until water sprinkled down my neck. *Nah, let's just go. She's gonna wind up hanging out with that guy tonight and I can't deal with it. Let 'em just come over here.*

Vacating the pool, we both stomped our feet clean, leaving it half full of mucky water. Inside, I changed into one of Brynn's shirts, too tight and small, but at least dry. It was pink with a rainbow across the front; a bright blue surfing wave said ALOHA over the bust.

We collected our bikes from where they leaned next to a tiny, rusted-out shed. I felt too hot and kind of sick, as if my skin were too tight for my body. We climbed on and pedaled through the sloppy front yard, weeds high up in our spokes, tires dipping down into the wet earth.

Marsha saw us when we finally hit the pavement. She yelled, waving her arms over her head, jogging after us. The sarong was a bright flag behind her.

Hurry up, Brynn said, standing up and pedaling hard.

Once we turned the corner out of the trailer park subdivision, I couldn't hear Marsha anymore.

Brynn laughed, and the sound floated back to me. *Please kill me if I'm ever like that*, she yelled. Her hair stuck out wildly behind her, crunchy from leftover hair spray. She wore her mother's mirrored sunglasses. They perched on the end of her nose and flashed in the sunlight.

8

Lolee rode between the prone bodies of the peacocks in the back of the truck. There was something feral about her, teeth gleaming in the hard bright light from the streetlamps, a yellow glow bouncing off her skin. Her canines seemed too sharp in her tiny elfin face. When she smacked her open palm against the back window to get my attention, I flinched and turned around to face front. Pretended like I didn't hear her howling and thumping around like a wild animal.

Despite the fact that my licenseless nephew was behind the wheel, I cracked open the last beer before we even turned onto the street in front of the shop. Bastien parked at the entrance, hopping out to lift Lolee from the back. They let down the tail, each of them grabbing a bird. I knew they expected me to get the third, the largest one, but I busied myself with the keys and let myself inside. The glow from outside gave me just enough light to see my shadow running ahead of me down the hall.

The usual burnished warmth of beer flooding my veins wasn't able to keep up with the horror of murdering three peacocks in cold blood. I sat down on the toilet in the rear of the shop, not even bothering to close the door. Bastien strutted past, then Lolee, staggering a bit under the weight of her bird.

I peed, the sound a loud rush, and closed my eyes, able only to focus on emptying my bladder.

"How many other animals have you killed this way?" I asked, reaching around in the dark for the toilet paper.

"Not many yet." Bastien walked past again, his boots heavy on the linoleum. "These today, that hawk two weeks ago. Some egrets. A red fox, maybe female? Oh, and the kittens."

"Kittens? You killed *kittens*?"

"Not me. Lolee."

There was a moment where I thought I'd need to get up so I could puke, pants around my ankles, urine splashing up into my own face. To think of my little niece strangling baby cats was too much to bear.

"C'mon. I didn't kill those." Lolee stopped and smiled in at me. She looked too thin. I worried about her hanging out with Bastien if he was taking her out to kill things in the middle of the night. That seemed like something a serial killer might do. Wasn't that something they said? That the first sign someone was a sociopath was animal murder?

"What did you do?" I asked, staring at her while she pranced around in the doorway.

"I found them, already drowned. Kaitlyn's stepdad did it, I think. Just a big, wet sack full of dead kittens. It was really sad. Kaitlyn cried for like a week."

"Do we have any more toilet paper?" The empty tube rattled under my fingers as I thought of the sweet little kittens with their sleeping faces; the ones I'd sheared and reconstituted just a week earlier. "I thought those belonged to somebody. That we were doing a pet consultation?"

"We're out. You need to go to the store." She shoved a fist-ful of fast food napkins at me. "Don't flush those."

Like I didn't already know better. I sat and wiped with a wad of them. I could hear them both out there, opening draw-ers, pulling out instruments. There'd be a lot of cleanup. I'd never skinned a whole peacock before, and there were three waiting for gutting.

"Bloody Mary," I whispered, face dark and wild in the mir-ror over the sink. I felt slightly buzzed. That helped. "Bloody Mary." I washed my hands and dried them on my pants. "What the hell are we doing?"

Gear was spread out on the countertops. Lolee and Bastien piled the birds onto the center table, necks knocking into each other loosely.

"This is too much work for now." I pulled my apron over my head and readied the gut tubs next to the table. "It's already after ten. Put two back in the freezer. We'll play around with this one; see what it needs for prep."

"I think we can do them all." Bastien slapped a hand against the back of the bird closest to him. Bits of fluff flew off and hung suspended in the air. "Let's gut 'em tonight, then we'll scrape in the morning."

I looked at Lolee, who was jumping up and down on the balls of her feet. "You're gonna help?" I asked.

She was already pulling on a spare apron—the one I'd got-ten from a garage sale that said LORD & MASTER OF THE GRILLE in yellow embroidery.

"Go grab the other table, then. Not enough elbow room here for three."

We each claimed a bird. I let Lolee choose first, because it reminded me of the first time Milo and I'd crowded around my father at the back of the shop. It was still exciting then, the fun of not knowing, both of us wondering what might happen. The bridge between the living and the dead, operating as the conduit between those lines. I wondered how much of my thirst for nostalgia I owed to my father, a man who'd sincerely loved looking backward, as if the past were a place he could visit any time he wished.

Lolee dragged hers over to the secondary metal table that Bastien had pulled out of the supply closet. I helped her settle the animal, back first, the feathers fanning out until they dipped close to the floor.

"Would've liked to read up on this first. Maybe research how to do it before we mangle them."

"How hard can it be?" Bastien had already ripped into his, slicing slightly below the gullet. Here I'd been thinking that we'd been lucking into an assortment of pricy work, when all along it'd been thanks to the murderous schemes of my nephew. How many animals had I cut into that he'd strangled the breath from? Run down with a car?

Maybe I just hadn't wanted to know.

But maybe that wasn't true. I was projecting again, like I always did. He was just trying to help out. Be what I needed, what the shop needed. Helping the family.

Though he was truly mangling his bird. He hadn't even put on work gloves. Clotted innards stained his hands all the way up to the wrist. I knew from experience that it would take a long time to come off, especially under the nails. Animal blood turned everything it touched nicotine yellow.

"Put these on." I grabbed some for Lolee and then pulled on my own, snapping them back over my wrists, pulling them up so far that the hair on my arms got twisted up in the latex. It was a good kind of feeling; like coming home after a long day out with strangers.

"How do I do it?" she asked, holding up the scalpel. The blade was neat and clean. "Show me."

I helped palm the edge, guiding it into her hand. Showed her the best way to make an initial incision; small and neat, something easy to cover with supplementary feathers and small stitching.

"Here's where we cut. Be tender, don't press too deep."

Her fingers were strong beneath mine, wrists corded with muscle, flexing hard below the joint. Bastien grunted as he stabbed into the torso, turning it into a sloppy mess we'd have to cover with a ton of extra stitching. It was unusual for him to jump right into butchering. Normally he stood back with me and assessed the situation. He made slow, specific cuts. But the kind of slicing he was doing now was rudimentary, a true hack job. He looked gleeful, hair stuck up in the back like a little kid. I wondered if it came from the thrill of running the birds down with the truck. His smile was too wide; his shoulders too tight. There was a dimple in his chin that dug in below the scrape of his beard. He looked like his mother whenever she got worked up over fight scenes in movies. Kind of bloodthirsty.

"If you go too hard you can mess up the torque of the neck." I said it loud enough for him to hear, but he just kept sawing. Lolee leaned into me and I could smell the unwashed scent of her hair, the soft dairy smell of her skin.

What was happening here was illegal. It was absolutely against the law. And I wasn't the only one who stood to benefit. My brain worked hard, flipping the idea over, rubbing at it like a coin between my fingertips. There was something else we could get out of this. Money aside, my mother had been working on pieces from the shop. Had possibly even used some of the illegal stuff for her art.

They couldn't put on a gallery showcase using illegally acquired animals.

Right?

Inside the peacock was a fascinating mess. We widened the slit large enough for Lolee to reach inside, pulling out innards as gently as she could: the twisting, looping swing of intestines, dark with feed and insects and bits of greenery; gristle and tendons; the fatty bits behind the haunches where all domesticated birds picked up weight.

"Open it a little wider, but careful. Flay it like a jacket."

As she pulled the knife downward, the skin slit seamlessly. I leaned down and pressed my cheek to her hair. She felt warm; her body heat radiated feverishly against me until I felt as if I were standing beside an open oven door.

"I can do it," she said, taking the knife from me and opening the bird the rest of the way. It lay spread, wet insides tender and red.

"You're doing real good. Just take out the big organs; we'll do everything else tomorrow."

I pulled the last peacock over to the opposite end of the metal counter, away from where Bastien hacked at his bird with lumberjack enthusiasm. The final one was the prettiest. Its feathers were wide and painted in rings of gold, green, indigo. It was a beautiful animal and probably very expensive.

"Are we gonna get in trouble for this?" I cut into the long line of its neck, working around the joints and smaller bones. "I mean, were there security cameras at that place?"

"Isn't that something you should've asked earlier?"

"Probably. Are we going to jail? Me, you, your little sister here in an orange jumpsuit?"

Bastien laughed and then coughed, a smoker's hack that lodged in his chest and stayed there rattling, wet and deep. "Nah. A guy owes me a favor. They've got like twenty of these birds. They won't miss three."

While that was probably true, it didn't make it any less illegal. The last thing our family needed was more stress. The art show, the illegal animals. Art show, animals. The coin, flipping between my fingers. It would be so easy to make a call. I was always looking for an out.

Nudging the gut bucket with my foot, I dumped out a large portion of the peacock's stomach and bowels, trying not to split anything open in the process. I scraped the interior using my favorite knife, the one with the long wooden handle, smoothed from years of use. It had been my grandfather's. My father had given it to me one afternoon when we finished cleaning eight deer in a row. I was so exhausted that the muscles in my forearms wouldn't stop twitching. When he handed me that knife, he told me I'd earned it. It glistened shiny silver in the light, and I wanted to gut another, just to prove I could. My father had skinned two more than I had. He was strong. When he talked about my grandfather, it was always to reference that kind of strength.

He never talked to me about anything, my father said one afternoon, the two of us drinking beer on the front porch as the
sun set, sinking blood red in the Florida heat. *Not like you and
me. Not like how we talk.*

"Would you ever do this with Mom?" Lolee asked, face
hidden behind a long swoop of hair. It was nearly trailing down
into the bird, and I tucked it back quick behind her ear so it
wouldn't collect any debris. "Did she do this kind of stuff?"

Lolee hardly ever asked about Brynn. She didn't have a lot
of concrete memories. Bastien was the one old enough to remember and hurt, the way I did. I shot him a look. He was
concentrating very hard on his knife work, pretending not to
listen.

That was the thing about Bastien. He might run down
some peacocks in the middle of a golf course, but at the end of
the day he had too much love in him to deal with how shitty
human beings were to each other.

"Not really." I slowed down, homing in on the tough meat
near the back of the bird. It would be so easy for the blade to
slip right through, to pierce the other side and ruin the shiny
plumage. "Sometimes she'd come hang out in the front of the
shop. She wasn't really into all the blood and guts."

"Not like you and Dad?" Lolee's eyes were big in her pale
face. They were wide-set like her mother's, but the color was all
Milo. Such a deep brown they bordered on black.

"Your dad doesn't really like it either." That was an un-
derstatement. If Milo thought too much about skinning, he
got queasy. Once he'd accidentally cut himself slicing tomatoes for a sandwich, and when he saw the blood pooling in

214

his palm, he'd passed out cold, right there on the floor. My mother walked into the kitchen, saw the knife and the spatter, and thought he'd been murdered. Brynn called me later to tell me about it and used the voice we always did for my mother, a kind of nasal-mucusy shriek.

You should have seen him, Brynn said, nearly cackling. *Classic Morton moment.*

I'd laughed along with her and thought about them there, at my parents': Milo and Brynn, my mother and father, the kids. Everyone spending time together, doing exactly what they were supposed to be doing. Living lives perfectly engineered to bring them happiness. What made a Morton moment classic? Couldn't it be that way only when I was there to be part of it? There was something in that image that made me feel I'd never understand it. That my family had absorbed Brynn, that it was whole without me. Jokes, personal stories, dumb shit that meant nothing to them and everything to me. It was a bad feeling, knowing my family could exist without me as an active participant. I'd gotten blackout drunk in my apartment afterward, thinking about that phrase and understanding I wasn't included in it: *classic Morton moment.*

"Only you?" Lolee pushed down on the back leg, trying for a better angle. It bounced back up again and knocked into her chest. "And Grandpa, I guess. I thought this was a family business. Why doesn't everybody work here?"

It was a question I'd asked before too, years ago. My father and I'd been closing the shop. It was quiet, and I was balancing the register while we had some Cokes. *Lemme tell you something,* he said, adjusting a mounted crow on the shelf behind the counter. *I love your mother, but if I had to see her at work all day and then at home we'd be divorced by now. People need space so they don't wind up killing each other.* We drank our Cokes in silence for a couple of minutes. *It would be better for your brother if he spent less time at home too. Brynn's got him by the short hairs.* He looked hard at me when he said this. It was one of the only times I felt an acknowledgment of the role I played in Milo's marriage.

But how to put it to Lolee, who wouldn't understand that explanation? "It takes a certain kind of person to do this work." I set my blade down and went over to where she was tearing at the back of the peacock, guiding her knife through a knot of bird flesh. "By the time I was your age, I'd mounted at least five deer. I'd learned tanning techniques too."

"Did Grandpa even like working here? I mean he killed himself, so that maybe shows how shitty this place is." Bastien hacked so hard through a tendon that the leg severed completely from the torso. He swore and threw it and the scalpel across the metal table. The leg slid across the floor and landed next to me. When I picked it up, there was a residue of thin spatter left behind on the concrete. Didn't that tell me everything I needed to know about this young man? Too much feeling in his body to handle anything appropriately.

"Don't be dumb, Grandpa loved this place." I handed him back the leg. Careful. "You shouldn't use a large-grade utility knife. This is finesse work; you need a smaller blade."

I understood why my father chose the shop. He was always happiest surrounded by his tools and the animals he'd pieced together. There was nothing he loved more than making a first incision. He once told me that cut was one of life's perfect moments. *When you still have that animal's future mapped out in front of you. Complete freedom to play God; to turn a creature into anything you choose.*

Watching his blood cool on that metal counter, I'd thought about fate and choice. He'd taken that power into his own hands, but in leaving his body behind, he'd forced me along with him. The letter, a thing that should've provided answers, was nothing but a load of unanswerable questions. *I trust you*, he'd written. *I trust that you'll do the right thing*. Duties, responsibilities. How could I choose my own fate when it was always assigned to me?

"That's enough for now." I snapped off my gloves and dropped them into the slop bucket. Lolee groaned. I took the scalpel from her and pushed her toward the sink. "Scrub everything. Up to here." I pointed well past my elbow. "Use lots of soap."

Bastien grabbed some rags and a bottle of cleanser we kept in a bin next to the tarps. We cleaned in silence, wrapping the birds in damp cloth, soaking the instruments in alcohol, mopping down the floors and tabletops until the room reeked of Clorox.

I bought them pizza and drove them back to my mother's house. Bastien turned and waved once, to shoo me off, but I stayed to watch them get inside. It was pitch-black, no lights on, not even the porch. I went back to my own dark apartment and sat up on the couch until daylight pinkened the sky.

An invitation arrived in my mailbox, stuffed between oil change coupons and overdue credit card statements. The envelope was generic, but the paper inside was creamy, the kind of expensive stuff I associated with weddings. Sandwiched between stiff squares of tissue paper sat a thick piece of cardstock, embossed with gold writing. When I stroked my fingers across it, it was so soft. It felt like petting a cat.

At the very top was a golden bull rutting atop a silver stallion. Also included was a scrawled note from my mother on a folded piece of notebook paper that asked me to *bring a couple gallons of iced tea* and to *wear something dressy. Dressy,* as if she knew I might have problems coming up with something appropriate. Was it my fault all formal wear felt like trying to zipper myself into a straitjacket?

"Fuck this."

I stuffed the envelope and all the coupons into my overflowing garbage can. I knew whose money had paid for the expensive paper. It was the same person who was paying for the rest of it, the woman I continued to sleep with, even though she was enabling my mother's descent into a pornographic void. A woman I knew was married to someone else. She held my family's well-being in the palm of her hand. Again I thought of the phone number still stashed in my bedside drawer. How easily I could call and put a stop to everything.

I just want to be with you, Lucinda said the last time we were together, and I wanted to believe it. But I'd heard it before, whispered by a much better liar.

Fearing the shaky grip I had on my resolve, I stopped answering Lucinda's calls. I deleted voicemails without ever listening to them. She dropped by the apartment once and I let her knock until she wore herself out. I could hear her breathing through the crack in the doorjamb, silhouette blocking the light for what felt like hours. She called my name and I turned up the volume on the television until my ears hurt. When she left, I drank the bottle of rum she'd left in my kitchen and passed out on the couch.

The next morning I got up with a hangover so bad it felt like the world was ready to split in two and I'd gladly plummet straight into the bowels of hell. Outside my apartment, a group of birds were chirping fit to wake the dead. Instead of getting up, I rolled over in my dirty sheets and rooted around in my nightstand until I found the magazine I'd stashed the number inside. I opened it and the paper slipped out, fluttering down to land on my bare stomach. I stared at it, bleary-eyed, and contemplated calling right then, but remembered we lived in the time of caller ID. There was a pay phone next to the gas station where Bastien and I bought coffee every morning, though I wasn't totally sure it worked.

Who even used a pay phone anymore?

I threw on dirty clothes and sunglasses and took the truck over, the magazine sitting beside me on the seat, paper slipped neatly back inside.

At the gas station, I bought the largest coffee they sold and a monstrous jelly doughnut that I knew I would not eat. Then I holed up in the phone booth and contemplated my next move. When we were growing up, Milo and I had sometimes used them to dial out to sex hotlines. The first few minutes were always free, and I delighted in listening to the breathy voice of the woman on the other end, begging me to stay on the line. There were a ton of quarters in my pocket, so I stuck one into the machine and listened to the clang and drop of it landing inside the empty belly of the phone. I got through one ring before hanging up and retrieving my change.

"Fuck," I whispered, tossing back some coffee. Cleared my throat. "Fuck, *fuck*."

I put the quarter back in and dialed the number, then waited.

It was a voicemail robot on the other end, but I startled when I realized she'd decided to say her own name. "Donna Franklin," she said, and that was it. The voice was softer than I'd imagined. Higher-pitched, sweet.

The beep sounded, signaling my time to leave a message. "There's some things I think you should know," I said. I paused. It felt like a big moment. "Your wife's cheating on you."

Then it all poured out. A garbled mess of half-truths: I talk-ed about the art show and the animals, mentioned that they'd been slaughtered inhumanely (they probably weren't). Said they were illegally acquired (they hadn't been). Told Donna that if something wasn't done to stop the art show, there'd be a protest (there absolutely would not be). That PETA would get involved. I tripped a little over the word *PETA*, stupefied that a taxidermist would even invoke such a group. Felt like saying the name Beetlejuice too many times: if you weren't careful, you could summon them like devils.

I hung up and hyperventilated for a few minutes. Then I drank my coffee, which had cooled, and got back into my truck and drove home to sleep off the rest of my hangover.

It was easier at work. I focused all my energy on the peacocks. They were gorgeous and shimmering; perfect mirrors. Observing them propped against each other on the metal surgical table, I saw the potential my father had spoken of: their myriad possibilities. By stitching rows of pale blue and green, I was able to reconnect the amputated leg until there was barely a visible mark. I strung copper wire inside their elegant necks, organizing the tail feathers into large, sculptured fans that reflected light like fiery opals.

I posed them several different ways before finally pinning them all together, flipping one of the tails around to the front to block the base of the mount. The beaks were sad little twists that took a lot of coaxing to set. I didn't want them grim and anxious, or terrified like they'd been in the moment of their death. I wanted them icy and regal. I wanted them beautiful.

Perched on a bolted branch of an apple tree, the peacocks were a crowning achievement. Their tricorn heads bent lovingly toward each other, glittering feathers coated with a shellac of protective spray to ward off dust.

When Bastien saw the finished product, he crowed with delight.

"Holy shit. We're gonna make a fortune off these." Brushing the back of his hand along the largest tail feathers, he smiled and tapped one of the clawed feet. Light gleamed off the peacocks' bodies, their plumage draped over them like jewelry.

"We're not selling them." I pushed past him with the cart and cleared a space near the goat, which needed dusting.

"What are you talking about? Of course we're gonna sell them." Bastien grabbed my arm when I went to lift the base. "We need money, right?"

We always needed money. Was there ever a time in anyone's life when they finally decided they didn't? "I don't want to sell these."

"Aunt Jessa, we don't have a choice."

A trio of perfect animals that complemented each other. One on its own was lovely, but there was something about the symmetry of three that made me feel as if the world had suddenly righted itself. Their feathers trembled in the sudden draft of the air-conditioning. "No." I shook my head. "These are mine."

"How are we gonna pay bills next month?"

I considered the fact that my nephew was in the business of murdering things for money. I loved that boy, could still see the little pinched face, doughy smile buried inside the new, leaner, adult one, but it didn't cover up his mercenary qualities. Something very much like Brynn: willing to do whatever it took to get what he wanted. I'd told Donna about the animals, but I hadn't mentioned Bastien by name. He was right, after all. We did need the money.

"We'll figure something out."

Bastien helped me move the mount onto the floor. It sat nicely next to our display of freshwater bass. The light was very good through the front window, but not bright enough to dull the feathers. Different times of day would bring altered colors to the setting. Purple in the midmorning, radiant blue in the early evening.

Bastien pushed a hand through his hair, which looked sparser than usual. "If I get more, can we sell those? That girl from before called back, said she wanted tail feathers to make some kind of Mardi Gras mask."

I'd already gotten what I wanted from the peacocks. Every time I looked at them I felt bone-deep satisfaction, as if a burden had been lifted. I wondered if this was how my mother felt about her own art, a selfish pleasure from forcing the work to give her what she wanted. For a short moment I was filled with guilt, to consider depriving her of that wildly good feeling. Then I remembered the father figure on top of the water buffalo, pale face peeking from the patent leather mask. The gray, bristling mustache fixed above its motionless lip. There was nothing redeeming about it. I couldn't allow it to live.

"I can fix up whatever you bring me," I said, adjusting the base until the feathers got maximum sunlight. They shone gold like pyrite. "I just want these."

MICROPTERUS SALMOIDES— LARGEMOUTH BASS

Here's what you need to do: hold the damn needle and keep your mouth shut.

My mother and I were crowded together on the love seat in our living room, the two of us leaning over a pair of jeans with a giant rip in the crotch. I'd been complaining nonstop since we'd gotten home from school, and my mother's patience had worn thin. Seventh grade had given me a *major attitude problem*, according to my parents. Our father was sick again, gray around the mouth and so sallow he appeared dipped in neon paint. My mother took the brunt of his short temper, swallowing it down as she cooked and cleaned and kept track of my brother and me. She looked haggard, clothes spotted with bits of food and coffee stains.

But how do we hide the seam? This wasn't what I wanted to be doing. There was a haul of fish at the shop, and my father was going to start mounting them that night. I'd never worked on the bass before because he said it was too easy to mess them up, especially around the gills. He tugged on the end of my braid, told me that sometimes girls weren't as steady when it came to detail work. It was odd to hear him say that when I

225

knew that my mother took care of so many sewing things at home. She made our clothes, Halloween costumes, blankets and curtains, Christmas tree skirts. But he was my father and he was always right. I trusted him.

This sucks. I set down the needle, thread dragging across the couch cushion. *Like super sucks.*

What did I say? Mouth shut. She grabbed my hand and directed it back to the fabric. The needle jammed in too hard and stabbed through to my leg.

Jeans were the only thing I wore other than a pair of cargo pants I'd taken from my brother. I hated going shopping, didn't like the dressing rooms with their bright fluorescent lights. My skin looked pocked in the mirror, as if someone had roughed it with a Brillo pad. The only time I liked going was with Brynn. She tried on sundresses, bathing suits, halter tops. I held the hangers and put the clothes away as she dropped them on my head. I watched her in the mirror as she changed, getting glimpses of secret skin, pink and white and soft.

I know you don't like the thimble, but use it.

My mother made most of her clothes. She'd had lessons when she was a little girl from an elderly preschool teacher who lived next door to her family. She'd learned embroidery; how to perfect a stitch, the best way to sew a hem.

Like this?

Not such a big knot. There'll be a lump and it'll be really uncomfortable when you sit.

My father was an expert, his stitches so tiny they were almost invisible. He always said you could tell when a piece of taxidermy was professionally done because there wasn't a single stitch in sight. The rabbits with their plush coats, doves with downy white breasts, even the deer mounts with their slick, oily hair looked pristine. I knew they were piecemeal; had seen him pry them apart, scrabbling with the flesher on the meatier animals, separating the pelts. But when he was done sewing, they were whole and clean again, ready to jump from the table in a wild bid for freedom.

It was well past time for me to learn the fancier stitches, the looped double threads that led behind the tanned skin, but my father had no time for it. He was barely in the shop most afternoons, so sick to his stomach he couldn't be out of bed for longer than an hour without vomiting, or falling asleep upright in his chair. When we asked why he looked so skeletal, our mother told us he had the flu. Only the flu, nothing to worry about. Milo and I waited to catch it, but we never got sick. Not even a sniffle.

Why are we using light blue here? Shouldn't we use gold, like the thread in the seam?

Blue matches the fabric. Because we're patching; it needs to look natural.

My mother didn't watch her hands while she worked. Unlike my father, who couldn't look away from his raccoons and possums, my mother looked around, her eyes flitting everywhere. From her hands, to the magazine held open on the arm of the chair, to the flashing television, and to my face. She made everything look too easy, like it was something anybody could do. That's how she always treated crafts. Simple things that meant nothing, just a way to make something a little prettier. She'd hand-painted mosaic tiles and put them up in our dumpy kitchen as a backsplash. Whenever people came over, they asked where we'd bought them and my mother just shrugged them off. The things she made felt valueless to me. How could I take her seriously when nobody else did? Even she didn't care.

Stew simmered on the stove and she'd made sourdough rolls, my father's favorite. I knew he wouldn't have any of it. When we ate, he stared at the food grimly, as if eating were a momentous, exhausting task.

I pulled too hard and the thread broke, taking some of the frayed material with it. Pieces flicked down onto my lap, meshing with the dog hairs pilled in the fabric of my sweatpants.

You'll have to pull those stitches. Carefully, or you'll wind up with an even bigger hole, and that's the last place you want an extra.

Cutting my eyes over to her in shock, I saw her smile into her own quilting square.

That's gross!

Sex isn't gross, Jessa. Her eyes went back to her work. *I know your father acts like it's the worst thing in the world, but sex is natural and normal. People should be able to talk about it. Even moms.*

No. That's weird.

She laughed at my serious expression. Her throat was scratchy from the cold she was trying to kick. Because she was busy taking care of us and my father, there was no one left to take care of her. She was so congested I'd seen her hack mucus into our kitchen sink while scrambling eggs for breakfast.

Using the stitch ripper, I dug into the knots that were pulling loose from the fabric. The jeans were too short, but I'd gotten them from Brynn last spring when she'd decided they were the wrong style for her. The fabric was pretty wrecked. Everything I ate wound up on my clothes: red Kool-Aid drips and butter from a toasted bagel. There were grease stains from the carport, blood-stains and rips in both knees from wiping out on the asphalt after Milo pulled me around on the skateboard behind his bike.

Why don't we just get you new ones? My mother put her hand on the back of my neck and ruffled her fingers through the short hairs that wouldn't stay in my braid. She caught a snarl and I yelped.

I like these.

You're gonna like lots of things in your life. She finished the coffee. *Lots and lots of things.*

I know what I like.

Milo lay on the rug by our feet, digging into a big Tupper-ware bowl of popcorn. He'd eaten almost all of it and was biting down on the uncooked kernels at the very bottom, licking salt from his fingers. His hair was getting long, which was good, be-cause he'd started to break out on his neck. On his treks to and from the shower, I saw the blotches covering his back, topped with pus, like boils. Brynn kept talking about how cute he was getting, and I wanted to show her that proof, to point out that, of the two of us, I was the one who didn't look like a plague victim.

Before, we'd make fun of him together. We'd ditch him at the house and sneak out the back so we wouldn't have to bring him along when we did things: bike rides, trips to the gro-cery for ice cream. But the past school year, she'd begun talk-ing about him the way she did the other guys from our grade. When she came over, she hung on his arm and tugged at his T-shirt sleeves. She laid proprietary hands on his stomach and leaned her head against his bony shoulder, as if it might of-fer some kind of comfort. Brynn laughed at the stupid things he said instead of mocking him for how dumb they were. My brother was a lot of things, but he'd never been funny.

Thinking about it put me in an even worse mood. It was hard to focus on sewing when I wanted to pinch the back of Milo's neck until he yelled.

Halfway through stitching the crotch, my thumb tore through the paperlike material at the seat of the jeans. It made a hole big enough to fit my hand inside.

Goddamn it. Enraged, I kicked the popcorn bowl. Milo jumped back and knocked a full glass of Coke onto the rug. *Stupid piece of shit!*

That's enough. My mother got up and grabbed one of the dishrags that hung from the fridge handle. She got down on her hands and knees and pressed it to the carpet, sopping up most of the spill. *Go get me the stain remover and a damp towel from my bathroom.*

I purposely ground the buttery popcorn bits into the rug on my way out of the room. Milo scuttled backward on his hands to get away from me.

And don't wake your father! He just got to sleep.

Our parents' bedroom was at the end of the hall. The lights were off and the door was closed. I inched it open, eyes slowly adjusting to the darkness. Their bed was heaped over with quilts, the lumps so high that I couldn't tell which of them was my father's body. I padded across the carpet, carefully avoiding an overflowing basket of laundry that my mother had yet to wash, and eased toward the bathroom.

The shell nightlight my mother had bought in St. Augustine glowed pink along the walls above the mirror. There was a weird noise, some kind of *hyuk-hyuk* sound that reminded me of dogs throwing up on the rug. I stepped inside and turned toward the tub.

My father stood in front of the toilet. The pale line of his back showed the entirety of his rib cage. He was shockingly skeletal, skin pale beneath a smattering of dark hair. He breathed heavily, grunting. At first, I thought he was trying not to get sick by holding it in, like how Milo did because he hated throwing up so much. Then I saw that his arm was moving, just the right one, stutteringly, the muscles in his biceps flexing and releasing spastically.

He was muttering something, words beneath the grunts that I couldn't quite make out. I heard the word *shit* and then I heard it twice more. My father sometimes swore in front of us, in the shop especially when he had messed up something with one of the mounts, but this kind of swearing sounded different. It came from deep inside his chest.

It scared me to hear those strange animal sounds coming from my father. I leaned away and hit the door. The handle smacked against the tile with a loud, resonating bang. My father spun around. He had his hand around his privates, gripping himself. He made a noise halfway between a bark and a cough. When I looked up at his face, I saw that he was crying. Mouth working up and down, he brought his other hand down to try to cover the soft mess of his genitals.

I turned and ran.

I dodged through the side door and into the carport, passing through the living room where my mother still knelt on the carpet. It was raining, and the wind blew leaves and pine needles across the yard and over the driveway. I sped into it, sliding wildly for a minute on the slick walk before righting myself and taking off down the street.

Rain fell into my eyes and half blinded me. I headed for the cemetery, bypassing the gate and launching myself over the chain-link fence. The ground was soft and mucky, and my feet slid there too, but I kept going. I ran between the new graves with their fresh white headstones, through the dripping trees, and past the mausoleum. Rain dashed across the stone benches with their lichen tops, crumbling legs dropping chunks of themselves into the dirt.

I crawled beneath a hedge that surrounded an oak near the oldest headstones. Lightning cracked hard overhead in rapid succession, bleaching the sky. The image of my father's bare back clung to my brain. Rubbing my eyes, I pressed into the sockets until colors swirled there, like fireworks, spangled red, blue, and gold in time with the lightning.

My father didn't talk about sex. He didn't kiss our mother in front of us; didn't hold us on his lap or even hug us too often. I'd never seen him naked. At least, I hadn't before that day, or couldn't remember it. His body was a mystery to me. I couldn't even remember him bathing us when we were little. Once I'd come out of my room wearing just underwear and a T-shirt and he'd yelled at me to cover myself.

I sat for a long time in the cold rain and worried what would happen next. If my father wouldn't want me to come help at the shop anymore since I'd seen him like that, naked and vulnerable. Would he look me in the eyes ever again? I wasn't sure I'd be able to face him at all.

I could hear Milo coming for me from a long way off, kicking through piles of leaves and jumping over downed limbs. He had a very specific way of walking, a kind of short-short-long pull to his step, a shuffling drag that always gave him away. He lost whenever we played manhunt.

Move over. He was soaked through. His Marlins T-shirt was a damp teal and looked like an entire Big Gulp could be wrung from it. *More. Like another foot.*

We sat together but didn't touch. Just huddled there in the brush. He was wearing only socks on his feet. They were covered in mud, the soles so dark I knew he'd have to throw them away. He'd just put a couple of sticks of Juicy Fruit in his mouth and the smell comforted me. It reminded me of home, like the corn-chip scent of our rugs and the cinnamon-apple candle my mother burned at Christmas.

He didn't ask me what happened and I was glad. He knew me so well. I liked that we could sit next to each other and just feel the warmth radiate off one another's bodies. Things couldn't be all bad if I had my brother.

There were three sticks of gum left. He gave me two and then shoved the last one in his mouth. We each licked the sugary stuff off the wrappers and ducked our heads to avoid the drips. The rain petered out, growing softer until the cemetery came back into focus. Everything was green again, leaves overhead dripping fat chunks of Spanish moss.

Both of us walked slowly back through the cemetery, glancing our hands off the headstones and avoiding some of the larger branches that had tumbled down in the storm. The air felt lighter again, humidity lifting briefly. My face was tight from crying and snot dripped down my chin. I wiped it off with the front of my shirt, a sheen of mucus sweeping across the front.

When we got home, I went straight to my room but left the light off. I wasn't sure where my father was. I didn't want to see him, and I wanted to think about it even less. I pulled off all my clothes and left them in a wet, muddy heap by the door. Then I crawled under the covers wearing only my damp underwear.

Low humming woke me. I was bundled in bed, the only light coming from the crack under the door. My mother sat beside me, stroking a hand through my long hair, which she'd taken out of its braid. My eyes were crusted shut from crying. They felt too big for my face, lids swollen.

I fixed your pants for you. Her cool hands felt good smoothing over my flushed cheeks and forehead.

You did?

It's patched. You can wear them tomorrow to school, if you want.

My mother turned on the bedside lamp. Rosy light pooled from the stained-glass shade. The owl peered at me from the belled center of the dome. It had wide eyes and a large brown body, surrounded by green leaves and blue water.

See? All fixed. The hole in the crotch was gone. I couldn't even tell where it had ripped. She flipped the pants over and stuck her open palm into the seat to present where the pockets had separated from the denim. She'd embroidered a twining vine of flowers there, the petals luminous in pink and yellow and blue. I followed the trail with my finger, feeling the slickness of the embroidery thread.

It's really pretty. How'd you do it?

I'll show you tomorrow. After school, okay?

Nodding, I burrowed my face into my mother's lap. She was warm and smelled like the powdery deodorant spray she always wore. I thought about school the next day, how jealous Brynn would be of my jeans. She'd probably want to come over and have my mom teach her how to do it so she could embroider all her clothes.

Everything all right? My father stopped in the doorway. He wore his regular flannel shirt and jeans and had on socks with his slippers. His reading glasses slid partway down his nose. He was normal again, just my dad, not the emaciated corpse I'd seen naked in their bathroom. He was looking at me and smiling. It didn't seem weird at all.

Everything's fine. My mother curled a long strand of my hair around her finger. She was pulling it a little, but I didn't care. I was tired and ready to forget everything, to pretend like none of it had ever happened. My life felt like it was supposed to again. Just like it should, with my mother and my father there and Milo just down the hall, and one of the dogs walked up behind my dad, sniffing at the leg of his jeans.

Can Brynn come over tomorrow and do embroidery with us?

Yes, sweetheart.

My breath came in slow pulls, drowsy, chest heavy. Smoothing down my hair once more, my mother stood up and turned off the lamp. She hung the jeans over the back of my wicker rocking chair and closed the door behind her.

9

Milo and I both showed up at our mother's on the night of the art opening. When I got there, he was already climbing out of his truck, wearing something snappy. That suit looked familiar: the navy-and-gold-striped tie, light blue shirt with the white collar peeking out over the matching navy jacket. Then I remembered. In my mind, there was Brynn standing at his side in a white linen sheath she'd bought at the mall, eyes cutting back and forth at the crowd in my parents' backyard. Worried someone else might have worn her wedding dress.

"You look fancy," I said, clearing my throat. The pants still fit. His shoes were the same scuffed brown loafers he'd worn his entire adult life. It was a miracle the soles hadn't fallen off. "Haven't seen that jacket in a while."

"Right." He darted a finger at me, taking in my clothes with a dismissive sweep. "I can see you spent a lot of time getting ready."

I hadn't worn something dressy. I'd come straight from the shop, still in my dirty jeans and a stretched-out T-shirt with the word *Bahamas* faded to crackling red bits across its front. My plan was to go inside and try to talk some sense into my mother. I had a tiny glimmer of hope that she'd listen to me, maybe see what she was doing was hurtful to the people around her. That maybe she'd hear me and decide not to go through with the night. I wasn't sure what good my phone call to Donna had done. I hadn't heard from Lucinda either way—not about the show and not about what I'd said regarding her cheating, either. There wasn't any way to know what would happen, not without calling again.

We started up the walk, overgrown with weeds, some sprouting up through the brick pavers. The flower boxes outside the front windows were full of moss and plants so far dead they looked like giant spiders, blackened vines twisting upward, trying to escape.

"Thought Bastien was gonna take care of this." I kicked a fallen palm limb out of the walk before ducking under the trellis. Black, mildewed gunk dripped from a corner of the eaves, leaching stains into the peeling paint. "Isn't that what he's here for? To help Mom?"

"I would say it's mutually beneficial. Besides, he's been too busy at work to handle all this shit. You know that."

"Right." The last time I'd seen Bastien, he'd been carrying a black Hefty bag into the back of the shop. He hadn't opened it to show me what was inside, but it was still moving. He was bringing more and more live fare back to the shop. It was beginning to feel like a slaughterhouse. "Where's Lolee?"

"I dunno. Probably with Kaitlyn."

"You don't know?"

"I've been at work."

I doubted that very much. More likely he hadn't checked in with his daughter for a few days and didn't like the fact that

I'd brought it up. I wasn't in a very good mood either and didn't have time for his pissy attitude. Our dad had constantly been on Milo's case about the lack of time he spent with Lolee. *Do you know a single thing about your own daughter? Do you know you missed her recital? Is this the kind of man you want to be? The kind of father who only pays attention to himself?*

Our father, who ignored Milo most of the time.

"She's been spending too much time with Bastien," I said, stepping back when Milo threw open the screen.

"What's that supposed to mean?"

A strong waft of cooking grease hit me, making my stomach rumble.

"And when she's not with him, what's she doing? You know what can happen when kids are left alone all the time," I said, thinking of Brynn and the swell of her stomach when she was only five months pregnant with Bastien. She'd looked like a preteen with a basketball stuffed beneath her shirt. Milo had seen it too. He'd been with us in the hospital. He knew all about how easy it was for your teen years to evaporate; gone forever, no way to get them back.

"Don't tell me how to raise my kids."

"Don't answer me in clichés," I replied, shoving past him into the house.

Only the blue glow of the television set lit the living room. It was always on, no matter what time of day. My mother liked it as background noise, said it made a house feel homier when she could hear people talking.

The hallway was full of newspaper and bits of tissue. Lucinda must have been over, helping my mother package up any

239

last-minute pieces. I imagined her over at the gallery, putting finishing touches on atrocities that shouldn't see the light of day. Or maybe not, maybe Donna had done something about it after all. I itched to call again, one last-ditch effort, but I figured I'd save up that stress for handling my mother.

Milo picked up the remote and switched off the TV. The room went dark. "What the hell do you want from me, Jessa? I'm doing my best."

I didn't believe that for a second. He was doing the least he could, especially when it came to his daughter. "I'm just saying, Lolee needs a parent. God knows that's not Mom right now."

"Shut up, Jessa. Just . . . shut up."

"Both of you shut up, you're giving me a headache." Our mother poked her head through the doorway. "I heated up a pot pie and threw some of those tater tots you like in the fryer. I put garlic salt on them." She turned and walked back through the kitchen. "Jessa, will you help me get ready?"

My mother had never once asked me for help getting dressed. I followed after Milo and snagged a paper towel from the rack, filling it up with tater tots and taking them with me into the bedroom. I hadn't eaten since that morning and thought I could use the fortification, though I was already feeling queasy.

She sat at the stool in front of her vanity. Her back was toward me, revealing the low zipper of her black satin evening dress. The band to her bra snicked around her torso, the soft skin over her ribs dimpling around the elastic. Her head was cleanly shaved this time, nearly glistening in the light from the ceiling fan fixture. The room was toasty-warm and smelled familiar: yeasty, like the bedclothes my mother seldom washed.

"Zip me. Then we can do the other stuff."

Alone with her in her room, I felt the beginnings of a panic attack flutter in my chest. Because I hadn't known what else to do, I'd brought my father's letter with me. It sat in the back pocket of my jeans, folded up, feeling like it wanted to burn a hole through the fabric.

There didn't seem to be any good way to bring it up, no specific opener that wouldn't immediately upset her. I wasn't used to saying difficult things. We didn't do that in our family. It was one thing for us all to process my father's suicide; it was another for me to present my mother with the last words he'd ever written. Words that weren't even addressed to her. The letter hadn't said specifically to keep everything to myself, but the contents made it seem like they were for me alone. All that duty. The vulnerability he'd shown. His overwhelming sadness and need.

She dug through the drawer in her vanity, grabbing a flat tin and a small paintbrush. I looked for the makeup, waiting for her to produce her stash of Mary Kay pale pink palettes, but that was it. No blush, no mascara. None of the eyeliner that always wound up smudged under her lids after a long day chasing after us or cooking for my dad.

She wriggled her shoulders at me impatiently, knocking the flap of the dress open wider to reveal another pale section of skin below her bra. I set my napkin full of tater tots on the bed and hurried over. The zipper was hard to grasp with my oily fingertips, and I left behind salt granules on her neck. She'd missed a tiny wisp of hair in her past few shavings. It peppered the base of her skull like a tiny soul patch, gray and wiry. It reminded me of Dad's hair. I wondered, if he were still alive, whether they'd have started to look more like each other, the way couples often did when they got really old. I touched the light fringe of it and imagined it was his mustache.

"Oh, that stupid piece." She handed back a pair of nail scissors. "Could you get that for me?"

A single snip and the hair was off, leaving just a dark smudge of stubble. For some reason, I couldn't stand to toss it. I stuffed the pinch into my jeans pocket.

"What do you need?" I asked, brushing some stray dog hairs off the back of her dress. I still wasn't ready to talk, though I'd had weeks to come up with something. I knew if I could say the exact right words, I wouldn't have to show her my father's letter. Something heartfelt, maybe, that would show her how I was hurting. That way we wouldn't have to deal with whatever fallout was going to happen at the gallery. Whatever Donna had decided to do.

She uncapped the tin. It was full of oily, bright-colored paints in tiny pots: teal, indigo, fuchsia, orange the neon of a nacho cheese Dorito. She dipped the paintbrush into the brightest red and swirled it there, handing it back to me the same way she'd done with the scissors.

"I want you to paint it. My head, I mean." Some dripped off the tip of the brush and landed on her dress. I swiped up the dot with my finger, using the cleanest edge of the paper towel to blot the excess. It left behind bits of white linty residue on the black fabric.

She held up a picture torn from a magazine. It was a full page of stained glass, light pouring through the colors like a geometric rainbow. "I want something like this."

I stood there, holding the paintbrush and staring down at my mother's pale scalp. "Mom," I said, speaking carefully. "This is extremely weird. All of this is very, very weird and it's making me uncomfortable. I would like you to stop."

"It doesn't have to look perfect. I just want the colors." She uncapped some ChapStick. It was a very yellowy old tube that smelled like VapoRub. I was positive she'd owned it since before Milo was born. She smoothed it on in concentric circles until her mouth looked tacky with it.

"You're not listening to me." I held the paintbrush in front of me, red end ready to drip again. "I don't want you to do this show. I think it's a bad idea, for you and for our family. It's upsetting, especially the stuff with Dad in it."

My mother groaned. "If you're not going to do it, just give it back."

"Fine." I decided I could talk to her while I clown-painted her bare head. It was bizarre, but I could get through it. I set the brush against the base of her scalp and drew a bright red line up the middle, bisecting her skull.

"Was that really so difficult? Think of all the times I did things for you and Milo." She leaned forward and I doubled up on the red line, nearly pressing her face down against the vanity. "Driving you places, cooking, cleaning up. This is just a couple minutes of your time."

My mother had done everything for us. The letter poked from my back pocket and all I could focus on was the feeling of it there; my father's hand in his exacting print. My name at the top written tight and controlled. How he'd ended it with the word *love*, something he hardly ever said when he was alive.

My mother told me she loved me constantly, said it so often I wondered how she could possibly mean it. *I love you*, please pass the butter. *I love you*, could you get the laundry from the dryer? *I love you*, I am going to hurt you, but *I love you*. Just remember that.

I dug the brush down into the tin and smeared a red heart onto the left side of her head. The oily slickness of the paint and the smoothness of her scalp moved the brush along. I felt myself relaxing into it, the way I did when I was piecing something together in the shop: sculpting a nose, perfecting the tiny, intricate stitches on rabbit pelts. I smeared blue circles near each of her ears, dipping indigo, then violet, the orange and yellow mixing together to make a nearly radioactive triangle at the spot over her brow. I created a pink starburst in the center, as if I were parting hair. I almost enjoyed it.

My mother sighed and leaned back into my hands. "Remember when we used to do watercolors out back on the porch? When you guys were little?"

"Yeah, I remember." It hadn't been fun. Brynn dumped an entire cup of water on my work after hers fell into a puddle on the corner of the porch. We were eight years old; Milo had just turned seven and had the chicken pox. He couldn't come out of his room—Brynn and I were going to slip the pictures under his door as get-well cards.

Those memories no longer gave me pleasure. Instead, there was a dull, constant ache, like a rotting tooth that had broken and needed to be pulled; a sharp fragment that I kept touching with the tip of my tongue. Every slide over the memories left behind the coppery taste of blood.

"I'm excited for you to see my art," she said. "I worked really hard on everything. I want my family there."

"Please don't do this." My voice broke and I paused with the brush pressed below her ear. "It makes me feel sick. I can't stand it."

"I'm sorry, Jessa. It's happening."

That was it. She'd left me no choice. I pulled the letter from my pocket and handed it to her over her shoulder, watching her reflection.

"What is this?" she asked.

"Open it."

She unfolded it and I stood rooted behind her, wishing I were the one who was dead. That seemed easier. To be gone, no longer dealing with the stress and trauma of managing my parents.

I read it over her shoulder, watched her eyes follow the cramped text down the page. That single-spaced letter that felt more like a list of demands. Ways I had to behave. Things I had to do to ensure our family's welfare.

She reached the end and looked up at me in the mirror. Then she ripped it in half; ripped it again, again. "This is garbage."

She'd taken the last memory of my father and destroyed it. "Why did you do that? It wasn't yours!"

Pieces littered the floor and the vanity. That last *love* at the bottom of the page; I'd never see it again. Gone forever.

"I miss your father, but I'm also very angry with him. He was a control freak. So uptight that he couldn't ever let things go." She met my eyes in the mirror. The glass needed to be

245

cleaned. There were streaks filling up the oval, making the two of us look like specters. "Sometimes I wish he were still here so I could have the satisfaction of shooting him myself."

"Is this what missing feels like?" I still held the paintbrush, globbed with acid green. "Mutilating memories? Making everyone else participate in them with you?"

She tilted her head and the brush skimmed the edge of her ear, dripping green down into the shell. I wiped it out with my finger and scraped it against my jeans.

"Your father was an asshole." She shook her head, eyes tearing up. "What he did to this family, to you, is inexcusable. That he would kill himself and let his own daughter find him like that. To leave a letter? To force you to bear that kind of burden. It's monstrous."

I was still holding the paintbrush. It dripped on the floor between us. "I just want all of this to stop. No more talking, no more gross art."

She slapped the top of the vanity so hard it upset a framed picture of Bastien and Lolee. "We have to deal with this." She reset the picture and sighed. "When you don't deal with things, like our family, people hurt themselves. They hurt each other. Look at what your father did. He loved you, and look what he did!"

"Dad had cancer." I jabbed the brush at her reflection. More paint flung and hit the mirror, leaving behind bright spatter. "He shot himself because it was too much to bear. And now you're going to show some strangers a replica of him that makes his whole life seem like a joke. People are going to *think* that's my father. And it's not."

246

Her hand snaked backward between our bodies, gripping my wrist so hard her fingernails broke the skin. "Your father was a lot of things. He was a good dad to you kids and I loved him, but what he did was shitty. And what Brynn did to you and Milo was shitty."

When I tried to yank away, she squeezed tighter. I couldn't feel my fingers. "Stop it," I said. "Stop talking." The brush pressed between our bodies, leaving paint smears on my pants and on her dress.

"This has gone on too long, and part of it's my fault for not making you deal with it. I had my own things that were hurting and I let your wounds fester. You and your brother."

"If you won't stop this, I will," I said. "And you won't like it. And I don't care. *Fuck*, I don't care!"

Straining backward, I finally broke free. I landed on the side of the bed and rolled downward onto the floor. The paintbrush jabbed into my belly, nearly impaling me. My mother tried to help me up, and I shook her off, half crawling to the door until I was able to pull myself up against the dresser. Bits of my father's ruined letter stuck to my sweaty palms.

She called after me as I lurched down the hall, but my head felt too full of static to stay another second. Milo sat on a stool at the counter. There was a napkin tucked into the front of his collar, covering his tie.

We looked at each other. He stood up and kept staring, the napkin dangling, then falling down onto the table to cover his plate.

"What the hell is going on?" he asked. "You gonna tell me what that was about? Did you just threaten Mom?"

"Fuck you. I have to go." I yanked my shirt up over my shoulder. The neck had pulled out wide and it lay strangely askew, as if I'd been attacked.

"I think you should stay," he said. "Let's get it all out in the open, right now."

I grabbed my purse and left.

There were four beers left, and then there were three. I drank each one perfunctorily, not even tasting when it hit my tongue. I'd stopped off at the convenience store before driving out to the lake, buying the cheapest beer they had. Brynn had loved shitty beer. She'd loved sugar cookies and sweet tea and those little red strawberry candies that elderly women always kept in their purse. Shitty candies, for sure. Brynn had been shitty. My brother had been shitty. My parents were shitty. I was the worst one of all, the shittiest one.

The air was the driest it had been in months. Still humid, but bearable. It was the kind of weather we'd always liked when we were kids, when going outside and staying out was our best option. Away from our families. Me, Milo, and Brynn just riding our bikes, and later driving around in Brynn's car with the windows down.

I wedged the can between my legs. Then I closed my eyes and listened to the drone of the cicadas in the oaks. Though the park was secluded, I could hear the steady buzz of the nearby highway. I wondered what life might have been like without Brynn. The decisions we'd made had wrecked us, keeping me here permanently, still attached to her, no matter how hard she'd tried to separate from me.

The last few sips were lukewarm and tasted like spit. I swallowed them anyway and cracked another, leaning back on my elbows on the wooden picnic table. I'd picked the one closest to the dock, sitting out on the lake like a splinter lodged in a fingertip.

It had been over an hour since the art show was slated to start. At least an hour, probably longer. I hoped Donna had done something. Stopped it. But who knew what had happened? Probably it'd just gone on as planned. I stared out at the lake and let myself feel real maudlin. I thought about starting everything over again, curling back up in the womb and getting a do-over, a reprieve from every bad decision I'd made in my life.

Once I drained the last beer, I walked the length of the dock. Stumbling on one of the older planks, I slapped my face a few times to try to sober up. I thought of my mother, of my brother, of the things people would know about my family before the night was over. I thought about Lucinda and hoped she could forgive me. Maybe she and Donna would work out their differences. I could almost imagine it: Donna, who looked so much like me, starting all over again with Lucinda. Making it work. She could use her carpentry skills to build them a giant bed where they could cuddle up together and have a million gay babies. Lucinda could forget she ever even met me.

"Fuck you, Donna Franklin."

Sweat blossomed under my arms and along my back. Staring into the cattails, I wished for a flashlight so I could call up the green glow of the gator eyes again. I knew it wouldn't be too long before someone showed up, and then I'd have to go back to reality. Taking off my shoes, I sat down at the edge and dangled my feet in the water. They looked fishy white beneath the surface, algae slinking along the tops.

Red and blue lights flashed out across the water. I looked back at the reeds, hopeful, but no eyes shone back at me.

MOUNTING

CANIS LUPUS FAMILIARIS—
DOMESTIC DOG

In the second-floor women's room, Brynn yakked up half a strawberry Toaster Strudel. She lay slumped over the toilet seat, the same one that nearly all the girls from our high school had sat their bare asses on.

She heaved again, a dry, hiccupping burp that her body seemed to feel more than expel, ribs jutting against the lip of the bowl as her back bowed. *I'm dying. I've got the super flu.*

No, you don't.

What else could this be? I'm so fucking sick. When she heaved again, a tiny bit of drool ran down her chin. There was some jelly from the Toaster Strudel in it; a lick of bright red that looked like blood.

Behind us, the door squealed open. I turned in the stall so that the heft of my backpack blocked most of Brynn from view. Two underclassmen stood in front of the mirror and poked at their dark, crispy bangs, sharing a tube of pinky-orange lipstick and blotting grease from their foreheads with brown paper towels from the dispenser.

Brynn's T-shirt had slipped up high enough that I could see the underside of her old gray sports bra. She usually wore the kind of underwear they sold at Victoria's Secret during the semiannual sale, stuff full of scratchy lace and underwire and inset mesh that let nipples play peekaboo.

She held back until the warning bell rang and the girls spilled out into the hallway. Then she heaved again, a desperate, choking sound. I rubbed her back and gathered the sweaty hair away from her mouth, sweeping it behind her ears. When she finally quieted, I yanked a long strip of toilet paper from the dispenser and rubbed the spit and vomit off her chin.

Have you taken a test yet?

Tears that had dripped during her dry heaving collected and trailed dark streaks of eyeliner down the side of her nose. Dragging a corner of clean toilet paper beneath her eye, I gathered as much of the runoff as I could. The paper was cheap. When I pressed it a little harder beneath her right eye, she hissed and backed away, knocking into the toilet bowl.

We can pick one up today. Then you'll know for sure. I knelt down and smoothed her shirt, which was still rucked over her bra. My butt knocked into my backpack. I felt like a turtle, crouched down on the sticky floor. A scrap of toilet paper was stuck to the bottom of my sneaker, and when I brushed it off, I nearly overturned myself.

I don't wanna know. She rubbed at her eyes, which were raw from where I'd scraped them.

Don't be stupid. You already know.

I helped her up and put her back together. She was like a wobbly, limp-limbed doll. I brushed her hair and reapplied her lip gloss, spritzing her body spray on her neck. The drops ran down into her cleavage and dotted the front of her T-shirt.

There was only one more period before school got out for the day, a trigonometry class that I was failing and Brynn was barely passing with the help of other people's homework. Instead of walking in late, we went straight to the parking lot. Her shitty car was parked next to the chain-link fence that surrounded the high school.

I took her keys and helped her into the passenger side, knocking fast food bags onto the floor. We drove directly to the gas station closest to my house, the one where we sometimes got beer when the right cashier was working. There was only one kind of pregnancy test on the shelf. The box was dusty and it wasn't a brand either of us had heard of, but we bought it along with a couple of Cokes and some Twizzlers. I heated up a decrepit-looking hot dog in the microwave, slathering it with nacho cheese and relish. Brynn bought a pack of Marlboro reds from the bored clerk, a woman so leathery her skin looked like something tanned in the shop.

We rolled down the car windows to let in the stagnant breeze. I drove slowly through the neighborhood while Brynn steadily consumed everything we'd bought. Biting off either end of a Twizzler, she stuck it in one of the Cokes and held it out to me for a sip.

It always tastes better with a Twizzler straw.

Yeah, it's good. Like Cherry Coke.

I put my free hand on her bare thigh while she fed me more sips, driving past houses that all looked the same. Repeating yards, carports, pollen-dusted mailboxes. When we got to the lake, we sat in the parking lot with our feet hanging out the windows of the car. It was so hot that most of the moms sat back beneath the trees, ignoring their kids while they splashed around and screamed.

I drank my Coke until the Twizzler was soggy and couldn't reach the soda. Then I gave it to Brynn, who'd already finished hers and was slurping away at the hot dog. She sucked the cheese-and-relish mixture from the ends and took bites from the side of the bun, like she didn't want the meat, just the juice of the thing.

Casey's going to be pissed. She picked at the bread, balling up bits of it and throwing them out the window.

Casey can suck my dick. I turned on the radio and punched in the cigarette lighter. Then I unwrapped the box from its cellophane and lit one for Brynn. *Plus you don't even know yet. Not for sure.* There was still hope, even if it was minuscule. Maybe she did have some weird flu.

Nodding, she tipped the cigarette so ash fell out the window and not onto her legs. Casey and Brynn had been fooling around for the past couple of months. They weren't really dating, and I couldn't see him getting mad about a baby. I actually couldn't see him reacting to anything at all. He was the kind of moonfaced guy who barely spoke more than two words at a time, spending most of his free time playing video games with his friends from the soccer team.

No way Casey would care either way, but there was something else. The other thing. A memory that floated through my mind whenever I saw Brynn and Milo standing too close together. I'd been sick with mono a few months earlier. I was bored out of my mind, and Brynn came over most nights to watch TV and keep me company. When I fell asleep, it was just her and Milo, hanging out for hours. They had their own inside jokes about movies they'd watched without me. They drew on my face with markers while I was passed out on the couch, oblivious. They went out for pizza and both ordered pineapple on it, which I hated. They drank our father's beer in the carport and got drunk enough to play tag in the graveyard next door. Later I'd seen something on the floor of his bedroom. A baby-pink polka-dotted bra with lace trim around the cups, poking out from beneath a pile of dirty shirts. Underwear I'd seen a thousand times. Brynn loved polka dots.

Slurping down the last of the soda, she threw the hot dog end out the window. It hit the car next to us and left a greasy ring, a circle of shine on the same level with the driver's head.

I'm gonna pee, she said, picking up the plastic bag and walking off toward the public bathroom.

It was too hot to stay in the car, so I took the leftover Twizzlers down to the water. Even the little kids had moved out of direct sunlight. They lounged on old bedsheets next to their mothers, sucking Capri Suns and tearing into oranges, eyes dulled flat by the heat.

I kicked off my sneakers and took off my socks, balling them up and stuffing them into the toes of my shoes. Cracked mussel shells and bits of stick poked into my sweat-softened soles. I focused on that painful feeling and tried not to think about what a baby would mean. A baby, when I was bleeding and maybe already staining the crotch of my too-wide jeans.

The dock was old and needed new boards in most places. The wood was going soft and mulchy along the edge and there were splinters. I walked down to the bench at the end and sat with the package of candy in my lap. Watched the light shine off the top of the water like slivers of aluminum foil winking in the sun.

Brynn had already applied for college. Lots of different ones. I'd seen the forms on the kitchenette table in the trailer, plopped down on the Formica, gathering food stains. I had some forms of my own, too, but I wasn't considering them. Of the two of us, Milo was the one who was actually interested in that shit, even though he was a grade behind us. He was looking at some of the same places as Brynn. I thought of the two of them, packing up their things and moving out of state. Abandoning me while they moved into an apartment together. Made new friends, attended classes. I'd be left with my father in the back of the shop.

Brynn stomped over to me, boards vibrating down to the end of the dock. I'd chewed a hole in my lip, biting at the dead skin until it was alive with blood, leaking down the pressed seam of my mouth. She dropped the pregnancy test. It hit the wood with a flat smack that knocked drops of pee onto my forearm. I wiped the mess on my jeans.

Guess I'm gonna be a mom, she said, and laughed.

The test had two little pink lines slicing through the center. *Looks like it.*

Unless I go somewhere. Take care of it.

Birds called in the trees near shore. The kids behind us finished their snacks and splashed back into the water. From somewhere out of sight, the humming drone of a boat filled the air with white noise. Brynn held her shoes. They were leather sandals that striped her feet tan and white. Her toes scrunched down into the dock, the nails coated in sparkly blue nail polish. I'd never wanted a baby in my life, but now I stared at Brynn's stomach and thought about the price of losing it.

You should keep it, I said, looping my arm around the back of the bench. There was still a droplet of pee on my skin and I left it there; let the sun cook it into my flesh. *We'll work it out.*

Walking to the edge of the dock, she dropped her shoes. One flipped over, sole bright with green gum.

I'm gonna be the worst mom ever. She took one giant step forward and dropped into the lake. Water splashed up onto the dock, leaving dark wet prints in starburst patterns.

10

The cop didn't arrest me, but he did make me perform all the sobriety tests in the middle of the parking lot. He took my driver's license and pointed me to the lines, refusing to let me leave until he'd done a full background check. After I listed the alphabet backward, twice, he told me that my truck would be towed and I was responsible for getting another ride. He stood there, flashlight beaming migraine rays into my skull, while I tried to remember how to operate a cell phone. The cab took twenty minutes to arrive.

When I reached my apartment, I walked inside and crawled onto the couch. My hangover was so intense that my tongue had dried to sandpaper in my mouth. I rolled around on the cushions until the sun came sliding through the window blinds, and then I abandoned the pretext of sleep altogether, trying not to think about what would happen next.

Milo showed up fifteen minutes later. He was still wearing his suit, though it was considerably rumpled. The shadow of his incoming beard was so thick it looked fake, like something he'd put on as a prop.

"You want some coffee?" I tossed some shit off the only other chair in the room. Milo threw himself down on the couch, and I perched on the edge of my seat. The apartment smelled like old food and rot. I hadn't taken the garbage out in a couple of weeks, and there was the cloying, syrupy scent of meat gone rancid permeating the air.

"I'd like a beer."

I hadn't expected that response. "What time is it?" I asked. It couldn't have been later than seven.

"Morning. Barely." He stretched out his legs until they nearly knocked over the coffee table. "And I don't care. Just gimme a fucking beer."

I went into the kitchen and rolled my shoulders, trying to relax. There were a couple of Millers stuffed in the door beside some ancient bottles of salad dressing, a two-liter of flat Coke, and an expensive jar of fancy champagne mustard Lucinda had left behind. I grabbed the beers and wondered if she ever thought about that stupid mustard. It cost more than fifteen dollars a jar, mustard that made your mouth tingle when you slathered it on crackers. It was an awful waste of money, and I couldn't help but be charmed by the fact that she'd buy something so pointlessly impractical.

Scrounging around for some kind of snack to settle my stomach, I unearthed a bag of stale chips in the back of the cabinet and brought everything back out to the living room. Milo hadn't turned on any of the lights. He lay flat on the sofa, legs extended over the arm. He'd tossed his shoes onto a pile of my dirty clothes.

I handed him one of the beers and took a long pull of mine, emptying a third of it. A tension headache brewed behind my eyes. I set down my beer on the edge of the coffee table and unplaited my braid; it loosened incrementally, a painful kind of pleasure. My hair still smelled like shampoo. I draped it over my face and inhaled.

"So you're not even going to ask?"

Milo stared up at the ceiling, as if he could see through the cheap speckled popcorn coating and into the steadily blueing sky above.

My fervent prayer was that Donna had pulled through to cancel the event. Milo showing up seemed to confirm that possibility, though maybe it was wishful thinking on my part. One voicemail didn't mean shit in the grand scheme of things. I thought of my mother with her painted head, standing next to the figure of my father she'd posed atop the water buffalo. The boar with its wounded sides, our family Christmas lights pouring and puddling on the ground like gore.

"Worse than we thought?"

He hummed, rubbing his cheek against a stained throw pillow. Lucinda had spilled a whole glass of wine on it and I'd never cleaned it up, so the fabric smelled like hell. I needed to throw it out.

"Never even went inside. The whole place burned down."

I nearly upset the beer into my lap. "The fuck are you talking about?"

"Yep." He shook his head, pressed the bottle to his temple. "Huge. Place smelled like burnt rubber."

Maybe he was lying to make me feel better.

Shrugging, he dug at the beer label with his thumbnail. "All of it, gone."

No, it couldn't be true. It was too convenient. A massive fire, suddenly obliterating all of my problems. All of my family's problems. Lucinda's problems. Donna's too.

"How'd it happen?"

"Who knows." He was biting his lip, hard. The skin looked ready to break open. "Unless you have something you'd like to tell me."

I did not want to tell him anything. Definitely not about the phone call, and not about Bastien murdering any of the animals. "I'm not even gonna respond to that."

We sat in silence for a minute. Birds chirped away outside, annoying as hell. But I couldn't let it go. It bugged me. My own brother, thinking I would commit arson. "You really think I did that?"

"I don't know what to think."

He dug the remote out from between the couch cushions and turned on the television. He muted it and surfed channels before stopping on a local news station. A reporter was on location at the gallery. Smoke drifted from the roof and wafted into the street. Yellow tape blocked traffic, orange cones set up to allow only news vans and fire trucks through. At the bottom of the screen, the ticker read: LOCAL GALLERY BURNS, ELECTRICAL FIRE SUSPECTED.

"Was anybody hurt?" Everyone we knew was supposed to be at that opening. My mother, the kids, Lucinda. All the people from the neighborhood. I couldn't imagine being trapped in a fire with all those taxidermied animals. The chemicals from their skins—the tanning fluids, the formaldehyde—would fill the air like a poisonous, smothering blanket.

"I don't know." Milo covered his eyes. "I don't think so. They didn't find anybody in the building. Mom's traumatized. Vera had to drive her home and give her a Xanax."

"Where are the kids?" The last time I'd seen Bastien, he'd

been tallying the register. There was gel in his hair and I remembered thinking how dumb it looked, spiking up the front.

"Lolee's over at Kaitlyn's. I haven't seen Bastien."

My stomach burbled so I stuffed a handful of potato chips into my mouth to try to tamp down the acid. There was a subtle, acrid smell coming from beside me, and I realized smoke and chemicals were embedded in the fibers of his jacket.

How had things gone wrong so quickly? Of all the things my father had wanted from me, the number one thing he'd stressed was everyone's safety and security. Not their happiness, not their wants, but that word again—the one he'd used against himself. *Need.*

What did my family need from me? What was it that I was supposed to give them?

The news switched over to a weather report. I turned off the TV and straightened some clothes piled on the floor next to my foot. Then I took the beer from Milo's slack hand and grabbed a semi-clean afghan from the closet in my bedroom. He was asleep before I'd even finished covering him up. Every wrinkle and vein around his eyes stood out, a burst blood vessel prominent in his nose.

I stared down at Milo and understood I was looking at a stranger. This was a person I'd allowed to grow apart from me, someone I'd never tried to understand out of the context of our relationship as children. I'd expected my family to understand me as an adult but somehow thought they'd always stay the same—a family encased in the skin I'd stretched over them, ill-fitting and irregular.

265

I called Bastien. He picked up after the second ring, and the relief I felt when I heard his voice was like a live thing scrabbling in my chest. I told him that he needed to get some animals into the shop immediately. He needed to find his sister and bring her there too. That I needed it all done by two that afternoon. When I hung up, I took a shower and put some clothes in the wash. I ate some toast. I brushed my hair.

The coffee in the cabinet was so old I worried it might poison me, but the smell as the first drip landed in the dirty machine made my mouth water. I chugged three cups, drinking until my body turned jittery. Woke up my brother by setting a cup on the table closest to his face.

He cracked a lid and peered up at me.

"Get up and go to work." I nudged the coffee in his direction until a little spilled over the lip. "I'll take care of the rest."

Bastien brought a muskrat, a coyote, two red-and-yellow parrots, a possum, a couple of raccoons that looked like they'd been scraped directly off the pavement, mallards, squirrels, and another peacock that was jaw-dropping in its iridescent splendor. When I stroked its tail feathers, they fanned magnificently, a beautiful spot in the dim gray of the workroom.

"What do you think?" He scratched at his chin and dug loose a zit. It sprouted blood and left a trail leaking down his neck.

"Not enough, but it's a start." I tapped one of the squirrels with a gloved finger. It was quickly settling into rigor and

266

was probably useless. I'd need him to go out and get us some more, but I was hesitant to send him out for anything live. Recently I'd noticed a pinched look to his face whenever he came back with something fresh. He didn't like it as much as he pretended; he was just very good at hiding his feelings. Very Morton of him.

Lolee snorted and rolled over on the cot, turning to face the wall. Bastien had picked her up at the bowling alley. She'd been hanging out at the snack bar with a senior from the high school, a boy with a rattail and a bottle-blue pickup truck with lightning bolts painted freehand on the sides. Bastien looked ready to strangle somebody, most likely Lolee, who kept growling at him whenever he walked too close to where she lay pouting.

"So should we gut these? What's first?"

"We head over to the gallery. I want to see what we can salvage."

Bastien laughed. "That stuff is wrecked. Toasted crispy. No way you're gonna be able to use any of it."

"We don't have enough here. Not for what I'm thinking. We can use some of the pieces from the front of the shop, but we're going to need more."

"I'll go clean out the truck."

I pulled an apron out of the clean stack at the back of the shop, and on second thought, grabbed a couple more. Lolee was still facing the wall, so I slapped her on the butt. She yelped and turned over, frowning ferociously at me.

"Wow, you look like your momma when you do that," I said. "Stop acting like a little asshole. Let's go get your grandma's shit."

Lolee and I loaded up on cleaning supplies and grabbed a supersized box of Hefty bags, my tool kit, tarps, and some paper towel rolls. We threw everything in the back of the truck when Bastien pulled around.

On the drive over, we rolled down the windows and listened to the afternoon traffic. None of us talked. We just sat and smelled the cool of fall finally coming on, everything in the air permeated by smoke. I thought about my mother and her art showcase. It was hard to imagine what she might be going through. I still found the work repugnant, but it had been hers. The one thing solely hers since my father died. To lose that must have felt catastrophic. So why did it take a catastrophe for me to recognize that fact? What had I thought was gonna happen when I'd decided to unleash hell?

Yellow tape fluttered on the sidewalk in front of the gallery, but there were no police cars or fire trucks. We went right up to the front and tried the door, which was unlocked.

"Come on," I said. "Let's get this over with." We picked up tarps and loaded them with supplies, carrying them with us into the building.

A heavy odor of chemicals and char hung in the air. "Careful," I said after Lolee walked across a bad piece of flooring. It creaked underfoot, giving the room a fun-house vibe. Standing water soaked the corners, full of wet ash. Lolee touched the wall and scowled at the black mess that came off on her hand, scrubbing it on her track shorts. I was glad to see she'd put on sneakers instead of her usual flip-flops. There were too many nails and sharp bits of debris that might scrape up bare feet.

At the center of the room, Bastien and I crouched near the skeletal remains of the water buffalo. Most of its exterior had charred. The insides were melted, gleaming wire wrapped around the remaining bones. Enough solid work remained inside to leave the animal standing like a half-drowned thing; the kind of black, gunky slop that resembled prehistoric remains in the La Brea Tar Pits. The replica of my father in the patent leather suit had liquefied and dripped down the side of the buffalo. A black puddle stained the floor.

Bastien dug a finger into the disintegrated fur. He wiped it off on his T-shirt. "Not sure we'll be able to salvage anything from this wreck. I mean, it's all pretty wet. Forget field prep. It'll mildew. Fast."

Ceiling insulation had dropped and scattered between the pieces. It was difficult to tell burned building from taxidermy. An elk lay supine near the door, as if it had fallen trying to escape.

"Just gather everything you think could work." I stepped over the melted pile and looked around. "Even little pieces. Skins, mounts. Skulls, especially."

I avoided shards of bone and scrap metal as I crossed toward the back. Lolee found the carcass of a tiger hidden beneath a fallen chunk of drywall. The back half of it was burned crispy black, but the front was still a vibrant, wild orange. It had a face like it wanted to bite the world.

"It smells bad." She grimaced. "Like dead animal stank."

"It *is* dead animal. Put it with the others."

She dragged it across the floor, its oversized paws collecting gunk from the muck. I picked up bits of antler and stuffed them into a plastic bag before shouldering my way into the fallen doorway of the back office.

All of Lucinda's paperwork had dwindled down to kindling. Her pinup comics were gone, but there was no glass on the floor, no remnants of the frames. I put my palm against the wall, remembering the first time we'd kissed in the office. How her whole body had swallowed mine. It felt good. Safe. I'd hated that because it didn't feel how I expected romance to feel: stressful and kind of blood-soaked, a constant power struggle.

I salvaged a deer skull, an alligator skin, what might have been part of a flamingo. Beneath the remnants of the desk there were several layers of thick, clear tarp. When I lifted a corner, water ran down the side and poured along my jeans, dripping into the top of my boot. A metal box covered whatever was below. I didn't remember seeing it before. It was very large and blocky, and it took up all the legroom beneath the desk. When I lifted the metal frame, I was confronted by the yellowed snarl of a carnivore. Kneeling there in the ashy mess, I dug my hands into the fur of a grizzly pelt.

I yelled for Lolee and Bastien. When they came in, I gave them each a corner. "Keep it up high, way off the floor," I said. The skin was heavy and very good quality. "I don't want it dragging in all this shit."

"Still smells." Lolee lifted hers high, higher than the two of us combined. The muscles in her biceps stuck out and trembled from the effort.

"Smells better than you." Bastien had trouble keeping his end over his waist. The bear's head drooped, snout nearly landing in a clump of charred, gummy paperwork.

"Goddamn it. Focus, please."

Outside smelled fresh and clean. Stars pinpricked the sky. Memories slammed into me. Being outside, the three of us. When it had still been good to be the three of us together.

"Your dad and mom and I used to go to this place to watch shooting stars." We put the bearskin into the back of the truck, alongside the garbage bags of stuff Lolee and Bastien had collected. "Paynes Prairie, just outside Gainesville."

"You could actually see them? Shooting stars?" Lolee petted the animal's head. It looked like an angry teddy bear in the yellow glow of the streetlight.

"Oh yeah. They're crazy bright because it's so far from city lights. We'd lie on the hood of your mom's car and hang out for hours, just watching the sky drip. There were gators out there too, and they'd come out of the water to watch us watching the sky."

"Gross," Lolee said, climbing into the truck. "I hate alligators. They look like dinosaurs."

"They're not that bad." Bastien tossed another bag of burnt parts on top. "How big were they, though? Big as here?"

"Bigger, definitely." I threw my tool kit on the floor of the front seat and hugged Lolee's neck. She yawned and leaned into my arm. I smelled her smoky hair, pressed my cheek against it. "Meteor showers. If it was clear out, they rained down over us for hours."

I didn't tell them how we drank cherry Slurpees mixed with vodka, ice and burn that left our mouths red and raw. Or how high we got, smoking right there on the hood, passing it to people on nearby cars. The stars were so low-hanging I imagined I could pluck them if I really wanted to.

271

That last time we drove out, everything had felt fuzzy and wonderful. I'd fallen asleep in the back seat afterward and woken up halfway home, my hair tangled around the seat belt. Rubbed the crust and sleep from my eyes. Saw Brynn and Milo holding hands, fingers laced together across the center console. She'd leaned over and put her head on his shoulder, smiling in a weird, soft way I'd never seen before.

"There's still a lot left to do." I threw a clean tarp over the bear and lashed it with a bungee cord. "If we hurry, we can stop and get dinner."

URSUS ARCTOS—BROWN BEAR

All the flowers had wilted in the heat, except for the silk ones. I stared at the cluster of silvery-gray asters in Brynn's hair and fought off the urge to pick out the seed pearls glued along the faux leaves. There were so many bobby pins jammed in her scalp that the flowers would probably be stuck there permanently.

You look so pretty, like an old-time movie star.

My mother was curling her own hair, leaning over the mirror. Brynn sat on the cushioned stool in front of the vanity. Her dress wasn't zipped all the way up the back, and her bra straps showed bright pink against the open triangle of tanned flesh.

I look like a pig. A sweaty, gross pig.

Vintage, my mother said, pulling the wand out of her hair and unraveling a curl. Smoke wafted from it. She'd already hair-sprayed the whole mess twice. *Like Greta Garbo.*

Brynn and I were very hungover. She was slurping from a bottle of Coke, and every time she set it down, she picked it right back up again. There was a lot of dark liner around her punched-looking eyes, which only exacerbated the circles.

My mother wore a dress she'd bought at Goodwill a few years prior. It sagged on her, khaki burlap belted in the middle with a green piece of ribbon. I had on my dirtiest pair of jeans

273

and didn't plan on changing anytime soon. They'd be lucky if I put on a bra.

Thumps came from outside, where the band sound-checked their instruments. It wasn't anybody decent, just a couple of Milo's old high school buddies who still lived in town and played out of a garage on weekends. They covered classic eighties ballads. I thought I heard the strains of "Total Eclipse of the Heart" coming from Dustin's guitar, but couldn't be sure. Bastien was screaming somewhere in the house. He was two and hated strangers. We had a house full of people nobody knew.

Can I have a sip of your Coke?

Brynn passed it to me over her shoulder. I took a few careful sips and managed to keep it down. It tasted too sweet, like someone had tipped sugar into the bottle.

I can't focus. Brynn pressed a tissue under her eye, trying to mop up some of the excess liner. *Can someone go shut him up?*

My mother sprayed a fat sausage curl, so crisp it looked as if it had sprung from a mattress. *Can I give him some juice?*

Hell, give him the rest of this Coke if it'll quiet him down.

I'll find him those animal crackers he likes.

She opened the door and left us there, hallway full of kitchen sounds and the steady hum of the vacuum.

He's gonna get icing all over his little suit, Brynn said. She rubbed at her neck. I stared at the ring that Milo had given her, barely a chip of diamond. I'd helped him pick it out at Sears. After he proposed, he came home and told me she was so happy she cried. I didn't really believe that. My brother was so overjoyed that he couldn't stop smiling. Who was I to tell him that the thing he thought was truth was really just a woman trying to manufacture a normal life for herself?

Do you really care? I lay back on my parents' bed and rolled onto my side, propping my head up with my fist. *Icing? Who gives a shit.*

She sighed and her bangs fluttered a little to the side, showing a big red pimple cropping up on her forehead. *Oh fuck.*

You can barely see it. I was lying; it was huge. White-capped and angry-looking, it could burst at any second. *Just put your bangs over it.*

I can't, it feels all weird now. I need to pop it.

That's a bad idea, I said, but she was already pressing it between her thumbs, biting down hard on her lip until her teeth were stained crimson with lipstick. She yelped and a bright splat of pus and blood hit the vanity mirror. A chunk of waxy buildup sat in the middle of it, an island of gore.

Are you kidding me? I pressed my face into a pillow, wanting to laugh at the absurdity of the situation. The love of my life popping her humongous zit in my mother's vanity mirror while she prepped herself to marry my brother. And here we were, pretending it was normal. Normal for me to feed her shots the night before, licking sweat from her neck. Totally acceptable to dance together at a club with some of her work friends, grinding to the bass notes until I could feel her dampness on my leg. Completely fine for me to fuck her in the back seat of her car later that night, Cheerio crumbs stuck to my ass as we sweat and cried and came, over and over.

What was normal? Normal for Brynn was marrying a man. That was what she wanted; that was what she'd get.

Help me, she said, waving. *The blood's gonna get on my dress.*

Grabbing the tissue, I pressed it hard to her forehead to stanch the blood. *I told you not to.*

Well, it's too late now.

We didn't look at each other. I watched my hand where it held the tissue, the cake of her makeup scrubbing off, showing the little line of freckles that dotted her skin, cinnamon-colored. I'd licked those freckles, tasted them to see if they were sweet and thought, yes, they were.

What if I throw up, right in front of everybody?

You won't.

I look fucking gross. She picked up a tube of lipstick and uncapped it before recapping it.

You look great. Lifting the tissue from her forehead, I waited to see if the blood would well again. It didn't. *You know you always look good.*

You're the only one that thinks that. She grabbed my wrist, fingers trembling. *I don't know if I can do this.*

It had been simple enough to set in motion. Like splashing my hand in the lake and watching the ripples spill out, farther and farther, until I had no control over them anymore. Brynn had a kid and needed someone to take care of her. She wanted a husband, stability. Milo loved her, I knew that. He would do anything for her. They'd been dating for only a few months before he told me he was ready to marry her. It was painful, but part of me wanted it too—her to feel secure, to have everything she needed. How could I complain of hurt when I was getting what I'd asked for?

Of course you can do it. Picking up the face powder, I dabbed it over the pimple, which was still red but not as severe as before. She closed her eyes and I lightly trailed the brush over her cheeks and down her nose, across her chin. *This will be easy.*

Her skin was pasty and damp from the alcohol she was still sweating off. She smelled like her fruity perfume and the very strong odor of her body, which curdled the edges of my heart. Everything inside me cooked at a low boil.

How do you know? She leaned back, and the spiny weight of the flowers in her hair stabbed through my T-shirt. *Tell me how you know.*

Smoothing gold shadow across her lid, I worked to cover the mess of black liner and tiny veins that had sprouted after her third time puking in my bathroom sink. *What's so hard about it? Just stand up there and repeat the lines. If Milo can do it, you sure as hell can.*

Brynn smiled up at me and her dimples deepened into crescents and I loved her, I knew, I loved her more than I'd ever love myself. Uncapping the mascara, I pulled the wand swiftly along her lashes, which were already so long and curled and golden that even a small amount made her look like a doll blinking.

What if he winds up hating me?

I laughed and blew against the mascara, trying to dry it. *He loves you. Don't be dumb.*

Yeah, now. Now he loves me.

Her blush was too dark. I dabbed at it with a tissue, tenderly, apples pinkening to a soft glow. I would not say what I felt, which was that we all loved her a little too much. That Milo was a smart choice because he had a job lined up at the dealership and that he was kind, and always giving, and that he would never ask her to be more than what she was. He was something I could never be for her, which was a husband, something her mother would envy. I knew if she stayed with Milo, she'd always be close, that I'd never have to lose her, even if I couldn't have her in the exact way I wanted. That was what mattered to me. Never losing her. Never losing what I wanted.

The one woman I'd ever loved. The person I'd allowed to see me at my most vulnerable, the only one who'd really known me at my worst and still wanted me around. A person that I found beautiful, even when she was terrible. I looked at her, looked hard, and she looked back at me, and I knew. She didn't want me to say it. Brynn wanted something else.

There. I closed the powder and leaned back, looking at her face. *All done.*

I pulled together the sides of the dress and zipped her up. We split what was left of the Coke, me taking the last few sips. She kissed me, leaving lipstick on my tongue that tasted like crayons. I left her there, in my parents' bedroom, wearing her dress from the mall, with beaded flowers in her hair that looked like they came from someone's homecoming corsage.

Bastien threw the rings on the floor as he walked in the procession. His little blue suit was stained with the icing from his cookies, white smears on his gold-striped vest. Everyone who wasn't in the wedding sat perched on folding chairs in the middle of our backyard. Everything was green, as if all the plants had soaked in the moisture and you could have wrung them out like washcloths, if you'd wanted. The overgrowth had been tamed a bit for the event, but there was still a wild amount of vines creeping up the fencing along the back. Our yard was mostly patchy weeds that got mown down to look like a lawn. Leftover pallets lined the left-hand side of the yard. The birdbath to the right had been sprayed out, and a few jays were squawking in the bowl of sun-warmed water. The plants were neon-fluorescent in the light. I wanted to remember everything, exactly as it was in that moment. Never, ever forget it.

There we were: my parents, Brynn's mother and her brother, who sat on his hands and tried not to bite his fingernails, Vera Leasey and her husband, who gnawed his wad of chew, spitting surreptitiously into a red Solo cup every few minutes, the guys from the cover band, some kids we'd gone to school with, and the pastor from Vera's church, who was officiating. His white, fluffy hair made him look like a stressed-out brood hen.

We held flowers that attracted bugs. Clutching our bouquets, we swatted and let the petals fall in wilted clumps on the grass. It clouded up and threatened rain for over an hour, but the sky refused to break open.

I wished that it would rain. I glowed greasy with oil and thought I'd pass out, hungover, chest aching and hollow. My brother was tall and handsome in his suit, looking suddenly very capable—the kind of person who should be getting married, someone who could handle a job and bills and responsibilities, despite his lackluster past in all those capacities. Brynn was powdered enough that she looked remarkably dry in the smothering humidity, sweet and pink and pretty. They each repeated the vows, holding hands like they'd been doing it for years, not going out on dates with Bastien in tow, like a tiny prefab family.

Their faces met chastely over the dying bouquet. Brynn's mouth left a pink imprint on my brother's lips that stayed for the rest of the evening. Their faces kept meeting, over and over again. They kissed while we ate fried chicken, grease coating their fingers, forks quivering with bites of macaroni and cheese with homemade croutons. They kissed while they danced on a makeshift floor that my father had assembled out of plywood in the center of the backyard, slowly swaying to the terrible music. Everyone drank pink champagne out of plastic flutes from the Dollar General. My father made a toast and so did Brynn's mother, who swayed drunkenly in her heels, crying, until someone helped her into the house.

I'd thought it would be like watching myself with her, but it wasn't. My brother seemed like a person I'd never met before. Stronger. He was as far away as she was, the both of them clinging to each other while they created something that had no space for me in it.

Milo kept his arm around Brynn's waist. They laughed together, heads ducked to whisper in each other's ear. When they left, they did it quietly, sneaking out the side door to his car. They drove off in the orange and purple evening light, heading toward the downtown Marriott where they'd stay for two days and three nights while my parents watched Bastien and they swam in the hotel pool.

I stayed in my folding chair and drank sweaty bottles of beer, ripping off the labels and sticking them to the top of the card table. Reeling from everything I refused to feel and still stuck in the clutches of my hangover, I burrowed down into myself. No one tried to talk with me. People continued dancing on the patio, hanging from each other in the flickering lights of the tiki torches. It was a warm night. Everything smelled like grease and citronella.

My mother, sweaty from serving food and dancing with my father, slipped a hand across my neck. She handed me a piece of cake, marble chocolate and vanilla from the Publix bakery. The bride-and-groom topper had sunk into the top before it was cut, making them look like quicksand victims. Bastien carried the plastic couple around like a trophy, sucking on the bride's feet.

I dug my fork down into the cake, which was still half-frozen. It bent back the plastic tines until they almost snapped. I took a bite of frosting and it sat slick on my tongue like unsalted butter.

11

I put Bastien in charge of any work up front and spent a week sifting through the detritus of my mother's art show. We laid out items on newspapers, tender bits of wing and thin, blackened legs, spindly and twisted from the heat. Every countertop was covered with parchment paper, tissue blotting up liquid, continually replaced with fresh sheets.

I felt like the administrator of a burn unit as I made the rounds. I flipped torsos, changed bandages, dabbed at seeping wounds that bled yellow and black liquid from tanned hides. The aftershocks of trauma lined up in pans on my tables. Most of the work was demolished, but I saw promise in the parts I tended, carefully applying fresh dressing to the boar's neck and snout, bleaching the dank crust off charcoaled bone matter. I reduced the remains by relegating any extraneous material to the garbage can: burnt copper wiring, soaked cotton padding, any foam forms that had twisted to crisp bits, adhered to bone like hot glue.

The smell was overwhelming. I made Lolee wear a mask when she helped, a white medical thing that scooped over her nose and kept sliding down her chin. Like a surgeon's assistant, she helped with the grisliest work—handing me cotton swabs or changing out linens, turning over pelts and heads on the damp floor.

We brought in fans that stirred the papers, creating breezes heavy with the odor of dead things and smoke. I wasn't sure I'd ever get the smell out of my nose or my hair. My clothes I tucked into garbage bags when I got home, hoping that after a few washes they'd smell normal again, but not placing any bets. When I scrubbed my face in the shower, I tried to focus on the freshness of the soap. I blew my nose often, sinuses so blocked I felt I might suffocate.

Bastien was good on his word. He collected new species for me, sometimes still fresh off the pavement where they'd been struck, others so deeply set in rigor I wondered if I'd be able to save the limbs, solid as statues. We kept them in the freezer while I worked endlessly on the burnt parts, trying to salvage pieces for my mother, who wouldn't leave the house.

She wouldn't talk to anyone. Not even Vera, who stood perplexed in the driveway, cradling a potato casserole after my mother refused to answer the door. I hadn't seen her either, but I hadn't tried to visit. I didn't exactly know what I was doing and wasn't sure how to broach the thoughts I had about her work and my feelings. It seemed smarter to wait; to make sure I knew the exact right thing to say before I went to the house. I didn't want a repeat of my last visit. I didn't want to hurt her more.

It was hard to leave the shop. I was there before the sun came up and stayed long after it set, subsisting on fast food that Bastien left out for me. I'd sit behind the counter in the moony glow of the front window, eating my cold burgers and fries as

I flipped through the day's receipts, tallying up the money that had come in and the bills left to pay.

For the first time in my life, I considered what it would be like to sell the shop. What freeing up my time would mean. I'd never lived anywhere else. There'd been only one neighborhood, one grocery store. The same gas station beer. Brynn had done it—just taken off without ever looking back. If it was something she could do, then I could do it too. But there were things holding me at home: family, and my memories. Nostalgia carved out my insides, padding my bones until my limbs stuck, splayed. Frozen in time, refusing to live.

Lolee brought in a food dehydrator and we stuffed in bits of hair, tiny rabbits' feet, birds' wings. We took turns toasting things with a hair dryer, close enough that the fur started smelling a different kind of burned. I took the bearskin rug to a dry cleaner down the street, the one who used to press my father's shirts. I kept the skin shrouded in a tarp until the cleaner came out from the back of the store; Mr. Gennaro with his overly white dentures, shorter even than me, skin leathery and wind-chapped.

"I have a special request, if you're up for it."

He nodded. "What is it? A sleeping bag?" He pulled out a handkerchief from his back pocket and scrubbed at his nose so hard I worried he'd give himself a nosebleed. "Smells like campfire."

"Something like that." I pulled free the head and sat it on the glass countertop. Mr. Gennaro stood there staring at the bear until I cleared my throat and put the plastic back down over its eyes.

"That's not something I can clean."

"Could you try?" When he didn't answer, I nudged the bear's head forward again until the snout poked under the tarp, a dark, quivering dog nose snuffling for treats.

Mr. Gennaro reached out and touched its cheek. He trailed a fingertip up the bristled fur, scratching at the hair behind its ears, as if trying to soothe it.

"Maybe. Be expensive."

"Just see what you can do."

"No guarantees." But he had that look in his eye that my father always got when he was appraising a really nice piece. I left it there on the counter, Mr. Gennaro fondling it, checking the teeth like a dental hygienist performing a cleaning.

Sitting with a singed piece of squirrel tail in my hands, I looked down at the ratted fur and couldn't understand what the hell I was doing. What was I trying to save? There were still so many things I didn't understand about what my mother had done. Things I didn't understand about myself and my feelings about all of it.

I threw out the animals that were too far gone to save.

"Goodbye," I told the chipmunk my father had mounted behind the wheel of its own small car. It sat looking up at me from the heap of trash, eyes accusing, legs singed to black lumps. "Sorry I couldn't do more."

I was bringing my mother a sampling of the pieces we'd salvaged. An assortment of specimen boxes sat sandwiched between furniture rugs in the bed of my truck. The sky was fairly clear—only a smattering of stringy clouds dotted the tree line near the horizon—but I decided to be cautious and put plastic sheeting down over everything. I pinned that down with bricks, then piled another blanket on for added security.

Bastien thought I'd lost my mind and said so, repeatedly.

"You sure you're okay?" He pulled another brick from the landscaping near the front walk and dusted it, sweeping free the dirt that clung to the bottom before setting it carefully alongside the others. "You want me to go with you or something?"

"Nah. It's fine."

"If that's true, why are you lining the bed of your truck like a goddamn bird's nest?"

I grabbed another brick and set it next to the one he'd just placed. "Just shut up and help me."

Once everything was done, Bastien handed me my keys. "I'm gonna go pick up a shipment. Got some ferrets and guinea pigs, some white mice."

"Tell me we're not pilfering dead boxes from pet shops now."

"Of course not." He smoothed the dirt where the bricks had been with the heel of his boot, divots all lined up next to each other, missing headstones in a graveyard. "Maybe gonna check out a couple penguins today. That something you'd be interested in?"

His eyes slid to mine and I was the one who looked away, ashamed to admit that I did want them very badly. "Maybe. Depends on the condition."

"Oh, probably pretty fresh." He grinned. So much of his happiness, I was learning, came from getting things for our family. He wanted to help provide for us. It was very sweet, in a morbid kinda way.

This was the new normal. Me and my nephew talking animal murder so we could keep the store afloat. I did like the idea of getting some penguins in, though. My inner child remembered all those SeaWorld field trips and couldn't wait to look at the bodies. Make my own dioramas. I bet I could do better than the theme park. Just needed some Styrofoam for snowbanks.

He slapped the tailgate as I took off down the road. It was October and the kitschy decor Halloween shops were back in business, one having taken up residence in the old T. J. Maxx where my mother had bought all the Easter dresses she hadn't sewn herself.

All the lights were out when I pulled into my parents' driveway. It was dark, Florida dark, which meant lots of bugs. Twilight was coming on quick, and I didn't want to leave the specimen boxes out in the truck, where God only knew what would start gnawing at them.

Knocking at the front door didn't elicit a response and neither did ringing the doorbell, which still played the tune my mother had set for Dad's last birthday. I knocked louder and called her name, hoping she'd at least turn on the light, but there was nothing. As I walked the perimeter of the house, I passed the scraggly flower boxes next to the front windows, burrs clinging to the cuffs of my jeans as I made my way to the backyard.

Grass had grown past my calves, weedy to my knees in some spots. White-lined moths fluttered as I waded through. It was past the point Bastien would be able to get to it with the push mower. It needed something industrial. Maybe a lawn service. What would it be like when my mother could no longer take care of herself? Would she live with me or Milo? Who'd handle the house and take care of her basic needs?

I tried the sliding glass door, but it was locked. Pressing my face to the glass, I peered inside but was unable to see anything other than the flashing blue 12:00 from the DVD/VCR combo. The heat from my breath fogged up around my mouth and made a Santa beard. I swiped my initials in the damp.

There was one last place to try: my bedroom window. The weeds were the highest there, wicking wet and full of mosquitoes. I felt along the ledge, looking for the place I kept the bamboo shard I'd used to sneak out with Brynn in high school. AC slipped through the tiny crack in the window and sliced at the warm skin of my cheek. I got it open a half inch, then a half inch more, finally yanking it wide enough to fit my whole head inside.

The room was musty. Nobody had used it since Milo and Brynn lived there with the kids. There was always an uncomfortable dampness to my old bedroom. Rot permeated the rugs. When I went over for dinners, I avoided the room as if its deterioration might infect me with the worst parts of me I'd left behind.

I slid the window all the way open, stumbled back through the wet mess of piled leaves, then jogged awkwardly up to the house and jumped onto the sill. My body wedged halfway inside, the ledge digging hard into my stomach. I used my arms to jettison myself through the opening. Falling into the room, I tried to brace myself against an old bookshelf, which promptly broke under my weight. I slid forward on a tidal wave of cheaply assembled MDF and books I hadn't read since elementary school.

I kicked a few of the books beneath the skirt of the bed, then opened the door to the hall.

"Mom?" My voice echoed and bounced back at me off the terrazzo. "You okay?"

It took a while to find her. She'd holed up in the master bathroom, sitting alone in the shower. When I snapped on the light, she flinched and ducked her head.

I crouched next to her and groaned at the strain it put on my back. "Is this what we're doing now? Hanging out on dirty bathroom floors?"

Strong body odor wafted from her armpits, powdery mother aroma, magnified by the smell of old underwear and used socks. Her favorite nightgown barely clung to one shoulder, nearly revealing her breasts.

Sir Charles sat beside the toilet. He'd seen better days. One of my father's stuffing jobs, completed in a big hurry after the dog had passed away from an obstructed bowel. His face was squinched and snarling, though I knew my father had been trying for sweet. It was too hard to make pets look friendly and alert; better to make them sleep, curled up in a little faux bed. But my mother had wanted the dog preserved that way and my father had done it for her, to make her happy. Even though he had a hard time saying the words, he tried his best to do things that showed he cared. I tried to keep that memory fresh in my mind whenever it felt easier to hate him.

"I've been working on some things for you." I brushed a hand across her head. The hair was growing back: a stark, shimmery silver that lit her scalp like tinsel. I wondered if she was cold. Tipping her face toward mine, I took in the make-up caked around her eyes. There was dirt or possibly smoke creased in the wrinkles of her neck.

"Let's get you a shower," I said. "Then we can talk."

It was hard getting her up off the floor. I sat her on the closed toilet seat and started the water, icy spray hitting my arms and spritzing my face before slowly heating up. I left the curtain half-open, trying to steam the room.

When I pulled her nightgown over her head, she leaned into me, body very soft and small. Her breasts pressed against my torso. The skin on her back was withered, so thin I felt I could break through her flesh with my fingertips. How strange, to think of the woman who raised me as defenseless as a baby.

Under the spray, she wilted further, until her chin nearly touched her chest. I soaped up a washcloth I found under the sink, one of the flowered relics from my childhood, faded into a muted gray from repeated washings. I scrubbed her head delicately, using care around her nose, sore and red around the nostrils. I washed under her arms, but between her legs I left for her, turning away for privacy.

She cried silently, tears and snot mixing with the water that sprayed out in wild directions from the lime buildup on the showerhead. I took the washcloth back from her and let her stand there, spray running down her face and chest, soap bubbles collecting in the bristly hair between her legs.

What was there to say? No lie would be believable. "It's all awful, I know," I said, squeezing the back of her neck. "It won't be like this forever." She turned and sagged into me, her body slick and still soapy.

"You can't know that." She nuzzled into my collarbone. Her head felt heavy, solid as a bowling ball. "I put everything I had into that work. It was the only thing that made me feel good."

Sorry was the only word that seemed right, but I couldn't get myself to say it. *Sorry* never fixed anything. It was just a word, no action behind it to make life any easier. My father's letter had been peppered with apologies: *sorry I failed, sorry I'm doing this, sorry I couldn't be the right kind of man.* What *was* the right kind of man? Was it a person who upheld his responsibilities? If he were truly sorry, wouldn't he have seen how he was about to destroy his family, and stopped?

Remnants of mascara dotted the corners of my mother's eyes like slimy dead gnats. "Your father abandoned me." Her mouth moved against my shirt, the fabric muffling her voice. "He was controlling and repressive, but he was my husband and I loved him. We built a life together and now he's gone. I've got nothing of my own."

Her breath was sharp and bitter. I let her sourness wash over me, took it in and didn't flinch. Took the foulness as my due, as she'd once taken it from my father. She was small and hurting and I loved her. I pulled out a clean white towel from the closet and bundled her in it. Sir Charles sat on the floor beside the toilet looking scraggly and damp, ringed with water from the drips falling from the shower curtain. I picked him up and handed him to my mother, who stuffed him under her arm like a teddy bear.

We went to the living room. For the first time in a while, the television was off. The animals sat propped on the shelves, dim and quiet, as if everything but us was asleep. I turned on the lamp my father kept beside his recliner, the one with the glowing green shade he'd called the tortoise.

Put on the tortoise, he'd say, shuffling newspaper pages, searching ads for old taxidermy pieces he could remount and flip. *Can't see shit in this house.*

Sitting her down on the edge of the chair, I wrapped the towel around her shoulders and used the edge to dry her face. Sir Charles sat beneath the tortoise's green glow, staring at the two of us with wide, glittering eyes. Water pooled beneath him on the wood, soaking into the paper coasters my father always liked to take from restaurants.

I held her hands as I squatted in front of her. They were smaller than mine and much, much softer. "What else do you want to talk about?"

"You didn't know your father."

"No," I replied, squeezing rhythmically, so I could focus on that sensation and not the one of my stomach falling through my body, down onto the floor between my feet. My body, piecemeal. "No, I didn't know him, I guess."

"And you don't know me, either."

Our faces were very close. I could see the tiny black pores that lined her nose. Her nostrils were crusted around the edges and beginning to flake. Hair grew near the corners of her mouth, bristly and dark. When she sighed, I could see that one of her front teeth had a white stain near the top. How strange, to single out pieces of the body I'd never seen before on a woman I'd known all my life.

"Do you know me?" I asked, cataloging the small defects in my mother's skin. The tags of flesh near her right eye, which was somehow lower than her left. A dark blotch lined her collarbone, what might have been a bruise or a birthmark. There was a mole on her cheek that looked nearly purple in the green light.

"Not now." She squeezed my hands again, rubbed her thumb against the center of my palm. "I knew you when you were little."

"Nobody can ever know another person."

There were times I'd thought I knew people. Brynn, who I'd loved more than anything. The other half of me. My father, a man I'd adored, someone I'd considered to be the strongest person on the planet. We spent so much time looking for pieces of ourselves in other people that we never realized they were busy searching for the same things in us.

She gently stroked my eyebrow. It was thick and overgrown, an inheritance from my father. "I'd like to know more about you, if you'd let me. I know it's hard for you to open up. To share things."

Her towel drooped and hung near one dark nipple. I tugged it back up for her and secured it beneath her armpit.

"Nobody knows me. I don't even know me, Mom."

"I don't know me, either. Nobody knew me but your father, and he's gone." The whites of her eyes were so red I worried I'd gotten soap in them. "I don't know if I can start over again."

"Nobody knew me but Brynn. Sometimes I wonder if she actually did, or if I told myself that so I'd feel less lonely."

My mother smiled. Her teeth were dark from years of coffee, chipped, pitted in the corners. Eyeteeth flat and no longer carnivorous. "Your brother knows you."

"That's not the same thing."

She shrugged and wiped at her nose, which was dripping again. "It's all intimacy. Just different kinds."

I knew who Milo used to be. But now I couldn't name his favorite movie. When was the last time he'd told me about a date he'd gone on, or if he preferred dogs or cats? Where did he like to eat lunch? Love was a thing that needed constant care. Our intimacy was an uprooted plant, shriveled and withered.

My legs had cramped while I hunched down in front of her. I sat down on the rug and picked at it; it was full of crumbs and needed vacuuming. Everything needed cleaning. I wanted to go around with a trash bag and start tossing things. All the dusty, unused stuff we didn't need anymore.

"Intimacy means giving up parts of yourself to someone, even when that means they can hurt you very badly. But sometimes we let them because pain can feel good too." She pressed her palm against my cheek.

I yawned until my jaw cracked. "I don't wanna try all the time. I'm just tired."

"That's okay." She petted my neck and smoothed back my hair. "It's hard to talk about the ugly parts. How we can be that terrible and still worthy of love."

"I don't want to feel anything." I leaned into her and she cradled my head against her chest. It was awkward and uncomfortable. I willed myself to go numb, to fill with white noise.

"It's scary to need people."

Burying my face into the crook of her neck, I felt my teeth denting the wrinkled flesh. I found it hard to speak without choking. "I do like feeling pain, feeling hurt about Brynn," I confessed, hating myself for saying it. "I like it because it's mine and it's the only thing I have left of her. If I stop feeling bad, then she's really gone."

My mother's fingers dug into my braid. I let myself cry then too. Both of us clinging to each other, the towel falling around her waist. Sir Charles stared down at us, little paws soaking ruin into the woodwork.

GOPHERUS AGASSIZII—
DESERT TORTOISE

We found the condoms in the lot behind Brynn's trailer. A whole box of them, unopened, like they'd just fallen out of someone's shopping bag. I'd seen condoms on TV before but never in person. Brynn told me her mother used them, but she wasn't sure where she kept them. She thought maybe the guys her mother dated were expected to bring them over. I didn't know if my parents used them, but it wasn't something I'd ask.

Let's blow 'em up, like balloons. She shook the box, held it overhead and shook it again, slapped it against her ass like a tambourine. *Fucking condoms!*

It was too hot to be outside. It was early August and we were smothering. I was breaking out bad on my back and wore a gray flannel to try to cover it, roasting myself alive. I'd ditched Milo at the 7-Eleven when he wouldn't share his Slurpee with me. He'd find us eventually, but for now it was just the two of us, which was better. Brynn was hanging on him a lot, touching him too often. Throwing her arm around his neck, poking at his underwear when the band popped up out of his shorts. It made him blush and then she'd laugh at the color in his cheeks, leaning in to giggle in his ear.

Brynn held the condoms out to me. *Let's do this. It'll be fun.* *Someone will see,* I said, crossing my arms. *We'll look stupid. We should find your brother. He'd like this.*

It put me in a really bad mood to think about the two of them together. I wasn't happy with anything; too broken out, my hair greasy from hormones. Brynn looked comfortable, snug in her cutoff jean shorts and white cami top. I could see her nipples through the thin fabric, and I told her so, but she just shrugged and wiggled her chest at me. I knew if Milo saw her he'd freak out and get that look on his face that always meant he was thinking about sex. It bothered me for a lot of reasons I couldn't reconcile. Brynn was mine, but Milo was mine too. I hated the idea of the two of them having each other without me.

No, let's just do it. You and me.

Yay! She skipped around in the grass, kicking up dirt with her flip-flops.

We drank hose water, pulled around from the front of the trailer to the back, where we could hide from prying eyes. Brynn's mother wasn't home, but she hardly ever was. She'd met a new guy and he was already living in the trailer. Brynn said he didn't have a job and he just sat around watching TV in his boxer shorts. It sounded gross to me, but Brynn said all the men her mother let move in were like that. The kind of guys who made her want to lock the bathroom door when she showered.

Fill them up with water. She held up one of the condoms, bloated and slick with lubricant. That was what Brynn had told me the shiny stuff was: *L-U-B-E* spelled out at me like I was an imbecile.

Like the Ripley's Believe It or Not! *of jizz.* Brynn shook it and it jiggled, so full it looked ready to burst.

That's nasty. I can't even look at it.

Get used to it. How else are you gonna have a baby? Gonna need some baby batter, dummy. She tossed it lightly, hand to hand, so slick she nearly dropped it. The hose had wet her cami, and now I could really see through it, tiny nipples hard as pencil erasers.

I don't want a baby.

Brynn snorted. *Of course you do. Everybody wants a baby.*

Well, I don't.

Most kids grossed me out. How babies were made especially disgusted me. I never wanted to think about having to do something like that with a boy, letting him lie on top of me and shoot weird gunk inside my body. It sounded like a horror movie. Made me sick even thinking about it.

I could smell the funk from my own crotch and underarms, got whiffs of the greasy mess of my hair, like old french fries. I didn't want to be in the field tossing condoms around. I wanted to swim in the community pool, spit chlorinated water from the gap between my front teeth. In the pool, I could feel light and weightless and like everybody else.

Taking a deep gulp of hose water, I held it in my mouth and wished it didn't taste so much like melting rubber. It was the tail end of summer and nothing felt good. Already my mother had put out the fall harvest leaves, the wreath on the table ringing the large white pillar candles we were never allowed to light.

Four, five, six condom water balloons stuffed into an old plastic Easter basket that Brynn had unearthed from beneath the trailer. Their place was a dump, so full of trash all the time. They never threw anything away, and it always smelled like pulpy, rotten wood. Usually I didn't mind. It was so different from my house and it reminded me of Brynn, how she loved things so much she couldn't bear to throw them out. But I was thinking of Milo, how he would find us soon, and then Brynn would ignore me to giggle at him, and it made me want to bite something. It was too hot. I just wanted to be alone.

Okay, we're ready. Come on.

I followed her back to the empty lot where we'd found the box, and she sat down with the basket of improvised water balloons. They jiggled obscenely. I waited for them to pop, stuffed next to sprigs of sharp plastic, but they stayed whole and glistening.

Wish I had a Coke. I threw myself down on a patch of grass and picked at some of the V-shaped weeds, pulling them apart and tossing the remnants to the side. *Or an ice cream Snickers.*

No, you don't. Remember last time?

I remembered. Brynn and I and some of our friends were hanging out while we waited for boys' track practice to end. Chocolate from the ice cream had melted onto my hands and face, but Brynn hadn't told me. She'd just licked at her strawberry Popsicle, holding the dripping mess away from her white overalls. Milo found us then and told me it looked like I'd gotten shit on my mouth. Brynn laughed so hard I thought she was going to piss herself. She'd given Milo the last of her Popsicle, and he'd crunched into it with his front teeth. The two of them had looked so cozy, like they knew everything about each other—every stupid secret, every bad idea. My skin felt tender and porous, as if their actions had actually scraped my flesh.

That was the funniest thing ever, she said now, laughing. *I wish I could see it all over again.*

Talking about it made me want to dig a hole in the earth so I could bury myself. I dropped the weed remnants and grabbed a rotten sliver of oak. I picked at the wood, the bits turning to dust in my hands, lodging up under my fingernails and turning my skin chalky.

What should we do with these? Throw them at passing cars?

There's not really anyone around, I said, dusting off my hands.

Brynn picked one up. She tossed it up, one foot, two, then almost three feet over her head, catching it each time. Pausing, she held it by the tied tip, staring into the microcosm of water and lubricant.

So oily in there. She tossed it again, lightly. *Catch!*

It hit me before I could put up my hands. Instead of breaking, the condom bounced off my face, smacking with enough force to turn my head. Stunned, I sat there with my hands pressed over my nose, which hurt so bad I could barely breathe without yelling.

What came out was a bullfroggy croak. Brynn laughed hysterically, running over to pick up the balloon from where it had rolled. It sat in a patch of weeds, lightly dusted with sand.

She threw it up and caught it again, bits of leaves flying off. The dirt coated her hands and she made a disgusted face. Dropping it, she wiped her fingers on the seat of her tiny shorts.

That hurt, you asshole.

Oh, get over it.

My nose felt swollen to three times its normal size. Carefully touching my nostrils, I searched for the blood that I was sure must be streaming down my face. There was only a bunch of clear snot.

You could have broken it. It's maybe broken.

No, it's not. It'd look way worse.

Brynn picked up a fresh balloon from the Easter basket and tossed it, higher and higher. I watched its trajectory as a plane flew overhead, the droning buzz loud as it lowered for landing. My nose throbbed. I wanted it to hurt anywhere else on my body, even for a second, just to give my face some relief.

It really, really hurts.

You're such a baby about everything. She rolled her eyes and squatted down. Thrusting up with a grunt, she threw it the highest yet. It wriggled into crazy, jiggling shapes in the air. Brynn ran for it, knocking into my legs and sprawling on the ground. It hit beside her and popped with terrific force, spraying water on her legs and top, drenching my jeans.

Ugh, what the hell. She kicked at me with her flip-flopped foot, digging her toes into my leg. *I was going to wear these tomorrow!*

When she kicked again, the muscles in my calf tensed, half cramping, and I snapped. I kicked her back, hard. It wasn't something I'd ever done to Brynn before. It was the kind of physical fight I'd have with my brother—the two of us reaching out and smacking, pinching, slapping. Brynn had never been on the receiving end. I was wearing sneakers and my heel jammed directly into her kneecap.

Oh! she exclaimed, eyes wide with shock. Then she kicked me again and I kicked her back, this time connecting solidly with the meat of her thigh.

We were a blur of tangled legs. Brynn's flip-flops had flown off and her bare feet struck me over and over again, gaining traction off my sweaty jeans. We struggled and grunted until my last kick went wild, connecting with the soft dough of her belly.

Then we both scrambled away from each other. My hair was tangled, half fallen out of its braid. Brynn looked demented. Lip gloss smeared red across her cheek and down her chin.

You dumb fucking cunt. She rubbed her face with shaky hands.

I'd heard kids say that word before, but I'd never heard it from Brynn. I sat there in the dirt and stared at her while she breathed heavily and collected her flip-flops, five feet away from each other.

Sorry, I said, scrubbing the dirt from my hands onto my jeans. It stung. There were tiny cuts and scrapes all over my palms. I hadn't even realized that I'd hurt myself. *I didn't mean it. I'm sorry.*

Fuck you! You are sorry.

I was crying and that hurt too. My nose was so swollen that it didn't want to let out any of the snot that was building in my sinuses. Sweat dripped from my hairline and mixed with my tears. I scrubbed at them with my palms and felt grit and dirt slide over my lids.

Stop crying! Shut up!

It was hard to hear her over the blood rushing in my ears and the whistling of my nose. I kept repeating the word *sorry*, wondering how many times I needed to say it before she calmed down. But then she was running away from me, stumbling over sticks and clumps of moss. When she got to the edge of the lot, she bent over and picked something up. She yelled again and threw it at me. It was a turtle shell.

Have another dead thing, you fucking freak!

Turning, she ran to the trailer. Her mother's boyfriend opened the door—leaning out in his white T-shirt and boxer shorts. She reared back a little and he leaned down into her face. I couldn't hear what he was saying, but I saw her respond to him. It looked like she was still yelling. He grabbed her by the arm, high up near the shoulder, and yanked her behind him into the trailer. She didn't look back.

12

My mother helped me pull the specimen boxes into the living room. They weren't heavy, but they were awkwardly shaped and some required both of us taking an end. After a couple of trips, her head drooped forward and she leaned against the wall to catch her breath. I sat her on the couch, put on a pot of coffee, and finished unloading the truck. It had stayed clear outside all night, but I wasn't sure how long that would last, or if the encroaching dew would harm any of the pieces we'd worked so hard to dry.

Mug in hand, she looked more human. She'd put on her reading glasses, and with every sip, they fogged over, little half-moons of opacity that she let dissolve on their own.

"Oh wow," she said, head rolling back on her neck, sinking into the overstuffed couch cushion. "Yes. Wow. This is very good."

"When's the last time you had any?"

"I don't know."

It was odd to think of my mother without coffee, a woman who got migraines if she went even six hours without a cup. She massaged the back of her neck. Clean, she gave off a soapy, comfortable odor. Her bathrobe smelled like too much laundry detergent.

Pointing out each item, I showed her the parts that I'd been able to gather. Bat wings, an armadillo shell, bird torsos, a salmon-pink flamingo neck with part of the beak still attached. We had pieces of coat and antler. There were legs from disparate animals—two hog hooves, a portion of elk femur. I'd conserved bones, bleaching what I could. It was hard to see any of my father in the remnants. It wasn't something he'd have appreciated or understood. I still didn't quite get what she'd been trying to do, but I thought I was willing to find out more. To be the kind of daughter who'd listen. Versus the kind of daughter who'd go out of her way to ruin something, who'd secretly call in threats because she was too much of a coward to deal with anything directly.

When she asked about the sex toys, I produced a solitary pair of handcuffs. All the fur trim had burned off, but the steel was pristine. She took them from me with trembling fingers and put them inside her robe pocket.

"Your father really loved those."

"Okay," I replied, trying to hide my grimace. "Great."

"He acted like a prude in front of everyone, but we actually had a very healthy sex life." She smiled. "We had some very good times with these."

"I'm going to get more coffee," I announced, taking our full cups back to the kitchen.

I'd left the bearskin back at the shop. Mr. Gennaro had done a fantastic job with the cleaning, though he'd threatened to charge me double if I ever brought in an animal again. The head was fluffy, coat so shiny it barely looked real. Even the teeth looked brighter.

Whitening toothpaste. He'd cleared his throat and busied himself with some receipts lined up on the countertop. *Tell your mother I said hello.*

I brought him up while I explained the bearskin, and she looked away too, stroking one of the soft rabbit ears between her fingers.

"What do we do with all this?" she asked. The boxes were spread around us, open, bits collected on the floor and on the coffee table next to our mugs.

"Honestly? I don't know." It was only pieces, a puzzle laid out, waiting for us to solve it. "I just ... wanted to give you back some of it. Show you that I want you to be happy, even if I don't understand what you're doing."

She took my hand. I looked away, down into an open box, to stare at the body of a platypus, legs twisted and broiled, but the face still sweet and earnest. "I appreciate that," she said. "I mean it."

"I don't know what that means. I don't know what I feel willing to help with. But I want to try." I lifted up the smallest box and held it in my lap. It held baby animal parts: raccoons' paws, singed feathers, and small, bristled tails.

"Try what?"

I patted the duck beaks and cow hooves, combed my fingers through part of a horse's mane. "Something. Anything."

My mother brushed the hair from my temple and curled it behind my ear. "I think that sounds nice."

Milo and I went to check out the empty building next to the shop. The property had been used for a lot of things, but in its last life, it had been a restaurant. When we got inside, it still smelled like one. There was a sweet, spoiled odor like milk gone sour.

A bar ran along the right wall with liquor bottles strewn across its top. Milo picked one up and shook it.

"Nada." He picked up another, then another. "Shit. You'd at least think I'd get a drink out of this."

Booths took up the front, slick menus still scattered over paper place-mats, ketchup bottles with tacky red rings at their bottoms twinned with little jars full of yellowed peppers soaking up juice.

"Let's check out the back," I said. "This isn't what we're here for."

There was a bank of freezers, stoves, and fryers. The heavy smell of rancid grease hung thick in the air. A stairwell stood at the back wall, a spiral that led up to the second floor. "Come on," I said, pulling Milo away from the refrigerators. He'd opened one of the doors and a rank funk emerged that reminded me of the Dumpster smell at an amusement park.

He put a hand over his nose and gagged. "Holy shit. I think there might be a dead body inside."

We proceeded upstairs single file. It was slow going. The stairs were rusty and creaked under our combined weight. The higher we rose, the more oppressive the heat became. When we reached the top, I was happy to see that all the stuff was still there.

"What the hell is this?" Milo walked ahead, boots marking tracks on the dusty linoleum.

It was an exhibition space. Dozens of glass cases formed pathways through the mess. Faded, ancient mannequins stood in some of them. None wore clothes, aside from a solitary figure in the first display. That one was dressed in a leafy loincloth and held a wooden club made from papier-mâché.

"They had that Christian historical museum here," I said, leaning down to look into a display full of old Bibles. "You remember. The anti-evolution stuff?" We walked around another case that contained oversized plastic dinosaurs and a dusty tree full of shiny, fake apples. "We had to come for a field trip."

Milo stopped in front of one that held remnants of palm trees. Wax animal figurines stood beside them, half melted from the heat. "I never did that. It was just you and Brynn."

One of the cases stood open. I reached inside to pluck a wreath of flowers. Its petals spilled clumps of dust when I shook it. "Only happened that one year. They got into a bunch of trouble for it."

Milo tapped an empty case. It made a hollow sound that reverberated off the walls. "What are we doing here, Jessa?"

"Looking to see if we're interested."

He turned in a circle, taking in the strange menagerie of creepy mannequins and faux greenery. "Interested in *what*?"

The whole place would have to be scrubbed down and disinfected, downstairs completely gutted. We could break through the walls of the shop and expand into the first floor, but that would take a lot more time and money. "We're going to rent this space. For Mom."

Milo sighed, long and heavy. His "exhausted with Jessa" sound. "Why?"

"It's right next door, it's cheap, and it'll make her happy."

"Couldn't we just give her the window display?"

I could have brought up the fact that he'd shit on that idea before, but I ignored that instinct and took my time answering. I set the wreath down on a mannequin's head like a crown. "It's a good location. It'll be a smart investment."

"You mean financially?"

"Yes. Maybe." I paused and thought for a second. "Also . . . artistically. I've got work I could display. I'm creative."

I picked up the wreath again, touching each of the flowers individually, counting them. Calming myself. "You could have some space too."

"I'm not an artist and I don't do taxidermy." His body language told me he was looking for a fight: chest outthrust, hands fisted. His jaw clenched rhythmically; it was something I'd never seen on him before. It reminded me of our father. "What the hell would I put on display?"

"I don't know. Something. It could be meaningful."

He looked confused, as if I'd spoken to him in a different language. "*Meaningful?* The fuck are you talking about?"

"I'm just saying we could get some closure."

The floor was so covered in grit that my feet slid every time I took a step. It was messy and would need a ton of work, but I could see it. Creating displays and putting together the light-ing. Assisting with the mounts, making backgrounds, crafting scenery. There could be spaces for me, for Mom. New work from Lolee and Bastien.

"I don't need closure. I've got closure!" Milo slapped his hand down on one of the cases. It made a sharp, clinking sound.

"Jesus, don't break them. They're not ours yet."

"You're not listening to me!" He grunted, throwing up his hands. "But you never listen. It's always about what *you* want. What's best for Jessa."

The sheer nerve it must have taken for him to say something like that. I was almost impressed. "That's not remotely true," I replied, pacing my words until each was nearly its own sentence. My face and neck felt hot, blistering. "Everything I do is for this family."

"You're completely selfish, and the worst part is you have a savior complex about it! Like any of us need you to save us? You're not God, Jessa. You're not in charge."

I lowered my voice, trying to calm him down. Calm *myself* down. "I know that. I just want everyone to be happy."

He laughed. "Yeah. Happy. We're all so fucking happy in this family. It's a regular Disney movie." His face contorted until I couldn't tell if he was about to yell at me again or cry. "This is stupid. It's just so fucking stupid." Turning away, he leaned over the case and braced himself against the top. His back rose and fell with labored breaths. "We should have made Mom go see somebody, you were right. Maybe you should see somebody."

"Maybe. But I'm gonna do this too." I walked closer to him and he jerked away. "And I think it'll be good. Why not try something different instead of the same old shit that's been making us miserable our whole lives?"

"I haven't been miserable my whole life!"

"Really? I've been pretty miserable." His shoulders were tense, raised nearly to his ears. "Neither of us can deal with anything because we refuse to let anything go. We learned it from Dad. Look at him, he killed himself rather than deal with anything. It shouldn't be like this."

One sharp slap and he broke straight through the glass. It rained down onto the animals inside and collected on the plastic baby Jesus's face. When he raised his hands, they were coated with blood. "Look what you made me do," he said, eyes watering. "I'm gonna get tetanus."

"You get tetanus from rusty metal, dumbass. Not glass." I grabbed his wrist and looked at the cuts in his palm. We were both shaking. "I know you don't want to talk about it, but we both know why we need to."

Blood dripped from his palm and licked across his forearm, down to the joint of my thumb. It dropped into the dusty linoleum and left behind bright patterns. "I hate talking about Brynn," he whispered. "It always fucks me up."

"I know, me too." I dug out some of the glass from his skin. The slivers were small, difficult to grasp. "But don't you think it's weird that we both loved her and neither of us can talk about that? She was mine, she was yours. That's something that won't change. Even if she's gone, that still happened."

Blood kept leaking from the cuts, making it difficult to see what I was doing. A shard stabbed into my thumb, near the nail. I hissed and shook my hand. More blood flew off and spattered the cabinet.

He pulled away and stuffed his fists into the hem of his shirt. Blood dotted the tops of his sneakers. There were stains on my pants.

Still not sure what to do with my hands, I picked the wreath up off the floor, plucking flower petals from their green plastic stems. "We both loved Brynn and she's gone. Left us for some person she'd only known for a month. This happened years ago, and we're still not over it."

"Okay, I get it." He tried to laugh, but all that came out was a rusty croak. "We're unlovable."

Once I started talking, everything spilled out: fetid and stagnant, a backlog of sewage. "Dad killed himself because he couldn't deal with his body breaking down. He couldn't stand being weak. So he did something horrible." I pulled more petals and let them drift onto the floor. Cornflower blue, bright pink. The fuzzy little heads of baby's breath. "Instead of talking to somebody, which would've taken actual courage, he shot himself."

With both his hands buried in the hem of his shirt, my brother looked like a shamed little kid. "You don't know that's why."

"Yes, it's exactly why." I sighed and set down the wreath again, this time on the broken top. "He left me a note."

Maybe I knew Milo better than I'd thought I did, after all. I could tell he wanted to read it. I could see by the twitchy way his eyes darted from my face and back down to the floor that he wondered if there was anything about him in that letter. And there were two things I could do: I could tell him the truth, that it didn't mention him at all, or I could do the other thing. I could say the thing he needed to hear.

"He said he was sorry. He said he wished he'd been a better father. That he loved you very much. That he was proud of you and of the kids you raised."

"Yeah, right," Milo replied, looking down at his bloodied hands. "Let me see it then."

"It's gone. And we don't need a fucking letter to tell us that."

Milo sagged so slowly he seemed to be deflating. Then we were both sitting on the floor. I drew my legs up to my chin. Milo sat with his hands clenching and unclenching in his shirt.

"Brynn's never coming back," I said, letting the words roll around in my mouth, like foreign objects. "She's gone. We act like if we wait long enough, she's going to come back again and things can be how they were." I rubbed my chin back and forth across my knee until the jeans chafed the skin. "But that's stupid. It's never gonna happen. She left because she didn't want the same things we wanted. She didn't want us."

Remembering it was bad enough; talking about it felt like chewing tinfoil. Milo wrung his hands in his shirt and the bloodstains spread.

"What does it say about me that the only person I've ever loved never loved me?" he asked. His voice sounded very young. If I'd closed my eyes, we could've been teenagers again.

"That's not true."

"She only ever loved you." Sweat beaded along his hairline and dripped down either side of his face. "She didn't love me, and we had a kid together."

Sitting on the floor should have felt awkward, but it was comfortable. Picking fuzz off the baseboards. Swirling prints into the dirt of the linoleum. I signed my name with a flourish. Drew a heart, then a star.

"Why did we have to love the same person?" Milo whispered.

"I don't know. We just did." Reaching over, I pulled his hands from the hem of his shirt. The blood had clotted. I examined them in the weak light. Glass was still trapped in the cuts, little slivers that glimmered like ice. "I think a better question is why we still love this person so much we can't love anyone else. She's gone. It's over."

He let me hold his hands as I began to pick out the glass again. "Did you and Brynn have sex when I was married to her?"

There was no use lying. "Yes."

Tiny slivers transferred from his palm to my fingers. I was stabbing myself with the shards. Our blood mingled, skin rubbing together.

"I knew it. I mean, I knew that you were." He laughed. "She and I didn't have sex very often."

"You don't have to tell me about it."

"I knew that you guys were together, even in high school. I didn't care. I just wanted her." Our blood darkened as it dried. It looked like menstrual blood, clots forming between our fingers. He looked up from our bloodied hands. "I saw you guys together. Lots of times."

"When?" It was hard to think back, all the places that she and I had been together. In my room, in her car. The couch at my parents' house. Outside, propped against the tree in the backyard.

"Lots of times. You guys weren't very careful. Dad even saw you once, in the shop."

"That's embarrassing." I wondered what my father had thought, seeing us there. He'd never once asked me about Brynn. If she was my girlfriend. "I didn't think anybody knew."

"Everybody knew, Jessa."

The room was stifling. Every breath I took seemed to contain a quart of dust. I coughed, then coughed again. My eyes burned from the dryness.

Something was under one of the cabinets. I leaned down and reached beneath as far as I could. My fingers brushed against something that jangled. I grabbed it and pulled it out. When I held it up in front of us, dust fell from the matted fur of a stuffed animal. The bell was still shiny and trilled when I shook it to dislodge the fuzz.

"Cat toy."

Milo winced. "You think there's still a cat up here?"

"Probably not a live one."

He dragged it around on the floor between our bodies, making patterns in the dirt. "You're a lesbian. How come you never got any cats?"

Grabbing it back, I beat him over the head with it until dust pillowed the air. "That's the stupidest thing you've ever said."

Coughing, he waved a hand in front of his face to dispel the cloud. "I find that hard to believe."

"Yeah. You've said stupider." I lay back on the floor, exhausted. "I think this place will work."

"We're gonna have to gut it."

I spread my arms and legs, knocking into Milo. "We'll have Lolee help. Child labor, right?"

"It's what Dad would've done."

Scraping my arms back and forth across the dirty wood, I pretended I was a dust angel. I'd never seen snow once in my life. That seemed very sad to me. I'd never traveled anywhere, or seen anything. Never left the United States. I didn't even own a passport. I wondered where would be the best place to see snow. Maybe I'd take Lolee with me. "Dad always made us work," I said. "He thought it was good for us. Built character."

"He always made *you* work." Milo reached for my leg and I kicked at him until he quit. "I didn't have to do half that shit. You're the one who liked it. You're the one who always wanted to be there."

"I still do like it. It's what I know. It's comfortable."

"Can you hear yourself?" He tapped at the bottom of my boot, prompting me to kick again. "You sound like you're sixty-five years old. Like you're describing life at a retirement village."

"Nothing wrong with that." I rolled over onto my side. There was something else beneath the case. I pressed my face closer to the opening between it and the linoleum, dirt grinding into my cheek. I couldn't quite make out what it was. Something dark and bundled. A mystery shape. "I like being comfortable."

"Maybe get a little uncomfortable and find a date."

"I don't want a date who makes me uncomfortable." I reached beneath the cabinet again, but my arm was too short to grab whatever it was. Huffing, I flopped over onto my back. The fluorescents were half-lit and spotty, flickering weakly.

"Is that what you like about Lucinda? It's comfortable?" Milo tossed the cat toy in the air, little puffs of dust flying out every time it smacked against his palms.

"What about Lucinda?"

"You guys are fucking, right?"

"Don't be gross."

"I'm not being gross." He threw the cat toy at me and it landed on my chest, rolling up to my neck, where it huddled like a scared live thing. I tossed it back.

"We were seeing each other. Now we're not."

"Why?"

One reason was she was married. The other reason was I'd anonymously called her wife and told her about Lucinda cheating. Did I need another reason? If so, I had one: I'd cost her her business. I had to assume she was pissed about that. On my next throw, I looped it up high, getting as close as I could to the light fixture without actually hitting it. "I don't know. I think I like emotionally unavailable women."

Milo arced it up the same way, coming even closer to the light. "You're emotionally unavailable, Jessa."

"You think I don't know that?"

"People aren't as emotionally unavailable as you think."

I aimed the next throw at his head. He tossed it back just as hard. "I know they aren't," I said. "I'm just not sure what I want."

"Maybe think about it."

"Sure. When's the last time you went on a date?"

My next throw hit the light. Bits of cracked plastic rained down on us. I sat up and tried to avoid debris falling into my eyes. I picked pieces out of my braid, remembering too late that my fingers were shredded from helping Milo with his palms. My hair dug into the cuts and it hurt.

"Shit. We need to clean up."

He got up and helped me to my feet, both of us careful with our wounded hands. "I bet we could pull this place together," he said.

I kicked the cat toy down the aisle, toward the doorway. I tried to yank the cabinet away from the wall, so I could see what I'd been reaching for. It was too heavy for me to lift alone.

"Help me with this."

Milo grabbed the opposite side and we both pulled. It scraped hard against the floor and moved a half foot forward. He looked behind.

"Found the cat," he said. "You want it?"

"I'll have Bastien bring a garbage bag."

CATHARTES AURA—TURKEY VULTURE

We weren't the kind of family that went on vacations. Our father thought it was a holiday if he took a day off work; even then, I couldn't remember a single time growing up when he'd willingly stayed out of his workshop.

I'm happiest when I'm busy, he told our mother when she'd pushed a Carnival Cruise brochure on him one Saturday morning. He was stitching a coonskin cap at the breakfast nook, even after my mother had given him the side-eye and told him to keep his taxidermy out of the margarine. *Can't imagine being trapped on a boat with all kinds of awful people. Rather be here, in my own house, with people I kinda like.*

So we played around the neighborhood during our summers off, making the lake our vacation spot. We rode our bikes through the cemetery, camping out in the tree house when it got cool and the roaches finally fled. And when I turned fourteen, my father brought me along with him once a week for our trek along the highways just outside of town. That's where we searched for discount taxidermy treasures. We were looking for roadkill.

We searched for animals that lay half in the crunchy dead grass, half in the road. We picked up squirrels and waterfowl, possums, armadillos, and snakes. Some had sat out too long and turned rancid; those we'd have to leave, unless my father decided that any of the parts were still usable: wings or beaks, legs or ears, possibly a tail if it was in good enough condition and the maggots hadn't gotten to it yet.

Morning's best. Before the sun comes up and cooks the meat.

That meant predawn on a Saturday. My father slouched at the kitchen counter, pounding strong black coffee while I forced down a bowl of Cheerios that stuck in my throat.

I liked how barren the streets were that early in the morning. The truck smelled like gasoline and heated vinyl. Receipts slid along the dashboard with a satisfying hiss every time he'd turn a corner or switch lanes. It was mostly quiet, but sometimes he'd put on the radio, and other times we'd talk about whatever was on his mind, which was usually the shop and what kind of animals he hoped we'd find.

As the sun came up, I'd surreptitiously watch my father drive the truck. I liked the specifics of his face. The creases near his mouth, the pockmark between his eyebrows. His skin was sallow, like mine, and oily, with a bristly dark beard on his chin and cheeks. His hair, still wet from his shower, dried into spikes that fluffed up birdlike along the crown of his head.

We raced down the empty streets, passing all the places I knew so well. They looked different in the darkness of early morning, like people I'd never met before. Even our shop was a stranger as we passed, all the lights off, the woodsy front porch with its rocking chairs lonely and dimmed with shadows. It was always good to know that it wouldn't be that way for long, that soon enough we'd pass all the same places and they'd look friendly and familiar again.

Most of the time we stuck to the highways near town, but I always liked it when there wasn't anything close and my father took us on the long drive toward Ocala. Fields flew past in green drags, rolls of hay stacked up like pecan pinwheels alongside pinpricks of black cows dotting the distance, peeking up through the mist.

I'd like a cow. I pointed toward one so close I could make out its chewing mouth, imagining the cud lodged inside its cheek.

To eat? He laughed, as if he hadn't already made that joke a thousand times.

As we passed the cows, all crowded safely together behind their fences, I thought how nice it was. How cozy and sweet to imagine that there were animals alive and kept in pens, not dead ones like we always dealt with. Then my father would remind me that the cows weren't long for this world either.

You gonna stop eating cheeseburgers? No more McDonald's for Jessa-Lynn? No steak so raw the blood pools on the plate?

I turned away and pretended to be upset, but I was smiling. Happy to have my father just to myself—knowing that we had these jokes, and these mornings together, and no one else got to share them. They were always going to be just ours.

Then one of us would spot a dark shape in the road. My father braked, and both of us guessed what kind of animal we'd found. He was almost always right. My father could tell from fifty yards if it was a bigger animal, like a deer or a turkey, could even narrow down the smaller kill, tell the difference between a possum and a raccoon.

See up there? Pointing through the windshield, he'd note the buzzards, circling overhead. *How many are there?*

As I counted, he'd nod along. The more vultures, the bigger the body. The back of his truck was already fitted out with tarps, blue ones he'd gotten for free from one of his better-paying customers, who owned a construction service.

My father decided our order of operations, different for each animal. He brought along garbage bags and nylon rope, the shovel from the garage, usually still coated with dog shit scooped from the yard. He always carried a small handsaw and a very sharp utility knife to separate the gristliest parts.

It was best when the animals were small and still intact. Then we'd load them into black trash bags, me holding the bags open while my father scraped them up with the shovel. Worse were the ones that my father would have to dissect right there on the road, eliciting a foul stench that wouldn't leave, even after we drove away. I could feel it on my skin, smell it in my hair and on my clothes. My father barely noticed when they were that rotten; couldn't seem to make himself care about the smashed faces, insides spread out from where the tires had made surrealist art of their organs.

Whole animals, shoveled into bags. If it was something like a possum or squirrel, then it was likely that we'd just leave them, although my father would always move them out of the road. He hated that cars just drove over them, continually, as if they couldn't see there had once been a live thing there.

There were times he'd hand me the knife or the saw, and then point to the pieces we could use. Always tails of foxes, deer antlers, hawks' wings. The few times we'd seen an alligator, my father would take only the head—tourists loved the gator skulls and paid good money for them, so we took them even if the flesh was falling from the skulls in mealy clumps. They were always worth our time, regardless of decomp.

Skinning gators is pointless work. My father stood with his boot pressed into one's back, anchoring the body while the blade sank into the rolls of its neck. The gator's head flapped up and down while he sawed at the gristle and bone, as if nodding along with what my father was saying.

Wouldn't someone buy the skin?

I couldn't understand why we wouldn't want the entire alligator. I could see us stuffing and mounting the eight-foot monster someone had hit with a car, spun out only a few feet from the edge of the grass. There was a look of surprise on its face, the look of a predator that had not understood there was a larger object that could blink out its existence without a hitch in the motor.

Too much work. Hard to get at the skin without ripping through the fat. He leaned over and ran a gloved finger along the ridges of its spine. It resembled dinosaurs from our textbooks, prehistoric, wandering around since the dawn of time, long before people like us had come along with cars to crush the life from them.

Couldn't you just price it really high?

I'm gonna finish sawing off this head. He gestured toward the truck. *Go get my knife out of the glove box. You're gonna skin that while I finish this. Then we can talk about it.*

The hunk of meat was heavy, but it didn't have the stench of rot on it. I found the knife, buried beneath folded maps of Florida and fast food restaurant napkins. Then I leaned against the warm grill, digging the sharp, flat blade into the flesh while my father finished up.

It was rough work. So gristly, the flesh unlike that of the mammals we regularly skinned—deer with their coarse hair, wild pigs, raccoons with thick fatty deposits in their stomachs. The gator's skin was nearly melded to the pink, tight muscle beneath, so brightly hued it resembled fresh tuna. Every time my knife slipped below, it poked through the skin I was trying to preserve. By the time my father had stuffed the gator head into a black garbage bag, I was only a quarter inch into the tip of the tail.

Leave it, he said, climbing into the truck and restarting the engine. *We've still got about a half hour before traffic starts up and the sun really gets cooking.*

I put the tail on top of the gator's torso. It still looked menacing, even without a head. I wasn't sure what made me feel so uneasy. But when we got back into the truck and drove past, I noticed no buzzards circled the body.

I was fine with most kill, but there were a few things I couldn't stomach. There were always too many dogs. Small and large alike, unlucky mutts with mottled fur, too skinny, ribs poking out so far you could see inside their bodies. I couldn't look at these animals; they made me feel too sad.

My father always stopped for dogs. He gently placed the bodies into whatever patch was grassiest. There were buzzards at dog kills, and my father had to shoo them off to move the body out of the road. Then we'd drive on and the birds would move back in, wings flapping against each other as they made room for themselves over the carcass.

Only once did we take one with us. It was a Sunday morning and there was no one around. The humidity was so thick it almost hurt to breathe. My father was talking about a customer who'd accidentally cooked up his largemouth bass when he was drunk, a fish he'd been saving in his freezer to mount. He was smiling, the sun just peeking up over the horizon like a bright slice of fruit. It colored the skin of his face fresh and bright. He laughed with his mouth hanging open so I could see the backs of his teeth. It made him seem young. It made me want to laugh too.

There was a horde of vultures circling the sky. The number seemed impressive, the most I'd seen in a long time. I knew my father must have thought so too, because his mouth snapped closed. He turned down the volume on the stereo, which was playing some loud morning talk show.

It must be something big, I said, trying to make out the shape. It was hard to see with the sun coming up hot and red orange, a bloody contusion welling up over the lip of the earth.

Slowing to a crawl, we approached the animal. It was covered in flapping, writhing vultures. So many we couldn't make out the lumped shape of the body. My father got out of the truck and pulled the shovel from the back before approaching the mass of birds. He brandished the tip like a blade. They flapped up and then landed again, too eager to pay much attention to anything that wasn't carrion.

My father pinged one with the shovel, smacking at it the way he would a golf ball. It made a deep, guttural squawk and flapped awkwardly to the side. The rest of the birds dispersed, settling down into the patchy weeds five feet from where my father crouched.

His arm went up, waving at me.

Bring me one of those blankets. When I didn't move right away, his head snapped around and he shouted my name.

I stumbled over my own legs as I jumped down from the cab. The smell outside was all wet, trampled grass and the funky odor of birds. Some were still circling overhead, but others were perched along the roadway. They reminded me of those cartoon vultures from that Disney movie. Those ones had been funny; these just looked menacing. Their necks and faces were ugly and wattled. They moved jaggedly, as if they didn't know how to operate their bodies.

My father kept a small pile of furniture blankets in the tool compartment. They smelled strongly of metal and oil. I hurried one over to my father, who was talking to the animal, making crooning noises, soft words I couldn't quite make out.

It was a black dog, maybe a Labrador. A deep gash ran along his neck, and a red collar that had once been bright tugged dirtily along the matted fur. Kneeling down beside my father, I put my hand out to try to touch the dog's side.

Don't, my father said, voice very sharp. *It might hurt him.*

He's alive? The animal looked dead to me. He was twisted up, body contorted in the way that I always associated with the bagged animals we carted back to our shop. There were already so many open wounds in the dog's torso. Blood dripped onto the asphalt.

My father shook his head, spread out the blanket. *Mostly dead, Jessa. Not all the way gone yet.*

The dog made a high whimper, a hurt sound that made me want to plug my ears. My father lifted him carefully onto the blanket, but still the animal cried.

My knee stung horribly. I looked down to see a wide trail of fire ants leading over from a huge pile next to the fence. They were crawling up my legs. I jumped up and smacked them off, sweeping them from my pants and my shoes. *Ants!* I yelled stupidly.

They're on me too. They're all over the goddamn dog.

And they were. Everywhere there was wet blood, there were ants. Scores of them. I tried to brush them off his leg, but it was so twisted up and bent that it only brushed them farther into his fur.

Move out of the way, I'm going to put him in the front seat. Hold his head, okay?

My father picked up the blanket, carrying the dog like a small child. He wasn't making noises anymore, or maybe he was and I just couldn't hear them over the sound of the vultures. They'd started shrieking, flapping around where the body had lain. Angry at the deprivation, they smacked into each other and pecked the earth.

I wanted to throw something at them. I looked around for a rock, anything to make them pay for putting that awful look on my father's face, but there was nothing. Aside from the birds, the ground was nearly swept clean.

My father called my name again, and I hurried back to the truck. It smelled heavy inside the closed cab, like iron, like the shed full of my father's tools.

We drove fast, my father pulling a U-turn so precise that we barely even drove over the grass. Vultures scattered, flocking outward in a dark mass. I couldn't see much of the dog, just the tip of his nose poking out from the blanket. It was very dry and cracked. I wondered whose dog he was. Who'd abandoned him, left him when he'd needed someone the most.

I held my fingers cupped in front of that nose, feeling for breath. Little puffs of air against my palm reassured me that he was still with us. My father reached over, across the dog's still body, and gripped my shoulder with his hand. He held on to me for the rest of the drive down the highway, not letting go, not even when we turned onto the state road leading back into town.

13

I spent most days in the rubble as we deconstructed the restaurant next door. Since it had been abandoned, we talked the rental agency into letting us keep the restaurant equipment as long as we took care of disposal ourselves. Some stuff we put on Craigslist. Booths, tables, countertops, stools—all older, but in pretty fair condition. Other items we sold to Winnie's: the large bank of commercial fridges, the glass pie counters. One of the new craft bars downtown took the taps and the vintage bar top. I let Bastien have the neon beer sign from the back wall, but told him he couldn't keep it in the shop.

"Grandma's porch," Bastien said, holding it in front of him. The lights were a clear, vivid blue. "That's where I've been keeping most of my stuff."

"At least it's cooler out now. Too hot during the summer."

"It's not so bad. Got a beer fridge." He set the sign carefully in the front seat of the truck. "She's gonna let me put a new shed out back so I can store things."

I thought of the old one, leaning rickety for so many years before it had finally collapsed on itself in a rusty heap. We'd barely been able to excavate the lawn mower from the pile.

"Maybe get a plastic one this time. Something squirrels won't nest in."

My mother was rebuilding her creations, but this time she and I both used the back of the workshop. Bastien had stopped procuring living creatures after I'd told him if he didn't knock it off, I'd start dumping the remains in his bed. I could tell he was relieved, but that didn't stop him from outsourcing labor to one of his seedier associates. There was a slew of new animals to take out of the freezer: an ocelot, a couple more peacocks, two otters, and a capybara with a face so much like an enormous hamster that Lolee screamed bloody murder when we unpacked it from the tarp. She climbed on top of the metal worktable to get away from it, shrieking.

"What, you can scrape the insides out of a deer, but you can't deal with an oversized rodent?" Bastien got down on the floor and flopped the thing's monstrous head back and forth while Lolee screeched. I unsuccessfully tried to hide my smile. She scowled and put out her arms, the way she'd done when she was little.

I couldn't lift her anymore, but I kicked off the brakes on the table and rolled her over to the other side of the room. She hopped down through the open doorway, middle fingers blazing.

"I'm going to Kaitlyn's. Call me when that thing is gone."

She walked to the front door with her purse strapped over her chest. I thought she looked older since her haircut. She'd shaved it underneath and cut the hair on top into a wedge. My mother had done it for her, and then Lolee had buzzed my mother's. I'd never realized how similar they looked. Looking at Lolee was like staring into a fuzzy picture coated over with the filmy residue of Brynn: shadows of it in her walk, the tilt of her hips, her long, slender arms, nearly disproportionate to her body.

"You need a ride?" I asked. "How will you get home?"

"Dad'll get me."

Milo had moved back into our mother's house with Lolee. He was fixing up a lot of the wiring and things that had gone to shit in my father's absence. The rugs were steamed, the sheets were washed, and he'd somehow tamed the overgrown backyard with the help of a borrowed lawn mower. His next project was tackling the leaky roof over the back porch.

My mother spent early mornings with Milo, supervising the cleanup, and then met me around noon at the shop. We'd sit up front and eat the sandwiches she'd prepped—me chewing on the pickle spears she'd packed in wax paper next to the ham on rye, her digging out the tomatoes she'd put on both sandwiches even though she hated them.

Then we'd head to the back.

It was weird; there was no other way to describe it. I still wasn't sure about the things my mother was creating. The kind of work she envisioned didn't speak to me, for a number of reasons, foremost being that it dealt so closely with my father and his sexuality. It made me uncomfortable, which made me wonder about discomfort in general. What about sex made me feel as if it couldn't be connected to emotion? Why was it something that made me cringe? I asked my mother questions about her work and, when I felt too overwhelmed, drank a beer or just went out to the lake. Tried to focus on what it was that made me shut down.

For so many years it had been only my father there, a strong, silent presence. Then suddenly it was my mother. We shared the tools and the workstations. Sometimes we put on music. I scraped and gutted, prepped and stitched. She went through bins of preserved animal parts and brought over big tubs full of crafting gear: plastic beads and strings of multicolored party lights, sequins, aluminum foil, old CDs. There were also boxes of art we'd done in elementary school, birthday cards she'd saved, family photo albums, and pictures of my father when he was younger than Bastien. It was strange to see him in those shots, looking so much like Milo. In one of my mother's favorites, he had a full head of dark hair and straddled a motorcycle in my parents' front yard.

When our hands cramped and we felt sick from the fumes wafting off the tanning solution, we'd take a break. Sometimes we wandered out to the front walk, lounging on metal folding chairs, soaking up the sun as we shared a cigarette. We'd face the store, checking out whatever new display my mother had come up with for the week. I'd encouraged her to take over the front; she could use it as a trial run.

"Are you sure you don't mind?" she'd asked, looking from the small, bare space in front of the window to my face. Back and forth, as if determining whether I really meant it. "You don't care what I put up?"

"It's your shop too. You get a say."

"You're right." Her eyes had turned sleepy, how they always got when she was focused on what was happening in her head: forming the structures, placing the animals, choosing the backdrops and furniture. Theme, she said, was the most important part. Everything else came second. I wondered why my father hadn't utilized her more in the shop. She was creative and good at putting things together. Even the stuff that made me uncomfortable made me think.

"It's a good thing when you can't stop thinking about a piece," she said. "That's when you know it's done the work. When you can't get it out of your head afterward."

That sounded right to me.

I kept the bearskin. I loved how alive it looked, even without the stuffing. Though it would have brought a good price, I couldn't stand to sell it. I spread the skin out over a couple of sawhorses, trying to decide how it looked best. My mother said theme was what mattered, but for my father it had been display. Display, he said, was the most important part of the process. It was the finishing touch to weeks of work put into an animal. If you didn't mount it correctly, it wouldn't matter that you'd sewn the skin perfectly or that the eyes were set exactly right. The mount meant that the animal had a place to live; it had a home. If the mount was wrong, everything looked fake. It took you out of the magic. Mount it right, my father said, and you gave your audience something to believe in.

The bear's face was well rendered. I loved to stare at the glinting red maw of its mouth, the sharp canines so perfectly placed beneath its curled lip. Its claws were fine and shiny, smoothed down to yellow points. I looked at it from every conceivable angle—sat upright like a floppy stuffed animal, pinned to the wall and snarling down at me, flat across the floor with limbs outstretched, as if reaching for every corner of the room at once. There was no way I posed it that I didn't like it; the bear was a companion and a pal. It looked at me with its glistening black eyes and seemed so alive I could almost hear it snuffling and breathing.

I took it home to my apartment and spread it on the couch, then moved it to my bedroom. The skin covered the entire mattress. That was where it looked best, welcoming me back every night. After long hours spent curled over the table with my needle and thread, scraping out the insides of things, I always had a friend waiting to greet me.

Lucinda Rex, her name already bigger than life, refused to leave my brain. Though I didn't call, I thought of her. I'd see her card on the counter beside the shop register or find her chicken-scratch handwriting in the bottom of my purse, notes about things to pick up from the store: eggs, bacon, sharp cheddar cheese. At my mother's house, invitations from the showcase migrated from the front of the fridge to the kitchen counter, even into my childhood bedroom.

When I went out, I drove past places I thought Lucinda might be: the bar where we used to spend our evenings, the seafood restaurant near the lake where she'd told me they had the best fried shrimp. I thought about her body in vague, ghostly ways that made me sad and aroused at the same time. At a moment's notice, I could conjure the smooth skin of her forearm and the hard, sharp jut of her jaw. The curly mass of her hair when she lifted it into a ponytail after sex, the smell of her neck when she was sweaty. She clenched her teeth so hard when she came, hard enough to break the skin of her lip and draw blood that tasted coppery when I kissed her. There were two moles dotting her right temple and three at the base of her spine, right above her ass. In the back of my mind she hovered, sometimes slipping out in the patterns of my speech or in how I set my hands on my own skin. I thought of her when I touched myself in bed at night. Afterward, I looked at the bear and wished she were there with me.

When I couldn't stand it anymore, I sat next to my mother in the kitchen as she basted a chicken and tapped a finger against another copy of the outdated invitation. It had somehow ended up in the breadbasket, poking out from where we kept the dinner rolls.

"Do you think we have everything?" I asked, tapping at the basket until it scooted along the countertop. "Is there anything else you're missing? Someone we should ask for help?"

My mother threw open the fridge and pulled out half a stick of butter, a tub of sour cream, and some bacon bits in a little plastic pouch. She slapped everything down beside the raw chicken. "All the pieces I have are good enough."

"Okay." I slid the card along the counter, back and forth. Lucinda's name glinted gold in the light, winking at me.

"Why do you ask?" She poked her head out from behind the fridge door. Her reading glasses were jammed on top of her head and she was squinting over at me as if it would help her see better. "Did you think of something I forgot?"

"I never got to see the whole thing. How would I know what's missing?"

"Just wondering."

Ripping open the inside of the bird, she took the serrated knife from the counter and dug a slit up the back end. "Can you get me some spinach from the crisper?"

"What the hell are you making?"

"Chicken ballotine. Or some variation of it." She gestured in the air with her knife, drawing a heart. "It's French. Found the recipe on the back of the Ritz box."

"If it's got bacon in it, I'll eat it." I pulled out the spinach, noting all the wrinkled apples at the bottom of the drawer that needed throwing out. "Why do you still buy the Red Delicious if Dad was the only one who ever ate them?"

"You don't eat them?"

"You know I don't. The skin's too tough. It's like gnawing plastic."

My mother flipped the chicken over and began smashing it with the rolling pin. "Lolee likes them."

I snatched a piece of bacon. "No, she doesn't. The last time you gave her one, she licked all the peanut butter off and stuffed the piece under the couch cushions."

"You wanna grab some red wine? I think there's a bottle of something in the cabinet." She pointed with the rolling pin. A bit of raw chicken was stuck to the end and flung off onto the floor.

"I'm gonna throw those apples out."

"Leave them. Lolee does like them."

That memory of the apple made me feel strange, as if time were slipping past in an oily ooze. I tried to remember what I'd felt at the time; I'd been angry because I sat on the couch and the pieces of apple had stuck to my pants. I'd yelled at Lolee until she cried. Then she'd tried to wash the pieces in the sink, assembling them into an apple shape before slipping them back inside the fridge. She'd written us all apology notes, drawing us as a stick-figure family. Our smiles were so big they'd outsized the circular faces. She'd even included Sir Charles in the drawings. Brynn had already been gone for a year, and Lolee had stopped putting her in any of the family art she created. I'd looked at that apology note and been so sad I thought my chest might cave in. It seemed I was the only one who remembered Brynn.

I unearthed a bottle of merlot left over from the ill-fated party. I uncorked it and took a whiff, grimacing at the vinegar smell. My mother was still bent over the bird, deboning it, yanking at the thigh.

Her back was turned to me as she peeled out the rib cage. I set the bottle of wine down beside the invitation, looking at the gallery's name and Lucinda's name next to it. Spun it in a circle until all the writing was upside down, then right side up, then upside down again. Lucinda's name in a loop until none of the letters looked real anymore.

"Do you know how that fire started?" I asked, pushing the card back and forth along the counter. It made a swishing sound along the Formica.

"I think you know who did it."

"Oh God," I said, picking up the bottle of wine. "You want some of this?"

"Yes, please." She yanked out the wings and flipped the bird over again. I watched her pound at the flesh with the rolling pin, muscles and tendons lining strong down her forearms.

I took a drink from the neck of the bottle. The opening was gunked and left grime on my tongue. "So Lucinda did that? To her own gallery?"

"I guess so."

"Her and her Donna. Probably."

I took another swig, then wiped the lip and pulled a couple of clean coffee mugs from the drainer in the sink, doling out half the bottle in one go. I handed one to my mother, who immediately took two long swallows.

"She told you about it?" I said. "About her and her wife. Needing the money."

"I didn't have to ask." My mother took another sip and then held the mug out to me, dangling it from her chicken-slippery fingers. I filled it up again and drank some more of my own. "I also don't think she was married anymore. Or at least she didn't want to be."

She stuffed the insides of the chicken with the spinach leaves and little pinches of salt and pepper. The cheese she'd already shredded in a pile next to the big bowl of bread crumbs.

"She sent me some money. After."

"Money from what?" I knew the investigation into the fire was still ongoing. I wasn't sure what would happen, if anyone would be prosecuted. "Insurance? How could they possibly pay out that quick?"

"Advance against a claim. Your father looked into that once for our shop. Just in case anything . . . happened."

That was news to me. But hey, I learned new things about my family all the time. Daily reminders that none of us were who we thought we were. God only knew what I'd have uncovered in a month's time. Or a year's.

"Aren't you mad? She destroyed all your work."

"I was. At first." She sucked in her lip for a second, then blew out. "But then again it wasn't really about keeping those things. It was about making them in the first place."

"Still."

"She destroyed her things too."

We were both quiet for a while, my mother stuffing in the bits of fatty bacon, rolling up the chicken and pressing it back down against a baking tray that was older than me. "Come help me tie these up, then we'll throw them in the oven."

Pushing down against the raw flesh, she tied the string twice around the flattened rolls, knotting it in loopy bows over my fingers. It reminded me of tying my shoes. Of my father teaching me, of me teaching Bastien. I didn't know who'd taught Lolee. Maybe she'd taught herself.

Looping the string, my mother tied while I helped knot. There were two rolls for each of us: Lolee, Bastien, my mother, Milo, and myself. There'd be a big pitcher of tea and there'd be bread and there'd be a salad that nobody ate but my mother. The same, the same. Even when things changed, everything still went back to equilibrium.

"You've been seeing her, haven't you?"

I pulled my finger from the last roll too quick and the insides spilled on the baking sheet. Bits of cheese and bacon coated a fragile leaf of spinach. She took my hand and pushed it down again, rolling the insides back up neatly.

"Does everyone in this family know my personal business?"

Tie, loop. The rolls pressed together like a savory gift. "Did you think you were being sneaky? You're not great at hiding, Jessa."

She put them in the oven and we both washed our hands clean of chicken guts, scrubbing the outsides of our mugs. I poured the last of the wine, splitting it evenly between us. My mother's lips were already stained with the purple kiss of it.

341

She called for Lolee and Bastien to set the table. They trooped in from the porch and took Tupperware from the cabinet, cups we'd had since I was a little kid. They poured the pitcher of tea, ice cracking in the still-warm liquid, and grabbed bowls and plates along with fistfuls of silverware. Milo came in from the living room and leaned into the open fridge, scrounging for leftovers even though we were just about to eat.

"You finish off that wine?"

"Course we did." I reached in behind him and took out the plastic bag of withering apples. I waited until my mother left to get a clean tablecloth and chucked the whole mess of them into the garbage.

"Good riddance," Milo said, gnawing a hunk of cheese. "Those are awful."

STRIX VARIA—BARRED OWL

One last, good memory:

We caught a baby owl that kept jumping from its nest. The mother had built it into the eaves at the back of our house, a small, cramped space stuffed with pine needles and bits of bark.

They're called leapers when they keep jumping. My father cradled the fluffy lump to his chest. *Damn thing has too much energy. Doesn't know he's nocturnal.*

After we'd called animal control, he and I sat in the backyard with the bird secreted in an Igloo cooler between us. We drank Arnold Palmers, heavy on the lemonade. I gave the owl baby little bits of grasshoppers I'd killed, a recent blight on the pink and white azalea bushes. The bird gulped legs, a head, meaty bits of a fatty torso.

Let's call him Oscar. That's a good name for an owl. I stroked its round head with a fingertip. The head was the size of a golf ball and very soft.

You shouldn't name wild animals. They're not pets. My father frowned and put the lid on the cooler, leaving just enough room for the baby to breathe.

Mites appeared once animal control took the bird. Everything itched: tiny, barely visible dots that crawled into my eyes and hair, tickling the insides of my ears until I thought I'd go crazy trying not to scratch at myself.

My mother had to scrub down everything. She made us strip out on the porch before letting us back inside the house. She boiled our clothes in a vat on the stove, wouldn't even consider putting them into the washing machine. I stood in the backyard, shivering in my underpants.

Milo watched from the safety of the house, pressing his mouth against the sliding glass door and blowing wet air. His tongue left behind heart-shaped spots. When Milo wasn't looking, our dad smacked a hand against the glass. It scared Milo so badly he fell backward and landed on his ass in the middle of the living room rug.

It was so funny I thought I'd never stop laughing.

14

I went to the mall to buy a new shirt because I didn't want to look like myself when I saw Lucinda.

I picked my way along the edges of the first store I recognized as I watched more experienced shoppers navigate the aisles, hangers dangling from fingertips, purses stuffed beneath their arms or shoved up onto their shoulders. Two girls near the back tried on tops over their clothes. One pocketed a silvery nail polish. She had bleached hair with dark roots and a *fuck you* expression that reminded me so much of Brynn. She caught my eye, staring hard until I turned away, embarrassed. The shirt I picked was blue and long-sleeved. It wasn't on sale and I refused to try it on in the dressing room. I went home and left it in a bag on the floor.

The storefront had been converted and the gallery was complete. That morning, my mother had been moving her finished pieces from the shop next door, directing the movers up into the recently renovated display space. New lighting had been installed. The cases had been cleaned out, the dead cat removed and buried beneath a patch of weeds in the back lot. I had finished the piece I'd been working on and was fiddling with it, posing the birds in different displays. Finding minute problems that I could hover over and pick at, opening up again and again like tiny scabs.

"You need to talk to Lucinda," my mother had said, packing up the last of her stuff into a cardboard box. She reminded me of a kid finally leaving for college. None of her children had gone away to school.

"I know. I'll do it."

"When? Today?"

"Tomorrow."

"Today," she'd said, and swept out of the room. The tail end of her dress had brushed a dust ball from the corner. I'd picked it up and stuffed it in the trash.

And then I'd gone home and realized I had nothing nice to wear. Hence the new shirt. I had bought it and afterward felt stupid as hell about it. I hadn't seen or heard from Lucinda in months. There was no reason to think that anything would happen, and I didn't expect it to; but I couldn't stand the thought of seeing her in something old and gross. So I put on the shirt and I brushed out my braid. I let my hair fall around my face and back, a protective curtain. A swath of me to protect myself from the world.

The street where she lived wasn't far from my parents' home. My mother gave me the address. It was a quiet residential area, set against a slip of woods near the lake. It was a condominium complex I recognized from high school. We'd gone to a party at one of them and Brynn had blacked out in the bathroom after drinking too much gin. Milo had to carry her out to the car.

Lucinda's condo was number four. I knocked, looking at the clean brick exterior, marred only by the spiderwebs plugging up the corners of the door. I wasn't sure if she'd be home. I hadn't wanted to try calling, nervous that if I heard her voice beforehand, I'd chicken out of driving over. So I waited. I hoped for a second that she wouldn't be there, but realized I'd only have to come back again, which seemed even worse.

It opened quicker than I wanted. She wore a bathrobe, a pink terry-cloth thing that looked like it was from Victoria's Secret. I'd brought a Publix bag with me, and the stuff inside banged against my waist.

"Hey," I said stupidly, after we'd stared at each other for several long, awkward moments. "Can I talk to you?"

"Give me a minute." She shut the door in my face.

A minute turned into fifteen. I contemplated knocking again, or sitting down on the curb, but worried one of her neighbors would think I was a Jehovah's Witness or selling magazines. So I just stood there like an idiot, hands stuffed into my back pockets.

Something crawled across my neck. I leaned forward and scrubbed wildly at my hair and screeched. My elbow knocked into the door and pushed it open a few inches. Once I was sure there wasn't a spider crawling into my cleavage, I went inside.

Lucinda sat at the kitchen counter. Her hair was piled on top of her head and one bare leg dangled through the slit in her robe. I sat down next to her in one of the tall chairs. My legs hung gracelessly and banged against the counter in front of me. They were stools for tall people.

"You look like a scared kid," she said. She was drinking whiskey out of a short glass. One giant square of ice sat in the middle of it, like a frozen island.

"Do you have a mold to make those?"

"Is that what you came here to talk about? Ice?"

A clock over the mantel ticked loudly. Its golden arms swung back and forth inside its body. There was a shelf against the far wall that held a lot of sculptures. The posters from her office were hanging at either side of the living room.

"I don't know how to start," I said. "I'm bad at this."

"That's something." Finishing the drink, she got up for another. "You want one?"

"No, that's okay."

"Have a drink." She poured a couple of inches into her own glass, then brought it back over to the counter and slid it in front of me. I looked down at the liquid, swirling over the giant ice cube.

"It's like an iceberg." I took a small sip and let it sit at the back of my throat for a minute. "Does it make it taste better? The special ice?"

She took it back, put her lips where mine had been. "It tastes better now," she said. We took turns sipping from the drink until it was gone. My nerves calmed a little, but I still felt electrified, like I'd rubbed my shoes against a carpet and at any moment I might touch a piece of metal and shock the both of us.

"What's that?" She pointed to the plastic grocery bag, which sat next to my chair on the floor. I leaned down to pick it up but couldn't quite reach the handle. Lucinda caught it with her big toe and held it out to me that way—leg extended, skin smooth and beautiful. I took it from her and she left her foot there, on the edge of my seat. I swallowed, took out the two items, and laid them flat on the countertop for her to see.

Lucinda dragged the invite in front of her. Unlike the ones she'd ordered for the gallery opening, these were simple and cheap. Printed on cardstock, bold font, with the Morton's Taxidermy logo on the front. "I'm supposed to come to this?"

"I'd like you to see the work."

"I thought you didn't like that kind of work."

I shrugged, touched a fingertip to her toenail. It was shiny and lacquered red. "I haven't known what I like for a very long time. Just now figuring it out."

"Why do you think I'd come?"

"I know what happened." I stroked up her leg. The skin was smooth, like satin. It was odd to feel skin so soft after dealing with furred pelts that made my own hands rough and cracked. "What you did. Or Donna, I guess. The gallery."

She shrugged. "It is what it is."

"Are you going to get into trouble?"

"Who knows. They're still looking into things. But I don't care."

She set down the card and picked up the other object, a tissue-wrapped ball closed with Scotch tape. "And what's this?"

I let her open it, waited for her to see and decide. Unwrapping it on the countertop, she held up the object. I'd brought her the carapace, the cicada shell so perfectly preserved.

"Something else about cicadas. They live underground for most of their lives."

"Really."

"Yeah. They leave these shells when they first come out, the last time they molt as adults. But it takes them a really long time. They live mostly blind, coating themselves. Waiting to emerge."

She cupped the shell in her palm and let it roll there, back and forth, tilting it to see better in the light. Then she closed her fingers, pressing down hard, harder, until I heard the crunch. When she opened her hand again, the husk lay like shards of broken plastic.

"Where's Donna?" I asked.

"Moved out." She dusted her palm, and the shards fell down into the carpet, dusty and inconsequential. "With the advance, I was able to buy out the condo. We could split everything. What we'd wanted."

I took her palm and licked the remnants. I felt her muscles give way, her arm moving to embrace me. I let her lead me to the bedroom, and this time I stayed with her the whole night. I wanted to. She didn't even have to ask.

As she hovered over me in the morning light, I watched her finger trace a line from my face down the naked center of my body. "Where's your seam?" Finger tickling, searching. "Where do you crawl out?"

I put her hand where I wanted. We kissed and she searched for the place where I'd break open. When she finally found it, my insides shook and all my skin felt replaced with something new. Lucinda stayed there with me, hand smoothing down my side, pulling me out of the wreck.

We invited all our close friends and neighbors and put up a sign in the shop: free admission for the first day. My mother put Lolee in charge of greeting guests. She'd been stationed outside at a card table and sat in a little sequined dress my mother had sewn for her.

While people milled around in front of the shop, we made lemonade in the gallon plastic jug and set up a stack of Solo cups. There was a cooler of beer and a couple of strawberry pies, one lemon meringue, and a peanut butter, for Milo, who loved peanut butter more than anybody I knew.

Lolee sliced them up and set them out on plates with plastic forks stabbed into their backs. People parked over by the Dollar General and wandered over to talk and eat. We all had pie, standing next to the plate-glass window where my mother had set up her latest display.

Though the temperature outside hovered in the mid-eighties, inside was frosted like a cake—spray-on snow and white cotton batting covered every surface. Glitter topped it all, little slivers of icy plastic that looked like bright diamond shards. In this winter wonderland sat Santa and Mrs. Claus. Two foxes, arctic and fluffy white. Except Mrs. Claus was wearing a teddy and propped up suggestively against a pillowy snowbank. Santa had his back turned to the window, his coat thrust wide open.

It was our single collaborative effort. I'd asked for the specifications of the animals—how my mother wanted them posed, how she saw them standing or leaning, what their limbs should look like. After that work was done, I gave them to her and let her take the reins. It was bizarre, to see how she'd taken the animals and anthropomorphized them, but I was starting to understand. At least a little bit. So much of who my mother was and who she was becoming was lodged in the past. It made her happy to make those pieces because she felt a wild kind of freedom that she'd never had access to before.

Vera Leasey, recently back with her husband from a two-week Norwegian cruise, leaned in and snagged a bite of strawberry off my mother's plate. "This setup right here looks really artistic. Saw some stuff like it when we went off ship. Europeans are very particular about their art."

"Maybe I should go on a cruise," my mother said.

"Oh, you definitely should! They got a lot of singles' cruises too."

Lolee took my mother's empty plate, and I followed her inside the shop. It was a relief to escape the sun and all the gathered people. I felt a little queasy, but I always felt queasy when I did new things. Every day lately made me feel like I was gonna puke, and that seemed like it was better than before. Like maybe I was actually living my life.

I brushed back Lolee's hair from where it had fallen at the side of her face. The cut looked very cute on her, even though I thought it made her look too old. It brought out the angles in her cheekbones. She looked very much like her mother.

Milo came in and tapped his watch. "Come on. Let's get this started."

Inside the new place was festooned in black bedsheets, which covered up the windows and gave the place a more intimate feel. The path to the back was lit with a variety of lights we'd culled from everyone's Christmas stash. Overhead blinked white, red, and green, twinkling. We'd taken out the rusted stairs in the back and replaced them with a new set. I followed up after the guests, my mother leading the way.

The chorus of oohs and gasps that came from the group was satisfying to hear. My mother preened under the attention. She stood to the side, watching everyone take in the displays. There was a lot for people to look at.

"Oh, Libby . . ." Vera leaned into the first box, a panorama of two caveman-styled possums making love next to a papier-mâché woolly mammoth. "This is so gorgeous."

My mother had put every single work together, with the exception of the one in the case at the back, a space she'd gifted to me. The group walked along silently, peering into the cases every few steps—pointing out the set designs, the scenery. The backdrops and the lighting. The animals in their provocative poses.

A hand settled on my waist. I nestled my fingers between Lucinda's and we walked along behind the group, enjoying the reactions of the people we knew and even the few stragglers who'd seen the signs and come in off the street.

"You're going to keep it open year-round?" Lucinda put her mouth very close to my ear. The hair on the back of my neck stood up.

"Most of it," I replied. "Come see my piece."

In the back corner stood a case separate from the others. It was a large one, a six-foot-tall curio cabinet that I'd replaced with a glass front. Inside stood my peacocks, all three just as beautiful as when I'd stuffed them, still mounted on their branch. Behind the peacocks, a replica of my parents' house, framed by a rendering of the lake and scrub pines done in felt and velvet. We looked at it together, Lucinda and I, and I let my head fall down onto her shoulder. I looked at the birds, and

I couldn't look away from the biggest, the brightest. The center star.

We left with the others and went downstairs to eat more pie. I gave Lucinda the last piece of strawberry, and we watched the cars drive past in the street until it was time to close the shop.

"Do you think this'll float?"

Milo looked down at the Styrofoam wedge we'd taken from a refrigerator box. On it sat the three birds. It wasn't dark yet, not completely, but the sky had taken on the violet tinge of near-dusk. We were out on the edge of the dock. I knew I was taking a chance, coming back at night when I'd already gotten in trouble twice before over it, but it seemed like the right place to perform a Viking burial.

"It only has to float for a second," I said. "As long as we get the thing lit, that's all that counts."

"Right."

Already we'd killed a six-pack, and we were working on our second. We'd taken the birds from their display and brought them out to the lake, carrying them down together, one of us at either end.

"Are you sure you want to do this?" Milo ran a hand along the fringe of feathers that fluffed up from the back of the biggest bird. "Maybe you should keep it. Put it in the apartment or something."

I picked up the accelerant I'd bought at the gas station and spritzed a healthy amount over top of them. "Nah. We're gonna roast 'em."

"I guess."

I looped a few more streams onto the birds, making sure to hit the tail feathers and the breasts. They darkened and wilted from the wet. Feathers drooped down over the head of the bird on the right until it looked as if it were wearing a hat.

"It definitely looks like you're pissing all over them."

"Shut up."

Birds sufficiently doused, I turned to Milo and held out my hand. "Lighter?"

Digging through his pocket, he unearthed a gunmetal-gray one with his name on it—the one Brynn had given him for Christmas a year after they'd been married. My brother didn't even smoke.

It lit on the first strike, glowing orange-red and warming my fingers.

"Put 'em in."

Milo gently lifted the end of the Styrofoam and scooted it off the edge of the dock. It wobbled there in the water for a minute, churning up a light wake, and then settled flat. "Huh. Thought it would tip over for sure."

We stared at it, bobbing there next to us. Then I took the lighter and leaned in, pressing the open flame to the neck of the center bird. Instantly the feathers caught; it was like watching a Christmas tree catch fire. Milo and I stood back and watched it spark light into the night sky and across the top of the lake. Pieces of it were already charring, fluffing off and breaking into the water, drifting overhead soft as down.

Milo raised his beer. I raised mine too. Then we drank the last of it. Behind us, I could hear the crunch of tires on gravel, see the purple smear of red and blue lights. We didn't turn around, just kept watching the disintegration of the birds in front of us. It was very beautiful. I felt as if I could watch it all night.

"Could you handle this guy? He's kind of a douche." I set my empty on the bench beside the others.

Milo walked to the edge of the dock to intercept the officer. Instead of going with him, I sat and watched the last peacock glint out, shining orange glimmer into the water. The sky was purple and full of clouds. The sun looked like a slice of heart on the horizon, drifting out there in the dark. I kept my eyes on it until it swam away.

I am so grateful to everyone who helped get this book into the world. Thank you to all the lovely people at Tin House who believed in my work (and in me). I knew you were my family right away. Thank you to Tony Perez for his wonderful edits and his patience with my extremely bad jokes and all the wild swears in my emails. Thank you to Jakob Vala for his kindness and for the beautiful cover he designed. Thank you to my agent, Serene Hakim, who saw promise in my book and helped coax out the very best version of it. Thank you to Vermont Studio Center for allowing me time to work on this book and for feeding me dinner when I would have just had beer. Thank you to my reader, Willie Fitzgerald—my wonder twin, my best beloved dummy. Thank you to Vivian Lee for being an endless well of support while I struggled through my edits and for always knowing the exact right thing to say. Thank you to Mattie and to Emily, the better parts of me. Thank you to Maria Jones for all the beach trips and for letting me talk about the book for hours even though you'd heard me say the same thing three thousand times. Thank you to Cathleen Bota, my Bota Mini, for her sweet kindness and her beautiful heart. Thank you to my 7-Eleven cashier. Thank you to everyone who put up with all my puns and still loved me anyway. I love you, too. I mean it. Thank you.